On the SPUR of SPEED

Other Books by J. E. Fender

Easy Victories (Houghton Mifflin, 1973)
   Under the pseudonym of James Trowbridge

The Private Revolution of Geoffrey Frost (UPNE, 2002)
   Book 1 of the Frost Saga

Audacity, *Privateer Out of Portsmouth* (UPNE, 2003)
   Book 2 of the Frost Saga

Our Lives, Our Fortunes (UPNE, 2004)
   Book 3 of the Frost Saga

Hardscrabble Books—Fiction of New England

Laurie Alberts, *Lost Daughters*

Laurie Alberts, *The Price of Land in Shelby*

Thomas Bailey Aldrich, *The Story of a Bad Boy*

Robert J. Begiebing, *The Adventures of Allegra Fullerton: Or, A Memoir of Startling and Amusing Episodes from Itinerant Life*

Robert J. Begiebing, *Rebecca Wentworth's Distraction*

Anne Bernays, *Professor Romeo*

Chris Bohjalian, *Water Witches*

Dona Brown, ed., *A Tourist's New England: Travel Fiction, 1820–1920*

Joseph Bruchac, *The Waters Between: A Novel of the Dawn Land*

Joseph A. Citro, *DEUS-X*

Joseph A. Citro, *The Gore*

Joseph A. Citro, *Guardian Angels*

Joseph A. Citro, *Lake Monsters*

Joseph A. Citro, *Shadow Child*

Sean Connolly, *A Great Place to Die*

Ellen Cooney, *Gun Ball Hill*

John R. Corrigan, *Center Cut*

John R. Corrigan, *Snap Hook*

Pamela S. Deane, *My Story Being This: Details of the Life of Mary Williams Magahee, Lady of Colour*

J. E. Fender, *The Frost Saga*

  The Private Revolution of Geoffrey Frost: Being an Account of the Life and Times of Geoffrey Frost, Mariner, of Portsmouth, in New Hampshire, as Faithfully Translated from the Ming Tsun Chronicles, and Diligently Compared with Other Contemporary Histories

  Audacity, *Privateer Out of Portsmouth*

  Our Lives, Our Fortunes

  On the Spur of Speed: Continuing the Account of the Life and Times of Geoffrey Frost, Mariner, of Portsmouth, in New Hampshire, as Faithfully Translated from the Ming Tsun Chronicles, and Incorporating an Account of Joseph Frost's and Juby's Conduct on Lake Champlain, all Diligently Compared with Other Contemporary Histories

Dorothy Canfield Fisher (Mark J. Madigan, ed.), *Seasoned Timber*

Dorothy Canfield Fisher, *Understood Betsy*

Joseph Freda, *Suburban Guerrillas*

Castle Freeman, Jr., *Judgment Hill*

Frank Gaspar, *Leaving Pico*

Robert Harnum, *Exile in the Kingdom*

Ernest Hebert, *The Dogs of March*

Ernest Hebert, *Live Free or Die*

Ernest Hebert, *The Old American*

Sarah Orne Jewett (Sarah Way Sherman, ed.), *The Country of the Pointed Firs and Other Stories*

Raymond Kennedy, *Ride a Cockhorse*

Raymond Kennedy, *The Romance of Eleanor Gray*

Lisa MacFarlane, ed., *This World Is Not Conclusion: Faith in Nineteenth-Century New England Fiction*

G. F. Michelsen, *Hard Bottom*

Don Mitchell, *The Nature Notebooks*

Anne Whitney Pierce, *Rain Line*

Kit Reed, *J. Eden*

Rowland E. Robinson (David Budbill, ed.), *Danvis Tales: Selected Stories*

Roxana Robinson, *Summer Light*

Rebecca Rule, *The Best Revenge: Short Stories*

Catharine Maria Sedgwick (Maria Karafilis, ed.), *The Linwoods: or, "Sixty Years Since" in America*

R. D. Skillings, *How Many Die*

R. D. Skillings, *Where the Time Goes*

Lynn Stegner, *Pipers at the Gates of Dawn: A Triptych*

Theodore Weesner, *Novemberfest*

W. D. Wetherell, *The Wisest Man in America*

Edith Wharton (Barbara A. White, ed.), *Wharton's New England: Seven Stories and* Ethan Frome

Thomas Williams, *The Hair of Harold Roux*

Suzi Wizowaty, *The Round Barn*

On the S P U R
of S P E E D

Continuing the Account of the *Life and Times*
of Geoffrey Frost, Mariner, of Portsmouth,
in New Hampshire, as *Faithfully Translated* from
the Ming Tsun Chronicles, and
Incorporating an *Account* of Joseph Frost's and
Juby's *Conduct* on Lake Champlain, all *Diligently
Compared* with Other Contemporary Histories

J. E. FENDER

University Press of New England
HANOVER AND LONDON

Published by University Press of New England,
One Court Street, Lebanon, NH 03766
www.upne.com
© 2005 by J. E. Fender
Printed in the United States of America
5 4 3 2 1

Library of Congress Cataloging-in-Publication Data

Fender, J. E.
On the spur of speed: continuing the account of the life and times of
Geoffrey Frost, mariner, of Portsmouth, in New Hampshire, as faithfully
translated from the Ming Tsun chronicles, and incorporating an account
of Joseph Frost's and Juby's conduct on Lake Champlain, all diligently
compared with other contemporary histories / J. E. Fender.
    p.   cm.—(Hardscrabble books)
ISBN 1–58465–475–9 (cloth : alk. paper)
1. Frost, Geoffrey (Fictitious character)—Fiction. 2. United States—
History—Revolution, 1775–1783—Fiction. 3. New Hampshire—
History—Revolution, 1775–1783—Fiction. 4. Portsmouth
(N.H.)—Fiction. 5. Sailors—Fiction. I. Title. II. Series.
PS3606.E53O5 2005
813'.6—dc22   2005000540

To All Who Were—

And Are—

Involved in the Pursuit

of American Independence

and Freedoms

On the SPUR of SPEED

KNEELING MING TSUN LIFTED HIS HEAD AFTER LISTENING INTENTLY TO JOSEPH FROST'S LABORED RESPIRATIONS. A DEEP FROWN DISTORTED HIS RAVAGED FACE AS he signed to Geoffrey Frost: "Your brother's heart is very faint, and he is consumed with fever."

"We must remove Joseph from this pest house," Frost said, rather than signed, engaged as he was in gently displacing two corpses rigid in the contortions of typhus so that there would be space for him to kneel on the broad pine boards of the Presbyterian Church. The dead men were scarcely more than youths, and they had been stripped of whatever remnants of uniforms they might once have worn. The church was one of the buildings in Philadelphia that had been sequestered as military hospitals to accommodate the hundreds of Continental Army soldiers stricken with camp fever in December 1776. Two very tired and haggard orderlies moved desultorily among the lumps of men and bodies lying on the church floor without benefit of mattress or blanket, dispensing what scant refreshments they could.

Frost pressed a finger against his brother's neck, greatly dismayed at the thinness of the pulse thread he felt there. "Dispatch Caleb Mansfield to discover a house nearby where Joseph can be removed," he commanded curtly. Frost chafed Joseph's cold wrists vigorously and spoke urgently: "Joseph, Joseph, if you hear me . . ." His voice broke as he recalled an earlier time when he had seen his younger brother nigh death, a result of Joseph's having stowed himself away in a coffin aboard Frost's privateer in order to join Frost's desperate expedition to free American prisoners of war held in the fortress of Louisbourg.

In the dim light filtering through a heavily overcast sky into the hospital Frost anxiously scanned Joseph's pinched, wan face for any sign that his brother heard him. Frost's fatigue threatened to overwhelm him—when had he last slept? Perhaps as long ago as the very early morning of Christmas Day. The weary miles he had ridden from George Washington's headquarters after Henry Knox had named where Joseph lay were of no consequence now. He had found his brother.

"Keep yere grubbin' hands offen that boy! Don't go thinkin' you can steal his clothes without a scrap with me," an accusatory voice behind Frost shrilled.

Startled, Frost turned to face a stooped gnome of a man, with a face squeezed like a winter apple. "This man is my brother," Frost snarled as the gnome knelt beside Joseph. The gnome flicked a ragged scarf of once-white cambric from around his neck, dribbled water from a cracked chamber pot onto the cloth, and gently laved Joseph's forehead. "A receptacle of multiple uses," the gnome said.

"I shall be grateful to know the name of my brother's friend," Frost said.

"Name's Stonecypher," the gnome said curtly. "Been with the boy this half-year, soldierin' with General Arnold 'til we wus chased offen the Lake. Then we went lookin' fer employment as cannoneers, though we done a lot more diggin' than we done cannoneerin'."

Frost found himself gagging on the stench permeating the hospital, a nauseous, gut-wrenching heave of lungs that foreclosed breath, the stench reeking of sour vomit, voided bowels, putrefying flesh, corruption from broken pustules. The gnome took no notice. "Can you tell me about Juby?" Frost asked, swallowing his gorge as he resumed chafing Joseph's wrists.

"Died a hero, a true hero," Stonecypher said simply. "Boy's been a hero right enough, though he's been more interested in gettin' hisself killed. Fer why, I got no clew, 'cept there be a woman sommers. Women's why I be here myself."

The overwhelming stench and the evident kindness of the man named Stonecypher forced open a hatchway long tightly battened into Frost's memory. Ming Tsun, stepping carefully over the bodies, approached, bearing a broad length of wood wrenched from a pew. "I once knew a man as kind as you. Come with us and tell us about my brother," Frost said spontaneously to Stonecypher, as he and Ming Tsun gently placed Joseph's rail-thin body on the makeshift stretcher. "Sorrowfully, you can do nothing else of use in this warehouse of dying men."

◦ I ◦

GEOFFREY FROST LAY CURLED INTO A FETAL POSITION IN A VAIN ATTEMPT TO EASE THE NAUSEA OF SEASICKNESS THAT HAD OVERWHELMED HIM THESE three days past. He huddled in wet, dung-matted straw foully reeking of sheep and pig urine, completely oblivious to his surroundings in the dark and malodorous manger in the fore-peak. The ship's motion was most violent and pronounced in the bow, as the *Bride of Derry* surged along under a fine top-gallant breeze from the south-southwest. The *Bride* was heeled slightly on a larboard tack, with jibsail, fore staysail, topsails, forecourse and trysail or spanker all drawing handsomely. Her motion was, in all truth, very slight as she thrust her dainty bow into moderate seas that were most unusual for late March weather in the North Atlantic just crossing through latitude forty.

None of this mattered a stitch to a Geoffrey Frost three months and a few weeks past his ninth birthday and out of sight of land for the first time in his brief life. The seasickness had gripped him in its vise before the *Bride* had sunk Nantucket Island, and the *Bride*'s master and captain had banished Geoffrey to the manger until such time as the youth recovered sufficiently to take up his duties as cabin boy and supernumerary. Wick Nichols had clearly indicated his complete indifference to Geoffrey's ultimate fate, though the captain would be personally inconvenienced by being denied the services Geoffrey had specifically shipped as the owner's generous favor to the youth's father to train him for the sea.

"Come now, laddie," a gentle voice said, "it be three days since ye hae et." Something pressed against Geoffrey's lips. Aware that he was also very cold as well as very ill, Frost shook his head vigorously, threw out his arms, and convulsed his body, driving away, with a mild, reproachful *baaah,* the young lamb that had snuggled against him for warmth. Geoffrey had heard the gentle voice before; it had been the only kind voice he had heard since taking his good-bye of his father on Brown's wharf. Three days? No, three years, three lifetimes ago. He had died a thousand times, had wished, prayed for death ten thousand times. He longed for death at this very moment. Geoffrey Frost had, in his brief life, absorbed enough of his mother's Catholicism and his father's Judaism to feel the moral horror of suicide and its attendant eternity spent dwelling in Hell. His understanding of this ethos, and the fact that he could under no circumstances muster the strength to climb out of the manger, ascend to the deck, and hurl himself overside, kept him from suicide. But he would have immensely welcomed a quick and final death by some other compassionate hand.

"It be pap, laddie, a bisket pounded to small crackers 'n' soaked with the milk from the she-goat. Tain't porridge, but it be nourishin', I'll warrant."

Geoffrey weakly averted his face as the bowl approached his lips. Nausea more miserable than anything Geoffrey had hitherto known writhed within body and brain, dry heaves so wracking that Geoffrey thought his stomach would be expelled through his mouth.

"All right, laddie dear, ye nae hae to think on the pap anon," the gentle voice said. "Yere stable-mate in grief hath licked the bowl as clean as a babe's arse. But ye must hae some water, that's a-sure." Gentle Voice's right hand gripped Geoffrey's jaw, not urgently, but firmly, and something liquid though vile-tasting was trickled into his mouth. Geoffrey tried to avert his head, but the hand held him immobile. Geoffrey felt as if he were drowning; his throat opened reflexively and he swallowed.

Gentle Voice kept dribbling the fluid into Geoffrey's mouth until whatever container Gentle Voice held was emptied.

"Now dear, we must get ye out o' this muck. Aaah, what be this? Yere pillar?" Gentle Voice prodded a small valise of heavy, brocaded cloth.

"Books," Geoffrey said through his nausea. "Consigned from my mother to further my education during leisure time." He was dimly aware of a pig's grunt and squeal somewhere nearby. "And my toothbrush, with two bottles of Doctor Weatherspoon's dentifrice powder."

"Aaah," Gentle Voice exclaimed with a mixture of respect and disbelief. "Kin ye truly read, laddie dear?"

"Not very well," Geoffrey said tremulously. "I must still read Virgil in the translation, but should I, most unhappily, live, I hope to improve my Latin enough to read Virgil in the language it was wrote in."

Gentle Voice laughed. "Aaah, so we's shipped a scholar in this guineaman! Doubt not ye'll live, young scholar. 'N all the years I've been tooin' and froin' over these seas I knows o' nae soul as was took away by *mal de mer,* 'n' hardly be a jot o' leisure time under Wick Nichols, captain o' this barky."

"Pray, what be *mal de mer?*" Geoffrey asked, extremely glad to find that conversing with the only human who had taken notice of him since his consignment to the manger served to distract him from his wretchedness.

"Why, dear Lord, love," Gentle Voice fairly cackled, "but I be a scholar meself, even I kin't read, 'n' *mal de mer* be the Frenchie for the sea's grippe. I've got me watch comin' on, but let's spread some new straw 'n this corner, 'n' brace ye up agin' the hull, do ye a world o' good if ye sit up more, rather 'n lie dog-fashion. Ye'll tolerate the motion more." Gentle Voice pulled several armfuls of straw from the sailcloth bag triced overhead, displaced three sheep by pressing the small flock into a more compact mass with the push of his body, and spread the straw along the larboard side of the manger. He then lifted Geoffrey's slender body onto the new straw, affording Geoffrey his first look at his benefactor as a shaft of light pierced through the small grated scuttle abaft the manger for ventilation of the cold and fetid space.

What Geoffrey Frost beheld in the dim light, dancing with dust motes, was a man, of middle age at least, bald except for a fringe of dirty, bluish-gray hair, his pate crossed with myriad scars and sun lesions, his heavy eyes deeply sunken in baggy sockets, a few yellowed, widely spaced teeth, fangs really, behind lips that were puffed with sun lesions. The man was also missing the majority of his right ear. Under other circumstances the man's features would have been hideous, but they gave Gentle Voice's face a kindly, compassionate cast. Yes, sitting up definitely eased the effect of the plunging motions of the bow. Geoffrey felt something warm squirm onto his stomach, though with hard little hooves—the orphan lamb. Geoffrey knew a glimmering, a flicker of hope that he might, despite all, somehow retain the faintly glowing coal of life.

"I would have known it for French was I not so wretched and sunk in the miasmal," Geoffrey said. "Maman is from Martinico, and we converse in French. Despite Papa's exhortations she refuses to speak English." Geoffrey tried to raise his hand but was so enfeebled he could lift it no more than a few inches. "I lament exceedingly that I am denied the pleasure of clasping your hand in gratitude, sir. My name is Frost, Geoffrey Frost. I pray the real pleasure of knowing your name."

"Garn," Gentle Voice cried, falling back on his heels, "but yere gab be educated fer such a child! I's never heard the like. I be Jabez McCool, rimes with fool, as me old granny said, a fool I was to leave the town o' Poole and take t' the sea fer me school. See, it all rimes!" McCool cackled with delight.

"I speak only as Maman and Master Graham, the pedagogue employed as tutor to the twins and me, have instructed," Geoffrey said with some asperity. "I am unaware of any other style of elocution, and it is English as exactly translated from the French, *vrai de vrai.*"

"Aaah," McCool said with even greater enthusiasm, "old

Jabez kens that word, too! Means talkin'! Me old granny wus a chambermaid to the quality, 'n' she used the word mickle, which I's kept the meanin' all these many years."

But Geoffrey had slipped back into his deep quagmire of misery bordering on the delirious and heaved up all the liquid that Gentle Voice had so laboriously trickled down his throat, coming up vile and evil tasting all in one watery jet.

Somehow he slept, though a menagerie of animals made themselves at home in his bosom. Some had sharp beaks and sharp talons and cluck-clucked in his face as they foraged in the fetid straw. Others had dainty hooves that nevertheless punched his stomach sharply, while others were long and sinuous and lay tucked into a heavy ball against his stomach. The sleep slightly assuaged Geoffrey's seasickness, so that it no longer enervated his entire body but localized with malevolent vengeance in his head and stomach. Still, it was with a sense of wonder and more than a little dismay that Geoffrey realized he was still alive the next time he fought up through the layers of turbulent nausea to wakefulness. "On yere feet, sonny-o, Captain been waitin' to gam with ye these four days past, and he's nowise disposed to let ye lie abed in ease while yere mates been standin' in for ye watch on watch."

The invisible, amorphous voice had a rough edge; though not unkind, it was nowise as soothing as Gentle Voice had been. Legs unwilling to obey him, Geoffrey flailed about for a wall, some support to help him rise to his feet, but all he could do was beat weakly and ineffectually at the straw. A chicken scratching industriously nearby cackled in alarm and scurried away, only to bang fiercely against the starboard bulkhead of the tiny manger and fall, flustered, onto the back of a sheep, then clapping on gamely. The voice sighed, and two strong hands grasped Geoffrey under the armpits and lifted his frail body to its feet. Geoffrey promptly fell back into the straw as soon as the hands released him.

"Gar," the voice sighed, "heaven ain't laid eyes on a more piteous sight since two cutpurses rode the cart one way to Tyburn Hill. Couldn't stand up atall in the cart, one nor the other, though the cart weren't pitchin' 'n' heavin' any more this barky be doin' now. Cryin' and pissin' their britches. At least ye ain't cryin' and pissin', though this bein' the manger and all, most like a right smart of that been goin' on. Come on, sonny-o, Wick Nichols, he don't like to be kept waitin', and he's likely to give me a rap or two with his staff lessen I get ye under his lee the next minute, no more." This time the hands picked up Geoffrey as if he weighed no more than a doll and their owner backed out of the manger, bent double at the waist to duck under the bowsprit where it was stepped into the bulkhead.

The pair emerged onto the main deck by a companionway just abaft the foremast, into a fair though very cold day with what clouds there were very high and shaped like the tails of horses. The voice, Geoffrey could now see, originated from a veritable giant, with a face as dark as the tan-colored sails drawing stiffly above them. The giant's hands set Geoffrey on the deck, carefully supporting him as he stood, unsteadily, on legs that seemingly contained no bones. "Nothin' be to it, so say ye, sonny-o? Most like ye would o' done better up here in the air than crammed into the manger with the sweet smells and all. Gar, ye look like a shirt on a beanpole! Here." Hands brushed at Geoffrey's dirty clothes, bits of straw flying aside. The giant produced a very dirty kerchief—Geoffrey guessed that it once may even have been a square of white linen—spat upon it and industriously scrubbed Geoffrey's forehead. Then the giant raked his fingers through Geoffrey's hair, scattering still more stems of straw about the deck.

"Indebted to you, sir, immensely," Geoffrey said, manfully thrusting out his hand. He still breasted his way through shoals of queasiness that flickered like the summer lightning over Maman's house above the great bay, but he concentrated on the giant's features to the exclusion of all else. Geoffrey marked the creases and folds beyond counting in the man's face, his faded, bloodshot brown eyes, the dark pouches beneath, and the hair that escaped the confines of a multicolored kerchief sun-bleached to the same color as the straw upon which Geoffrey had so recently and so wretchedly reclined.

"Wolcott Crowninshield," the giant said, lips parting in a caricature of a grin, enclosing Geoffrey's small hand in his great paw. "I be first mate to Captain Nichols on this barky, and ye are to call me Mister Mate because I hold an awesome position, ye'll warrant. And yonder on his quarterdeck be Wick Nichols, known throughout the trade as Beelzebub Nichols, though havin' been foretold his nickname ye are forever enjoined from the mention of it in his presence." The mate turned Geoffrey around so he faced the stern, then prodded him.

"Make yere presence known to Captain Nichols, but mind, no speakin' to him until he speaks to ye first."

"But how am I to make my presence known unless I speak?" Geoffrey said, taking a tentative step, staggering and almost falling. How could anyone maintain his footing on this chip of wood pitching violently on this malignant sea, first to the left, then to the right, then up and down, and then a heaving, shuddering corkscrew motion reminiscent of a large dog shaking himself violently, the movements then repeating in no particular order? Crowninshield caught him quickly.

"Still a bit giddy, eh? Light in the head ye be, but fix on a mark that don't move so much—that wrap of iron around the mainmast a man's height above the deck, say. Don't look at the water," the mate said cheerfully. "Just walk up to the captain and raise a knuckle to yere forehead, a proper salute like, when he speaks to ye. Captain Nichols, he'll tell ye what he expects of ye right quick." Crowninshield urged Geoffrey forward a step.

And Geoffrey, though curiously lightheaded, was remarkably revived by the zephyr brushing his left cheek. He tottered forward precariously, instinctively knowing that the mate would not accompany him further, and steadied himself by grasping a nearby rope affixed to the vessel's bulwark and extending upward at an acute angle. Geoffrey did not attempt to raise his eyes skyward but kept them fastened on the iron band around the mast, noting, without amazement, that a pig and two goats were tethered there. He shuffled past the ship's open launch, raised above the deck on blocks and filled with a turmoil of chicken coops woven from sea grass.

It took him the better part of two minutes to cover the fifty feet of cluttered space to the break of the quarterdeck, and all the time he was keenly aware that the hooded obsidian eyes of Captain Wick Nichols were unblinkingly marking his progress. Geoffrey paused when he reached the break and stared up at the figure on the quarterdeck, alone except for two men standing on either side of the large steering wheel. Geoffrey coughed hesitantly and saw the hard eyes, peering from a face sun-scoured the bronze color of a weathered acorn though now sheltered beneath an incongruous round Quaker hat, fasten more keenly on him. He raised his right knuckles to his forehead. "Geoffrey Frost, your servant, sir."

"My servant indeed, young Frost," Wick Nichols snapped. "A servant who has absented himself voluntarily—voluntarily! —from his contracted billet these three days past, and more— to lie with animals. I agreed to ship you as captain's servant and supernumerary only because your father, and Aaron Lopez, importuned me incessantly. I castigate myself fervently that I did not list to the better spirit within me that argued my material wants would be more adequately served by a foremast hand. Instead, I listed to the devil spirit who counseled how my great burdens of command would be lightened by a person to tend my wants while I devoted my energies to the husbandry of this vessel of John Brown's. Faith, I have shipped a lollygag fitted more to the counting house than the commerce that generates profits—profits that permit the gentry to dress their whores in fine silks and be driven behind proud horseflesh that cost one hundred pounds the pair."

Wick Nichols thrust out the staff he held in a gesture pregnant with disgust, causing Geoffrey to note it for the first but by no means the last time. He would quickly learn that the staff was always in Nichols' hand or within close reach. The staff, an inch or so more than five feet, was something between a cudgel and a quarterstaff in length and included a brass ball the size of a closed fist surmounting its thick, dark, gnarled wood, which was almost the color of old, dried blood. Nichols took a turn about his quarterdeck, all of eighteen feet on a side, blocked and crowded as it was with tackles and ropes and barrels and chests still unstowed. He glowered at Geoffrey Frost for a moment, then past him. "Mister Mate! That idiot hand acquired from Jamestown, much to the town's delight and our sorrow, still has not learned the difference between halyards and braces! See to his instruction afore he ruins the shape of the fore course we've just gotten drawing properly."

Then his gaze went immediately back to Geoffrey: "Young Frost, it has been represented to me that you can cypher a lunar, have divined the secrets of the rhumb line, and can conjure a wind from the most oppressive doldrums by whistling. Say to me that these representations be true."

Geoffrey lowered his eyes. "Alas, sir, I ken my cyphers through geometry, and I ken the meaning of the rhumb line, but 'cyphering a lunar' is alien to me, and I know nothing of the doldrums." Geoffrey paused, then continued cheerfully: "I am marvelously keen on whistling, and believe I do a capital job of it."

"Your hand, then, young Frost. How do you represent your hand?" Wick Nichols advanced to the fife rail, leaned on it and over until his face was no more than two feet from Geoffrey's.

"A fair hand, sir," Frost said hesitantly. "Not as accomplished as Tad Barefoot's or Henry Remington's. I was made by the pedagogue to hold the chalk in my right hand, my left arm pinned behind me, until Maman heard of it and beat the pedagogue unmercifully with her umbrella. He desisted, and I write tolerably well with my left hand, which I favor, sir, though Tad's and Henry's hands are marvels of cursive penmanship."

"Are this Tad and this Henry shipped aboard this *Bride of Derry?*" Wick Nichols demanded.

"I believe not, sir, " Geoffrey said hesitantly, thinking that he was being made the fool. "Leastwise I would have known of it before my father gave me over to you to learn the sea."

"Young Frost," Wick Nichols snapped, "how old be you?"

"I am rising ten, sir," Geoffrey said fearfully, knowing full well that he was still nine months shy of that birthday.

"Young Frost, I have been afloat on the bosom of the sea for thrice your years, and mark you, one does not learn the sea. The sea is like a catamount you think to have gentled. Then she turns upon you and rends your limbs, leaving you broken but alive if you be blessed by fortune. Or dead, most like." Wick Nichols glared at Geoffrey. "Never be such the clodpoll that you think you have learned the sea, and if I teach you nothing else during your career aboard the *Bride of Derry,* never turn your back upon the sea, even in the sea's best moods."

"I ken your words, sir," Geoffrey said meekly. "I shan't forget them."

"Good," Wick Nichols said bluntly, turning his back to Geoffrey to signify that the interview was over. "Repair to my cabin; it must be pridied and set in order. And at eight bells promptly I shall take dinner in my cabin."

"Yes, sir," Geoffrey replied, and turned away, not knowing what was expected of him, or where he was to go, or certainly what a bell signified. He was brought up short as he bumped into Wolcott Crowninshield.

"Make yere manners to the captain, sonny-o," Crowninshield said, not unkindly. As Frost turned and hurriedly knuckled his forehead, he continued, "Sails all drawing well with no attention needed in the tops, so old Jabez can take ye in tow fer the next hour. Keep yere ears unstoppered. Captain Nichols, he don't like to chew his cabbage twice, if ye twig my drift." Crowninshield led Geoffrey toward a scuttle. "Foot of the ladder and straight ahead a fathom, through the door and ye'll be in the captain's cabin. Get to sortin' it out, and I'll send Jabez along soon as I kin roust him. Mind what the captain said about dinner; he's partial to sittin' down as soon as the last bell's struck."

"Yes, Mister Mate," Geoffrey said miserably, hoping mightily that a bolt of lightning might materialize out of the clear sky and strike him down dead to spare him the loneliness and sickness that now churned his body and mind into complete turmoil. But he got to the scuttle somehow, made it down the ladder without falling, and found the strength to push open the door to Captain Nichols' cabin just enough to slip through; something was weighing against the door from the other side. It was an open chest of clothes, and behind it the cabin was in utter chaos.

Geoffrey stood dumfounded. He had not the slightest idea of how he was to go about his duties. Set the cabin in proper order, Captain Nichols had said. Geoffrey supposed that meant cleaning the cabin, finding spaces to stow the tumble of clothing, boxes, ledgers, dishes, candles, bundles of quills and papers, bottles and tarpaulin jackets. He wondered if the bolt of lightning could strike him through the wood surrounding him without damaging the ship, because Geoffrey did not wish the crew of the *Bride of Derry* to die with him.

"Now, laddie, let's see what we's got to work with . . . gobsmack me, but I've to allow the captain bain't got no one to pick up atter him or keep him shipshape, all Bristol fashion." Jabez McCool bustled into the small cabin, immensely crowding it.

"What is needed, Mister McCool," Geoffrey said with great feeling, "is Prudence, or better yet, both Prudence and her sister, Patience. They could set this room a-tidy in no time at all."

"'N' who be these Prudence and Patience, now laddie, save for two of the virtues parsons harp about most every sermon? 'N' by the by, this Mister McCool bain't my style. Just plain Jabez I be." Jabez waded into the clutter. "Bound to be a desk somewhere in here, most like a chair, and there be some cupboards to larboard what's likely empty 'n' can stow some of the captain's kit."

"Prudence and Patience be Maman's chambermaids," Geoffrey said, a trifle smugly. "They keep my chambers in good order—shipshape, as you call it." He put a hand on an open locker to steady himself as the ship rolled and touched a large leather-bound Bible, to all appearances well used, and behind it a leather-bound copy of More's *Utopia*.

"Chambers? Did ye say chambers, laddie?" Jabez asked incredulously.

"Why, yes," Geoffrey said, "my brother and sister and I each have two chambers allotted us, one chamber for sleeping and another as a study where we may do as we wish. Joseph shall have his two chambers when he is old enough, though now he is but two years old and sleeps in the trundle bed in Maman's bedchamber. And what is that horrid smell permeating this chamber? Faith, it be far worse than the aromas of the manger."

"Waal, yere little brother mought be moved into yere cabins—chambers, ye know 'em by, time ye finish this voyage," Jabez said testily, "'n' old Jabez don't collect Patience or Prudence be among the crew. Matter of fact, laddie, we be powerful short-handed. Most *négriers* in the trade, specially the ones out of Liverpool and all the Frenchies, have one hand for each two and a half tonnes burthen. The old *Bride,* now she be nigh on one hundret and ninety tonnes, so by rights we should number no less than eighty seasoned hands, able to reef, hand and steer." Jabez broke off and peered archly at Geoffrey: "How many hands, including captain and mate, cook and bosun, cooper and surgeon, though we ain't got no real surgeon, think ye now be afloat in the old *Bride?*"

"Seventy-five?" Geoffrey said hopefully, though knowing that would not be anywhere near the answer. "And what is a *négrier?*"

"Thirty-three souls be in the hands of Wick Nichols," Jabez said, "thirty-four countin' yeres, though ye'll understand that I hesitate to number ye as a proper hand. 'N' if ye speak the French ye'll sure know what a *négrier* be."

"Yes," Geoffrey said, haltingly, "it translates as a transport for blackamoors. I do not understand your term."

Jabez McCool sank down on a much-scarred and battered sea chest of unpainted pine, unintentionally knocking over a basket of clothes, from which a serpent of indeterminate length tumbled, then gathered itself in an accusatory coil on the cabin sole to survey Geoffrey and Jabez balefully. The serpent lowered its head and slithered slowly, insolently, through the open passageway. "Oh Jesus, that be Ali, the cook's special pet 'cause he keeps down the rats in the stores. But the capt'n, he hates Ali all of a passion. Cook Holly's got to keep Ali out o' the capt'n's way, and yere bound to do the same, hear me there?" Jabez said loudly.

Geoffrey nodded dumbly. He was not sure, but it was entirely possible he had already made Ali's acquaintance in the manger. Jabez looked at Geoffrey pityingly. "Laddie, ye truly do not know what kind of trade ye be engaged in? Don't ye mind my tellin' ye when ye wus in the manger that ye were aboard a guineaman? That is the reason for the smell, ye ken, because you be young 'n' never known tobacco, while to me the smell bain't no more noticeable than October apples to a farmer."

"I recall little of my time in the manger," Geoffrey said truthfully, "save that you are possessed of a gentle voice and were exceedingly kind to me. And there were smells, though not this foul."

"Your folks, they tell ye what kind of vessel ye be given over to learn the sea?"

"My father was pleased to tell Maman that he had found a place for me aboard a vessel trading with the Spanish and the Portuguese, and that I would learn the sea with a successful captain."

"I dinna want to go hard on yere father," Jabez said, "and in a manner of speakin' we do be tradin' with the Portugee 'n' the Spaniard, but the trade of a guineaman or a *négrier* be in livin' flesh 'n' blood, laddie, human flesh 'n' blood, covered with black skin. 'N' the smell goes with the barky, laddie. The old *Bride* never be rid o' it."

"You cannot mean that this *Bride of Derry* is a slaving vessel!" Geoffrey said with great indignation, almost hooting in disbelief. "My father would never have any truck with such a nefarious trade, much less sign me aboard a vessel that is a," he sought the word that Master Graham had once used to illustrate a lesson in geography, "blackbirder!" Geoffrey exclaimed, pleased that he had recalled it.

"The *Bride of Derry* be a slaver, a blackbirder if ye will, laddie, and a crack one if'en ever one there was. Yere pa had to know afore he bound ye over to Wick Nichols."

oseph Frost watched Hannah Devon undress, his desire
and his groin swelling equally to the point of burst-
J ing. "She is a wonton, a total wonton," Joseph breathed
heavily through his lust, and he would have thrown
himself from the bed to hasten Hannah's disrobing, but with
seductive, promising words Hannah had cunningly bound
him, hand and foot, to the bed posts after stripping him of his
clothing. He was bound with the heavy, ornate, silver-colored
cords that normally held back the purplish-brown draperies of
the bedchamber Hannah shared with her two sisters on the second floor of Parson Devon's newly built garrison, at the end of
Bartlett Street looking out over Islington Creek. The garrison
was severe and aesthetic when viewed without but extremely
luxurious within. It was by Islington Creek, in an Abanaqui
canoe paddled with the assistance of a sour-faced Juby, his
father's major-domo, that Joseph had arrived the hour after
sunset.

Parson Devon, his sharp-featured wasp of a wife, whose
name Joseph could not for his life recall, and the two younger
Devon daughters, Deborah and Mariah, were gone away to
visit relatives in Boston. The relatives were still hysterical three
months after General Howe had precipitously withdrawn all
British forces from that city when cannon raised on Dorches-
ter Heights had unexpectedly appeared to besiege it. Joseph
was intimately familiar with the cannons, for he had been with
the men commanded by Henry Knox who had drayed the sixty

tons of dead metal over three hundred miles from the place of their capture, Fort Tyonderoga on Lake Champlain. Happily, the family Devon would not have to lodge with their afflicted kin, for they were accompanied by the studiously melancholy Lancelot Duford, in Joseph's opinion an affected dandy. Lancelot was a matriculate of John Harvard's university with aspirations of becoming a prelate of some congregation. For the past several months an obsequious Lancelot had been keeping in the room over the Devon barn while attending Parson Devon in his fanatical quest for souls. It was widely known throughout Portsmouth that the Duford family, poised on the cusp between patriot and loyalist, though obviously keen to remain absolutely neutral, was possessed of a large mansion in Cambridge. And it was with the Duford family that the Devon family intended to lodge.

Hannah had remained behind, pleading some sewing to be done, not to mention the heartfelt desire to spare herself the sanctimonious and specious shrills of the Devon relatives' penury. She had also cited the common sense that the house should remain occupied during this time of wicked turmoil in the colony of New Hampshire, which had recently, along with twelve other colonies, declared itself a state free of domination by the British Crown. Upon their arrival, the disapproving but rigidly silent and subservient Juby—he might be Marlborough Frost's major-domo, but he was, nevertheless, a slave and his master's property—had drawn the canoe out of the water and secreted it in the barn behind the garrison. Juby was maintaining a surveillance from there.

Hannah took an inordinate amount of time moving about the bedchamber, striking a flint to kindle a taper and then lighting a candelabra of three stems. "She is completely aware of the fact that the candles' light easily penetrates her muslin shift and highlights her charms wondrously," Joseph said to himself. He strained mightily but futilely against his bonds, for Hannah had indeed bound him most ingeniously. How had this demure maid learned to shape a bond tight enough to snug one of his father's ships against the company's wharf at Christian Shore?

Hannah advanced slowly, candles in hand, languidly unbuttoning the bodice of her shift. "La, Mister Frost," she mewed demurely, "how came you to be trussed so in a poor maid's bedchamber?" She sat down on a small stool several feet from the bed.

"Hannah," Joseph said huskily, "you know very well how I came to be trussed like a turtle, but why I agreed to be bound so submissively is beyond my ken. Come hither, though, and unbind me, so that I may address and caress you properly."

"Address me, sir, caress me, sir? La! I believe your intent is the ravishment of me. And the comparison to a turtle does not cypher. The world knows that a turtle turned upon its back is rendered helpless without need of trusses. My family enjoyed excellent dining recently upon a sea-terrapin brought from the Caribbean Isles. I recall how doleful the doomed creature appeared, waving its legs haplessly as Mother approached the knife near its neck. A turtle menaces me not at all, but you, sir, menace my virtue extremely." Hannah slipped her shift off one shoulder, exposing a firm, silky breast the color of ivory in the candlelight. "To guard my virtue should not I approach you with a knife?"

"Your virtue is safe when entrusted to me," Joseph said somewhat querulously, hoping he kept the edge of unease out of his voice. Why had he permitted himself to be so bound? He had lain with Hannah just once before, but he had long desired her and doubted not that she had long desired him. They had submitted to mutual passion during a fleeting but opportune moment when they had been alone the month before, following a service of thanksgiving for the return of his brother-in-law, Marcus Whipple, and other American prisoners of war from British captivity in the horrific conditions of the gaol in the Fortress of Louisbourg. But this tryst had been initiated by Hannah. Joseph acknowledged with more than a little chagrin and dismay that Hannah could well do with him whatever she wished.

"Approach me with a knife, fair Hannah? Why, your scandalous suggestion would deprive us both of exquisite pleasure."

Joseph said the words lightly, though with more foreboding than he wished to acknowledge. Above all, Hannah was a parson's daughter. Had she been overcome by some shame, some remorse, and now intended to seek absolution by inflicting some excruciating barbarism on him? And how could he possibly cry out? In a room with a parson's daughter, both of them as naked as the day they were breached—well, Hannah still had a small portion of her shift clinging to her. The parson's garrison was well away from other habitations, so no one, with the possible exception of Juby waiting morosely in the barn, would be likely to hear his cries. Joseph cringed inwardly, flesh shriveling; no matter how intense the pain Hannah might inflict, shame would keep him from uttering the slightest sound.

Hannah twitched her shift away and stood before Joseph. Despite his growing apprehension, Joseph marveled at how the smooth paleness of her skin set off the dark pubic hair around her womanhood. Then Hannah disappeared from his view momentarily, to reappear with a sly smile, the candelabra in one hand and a long knife in the other.

"La, Mister Frost, do you not ken that years past there were women in Salem who flew through the night air, danced the abandon, and had congress with the devil? You ken there were men who begrudged those women such abandon and condemned them as witches? La, those women condemned as witches, among them a sister of my great-grandmother on the maternal, were put to death in devious, painful fashions." Hannah laid the knife's blade on Joseph's belly.

"Hannah," Joseph said quickly, "it is decidedly old-fashioned to believe in witches, and you and I are too modern to do so." He dared not glance at the knife, though he felt its weight exceedingly. He fastened his gaze intently on Hannah, noting how her eyes were wild and unfocused, the pupils enlarged, and her face suffused with blood. "Though I confess I am totally bewitched by your beauty and entirely at your mercy."

"La, Mister Frost, you as a man say those words, but it was men who hanged my great-grandma's sister." Hannah moved the knife downward until the blade touched Joseph's manhood.

Joseph felt all desire leave him, driven out by a sickening fear.

"Oh, I can't have that," Hannah cried. She slid one hand onto Joseph and manipulated him into erection again. Then she hitched herself across his lower body, supporting herself on her knees, and seized and guided him. Hannah slid down upon him, then the knife gleamed again. Hannah smiled that taut, wicked smile and reached behind her, the movement bringing an unbelievable spasm of pleasure to Joseph. The knife flicked, and his legs were free, instantly twining behind her. Hannah then leaned forward, bringing her breasts tantalizingly close to Joseph's mouth. He strained upward as Hannah touched the knife's blade first to one cord binding a hand, then the other. The knife then flew from her hand as Hannah covered his mouth with hers.

"La!" Hannah gasped, breaking away for a moment, "Mister Frost, but you do know how to bring pleasure to a simple maid." Then the frenzy of her riding motion increased, until their motions were fair rocking the bedstead. "Yes! Yes!" Hannah breathed as their hot, perspiring flesh became one. "Yes! Yes!"

For many long minutes they lay pressed together, exhausted, bathed in perspiration and the wan light of the three softly guttering tapers. Then Hannah reached his mouth with hers while with her fingers she manipulated his manhood, until at length they were able to resume their lovemaking, with all the passion and ardor though not quite the strength of their first coupling. And then they were entirely spent, the sheets beneath them soaked with perspiration. Joseph rolled over onto the other side of the bed, a much cooler side in the late June heat, drew Hannah's head onto his chest, stroked her hair gently, and gathered air to speak.

"Has your brother ever known a woman?" Hannah murmured.

It was the last question that Joseph could have anticipated, and he stiffened, hand arrested in mid-stroke. "I ken your reference is to my brother Geoffrey, since my brother Jonathan,

Charity's twin, departed this life as near as any one in the family can cypher in the autumn of the year seventy."

"La, Mister Frost, I inquire about your brother Geoffrey, for I have no knowledge of the middle Frost." Hannah snuggled her body against Joseph's and drew his arm over her shoulders, calculatedly so his hand would brush against her breasts.

"My brother is a complete enigma to me," Joseph answered truthfully. "Faith, he is an enigma to all the family. But I misdoubt much Geoffrey's ever knowing a woman carnally."

"Carnally," Hannah fairly purred, "that be quite a word, but nevertheless I ken its meaning. My sisters have told me," she said mischievously, hitching herself closer against Joseph's body. "Why do you profess to know so little about your brother? Is it because he is so many years older than you?"

"But eight," Joseph said.

"Oh, then he be but twenty-six," Hannah said. "I had thought him to be so much older, practically of an age with Father." Hannah giggled. "But he is so much fairer to gaze upon than Father."

"Or fairer to gaze upon than I who lie here in your arms," Joseph said, somewhat more abruptly that he wished.

"Oh, dear Joseph, I did not mean to compare you unfairly with your brother, but I have known you close these ten, no, eleven years past, and I have glimpsed your brother but twice. Once when Charity was wed to Marcus Whipple, and lately when he fetched in that British warship taken so grandly off the Isles of Shoals. Mariah and Deborah tell me there was never anything like it in all New Hampshire! A bluff-bowed Chinee trading vessel besting an awesome Royal Navy warship but ten miles off our coast! Had there been no storm the thunder of the great cannons would have carried even to this house!" Hannah burrowed deeper into the hollow of Joseph's arm.

"It was not a really great British warship," Joseph said quickly, hating himself immediately for the hasty words but continuing nevertheless. "A sloop-o-war, something the British Navy terms a sixth-rate, eighteen cannons—"

Hannah raised herself on an elbow and looked directly into

Joseph's eyes. "Why, Joseph Frost, you are all a-prickle with envy that it was your brother who fetched in the *Jaguar* sloop-of-war and not yourself. Yet all Portsmouth knows and pays you honor as to how you went so artfully aboard your brother's new vessel disguised in a coffin, and returned to us the hero! But lo! Had you earlier looked upon the face of the British officer during the funeral for all the British dead, and marked how close he resembled Geoffrey?"

Joseph squirmed in embarrassment. "The coffin was open but for a moment—"

"But save for the fact your brother has dark hair and the British commander had fair hair, they were as alike as two peas from the same pod, so I am reliably informed," Hannah said haughtily. "So great was the press of people about the coffins of the British dead that my sisters and I could see naught. And think you that would have been unseemly for young ladies, particularly the daughters of a clergyman, to have pressed closer? We could have done so with impunity, indeed, have stood graves' side, had Father delivered the eulogies, but it was that pompous Anglican from Hampton, Shalom Cutts, who was tipped the nod by Mister High-and-Mighty Langdon to consign the souls of British and American dead straight to God's bosom."

Joseph was more than a little aghast. "Hannah, Reverend Cutts be as much a man of the cloth as your sainted father—"

"I ken, yes, I ken," Hannah said irritably, "but we were talking about your brother. As the elder issue of Marlborough and Thérèse Frost, stands not he to inherit all the Frost properties in New Hampshire and the Martinico?"

"I know not how reads my father's testament," Joseph said truthfully, "nor do I care." This was also a truthful answer. "But truly sad to admit, Marlborough and Geoffrey are separated by the great gulf attending Jonathan's death. I fear it is so vast a gulf that it shall never be bridged in this life."

"You allude to things that intrigue me, Joseph," Hannah said in a low, throaty voice. "I have heard the gossip about your brother, including the tale that your brother is impotent, or given over to the affection of other men—"

"The gossips are fantastic concoctions of idle minds lacking sufficient occupation to preserve them from sloth, God condemn their putrid souls!" Joseph said forcefully, squirming away from the sticky perspiration beading Hannah's body to cooler sheets. "Something horrific, perhaps numerous things horrific, transpired—he has never spoken even to Maman of those events—those events that transpired in the six long years he was at sea before he was returned to us."

"Why, Joseph," Hannah mewed, "you have taken the Lord's name exceedingly in vain, and as surely as I could spell my name backwards as well as forwards by the time I was four years of age, there shall be the Lord's reward for such hubris in due course."

"I meant not to provoke the Almighty, Hannah," Joseph expostulated, wishing he could cross himself furtively and unseen, "but examining their conduct objectively, as Master Graham always taught that we should measure, the gossips know not my brother, though they malign him shamelessly. I vow there is not a gossip in Portsmouth, or any of the surrounding towns, for that matter, who would dare breathe such falsehoods in Geoffrey's presence. They fear his cold eye as much, if not more, than his indifference."

"And what of your sister, Charity, and her husband, Marcus Whipple? What portion of the Frost properties stand they to inherit?" Hannah inched her way, serpent-like, into the hollow of Joseph's arm and nestled there with evident contentment.

"I know not," he retorted to the question, which was again completely unanticipated and without predicate. Joseph flailed about for an answer, wondering all the while if he should provide any response at all. "Our parents, Charity's and mine, are in robust health—"

"Your father is continuously plagued by gout and your mother is demented," Hannah said amicably.

"Hannah!" Joseph raised himself on an elbow to stare hard at the woman naked beside him. "I shall entertain no further talk regarding the health of my parents. When he adheres to the low diet prescribed by Doctor Ezra Green, Father is spared gout's pain. Maman suffers perpetual anguish over the death of Jonathan and has chosen to console herself with meditation and prayer. This your father knows well, for he attends Maman assiduously. Surely you have exhausted all your questions about my brother, my parents, and my sister—for I shall answer none further."

"But there has been a purpose to my questions, Joseph, my dearest," Hannah crooned, throwing an arm across his chest. "I ask from the curiosity of what provisions its paternal grandparents shall make for the life growing within me." Hannah sought Joseph's mouth eagerly, smothering him with kisses to forestall any reply. "Joseph!" Hannah breathed excitedly, "I willingly gifted you with my virginity—you cannot imagine how happy, nay, happy and proud I be to bear the child we both have produced."

Joseph felt his heart smite his throat, and he lay back against the horsehair mattress in a state of disbelief. After a moment Hannah's kisses grew less frequent, but she grasped his right hand in her own and guided it down to her belly. "Here, Joseph—do not fret, my dearest, I shall never ask where you learned your myriad ways to please a maid—you can feel our child, just a slight thickening of my belly for the moment, but life within me quickens, and we must ask Father to announce our banns at services this coming Sabbath."

Joseph's hand explored Hannah's belly, and truth, there was a swelling. He drew back his hand as if it were aflame. Oh, Almighty God—

"I believe we may fairly contemplate a wedding within this next fortnight, certainly before the middle of July," Hannah said, happily nestling against Joseph. "We shall consult Father about the date as soon as he and Mother return from Boston. Oh! How envious Deborah and Mariah shall be! And how glad they will be no longer to share this bedroom with me—no less glad I to be shut of them! I doubt not that Marlborough will be glad to let you expand out of the apartment you have in his great townhouse. Do not you think that we shall find your father's townhouse better suited to our needs than being sequestered on your mother's farm—what does she call it? Bois de Jonathan? A noble house indeed, from Father's descriptions, but so far away from the bustle of the town!" Hannah threw both arms around Joseph's neck. "Oh, Joseph! Promise me that we shall begin our married life at your father's townhouse and not your mother's farm, elaborate though it may be. And I am sure your father won't begrudge us the black people who wait upon him. I quite fancy that Marlborough will rejoice to have the sound of a child's voice in his house again."

Joseph made small, soothing noises, but he had quite lost his voice, though he continued to brush Hannah's hair mechanically.

"We shall be so happy, Joseph!" Hannah cried rapturously. "If ours is a male child we shall name him for Father! A girl child you may name. Perhaps after we are married we may elect not to live in this colony of New Hampshire at all, even in Marlborough's elegant townhouse, and shall take ship to England, there to wait out this war that portends so hideous! I would prefer our child to be born in England, as I am sure your desire is also." Hannah yawned. "We have some hours yet before the cock summons the sun, so sleep you now, my darling, but I beg, wake me a-fore leaving." And Hannah Devon went promptly to sleep, apparently much satisfied.

Joseph Frost lay rigid and unmoving, except to breathe, for several overly long hours. Somewhere in the floor below he heard a clock chime eleven, and an interminable time later strike the midnight hour. He very cautiously pushed himself away from Hannah, who had curled into a ball on her left side and was incongruously snoring gently. Joseph's mind was in absolute turmoil. He had never lain with a woman before Hannah, and the fact that his seed was the cause of a new life was strange and disturbing. Though he was woefully unlettered in matters of sex, Joseph resolutely absolved Hannah of any and all blame for the predicament in which the couple now unexpectedly found themselves.

Joseph remained completely still, listening to Hannah's snoring, though the thoughts and emotions churning through his mind had yet to arrange themselves into any semblance of logic. Two of the three candles had guttered out, and the flickering third candle was down to its last dregs of liquid beeswax. Its weak flame would not survive another five minutes. Joseph eased himself slowly out of the bed and gathered his clothes. The candle extinguished itself before he located his shoes, but he did not panic. Service with Knox and his brother had taught him that panic was much more to be feared than fear absolute. Joseph waited until his eyes adjusted to the darkness of the bedchamber as much as they could, and then he noiselessly felt on hands and knees for his shoes. Having found his shoes and stockings and tucked them under one arm, Joseph felt his way to the chamber door and continued to grope barefooted along the hallway and down the stairway to the ground floor, testing his footing and weight carefully on the treads to avoid any sound. He found the kitchen window by which he had entered Parson Devon's garrison, pulled on his stockings and shoes, and carefully eased aside the Indian shutters, flowing through the window without sound or shadow.

The night was overcast, but Joseph found the parson's barn quickly enough, and he knew that Juby would be awake and waiting for him. "Don't touch them doors," Juby cautioned in the lowest of voices, "she be plenty wide enough for the canoe's git out." Juby seized Joseph's hand and guided it to the canoe's left gunwale, then along the canoe to its stern. Juby lifted the canoe from the bow and carefully navigated it through the small opening between the barn doors without the slightest scrape or noise to betray their passage.

Joseph and Juby freighted the canoe down to Islington Creek through knee-high grass saturated with dew, and Joseph knew that anyone with half a woodsman's eye would be able to mark their passage from barn to creek until at least mid-day, when the sun had evaporated the heavy dew. Joseph could not help that; he was rapidly learning not to be turned aside by events over which he had no control. He was knee deep in the creek before he lifted himself into the canoe and took up the paddle he knew would be just behind him, resting against a thwart.

Joseph paddled silently, feeling the incoming tide and welcoming the physical exertion of working roughly northeast toward the creek's mouth, where it joined with the great Piscataqua. The tide was coming on strong, and both Joseph and Juby were leaning heavily into their paddles, approaching the bridge spanning Islington Creek on either side of the Board Road.

The early morning suddenly came alive with the shrill shouts and curses of drovers, the squeal and protest of ungreased axles, and the squeak of harness and chain. A long parade of lanterns and torches appeared on the Board Road from the direction of Portsmouth. The canoe was still some hundred yards away from the bridge on the making tide, and the temptation was strong to turn and flee upstream, but there were many houses inland on the creek, and Joseph had a fervent wish not to be seen. He lengthened his stroke, knowing that behind him Juby was doing the same, though he was certainly no expert with a paddle. The canoe shot under the bridge a minute before the first wagon rumbled over the boards, hooves and the iron rims of wheels sending vibrations down through the bridge's timbers to resonate loudly in Joseph's skull. He held the canoe immobile in the darkest shadows beneath the bridge by thrusting his paddle deep into the mud along the western bank of Islington Creek and clinging to it as the train of protesting teams and wagons lumbered by overhead.

Joseph prayed that the drovers would continue without pause, and the drovers did, though so slow was their passage that every now and again Joseph could distinguish muffled words shouted among them. *St. Jean. Chambly. Montreal.* A stand at Montreal to win all. *Sullivan.* New Hampshire's own General Sullivan was in command, having relieved the gallant Thomas, carried off by the small pox. *Arnold. General Arnold.* Withdrawal from Quebec in the face of a British fleet arrived the first of May, the British and the small pox forcing the dispirited Americans to flee up the Lake. *The head of the Lake. Retreat.* The Continental forces cut off if the British bypassed Montreal and marched directly to St. Jean and Chambly. And then a name that Joseph knew so very well. *Knox. Henry Knox.* Cannon still left at Tyonderoga. *Could best the British yet if control of the Lake was denied them.* Joseph listened to the fragments of speech stridently shouted by the drovers passing overhead; many of the words were too low to be understood, but he instinctively filled in the gaps in the shouted conversations.

Yes, Henry Knox had gifted General Washington with sixty tons of cannons hauled away from Fort Tyonderoga, but there had been dozens of smaller cannons left, and rumors of dozens more dismounted from their carriages and stored in warehouses, even buried. Cannons that had been brought to Tyonderoga by the British after they took Fort Carillon from the French, and cannons that the French had taken to the narrows at the head of Lake Champlain when they had built that grand star-shaped fortress.

The train of wagons took an inordinately long time to cross the bridge, far more than fifteen minutes, and Joseph's arms, clinging to the paddle thrust into the mud, were tiring as he silently held position beneath the bridge against the incoming tide. Then the tide slackened, as did the traffic over the bridge, and Joseph hesitated wondering whither he should direct the canoe once abroad on the Piscataqua. To the left and upstream would bring him to the Frost warehouse on Christian Shore. An hour's pull beyond the warehouse, stroking lustily and without pause, the canoe would deliver him to the foreshore in front of his mother's house overlooking the Great Bay, *Bois de Jonathan,* where he would surely find a haven. To the right and downstream was the town of Portsmouth, and beyond the town the creek that was actually the Pool, and the high point overlooking the Pool where Marlborough Frost had built his townhouse. From the porch of his townhouse Marlborough could oversee all the shipping in the Pool, count his ships in from distant ports, and estimate to the shilling the increase in his wealth. Joseph turned right. Just as the last day of June in the eventful year of 1776 dawned fully, he and Juby brought the canoe to ground amidst the fishing sheds and punt yards at the south end of the Pool.

❧ III ❧

"✱✱✱✱✱ AH, LADDIE, YE'VE GOT THE TAG OF
✱ A ✱ IT," JABEZ MCCOOL SAID WITH EVI-
✱ ✱ DENT SATISFACTION AS HE AND GEOF-
✱✱✱✱✱ FREY FROST SAT COMPANIONABLY IN
the main topmast crosstrees, their bodies pleasurably adjusted
without conscious thought to the roll, pitch and sway of the
Bride's passage through the swells of an azure sea. Geoffrey was
long past his bout with seasickness—indeed, with the resilience
of youth, had forgotten it completely. All plain sail was drawing fully, with the exception of the main course, which was
brailed up in order not to block the draw of the fore course. The
fine spread of canvas was momentarily capturing a steady ten-
knot breeze from the north-northwest, and the *Bride of Derry*
was sailing close-hauled with the bowlines steadied out on the
weather side, holding the weather leeches taut.

Jabez had just finished combing and clubbing Geoffrey's hair
into a neat queue. "Soon yere hair'll be long enough to mark
ye as a right sailor-laddie. Now, before it be time fer ye to skin
down and wait table on Captain Beelzebub, please to name me
the sails our *Bride*'s be spreading." Jabez spat a stream of dark
brown tobacco juice to leeward, carefully waiting for the roll
of the vessel to starboard so as not to risk staining a sail. "First,
though, what manner o' vessel contains us? It must go hard can
ye not name us proper, seein' that I hae paid exclusive drill the
past two months to yere schoolin'."

Geoffrey looked around him and dreamily down with as

great a degree of contentment as he had known since coming aboard the *Bride of Derry* two months previously. He was quite happy here in the tops; though only sixty or so feet above the sea's surface, he was far away from the malevolence of the quarterdeck and Wick Nichols. Geoffrey was no longer fearful of heights and could skin up and down the ratlines as swiftly as any topman. In fact, he had twice experienced the unspeakable thrill of gaining the deck by grasping the main topgallant backstay firmly and sliding down, though he had burned the palms of his hands something fierce. Geoffrey surveyed with equanimity the length of the *Bride,* from the foam crest of the *Bride*'s bow wave, in which dolphins gamboled, to the smother of the vessel's wake.

"We be contained in a vessel known famously throughout the surveyed world as a snow, a square-rigged vessel with two masts. Beginning at the forward spar . . ."

"Which rightly be called the bowsprit," Jabez growled, "as any lubber been aboard two months, 'n' fair wallowin' in luxury, would know. But hold! What be this business o' two masts? What think ye be thet stick o' wood snugged abaft the mainmast, and clamped on with a tight ring of iron just beneath the main top?"

Geoffrey's throat tightened, and he swallowed several times. "Aye, Jabez, you remind me well a-fore I advance too far. There be a small mast, belike the lower trunk of a mizzen, set close a-hind the mainmast, stepped on the deck with head held in iron jaws immediately aft the mainmast and just beneath the trestle trees of the main top."

"'N' what be the name 'n' purpose o' this curious stick of wood?" Jabez demanded. "I hae complete forgot."

"Why, Jabez," Geoffrey dared to taunt, "it was you who taught me its name an' purpose. It is a trysail mast, and it sets a fore-'n'-aft trysail raised with hoops on the trysail mast. Though it seems to me that you could as easily term that sail a fore-'n'-aft mainsail, since both the mainsail and the trysail have no boom at the foot, though the mainsail is suspended from its yard, and the trysail is suspended from its gaff."

"As ye say, we already got a considerable mainsail square-rigged from its own main yard," Jabez said accusingly. "'N' strikes me there be others who call that puny little spar by other names."

"Yes, sir," Geoffrey said meekly. "Others contend that the mast stepped aft of the mainmast should rightly be called a snowmast, and the sail it carries a brigsail, or even a snowsail."

"All the same as a proper spanker laying aft on a three-masted ship-rigged vessel," Jabez sniffed. "So why all the hum and bustle about a name for a particular sail?"

"I admit to perplexity," Geoffrey said earnestly. He had taken readily to Jabez' instruction and thought that the sail plan of a vessel should be something that obeyed in some wise the same rules as the inflectional forms of Latin nouns of the second declension.

Jabez snorted derisively. "Yere ears be stopped by cheese, and I ferget ye be but a child, though a fast learnin' 'un, I grant. We agree that the snow rig be wondrous efficient for navigation, and whether the term be but the way we English pronounce the Dutch *snausnout,* so the cheeseheads pronounce this rig, or somethin' else, ain't worth the inquirin'. Some sailors I've shared a tankard o' ale with 'n a port or two would call our rig a hermaphrodite brig, since we can be a brig or a snow, just so as we elect. But withal, a snow be but a bastard brig, though, ye ken, the largest of the type."

"You be wondrously patient with me," Geoffrey said gratefully. "And I appreciate comprehending the term herma," he stumbled over the word, "hermadite, meaning one or the other. All I can deduce from the facts you have marshaled for my observation is that there be a prodigious amount of peculiarities among rigs. Of a certainty the rig of this snow bowls us along at a prodigious rate."

"Aye, laddie," Jabez agreed. "We need all the speed across the ocean we can muster. We be at war with the Frenchies, and there always be the chance we may come in sight of a Frog cruiser or privateer. We got them six 4-pounder popguns on the deck, three a side so's to spread the weight, though they'd be better restin' on the ballast. And Wick Nichols bain't had no gun drill, not even dumb show haulin' er clearin' one cannon. The capt'n may have served 'n' sighted a gun, but nobody else aboard this barky," and here Jabez puffed with pardonable pride, "savin' yere present company has ever served a gun on a King's ship. Faith, mayhap no powder ner shot be shipped, so them guns 'bout as useful as tits on a boar hog. Speed, 'n' only speed, kin save us from bein' guests o' the Frogs for a smart long piece. Speed also be necessary 'n our particular line o' work 'n gettin' the cargo to market quick as possible." Jabez changed the subject.

"Every sail, every line, every piece of wood on any vessel leaves sight o' land has its particular purpose, there's no accounting for the likes of 'em as wants this done better or that to go faster. My faith, hardly any two vessels appear alike, even the warships of good ol' England, our ancestral home, and I'm hoping the receptacle o' my bones when I cross the bar markin' the end to this mortal life. A snow truly be a hermaphrodite rig, so that we can take our two mainsails, and call one a boom mainsail when we wants to call ourselves a brig, then we can trice up a square mainsail when we wants to call ourselves a snow. Sometimes we show a boom mainsail bent to the mainmast as a brig, or tack it onto the trysail mast and call it a snow. But tell me," Jabez said, more than a little testily, "ye earlier twigged why this snow rig of ours uses a trysail mast when we spread a square mainsail, so out with it quick!"

"Jabez, surely you know the answer, so as the squaresail suspended on the mainmast cannot be fouled by the hoops of the snowsail—the trysail, as it is lowered and hoisted."

"Truth. Now directin' yere attention to the bowsprit, it be a spar, but the name most used be bowsprit. Bain't ye able to collect anything I've learned ye?"

"Beginning at the bowsprit," Geoffrey said quickly, "actually, under the bowsprit, we have spread the spritsail . . ."

"'N' the spritsail be trimmed how?" Jabez demanded.

"You asked only I name the sails," Geoffrey remonstrated. "Can't you inquire about their trim and tricing later?"

"Ye be the star pupil in the McCool School of sails 'n' riggin'," Jabez said, shifting his quid to the right cheek. He waited for the *Bride* to heel to starboard sufficiently, then spat a stream of tobacco juice arching downward. "So ye have to be ready when things change."

"Yes, I be the only pupil in the McCool School of sails and rigging," Frost said, his quick, juvenile anger at the perceived injustice of a sudden change in the rules already forgotten. "The spritsail be bent to the spritsail yard same as any square sail, with earings and robbands. The sail be not gored at foot or leech but has buntline cringles at the foot. Being apt to dousing in any seaway, the spritsail being situated beneath the bowsprit and close to the water, there are waterholes cut in the leeches for the water to run out and not bag in the sail." Geoffrey paused, visualizing the spritsail in full draw, then continued: "The spritsail sheets are reeved through a strap-block and made fast to eyebolts in the bows. The buntlines are reeved through their own blocks, attached either side of the bowsprit, then led through thimbles on the spritsail yard itself and down to the cringles at the foot of the sail. When sailing by the wind, the yard is topped up by its lee brace, and the spritsail is then obliged to be reefed, else it would drag in the water and offer resistance. You have averred much that the spritsail be a right handy sail, even though the jib sails make coming about easy in the comparison."

"Ye's got the sense o' it," Jabez said grudgingly, scrutinizing Geoffrey's head as he shifted his quid. "Some ships have laid the spritsail aside, but should some mischance cause loss to the foremast, the spritsail would permit the handy wearing of the ship. Does ye want me to renew the poultice on yere noggin? I've got the makin's right here. Our discourse on the employment o' the other sails must wait for another time."

Geoffrey grimaced, then hesitantly palpitated the gash above his right ear. The wound had crusted over, but the seam of proud flesh was still painful, very painful, to the touch. "Thankee, Jabez, but I ken my noggin will right itself the faster without another tobacco poultice. And the other bruises on my back are tolerable, not worth the mentioning."

Jabez sighed. "It were a close thing, laddie, and the Dear saw to it that Captain Beelzebub struck ye with the tip o' his staff rather than smiting ye with the broad side o' the cane. The heads of youngun's be not as harded up as a man with his full growth." Jabez waited for the roll to starboard and spat another stream of tobacco juice. "Wicked Nichols be a powerful sinful man. Killed the bosun last voyage—threw a belayin' pin at him, dashed his brains on the mainmast. Entered the death in the log as a fall from the fore topgallant yard, at least that was what Wick Nichols said was in the paper he wrote out and had every man-jack in the crew witness with their X's. Could hae been a paper sayin' I hae killed the bosun, but nothin' was said 'bout it, not in Charles Town in South Carolina, where the cargo was turned over to a Mister Laurens, prominent of that town. Nor was anythin' said when the *Bride* paid off in Newport. That be a piece yere pa nor John Brown nor that Lopez fella never heard."

"Then why did you agree to ship with this Wicked Nichols on this voyage?" Geoffrey demanded in his high, immature voice.

Jabez sighed again. "Got my reasons, laddie, got my reasons. Now, we better shinny to the main deck, 'cause ye got to wait table on Captain Beelzebub in two shakes o' a dead sheep's tail. Oh, I be awful sorry, laddie, I dinna think a-fore I spoke." Jabez said contritely.

Geoffrey nodded miserably and mumbled: "It's all right, Jabez." He leaped and caught the shrouds handily, then scampered nimbly down to the main deck.

"Would you care for a piece of this kid, young Frost?" Wick Nichols asked, raising a questioning eyebrow.

"Thank you, no, Captain Nichols," Geoffrey said from where he stood stiffly beside the desk that served also as Wick Nichols' dining table, his arms bracing the tureen of stew to the table against the pitch and roll of the ship. "Young boys, growing boys, need much food to keep up their strength, particularly on a sea voyage, young Frost," Nichols taunted. "And this be the last fresh meat we can expect until we can re-provision, either somewhere on the Bulge, or the Bight, or the worst of it, waiting until Freddie Po."

"Yes, sir," Geoffrey said, in what he hoped was a noncommittal voice, though he was swallowing hard to keep his gorge from rising. He knew that Wick Nichols had deliberately ordered the slaughter of the young lamb that morning to be long and drawn out, causing the piteously bleating lamb a needlessly painful death. The lamb had been Geoffrey's only other friend aboard the *Bride of Derry* save Jabez McCool, and Geoffrey had shared the better portion of his stale and virtually uneatable ship's biscuit with the affectionate and equally lonely little animal, grown to a ten-pound weight. Perspiration coursed down Geoffrey's spine as he rigidly held the tureen, more from the smell of the lamb stew—a sickening stench in his nostrils—than from the fact that two months of sailing east of south had brought the ship into tropical waters.

Wick Nichols spooned the last of the stew into his mouth, tossed the spoon onto the pewter plate, and wiped his mouth with the back of a hand. "Well, you can take it to Damon, then. Reckon he will enjoy it. Then hasten you back. I grudge that you have learned something of the ship's management, and how to obey. It be time you learn the trade, and perhaps, just perhaps, one day to be a proper merchant, to command your own vessel even." Nichols snorted in disgust. "If you were to wish the command of a vessel in trade, to have the heavy responsibility of every failure, every disability, no matter how obtained, no matter how slight, marked against you." Nichols held out his empty cup imperiously; Geoffrey moved as quickly as the ship's motion permitted to a locker, from which he withdrew a demijohn; holding it carefully, he removed the cork and, bracing against the ship's movement, filled the cup almost brim full without spilling a drop of the rum.

"But most like, you will be exceeding glad to plot a career in the counting house after this one voyage, eh, young Frost?" Nichols fairly sneered. "Tally the profits made for your father's mercantile and banking company by the likes of people like me who have no use for counting houses. Nay, we would be run from them by their proprietors should our shadows fall athwart their door sills, those of us who know only the sea routes in pursuit of a fair cargo."

"Yes, sir," Geoffrey said, not daring to voice his thoughts on the "fair cargo" Wick Nichols was pursuing. He steadfastly denied to himself that his father could even remotely be involved in the heinous trade of human bodies.

"Feed Damon the rest of that slop, then attend," Nichols said shortly, sucking a tooth. "Present him the wafer of biskit; the flour and weevil dust should stand in equal portions these two months into the voyage. You'll most likely regret having passed on the kid. You are to return with my coffee."

"Yes, sir," Geoffrey said quickly, dutifully clapping the lid on the tureen and hugging the tureen closely, afraid he might spill the contents, or worse, drop and break the tureen. He fled the reek of the stifling cabin into the relative openness of the berth deck, there briefly considering running topside for a lungful of fresh air. But he dared not chance being found out. He paused before the flap of canvas just in front of the thick shaft of the mainmast that pierced down from the main deck on its way to its step on the keelson. The canvas enclosed a cabin space hardly wider than a coffin.

Geoffrey coughed, then said in a middling loud voice, a supplicating voice: "Damon, I bring you food from the captain's table. Please allow me to serve you."

The flap of canvas flipped aside and Damon, ship's surgeon, rose eagerly from his pallet, nose aquiver like a hound in pursuit of a rabbit. "Aaah, my brother acknowledges me at last," Damon said triumphantly. "All this voyage without a word from him, and now he favors me with the offal he cannot force past his gullet." Damon glared at Geoffrey so malevolently that the boy shrank back.

"This be not offal, Damon," Geoffrey said quietly. "It be the last flesh of an innocent young lamb."

"And you haven't swilled it yourself?" Damon said, accusingly, wiping away a glob of saliva as he eyed the tureen hungrily, then reached for it.

"It would be the devouring of a friend," Geoffrey said, attempting to keep the note of sadness from his voice.

"Give me the bowl," Damon demanded.

"Have you no firkin or plate? The tureen is the captain's, and he bid me return quickly."

"No firkin, no plate," Damon said, "but hold, I can empty this bowl quickly enough." Damon sat down, cross-legged, on the deck, and held out his arms for the tureen. "May as well join me on this deck, young Frost. I have no stool or chest to offer you."

Geoffrey sat on the deck and drew his arms around his knees as only the young and supple can, watching in fascination as Damon tilted back the tureen, tipped the contents into his mouth and swallowed quickly and steadily. Damon emptied the tureen, then set it between his legs and scraped the interior of the bowl with the hard wafer of ship's biscuit Geoffrey gave him, sucking the gravy off the biscuit, and repeating the maneuver again and again until the tureen was swabbed clean. The hard wafer of bread crunched between his strong, even teeth. Damon uttered a contented sigh, belched, and dried his hands by running them through his skullcap of kinky hair.

Geoffrey collected the tureen and lid and hurried forward to the galley to tender the tureen to plump, good-natured Holly, the cook, who promptly set the pots and pans boy to scrubbing it in a wooden tub of gray water with lumps of congealed grease floating on the surface. "Masta Wick happy wit' him feed, Geefroy?" Holly's oiled cheeks and belly shook as he laughed. "Feed good that, eh? Geef-roy got some dat feed, eh?"

"No, Holly," Geoffrey said truthfully. "Captain Nichols and Damon had the full enjoyment of the last little inhabitant of the manger. I dared not abridge their gustatory delight."

Holly slapped his knee and exploded into another gale of laughter. "How you talk, Geef-roy. Holly neber hear nobody talk lak you. 'N' how old you be, Geef-roy?"

"Never mind how old I be, Holly, I must return to Captain

Nichols with his coffee." Geoffrey looked around desperately for the coffeepot.

Holly threw back the piece of rumbowline canvas shrouding a bucket of sand placed for warming near the brick galley oven and drew out a battered pewter pot. "Ali! So this be where you got yourself off to!" Holly flipped the ball python's good fathom-and-a-half length out of the bucket of sand, where it had twined itself around the pewter pot. The snake writhed languidly across the deck and wound itself into a wicker basket seemingly too small to contain its length. Holly laughed as he picked up the basket and hung it from a low beam ten feet or so from the brick stove. "Did you see that bulge in Ali's gut, Geef-roy? Ali got hisself a rat from out the hold 'n' now requires a place of ease to enjoy his repast. Ali, now, he's pert much o' a sluggard 'n those high climes, but once we sailed below thirty latitude he picked right up, 'n' we won't be bothered overmuch with the rodent kind."

Holly wiped the sand adhering to the pot with a huge black hand and placed it on a small tray. "Don't you go forgettin' the captain's flavorin', Geef-roy. Beelzebub, now he likes his bumper of brimstone dashed up with liquid sin. Be in that demijohn in the settee locker, sure. Best Jamaica. Wished I be possessed o' sum o' it, but take the capt'n's rum 'n' he take the meat off ma back down to the bone, he would."

Geoffrey's various meetings with Ali had engendered a tolerance for the royal python now developed into an affection as keen as Holly's own, though Geoffrey innately grasped enough of the mentality of the serpent to understand him as neither moral nor immoral, simply amoral. He grasped the tray, first feeling the pot to ensure that its contents were sufficiently hot. Then, hunching his shoulders to clear the overhead of the cramped 'tween decks space where men with their full growth had to bend double, he scurried aft, Holly's booming voice following him. "Hard to credit they be brothers, Geef-roy, but they be twins, both born the same hour o' the same dam, though one was sired black and one was sired white."

Geoffrey knocked twice on the cabin door and went in

without waiting for the command to enter. "Took you long enough, young Frost," Wick Nichols snapped querulously, looking up from the charts spread on his desk. "I hope to God the coffee's hot, otherwise I'll start the bung of that hogshead of bilge water passing for a cook." Nichols thrust out his empty cup. "Half the cup, 'n' flavor the coffee with the rum in the settee locker. As you know it, half with the half."

Geoffrey obeyed, again fishing out and struggling with the large demijohn, carefully pouring the glazed clay mug half full of the pure spirits of distilled cane, scarce six months old, then stoppering the demijohn and filling the mug just shy of the brim with coffee. The mug gave off the disagreeable aroma of raw alcohol as Geoffrey placed it on Wick Nichols' desk.

"At least it is hot enough," Nichols said, swallowing half the contents of the mug at a gulp, "though the rum certainly seems to be losing its ginger." He fixed Geoffrey with an accusing eye. "You have not been swilling my rum and replacing it with water, have you, young Frost?" Nichols said softly.

"No, sir, surely not, sir," Geoffrey said immediately, suddenly greatly afraid. "The smell of the raw cane is violently disagreeable to me, Captain Nichols. I draw out the demijohn only to flavor your coffee."

"Place a hair in the neck of the demijohn afore you drive home the cork, and we shall determine if it be missing later whether any of the crew mayhap be making free with my rum, then." Wick Nichols drained the mug, and Geoffrey obediently filled the mug again, half with rum and then with coffee. Wick Nichols pulled a chart nearer to him, scrutinized it, and then pricked a location with the point of a divider. "I confess I represent not the paragon of navigation John Brown considers me, young Frost. That is why I eagerly awaited you as supernumerary. I had been given to understand you have a head for figures." Nichols shrugged. "But you are just a school boy with no notion at all of the fundamentals of navigation. But it is a great ocean, and I can solve for latitude as well as anyone. I generally pick up the bulge of Africa within one hundred leagues of the out-thrusting coast. Coastwise navigation is far easier, you'll warrant."

"I have not been afforded the opportunity to apply my sums to the navigation of this vessel, sir," Geoffrey said, knowing that he had to speak the truth and at the same time steeling himself for the blow he expected to fall his lot.

To Geoffrey's amazement Wick Nichols simply nodded. "'Tis true, I have seen first to your instruction in other areas, primarily that of obedience and sail trimming, as your father would wish. Your cyphers can begin now. When I dismiss you, your task will be to inventory the trade goods enshipped. After I have that tally to compare with the manifest given me—one I trust not—we must find time to devote ourselves to the principles of navigation." Wick Nichols gestured with the steel dividers to the chart. "Yonder be the bulge of Africa. I cypher we are a month, perhaps only three weeks, if the trades hold fair, from sighting the islands off the Green Cape as we run down to fifteen degrees north. Once we confirm our transit we shall run down the easterly islands to determine the land, which I expect to be very near the Green Cape. We shall quickly look into the island of Gorée for a possible cargo." Wick Nichols drained his second cup of coffee and gestured for it to be refilled.

"Other guineamen will have preceded us, more likely than not, out of Liverpool or the Denmark. I mind it far easier to take aboard stock at one place only, so if denied a full complement in Gorée we shall sail southeast along the Guinea Coast, looking in at the factories at the mouth of the Gambia, the Bissagos, Verga Cape, or even along the Grain Coast past Cape Mount. We shall surely find a cargo between the Capes of Mesurado and Palmas."

Wick Nichols applied himself more closely to the chart. "Ask the first mate to deliver a pallet. You are to make your berth in the passageway outside my cabin. You are relieved of all watch and deck duties save serving upon me. Your supernumerary duties are to tally the trade goods accurately, ensure the satisfaction of their goodness, and see to their proper storage." Nichols paused and looked at Geoffrey sharply. "Is something wrong, young Frost? Your appearance is querulous."

"Oh, no, sir," Geoffrey said quickly. He was not at all inclined to be querulous, though apparently he had allowed his features to betray his incredulity that the master of the *Bride of Derry* had delayed until the end of the second month of a three-month voyage to ascertain the accuracy and condition of his trade goods. He continued hastily, knowing that something else needed to be said: "I was quite reflecting upon the trust you repose in me."

Wick Nichols allowed himself to be mollified. "Better get on with it then." He waved a hand in the direction of his sparse book rack: "You may browse my books as you wish, but you are not to touch my quadrant save under my instruction."

Geoffrey stepped to the book rack and peered intently at the books beside the Bible and More's *Utopia,* noting for the first time Robertson's *Elements of Navigation,* well thumbed, and a copy of *Navigatio Britannica,* by Barrow, the 1750 printing, the year of his birth, by the house of Mount and Page. There was also a copy of *Connaissance des Temps* issued by the French National Observatory. The latter appeared little used. He regretted highly the loss of his copy of the *Aeneid;* he had taken quite a liking to the retiring, shy poet and scholar of the era immediately preceding the birth of Christ. And he missed equally the book of sonnets composed by the inestimable Mister Shakespeare. He had it from Jabez that the pages of the books he had prized had been equally prized by the crew—as toilet paper. *Aeneid* and the sonnets had long ago vanished, sheet by sheet, into the *Bride*'s wake. But at least the crew had left him his toothbrush in its silver case, and the bottles of herbal dentifrice.

Nichols saw the direction of Geoffrey's gaze: "The British is sometimes obtuse, but I've always been able to get the gist of it. I have not a clew as to the French, won in a card game against the captain of a French *négrier* at El Mina."

"I appreciate the French, sir." Geoffrey said quietly, believing it best not to lament upon the loss of the books he had brought aboard. Twigging that Wick Nichols had no further requirement for the jug of cane, he tweaked out a single hair from the curls overhanging his forehead and placed the hair in the jug's neck before carefully pushing in the corncob stopper. He sighed regretfully, all the same, unable to repress the pain over the loss of the books his mother had sent with him.

❧ IV ❧

❊❊❊❊❊ oseph Frost was grateful, exceedingly grateful, to
❊   ❊ learn from Clio, his father's cook and housekeeper,
❊ J ❊ who scolded his disheveled, distracted appearance with
❊❊❊❊❊ clucks of motherly disapproval, that Marlborough Frost
had departed the townhouse via the front door scant five minutes before Joseph had surreptitiously entered via the kitchen. In
point of fact, Master John Langdon had sent his coach to fetch
Master Marlborough, and the two great men were expected to
confer on various important matters for the majority of the day.
Moreover, Master Marlborough would be joining Master John
and Mistress Elizabeth for supper, and if Joseph was desirous of
conversing with his parent this day, his tardy arrival had completely obviated all chance of discourse.

Joseph contritely asked Clio if there was any possibility of
breakfast and was grudgingly assured that a simple meal of
ham, bread, butter and applesauce, with buttermilk and coffee,
might possibly be arranged. Clio tartly reminded Young Master
Joseph that the scarcities caused by this ruinous war would pre-
clude any meal more elaborate, and to think not that the portions would be abundant.

Joseph refreshed himself as best he was able in his bedchamber, brushing both hair and teeth, but decided that shaving
would consume too much time, not that his eighteen-year-
old face required the razor's daily attention. He recalled with
wry amusement how he had shaved his brother, following
Geoffrey's triumphant entry into Portsmouth Harbor scarce

two months earlier. Once again in the kitchen he was not surprised to find a plentitude of food set out, for he was beloved by all the household slaves. Joseph feasted on freshly baked bread slathered with butter only hours from the churn, and he heaped the crusty bread with tangy fig preserves put up the summer past and slices of lean ham carved from a shoulder salted, cured and smoked by Jacob Moore of Durham, whose hogs were the finest in the world. He drank the better part of a quart of buttermilk, but the food and drink could not banish the remorse, dismay, self-loathing, and shame that weighed so heavily upon him. The food became lead in his stomach. Joseph took the pot of coffee and retired to his father's study.

Only in the last two years had Joseph been permitted access of Marlborough Frost's study without his father's express invitation, and he had been in the room by himself no more than half a dozen times. But Joseph required the solace and silence of books to bring some semblance of order to the confused state in which he found himself. The heavy breakfast so hastily bolted was unsettling his stomach, and his demons were attacking with a fresh vengeance. A deeply shamed and contrite Joseph Frost seated himself at his father's desk and contemplated the ruination of his family.

He had allowed his lust and sexual appetite to overwhelm him. His thoughtless, irresponsible, hasty, irreversible actions would definitely be found out, and sooner rather than later. Possibly as soon as the end of the current week, when Parson Devon was due to return from Cambridge with his family. Joseph put down the coffee cup, unable to swallow against the lump of shame stoppering his throat. What was he to do? He could not return to the Saugus works, where he rightly should be this morning had he not stolen back to Portsmouth to keep the tryst arranged by Hannah. Dear, simple, trusting Hannah. But he did not love Hannah; he felt nothing for her, certainly nothing like the love that was so evident between his sister and Marcus Whipple, nor the bonds of affection between his father and afflicted mother. But he had lain with Hannah twice now, and gotten her with child. Shame and ruination and ridicule would be heaped upon his family—humiliation such that his family would not dare appear in public in Portsmouth.

But he could not think solely of his family. Hannah would bear a bastard. She would be ostracized, a pariah. Her family would have nothing to do with her. She would be driven from the Devon household once her condition revealed itself. Should he approach Parson Devon and ask for his eldest daughter's hand in marriage? What business had he, Joseph Frost, barely eighteen, in marrying? What were his prospects? What could he offer a wife? He was entirely dependent upon his father for allowances and lodging, not that Marlborough Frost was in the least stinting in those regards, and it was understood and tacitly agreed that he would follow his father into merchant banking, eventually becoming Geoffrey's partner in the Frost Trading Company. So he had prospects—distant prospects.

And now that he had conjured Geoffrey Frost to mind, what would his brother do in such a situation? But Joseph knew that his austere and chaste older brother would never in life so blatantly and shamelessly compromise himself. He knew he would have to find his own way out of the labyrinth into which his carnal desire had led him. "No, that be not true," Joseph reminded himself. "I was not led to Hannah's bed. I went there willingly, all too willingly." He assayed another sip of the coffee, but it was as cold and foreboding as the obsidian Abanaqui war axe head Marlborough Frost used as a paperweight.

Joseph got up and paced the study, then wished he had not, for his pacing brought him near the small, perfect miniature of Thérèse de Villette Frost painted by the great portraitiste Roger DePoinois during his triumphant tour of the New England colonies in the year seventy. The exquisitely colored miniature had been painted the year before Jonathan's death, and DePoinois had captured all of Thérèse Frost's charm, health and love of her family. The beautiful miniature made Joseph's heart ache, for he realized with indescribable pain how much his base, craven actions would disgrace his family. He bit his lower lip to keep from crying, and he had to wipe away the nascent tears with his fingers, since he could locate no kerchief in any pocket.

Joseph's self-loathing knew no bounds or depths. For a desperate moment he thought that he should dash for the necessary situated in the orchard one hundred feet from the kitchen door while he still could. But he fought against the convulsions of his gorge until they subsided, and Joseph sat down at his father's desk and, drawing a fragment of foolscap, a turkey quill and an inkwell toward him, willed himself to take stock of his situation.

He had debauched Hannah Devon and she was springing with his child. Joseph made a tick on the foolscap. He did not love Hannah. Another tick. He possessed in this world no more than the equivalent of fifteen pounds sterling disposable money of account. Another tick. Joseph used his father's small penknife to freshen the nib of the quill, then tentatively dipped the quill in the inkwell. At a mere eighteen years of age he had no immediate prospects of earning a livelihood on his own, dependent upon his father as he was. Another tick. His debauching of Hannah Devon would hold his entire family up to ridicule and infamy. Joseph threw down the quill, spattering ink on the foolscap.

"I must away," he told himself. "My presence in Portsmouth will bring nothing but reproach and disapprobation to our name. Thankfully, Maman will not know of it." But what of Marlborough, Charity, Marcus? Geoffrey, upon his next return from privateering? "I wish the cannons of the light frigate we engaged off Nova Scotia had marked paid in the column of my accounts," Joseph whispered, bitterly but devoutly. "This trial would never had come to pass, Hannah would still be a virgin, and my family would be spared the disgrace sure to accrue, for I can no more marry Hannah than I can fly to the moon, and the world shall know me for a despoiler of woman, and the name Frost shall be uttered only in extreme derision."

Yes, away. Disgrace would attach when all would be known, but perhaps there might be some atonement, some expiation—yes! There was the expiation of blood, of death! Death would resolve all his problems. Hold! He could do nothing as desperate as Jonathan had done in taking his own life. Had he been fortunate enough to die aboard the cat in the sharp but brief engagement with HM *Lark* his memory would have been lauded and esteemed. Women and men would have wept over his promise cut short by so noble a death. Yes! That was it! Death would lave away the blot he had so carelessly cast upon his family's escutcheon. And Joseph remembered the wagons that had rumbled over the Islington Creek Bridge earlier this morning while he fought to hold the canoe stationary in the tide.

There was fighting in Quebec, desperate fighting, and his father's friend, John Sullivan, was leading the American forces struggling to bring that Canadian province into the American fold. What greater cause to serve, one sanctioned by that great patriot, Benjamin Franklin, who had journeyed to Quebec in March of this year to convince the Quebecois that their future lay with the rebel American colonies, not the United Kingdoms? Joseph's decision to join Knox's expedition to Fort Tyonderoga had been born of a boyish desire for adventure, and to show his father and elder brother that he was worthy of bearing the name Frost. And Henry Knox has asked Joseph specifically to join him in that mighty endeavor. But his father had sourly bade Joseph return to the manufacture of iron articles for the revolution—nails and bolts and hinges and spikes and cannon balls and, just perhaps, cannons!

But the Quebec campaign had much to recommend it. There were New Hampshire men fighting there, led by a Continental Army brigadier general from New Hampshire. Joseph would at least be assured of a welcome, and an opportunity to be of some service in fighting the cynical agents of the tyrannical British, who should, by all rights, leave the American colonists who had prospered without British assistance to their own devices and forms of governance.

Joseph pulled a fresh rectangle of foolscap toward him. He would write Hannah a letter explaining his reasons for going away—she would surely understand! He dipped the pen's nib in the ornate silver inkwell on his father's desk, then stayed his hand. There was no explanation he could make Hannah for abandoning her to such a distressed and disconsolate state of being the mother of a bastard whose father had skipped away from cowardice. Absolutely none. He could not face Hannah, he could not face his family, so he was going to run away. No way to put a false polish on his ignominy. No possible way to explain his flight. His stomach heaved again. Coward. Craven. Poltroon. Better to acknowledge himself objectively for what he was and be dished for it than attempt to cover himself with some façade of patriotism or bonhomie to merit acclaim. He, Joseph Frost, was a completely vile and utter coward who was no true son of Marlborough and Thérèse; no true brother to the virtuous Jonathan and Charity; certainly no true brother to the enigmatic and taciturn Geoffrey.

Joseph anchored the rectangle of foolscap with his left hand and quickly scrawled:

Father, I beg your forbearance, but just as I was willed away to assist Colonel Knox in fetching those cannons from Tyonderoga to General Washington by a mysterious power outside myself, just as I was willed away to join with Geoffrey in freeing Marcus from the horrors of imprisonment in Louisbourg by a mysterious power outside myself—I now find that same power compelling me to seek out our valiant General Sullivan in Quebec to succor our Cause there as best my humble abilities shall permit. It galls me exceedingly that I have not the courage to advise you of my decision in this matter directly, for I acknowledge all too poignantly the anguish and opprobrium my precipitant past actions have caused you and Maman. Please know that I could not make such decisions regarding our country and our relatives absent the fine and punctilious sensibilities of honor that you and Maman have inculcated in my innermost being.

Joseph laid aside the quill and wrung his hands—no, he realized he was going through the motions of washing them. "Like Pilate attempted to wash the blood of Christ from his hands," he told himself bitterly. "And like Pilate there is no absolution for me." He picked up the quill and with tremulous hand finished the letter: "Your affectionate and dutiful son, Joseph."

Joseph sanded the foolscap and, hands trembling, arose from his father's desk to consider his next move. He peered out the study window overlooking the kitchen yard and saw Clio's two children, Erato and Terpsichore, seven and nine years old respectively, playing by the water pump. Joseph raised the sash and leaned out to call: "Terpsichore, Juby is much fatigued and must not have his rest disturbed. Please to fetch the golden-bay gelding, the one with the roman nose, from the paddock into the stable and saddle him, for I must dine with my mother at Jonathan's Woods this noon, and already the hour hand of the clock approaches the eighth division."

Joseph quietly lowered the sash and chewed his nether lip reflectively. He must take his leave of his father's house without arousing suspicion; therefore no clothes, no provisions. It must appear that he was merely riding out to *Bois de Jonathan* to take lunch with his mother. And which of Thérèse de Villette Frost's three sons would visit her this day? "I shall be myself today," Joseph told himself. "Hopefully Maman can find forgiveness and a prayer for me in her heart. Perhaps in God's own image of time there can be absolution." He morosely doubted, though, that his sins would admit of absolution.

Joseph swallowed the dregs of the coffee with a pronounced shudder and despite the gravity of his spirits managed a cheerful whistle or two as he returned to his bedchamber and selected the sturdiest shoes from his armoire. He swept all the coins in his desk into a leather wallet that he tucked into his waistcoat. He went out through the kitchen and gave Clio a buss on her forehead and an elaborate bow to thank her for the elaborate breakfast, snatched up a handful of tea cakes kept warm on the brick hearth, and bundled them into a napkin taken from the breakfast table. Joseph forced the appearance of light-heartedness as he walked across the backyard to the stable.

Joseph gave each of the children a tea cake and a smile as he led Nimble, the golden-bay gelding, to the mounting block, balanced the cache of tea cakes atop the block, and tightened the girth. Erato and Terpsichore had not yet the growth or strength to accomplish that important task. He wished he could take a saddlebag filled with food and clothing, but ostensibly he was off to visit his mother, a brief ride of no more than one hour each way. Joseph thrust the napkin of tea cakes, feeling suddenly and intensely possessive, into a pocket of his coat.

V

ABEZ MCCOOL WAS ABLE TO LEND GEOF-FREY AN OCCASIONAL HAND WITH TUM-BLING OUT BARRELS, BAGS AND BOXES OF TRADE GOODS WHEN HE WAS OFF watch, a greatly appreciated hand, for the casks and boxes were heavy and closely packed in the dank, airless holds, permeated with the suffocating reek off the bilges. Geoffrey applied himself as diligently and methodically to the tally as he had always applied to his pedagogy. His studious nature had pleased both parents, and more than anything else in life Geoffrey wanted to please Marlborough and Thérèse Frost, though they were some thousands of miles to the northwest, and at least twenty degrees of latitude separated them from the tiny chip of wood that encompassed all of Geoffrey's world. He had learned to derive pleasure from performing any task worth doing to the maximum of his competence.

The inventory consumed his every waking moment for three days. Geoffrey laboriously inscribed his initial findings on a broken slate with a knuckle of hard chalk in the fitful light of a small bull's-eye lantern, then transferred the rough count in a neater, smaller hand onto a page of water-stained foolscap torn from a ledger. The final inventory Geoffrey copied in his fairest script, kept simple and therefore highly legible, penned with a gull's-wing quill onto a rectangle scroll of foolscap he found tucked into a pigeonhole in Wick Nichols' desk.

"Captain Nichols, here is the tally for your inspection,"

Geoffrey said, proffering the rolled foolscap and putting all the confidence he could muster into his voice, hoping he hid his trepidation convincingly. Geoffrey knew he had done a very creditable job of identifying and inventorying all of the trade goods the *Bride* was conveying. But the boxes and bales in the hold had been densely packed and recalcitrant to maneuver and open except with the infrequent assistance of Jabez. There was the possibility, however slight, that he may not have located all of the trade goods.

"You attest to the accuracy of your tally, young Frost?" Wick Nichols asked with a hint of menace in his voice.

"I do, sir," Geoffrey said respectfully. He faced down the fear that perhaps he had overlooked something. He had done his best.

"Let us now compare." Wick Nichols opened his shirt to pull a string from around his neck and used the key suspended there to open the locked drawer on the lower left side of his desk, plucking out a sheaf of papers. Nichols selected one folded paper, smoothed it with the palm of his hand, did the same with Geoffrey's scroll, and laid the papers side by side, musing over them for a moment.

"Two hundred and fifty hogsheads of Newport distilled Guinea rum at fifty-four gallons the cask. Fifty ha-barrels of English corned gunpowder at fifty pounds the ha-barrel. Twenty bales of heavy woolen cloth, variously colored in bright hues, woven into lambens by mills in Manchester, at two hundred pounds the bale. Five hundred bars of raw iron smelted at Saugus, each ten inches long and weighing five pounds. Two hundred and fifty cutlasses with brass guards, forged in Birmingham. Two thousand pounds or one ton of codfish, dried and salted on the Isles of Shoals. Six hundred chamber pots of Spanish porcelain. One thousand pounds of brass *manillas,* or bracelets, of various sizes, of indeterminate manufacture, probably German. Five hundred weight of glass beads, various sizes and colors, but with much amber color, from factories in Venice in Italy.

"One thousand pieces of kitchen wares, knives and forks

of pewter, ladles of iron. One hundred and twenty muskets of indifferent quality among five chests. Unable to distinguish origin from examination of firelocks, either Danish or Birmingham in origin." Wick Nichols glanced at Geoffrey, head inclined in mockery. "'Indifferent quality,' young Frost. Rising ten years on this planet and already expert in matters martial?"

"I have shot both musket and pistol under my father's supervision, Captain," Geoffrey said stiffly. "I make no claim of familiarity with firearms, but the condition of the muskets, as with any mechanical contrivance, was easily discernible. They were much mended, broken cocks crudely welded rather than replaced, some with springs much rusted, others with frizzens much scored and bent. None possessed flints, but even with flints I much doubt any of the muskets giving fire upon demand."

"I accept your observations. Five chests of shells of some small sea animal, one hundred weight the chest. A competent tally, young Frost," Nichols said gruffly, placing Geoffrey's scroll with the sheaf of papers and thrusting them back into the desk drawer. "It agrees with the tally of goods given me by Lopez to a slight variance only. I am glad to know that the Jews of Newport did not skimp on the quantity, whatever may be the case with the quality."

"Jabez was of great assistance to me, sir," Geoffrey said quickly. "He aided me every moment he could spare when he was not on watch or sleeping. I could not have made the tally but for Jabez."

Nichols nodded and glanced at the barometer attached to the bulkhead near the cabin's entry. "I warrant you have toughed up a bit, wrestling with them barrels 'n' suchlike. But mind, I have only this one voyage to make a man of you, so I of a certainty am obliged to press you hard. Very hard. The glass has been steady these two days past, a convenience to your rummage, no doubt. After dinner I shall roust out the chests of cowries and those with idle hands can string them."

"Cowries, sir?" Geoffrey inquired.

"The shells of the small sea animals. They are a medium of exchange recognized in all the bulge of Africa. A single shell has so little value that a farthing, half a ha-pence, will purchase the thirty in Liverpool. They are cumbersome to transport in bulk, God's truth. But they are valued for their appearance and their shape. They feel good in the hand, can be used for decoration by the savages, and unlike coin have the advantage of proof against counterfeit." Nichols opened a desk drawer, shuffled some broken clay pipes, and drew out a single cowry that he tossed to Geoffrey. Truly, the weight and shape of the small seashell were pleasurable in Geoffrey's hand, and the shell bore a lustrous sheen over the swirls of amber and mahogany colors splashed with whitish, irregularly shaped dots.

"Since idle hands may turn to mischief, apportioning the cowries into lengths on string will answer for useful employment," Nichols said as Geoffrey returned the cowry. "Forty served together make a convenient length, commonly called a *tocky*. Five *tockies* make a *galinha*, that is, a chicken. It takes one hundred and twenty-five *tockies* to make a *cabeça*, or a head." Nichols tossed the cowry back to Geoffrey and demanded: "How many cowries in a *cabeça*, young Frost?"

"Five thousand, sir," Geoffrey said without hesitation, even as he caught the shell of the sea animal.

Nichols nodded his satisfaction. "One *cabeça* has the value of one bar of iron. Two voyages back I was able to purchase a healthy man of no more than eighteen years in Ouidah for twenty *cabeças*. Last voyage when I was able to complete a cargo between Cape Mesurado and Grand Bassa, it was impossible to buy a man completely with cowries, but some partial payment in cowries was demanded."

Geoffrey Frost's palm felt as if it held a glowing coal straight from Holly's galley. He hastily placed the cowry on Wick Nichols' desk, awash with dismay and apprehension, sickness and dread, and horror that something so small and so beautiful—so inert—could be exchanged for a human life. He wanted to be anywhere in the world so long as he was not standing by Wick

Nichols in the *Bride of Derry*. Nichols stepped over to the locker that contained his chamber pot, unbuttoning his breeches. "My dinner now, young Frost, it is approaching eight bells, and then we shall take our turn on deck."

VI

A n extremely fatigued Joseph Frost rode his equally tired golden-bay roman-nosed gelding through the great iron gates of the thrown-down old stone walls of the disheveled fortifications of Crown Point, the old Fort Amherst located on a bluff high above the Champlain Lake. The lakeshore below the bluff on this hot summer afternoon of seventh July was indiscriminately strewn with a jumble of abandoned bateaux, and Joseph rode into a preview of the Hell he knew surely awaited him for his sins of the flesh. Joseph had never experienced such squalor and shambles in his brief life, nor the smells, as his horse slowly paced among the rabble of silent, skeletal soldiers squatting haphazardly around smoky fires of green wood not lighted for cooking but in the vain hope that the mosquitoes, black flies and midges would be fended off by the roils of acrid smoke.

The horrors of the squalor and smells were exacerbated by the sounds that arose seemingly from nowhere and yet from everywhere. Joseph had never heard such sounds before, and after he identified them he hoped with all his soul never to hear them again. The sounds were incredible blends of the buzzing whines of the milling, noisome insects and the muffled keenings of men muttering out in delirium.

He skirted the new cemetery in a corner of the fort, not daring to estimate the number of bedraggled, unmarked clumps of newly spaded earth, and then started at the sight of one long open pit, at least fifty yards in length but only a little more than six feet in breadth. "Every man-jack who dies on behalf of this new country of ours deserves a private grave," Joseph thought, the notion prompted by his stunned and disbelieving survey of the hundreds, no, thousands of men suffering the horrors of smallpox who lay in the hot sun, unattended amid the stench of their voided bladders and bowels.

"Houdie. Would ye perchance have any 'bacca?" a haggard, shrunken, slack-mouthed soldier in the remnants of a mud-colored uniform, his upper body pillowed against a broken wagon wheel, called out hopefully. His face was a mask of black flies. "Mayhap a thimble o' rum, er better yet some flip."

"No," Joseph said hesitantly, "but I do have some water, if you crave that."

"Water," the soldier said dreamily. "I ain't had no water since my mates bore me up from the Lake. Water, fer sure, if'en ye don't mind givin' it to a dead man."

"You don't look dead to me. And dead men don't talk, and you be talking," Joseph said uneasily as he dismounted. "Nothing you need but decent food, a shelter from this scourge of high sun, a bath of clean water and a change of clothes."

The soldier uttered a faint, sepulchral laugh. "Kind o' ye to say so." He pawed feebly at the mask of black flies. "Ain't no idea who ye be. Don't recognize yere step. I be blind from the small Pox 'n' kin't descry who ye be. Did ye come up the Lake with us from Isle aux Noix? There ware ten thousand o' us in Canada, so I kin't be knowin' everyone o' the officers."

Joseph fanned the cloud of flies away, drew the cork of his canteen and raised the man's head off the wagon wheel. "I'm no officer, certainly no soldier, though I've come a-seeking a particular officer. General Sullivan, from New Hampshire. Mayhap you have marked him?"

The soldier laughed, the sound choked off as Joseph tilted a small gurgle of water into the soldier's mouth. "I know Sullivan right enough. Took over from Thomas atter old Thomas died o' the pox in Chambly, though it ware better had thet silly Congress gave Arnold the charge o' the army in Canada. Sullivan, he be all talk 'n' bluster. Quick to act, but don't take no thought first. We could have held Canada if we'd had better generals, but our best, Montgomery, got hisself killed, 'n' Arnold wus wounded. Think on it. With Quebec throwin' in with us them Britishers would be denied the Saint Lawrence. But the generals took their places, Sullivan fer sure, wus mad for the retreat once they saw the numbers of Britishers."

"Easy," Joseph said harshly, "you are talking about a New Hampshire man."

The soldier bristled. "As if'en I wusn't a sergent with Colonel Poor's Regiment, Second New Hampshire. Went all the way to Sorel on the Saint Lawrence with him, 'n' Poor's a New Hampshire man right enough! Trapped 'n' roamed the northern Connecticut River these past ten years. Wus at Fort Number Four when Rogers brought in the first o' his rangers what settled with the Saint Francis Abanaquis. So I kin talk about a New Hampshire man all day, should I want." The soldier lay back exhausted. "Water wus mighty fine. Sure ye ain't got no 'bacca? Not to chaw, but to smoke, seein' it keeps the flies away."

"If I can locate some tobacco in this place I'll hasten it back to you," Joseph promised, stoppering his canteen.

"No hurry 'tall," the soldier said stoically. "I'll be here if'en ye get back with some 'bacca. I'll be here if'en ye don't get back." The soldier feebly brushed a hand across his stubbled beard and momentarily stirred the mask of flies, revealing a face grotesquely swollen and besmeared with blood.

"Ye've had the inoculate agin the small Pox?"

"Yes," Joseph said, remembering how his mother had taken him and Jonathan and Charity to a house in Portsmouth where a young milkmaid had broken out with the cowpox, and their resultant sickness, when the children were carefully tended by their mother. That had been at least seven years ago—two years before Jonathan went to sea with Geoffrey.

"Good," the soldier sighed. "Ye'll mayhap live then. Ye took the small Pox minute ye rode into here. Arnold, now, while we wus in Chambly Arnold ordered us all to get the inoculate, a pinprick under a fingernail, a thorn usually, pushin' in some of the pus from one's already broken out with the sores.

Old Thomas, he came along 'n' countermanded Arnold's order. Thomas wus a Puritan, see? Thought the inoculate was goin' agin the Power o' God by givin' disease deliberate. Two weeks later, Thomas, he wus dead."

"I shall willingly do more for you," Joseph said disconsolately, "though there are so many of you hereabouts that I cannot succor the half of you should my canteen hold all the water of the lake below."

"Waal, as to that I've no idea," the soldier said tiredly. "I kin hear though I kin't see, which be right enough since the Pox makes ye long for 'bacca, rum er flip. If'en ye want to find yere Sullivan he'll most likely be over where the barracks that wus fired been repaired; he be jawin' with the other generals. But be warned, Arnold's the only general knows his cock from a musket, 'n' which one's fer killin' 'n' which one's fer fun." The soldier relaxed back against the wagon wheel.

"I must move you into a tent," Joseph said helplessly.

"Tents be all full o' the real sick, that's why I be layin' here," the soldier said philosophically.

"Then into shade, surely."

"Tell the truth, I'm right comfortable layin' here 'n' rather not move a-tall, though the flies be a bother, as ye'll warrant. I'd be proud to be shut o' them."

Joseph was struck by the simplicity of the soldier's request. "I believe I can help you." He pulled his kerchief from a pocket of his coat and incredibly enough found contained in it a hardened lump of teacake. No, it was a lump of brown sugar he had meant for his horse. "Here is a bit of sweet for you," Joseph said, gently fumbling the hard lump to the man's lips. "Hold it in your mouth and let it dissolve." Joseph dribbled water from the canteen onto his kerchief, then placed the kerchief over the man's face.

"Why, thankee a right smart," the man said appreciatively. "Kin't remember when I last had a sweet." He sighed in contentment as Joseph draped the dampened kerchief over his face. "Name's Knowles, Charles Knowles. Mother moved to Rumford atter my pa died. Keeps a tavern on the Boston Post Road.

If ye wus to pass by Rumford anytime soon I'd take it kindly if ye'd let my mother know I died a true soljer."

"I'll do that," Joseph said wretchedly, wringing his hands in despair. He knew the man was dying, and he was painfully aware there was nothing he or anyone else could do for him. Just as there was nothing he could do for the hundreds of men in this charnel house dying of smallpox and hunger and loss of hope in their cause and in their leaders at Crown Point. He walked his horse back to the rude cemetery, rigged a makeshift halter and tied the horse so he could easily reach a patch of good grass. Joseph straightened his shoulders and collected two wooden buckets with rope handles at a stock watering trough. He filled the buckets with water from the trough and moved among the dying men, giving them drink.

On Joseph's second trip from the watering trough a soldier, barefoot, with no garment except a thin, ragged blanket draped around his emaciated shoulders, got up from the smoky fire where he had been squatting and wordlessly began assisting him. A man died even as Joseph lifted the man's head to give him a drink of water. The weathered tailboard of a Conestoga wagon lay on a patch of stony ground nearby. Joseph fetched the tailboard and he and the soldier lifted the body onto it and bore the body to the rude cemetery. Joseph and his nameless assistant went about their gruesome tasks before a thousand shrunken idle men who studiously averted their dispirited eyes.

"What's this! What's this! Idling jackanapes letting others do for your comrades while you wrap yourselves in pity, too glum even to lift a finger! Where are my majors, my captains, my lieutenants, my ensigns, my sergeants! Were none here to give orders while I attend a council of war? None of this, sirs, none of this!" A disbelieving Joseph saw a squat, swarthy dervish of a man in buff-colored breeches and a faded blue coat with buff facings dash from one group of idlers to another, pulling men to their feet, berating them, shaming them, pushing them. "You, Christopher Shays, you hail from New Haven same as George Maxfield lying not five yards away, and you ain't lifted a finger to comfort him. Oh shame, shame, sir!"

"We all be dead men, General," the man named Shays whined. "What the Pox ain't kilt be kilt by the Britishers come boilin' up the Lake pert quick."

"By God, you are a sorry shit who ain't earned the right to die," the man thundered. "Not yet you ain't! I'll tell you when you can tuck your nose under your tail like a porcupine and die. But I know for a fact certain that if George Maxfield was on his feet and you were lying there not five yards away, George Maxfield would be tending you. Now do your duty to your mates, or by God you'll have my boot up your arse, and ill words from every man who fought in front of Quebec!"

The whiner furtively attempted to slink away, but the man in the blue coat collared him and handed him over to another soldier. "Sergeant Jenkins, take Shays here and put him on the useful end of a shovel. Then send for my adjutant and advise him, though distasteful as it may be, his duty, and the duty of everyone attached to my headquarters, is to identify each man presented for burial." The man turned aside and muttered in a voice so low that only Joseph heard it. "So much as any of these poor wretches who followed so willingly into the wilderness can be identified."

The man in the blue coat stumped purposely toward Joseph, who studied the scowling, wide-shouldered character as he approached. The man's lower lip thrust out obstinately, and his slate-gray eyes seemed to protrude from their sockets above cheekbones dark with beard stubble. The man's prominent nose had been broken more than once, yet he radiated more charisma, personal magnetism and fiery energy than Joseph had ever seen anyone save his older brother exude. He thrust out his right hand. "Name's Arnold. I don't mark you from any campfire that's warmed me since September last, when I set out with a thousand men from Newburyport to bring the Quebeckers into this war on our side."

"Joseph Frost, of Portsmouth. I've come seeking General Sullivan."

Arnold winced as if struck a physical blow. "You'd best kick up a dust then. Brigadier General Sullivan is on the wing to join General Washington in New York even as we speak. He doubtlessly shall be anointed a major general this time next month. Major Generals Schuyler and Gates, together with Brigadier General Sullivan and Brigadier General De Woedke and yours truly, have just concluded a council of war where the aforesaid General Sullivan has declared himself indispensable to General Washington's defense of New York. For myself, I have resolved that the most effectual measures to be taken to secure our superiority on Lake Champlain be a naval armament of gundalos, row gallies and armed bateaux."

"Well, before you go declaring effectual measures to be taken to secure your superiority on Lake Champlain, General," Joseph Frost said indignantly, "and I'm sure you'll excuse my impertinence, but you should separate out from these men who are sick those who are well enough to execute your purposes, and convey those sick to a place where they may receive the attention their conditions warrant."

"Well spoke, Joseph Frost of Portsmouth," Benedict Arnold said. "But now that you have come all the way from prosperous Portsmouth to this outpost of misery and defeated American arms to discover Brigadier General Sullivan," Arnold drew out the word brigadier as he threw out an arm to encompass half the encampment, "I imagine you will be accompanying him to New York."

Joseph locked gazes with Arnold. "Tell me, General Arnold, where is a glorious death more likely to be found?" he said theatrically. "Here defending Crown Point, or accompanying General Sullivan to New York?"

Arnold grasped Joseph's arm. "Allow me to escort you to a point of vantage in order to add further dismay to this already overburdened abyss of death, despair and desolation." Arnold led Joseph a hundred or so yards to the overlook at the northernmost point of the bluff. "This fortification was originally built by the French to protect against a British advance from the south. From the south, mind. As built by the French engineers this Crown Point would be a tough nut to crack—from the west and south. The French are grand engineers of fortifications, as I found to my sorrow before Quebec. Christ's eyeballs, but Montcalm easily held Carillon just south of here in fifty-eight against fifteen thousand crack British troops with less than four thousand men of his own."

Arnold sat down on a boulder that had been roughly squared by long dead French stonecutters and absently massaged his right leg. "But the French weren't concerned about an attack from the north, since they owned the north. But a deadly threat to our United Colonies will come from the north, laden aboard the fleet Carleton will assemble. Hugging the west shore of the Lake, Carleton would be under our noses here at Crown Point before we sniffed him. Building up and extending the fortification on this side of the fishhook so as to contest successfully a British passage up the Lake would take us until December. And Carleton's got to force his way up the Lake before the ice comes. So we ain't got until December. We send the sick—by now there ain't no wounded, they've done died—down to the narrows 'cross from Tyonderoga. 'Cause, you see, Tyonderoga looks south, just as this fortress. So the need is to raise fortifications facing north. And I somehow must find a fleet of ships, and the crews for them, to meet Carleton as he sails out of the north."

"Yes, I knew it as Tyonderoga, not Carillon, when I was there December last with Henry Knox," Joseph said in a matter-of-fact tone.

Arnold looked up sharply at Joseph. "In a pig's eye you've ever been to Tyonderoga! I'll have you know I captured Tyonderoga from the British."

Joseph's face reddened as he bristled. "I have no quarrel whether it was you or Ethan Allen gets credit for crossing by boat from the Verdmont side and walking into an isolated garrison of a handful of soldiers who considered themselves abandoned by their empire and declaring their fortress a prize of war, General Arnold. But Henry Knox, though he got his learning about cannons from books, certainly removed sixty tons of dead metal cast in the shapes of cannons from Tyonderoga to

General Washington's aid in front of Boston, and I was with him every weary step of the way."

Arnold continued massaging his leg thoughtfully. "If, as you aver, you were ever at Tyonderoga, who consigned the cannons over to Knox?"

"General Schuyler, who at that time was making his head-quarters at Tyonderoga," Joseph said readily, "though I saw him only from a distance, since Colonel Knox bade his brother, William, and me assist in constructing sledges to skid the cannons down to the lakeshore."

"I recollect the cannons were kept on the lakeshore until the Lake froze," Arnold said, his voice cracking with apparent dis-belief. "Then it was ever so much easier to dray their loads."

"I regret you are so grievously misinformed, sir," Joseph said, his jaws tightening. "Colonel Knox was goaded to all speed and diligence, sir. It would not do to wait for the ice. We made the uphill portage to Lake George and took barge to head of the Lake."

"What was your route?" Arnold snapped.

"Directly south from Fort George, then across the Mohawk River and then Hudson's River at Albany. We turned eastward at a place called Claverack. In all it was three hundred weary miles that Colonel Knox led us to Cambridge."

Arnold stood up and began pacing excitedly, much as his brother might pace, Joseph mused, though Geoffrey would have been more methodical and less excited in it. "God's teeth! So you really were with Knox!" Arnold exclaimed. "Have you any experience in the employment of cannons?"

"I'm six weeks returned from a privateerman's cruize in which I learned the trade of matross from Master Gunner Roderick Rawbone, who hails from Connecticut." Joseph said with pride. "I believe you are also Connecticut born."

"Rawbone?" Arnold squinted sharply at Joseph. "Bless me! He's the best there is. I sent for him to come up to Canada but heard that he had gone to sea in venal search of vast sums of prize money. Rawbone taught you the trade? If so, and you were with Knox, then you are a right marvel, young man."

"I shall never possess Gunner Rawbone's skills," Joseph said in all truth, "but I believe he would vouch me as acceptable to serve in his gun crew."

"Knox took only half the cannons there was at Tyonderoga. Can you instruct others in the science of the matross?"

"Yes, sir," Joseph said.

Arnold grinned. "And you have a horse. Come with me. I'm going to ask Major General Gates to attach you to his command as a gentleman volunteer with particular knowledge of artillery employment when he goes to Tyonderoga. Though don't expect no pay for it. I ain't been paid nor my accounts settled by our esteemed Congress of Conjurers for any of my forays into Canada. Major General Schuyler goes to Albany to gather supplies to send to us. I'm here at Crown Point for a few days to strip everything that can be used at the Tyonderoga fortifications. You'll be charged with assembling all the cannons you can and sledge them down to the water. I have cannons taken from the British during our retreat from Canada that will be delivered to Tyonderoga presently. Right now we've got to concentrate on building a fleet, and on getting men, powder, nails, canvas, ropes, oakum, everything that a fleet needs and that we don't have at all. But once we start getting hulls built you can set up cannons on them, and train matrosses in how to employ them.

"This bankrupt Continental Army of ours has but three vessels afloat on the lake: the schooner *Liberty,* taken from the Tory Philip Skene, the sloop *Enterprise,* built by the British at St. John's and called by them the *George,* and the *Royal Savage* schooner that we raised after she was sunk by our own cannons. And there ain't a cannon mounted on the three, and even if there was they wouldn't throw a scare into Carleton, no way. So we've got to build a passel of row gallies and gundalos. They can be built quick—if I can get the shipwrights—and oh will they give Carleton occasion to gnaw his navel—if I can get the crews. And if I could transport myself to London by thought alone and kick the King of Hanover's butt off the throne then I could style myself the King of Hell and Gone.

"Then," Arnold continued triumphantly, "assuming you're still looking for some glorious end to your young life, I promise you will realize such a fate sooner with me on this Lake than you'll find it chasing after Sullivan, though he hails from your colony—your state, that is." Arnold gestured toward the north. "Carleton's got to reach Hudson's River in order to control the Mohawk and Hudson valleys and keep Washington from even thinking about retreating up the Hudson ahead of Howe. Carleton will be coming up the Lake soon's he's got the means to protect his force. He could build enough bateaux by the end of July to ship every redcoat and German hireling toward the headwaters—and he'll have over ten thousand all told, likely more, the way King George's ministers are filling troop ships to Quebec and New York. His Indians don't need no bateaux, they'll fetch along their canoes. But Carleton's going to know I'll be contesting his passage, and without ships we can run among his bateaux and slaughter with impunity. So he'll have to build ships to protect his troops. So spurred to speed, let's kick up an almighty amount of dust, for Carleton's got to start up the Lake before the ice comes, for come it shall."

Arnold limped away toward the encampment, which was now a-bustle, and though he limped Joseph was hard pressed to keep up with this intense brigadier general who had the unmitigated gall to believe he could create a fleet on Lake Champlain. And Joseph knew he could—and would—do it. Joseph hoped that Arnold might be in a position to offer him something to eat. He could not recall when last he had eaten. But as he followed Arnold toward the barracks where the generals had earlier conferred, he came abreast of two scarecrows. These caricatures of men were struggling along under the weight of a slight body they carried on a door. The body was almost completely a-swarm with flies.

"Don't tumble him into the burial pit like he's a rock without feeling," Joseph said sharply to the two scarecrows. "His name was Charles Knowles, and I'll tell his mother and the world entire that he died a true soldier."

ᴄᴇ V I I ᕲ

T HERE WERE NO SLAVES TO BE HAD ON THE ISLAND OF GORÉE. TWO VESSELS OUT OF LIVERPOOL HAD EMBARKED FULL CARGOES OF SLAVES TO BE DIS-charged at the appropriately named Gorée Wharf in the city flourishing at the mouth of the Mersey River, and a small brig, the *Nancy Jane* out of Bristol, Rhode Island, and returning there, where a parish had been given that singular name, had removed the remainder of the stock.

Geoffrey went ashore with Wick Nichols to the long, low island just south of the Green Cape, on which the forts protecting Gorée, Saint-Michel and Saint-François were sited. They rode in the ship's gig, since the barrier bar of sand was swept clear by the currents swirling around the Green Cape and could be crossed without trepidation, though the *Bride of Derry* was anchored a prudent good sea mile off. Geoffrey waited with the crew of the gig while Wick Nichols visited with the English factors. Harpwell, a loquacious carpenter's mate of some thirty years, fifteen spent at sea, who acknowledged some obscure village north of Providence, Seekonk, as his home, and who had been pressed into service as an oarsman, had touched at Gorée twice before with Wick Nichols and knew something of the island's history. He was quick to impress upon Geoffrey and the oarsmen the affinity between him and the captain.

"Now Capt'n Wick 'n' me, we's wus here two years be past, 'n' last year. Capital place, stunning really. The Portagoose wus the first to establish a post here. The Cheeseheads came along later and swindled the Portagoose out of their post, most like with a few score cannon pointed shoreward, God's truth no lie. The Portagoose and the Cheeseheads went back 'n' forth over the years, one possessin' it, then the other. When Charles Number Two was premier of all the world, we took the Gorée, only to have the Cheeseheads come back agin when we wusn't lookin'. But the Frenchies wus keepin' 'n eye on the Gorée, 'n' when the Cheeseheads weren't lookin', gar, the Frenchies came'n. They be the ones which built them forts."

"Then why us English possess Gorée now?" queried a man by the name of Evans, out of a whaler from Nantucket and on his first voyage to Africa.

"We took it square 'n' fair first year of the current war," Harpwell said. "Good thing I say, Frenchies ain't got no claim to anythin' but the land the Pope give 'em. 'N' all that be situated across the Channel from the Fair Isles. No popery 'n our America, not by a long shot. Keep out all popery, and Jewry, too. We don't should never give back the Gorée!"

"Well, why don't we find the black peoples here," demanded a cross-eyed topman named Fernald, who came from some poor fishing village toward the end of Cape Cod's fist.

Harpwell shrugged. "All took off. The *captiveries* hereabouts kin hold some thousand, two hundred, three hundred of the blacks."

Geoffrey Frost had been walking about with great excitement in the fine white sand of the beach before what passed as the administrative center of Gorée Island. He was entranced by the long, curving beach, the sand so brilliant in the sun of noontime that it hurt the eye, and by the relaxed murmur of surf testing its strength with the sand. The exotic architecture of the low buildings, constructed of unpainted tabby, was very different from the ordinary scenes of his upbringing in New Hampshire. His ambulating left much to be desired, for the land was no longer the *Bride of Derry,* pitching, shrugging, trembling and rolling. Geoffrey staggered about as if he were inebriated, though truth to say, he had never imbibed so much as a drop of alcohol in his very young life. He knew a queer feeling in the pit of his stomach as one unsteady leg collapsed and he rolled upon the fine sand. He looked up at the palm trees, so alien from the pines, oaks, maples and birches of New Hampshire, and shut his eyes in an attempt, largely unsuccessful, to overcome the vertigo of suddenly adapting to the placid earth after having been so long upon the restless sea.

After a long while his whirling sense of heavens spinning reached some semblance of equilibrium with his surroundings. Geoffrey gratefully composed himself for sleep. but it was to be denied. A rough boot in the ribs shoved him bodily half a foot from where he had formed a pleasant hollow in the warm sand and then snuggled down. One arm was draped over his forehead to shade his eyes from the sun, and his left thumb hovered anxiously near his mouth: *oh, how he had delighted in sucking his thumb as a child!* Geoffrey was oblivious to the conversation of his mates and half expected his mother to lean over him with a good-night kiss.

"Back to our barky," Wick Nichols shouted venomously. "There be no trade here. All the stock gone off in other bottoms, and I don't fancy waiting offshore while the harlequins about this place stroke me that, sure, the stock be replenished from wars between the Mohammedan in the interior. Mayhap so, but we ain't tarryin' here while they does!" Wick Nichols kicked Geoffrey again, a mild, disinterested kick, and at the same time tossed a leather bag, heavy with metallic coins, into Geoffrey's lap, overbalancing him as he attempted to stand.

"Gorée's the first place on the Slave Coast where something close to real currency kin be used," Wick Nichols leered at Geoffrey Frost. "Never knew about these Dutch stuiver pieces, did you, young Frost? Of silver they be. A good inventory, sure you did, but you did not ask for coin to tally, and see, I didn't volunteer the exchequer. Only in this Gorée is there coin recognized so as to avoid the tedium of determining equivalency in iron bars, cowries, cloth, guns, rum, the whole damn lot, for a set of hands wrapped around with black skin."

The crew goodnaturedly applauded Geoffrey's valiant efforts

to assist them, putting his back and young strength into leaning, grunting, against the bow post to skid the gig back to the water across sand wetted by the retreating tide. The crew let Geoffrey do most of the work, then tumbled in and began the long row back to the *Bride of Derry.* "Does your father own slaves, young Frost?" Wick Nichols said, turning to address Geoffrey, who sat beside him in the stern sheets as the oars dipped symmetrically in an even, strong pull. "I have been meaning to ask."

Geoffrey considered his reply before answering. "My father has black people in his employ, sir, but I have ever considered them part of our family."

"How many?"

"There be Juby, his major-domo and coach driver, and the women, Patience and Prudence, who assist my mother in the management of the house."

Wick Nichols hawked and spat overside the gig. "Juby. A cape north on this continent, on latitude twenty-eight, with the Canaries lying to the westward. Last sight of Africa those taken off by way of the Canaries would ever see. Other slaves in your family?"

"A variety of men who work in the warehouses and barns, and one delightful soul who induces the garden to surrender an abundance of beans, peas, cabbages, potatoes, asparagus, strawberries and other luscious fruits."

"Your parent's friends, mayhap they own slaves?" Nichols asked calculatingly.

"Yes, sir," Geoffrey replied soberly. ""I have observed black people assisting friends of my parents in divers ways, such as house management, carriage driving, and warehouse work. There be many such in Portsmouth, servants really."

Wick Nichols did not speak again until the gig hooked into the starboard foremast chains. "Happy in their lot, be they? Afford you a life of privilege and ease, eh? No gettin' along without them. You have a lot to learn about this trade in *ser-vants,* young Frost," Nichols said with a sardonic grin. "There weren't no trade goods in the island of Gorée, so we must trend southeast along the coast. It is past eight bells, and my dinner is delayed. Afterwards we shall begin your education in coast-wise navigation."

The *Bride of Derry* crept down the bulge of the ancient, long-suffering and war-wracked, beautiful continent of Africa. She stood off from the land at least a league to remain well away from bars and reefs that made any approach perilous in the extreme. Now that they were in constant sight of land, Wick Nichols began Geoffrey's lessons in navigation, showing the youth how to use the quadrant to determine the angles between the *Bride* and various headlands and then solve for distance offshore with simple trigonometry. Geoffrey had been briefly exposed to trig-onometry by his pedagogue, Graham, and he took to its math-ematical delights with enthusiasm.

"You know already far more than me about mathematic extrapolation, young Frost," Wick Nichols conceded grudg-ingly, returning his quadrant to Frost and consulting once again the skewed column of figures marching haphazardly across his slate. "I grant your plot of our current position more accurate than mine." Nichols reflectively sucked a tooth. "I claim no great shakes with the mathematic when close in shore, though ten voyages, all successful in the extreme, between these shores and North America attest to more than adequate competence in the practicals of ocean navigation. We have passed the mouth of the Rio Gambia and are bearing down on the Rio Casamange, with Cape Roxo in the offing south-southeast by south." Nich-ols unfastened the kerchief around his neck and mopped his brow.

"Insufferable heat would prostrate us all save for the breeze off the land this time of the afternoon. Know you, young Frost, how translates the Rio Casamange?"

"If I be permitted the French of it, Captain," Geoffrey said diffidently, carefully fitting the brass quadrant into its wooden case, "it would translate as the 'eater of the house.'"

"There have been much larger objects than houses borne sea-ward and eaten by these great torrents, whose genesis in the mountains and forests of the Senegal is beyond comprehend-ing." Nichols opened and focused his telescope with a comforting metallic snick. "There are mixed and muddied currents hereabouts, running all crosswise. Had I attended my initial instincts and stood in half a league more toward Cape Roxo, I fear our vessel would have come under the influence of the easterly trending current just riffling the bar there!" Wick Nichols threw out an arm, pointing. He collapsed the telescope, thrust it under his arm, and began pacing his quarterdeck, hands firmly clasped behind his back.

"Young Frost," Nichols said fiercely, "have you the idea of our occupation had we but come one sea mile closer to Cape Roxo than we bear now?"

Indeed, Geoffrey's intuition of how currents met, co-mingled, and brawled savagely with each other along this African coast had given him a very good idea of how a vessel could be entrapped in a strong, landward trending current, though seduced by a breeze off the land. But his diplomatic instincts were sound. "I have never glimpsed this coast, Captain Nichols, while you have descried it numerous times."

Nichols snorted a short laugh. "Last voyage I saw two Danes coming out of the Bissagos with overly full cargoes of blackbirds. They hoped the currents close inshore would catapult them northward at a faster clip. They wus fools." Nichols prodded Geoffrey in the ribs with the telescope. "Fasten upon that weathered spar protruding from the sea less than a cable off the bar."

Geoffrey did as he was bid. "I descry the weathered spar, a splintered mast apparently still attached to its hull, as you describe, Captain, half a league off the beach."

"Off the bar, not the beach," Nichols growled. "The bar protects the beach and keeps vessels like ours from approaching muchly close. That spar solitaire marks the wreck of two Danes, and above six hundred lives."

"The wreck lies close against the shore, Captain, less than half a cable," Geoffrey said urgently. "Surely some of the company must have lived through the surf."

"Know you what kind of animal a sea-shark be?" Nichols demanded, advancing to the mainmast windward shrouds and seizing one with a vengeance. "I observed both vessels over-turn, at the same time, actually. Their keels touched the sand beneath the water and arrested their progress. Then they were over-tipped by the force of water sweeping from the west. I confess to having seen people of the crew bobbing around in the swells, striving mightily toward the bar, only yards away. Then the sharks were among them. You should know, young Frost, that sharks always follow a slaver! Always! I am certain your father instructed you to note useful things. The fact that sharks always follow a guineaman is worthy of note. So no one reached the bar."

"But what of the people aboard!" Frost exclaimed. "Even with the vessels over-tipped, the depth of water could not have been too great, and the bar must have been in communication with the masts of the vessels so that the slaves easily could have won the security of the bar!"

Wick Nichols chuckled, "Now, you must concede that it would be inadvisable in the extreme to let slaves out of their fetters simply because of a foul shore, young Frost. I misdoubt any among the cargo survived the overturning of the hulls, con-fined as they were inside."

Geoffrey fought hard to keep his emotions from betraying him. He had no high opinion that he would live long enough to return to New Hampshire. Once he had emerged—miracu-lously now it seemed—from the bane Geoffrey had determined that he would live only the current day. He loved his father, wanted in all things to please him, but of a certainty his father had known precisely the nature of the trading voyage upon which the *Bride of Derry* was embarked. The voyage thus far in the *Bride* had thrust upon Geoffrey the crushing realization that he had been extremely naïve in his young life, focused overly much on his studies and family, shielded by his doting mother from all alarms and harms, real or imagined.

His father, obviously entertaining great expectations of him, had arranged with his fellow merchant John Brown to send Geoffrey out into the world under the auspices of a successful, even brilliant sea captain. But Geoffrey marked the spar rising from the edge of the surf that was the only monument, so Wick Nichols opined, to above six hundred lives. It did not matter to Geoffrey that some of the people who had perished there had white skins and others had black skins. They had all been people, lives and souls. With the stark evidence under the *Bride*'s lee of just how exceedingly easy it was to perish on the bulge of Africa, Geoffrey had no illusion that he would see his mother or father again. But were a benevolent God to vouchsafe sight of his family once more, no matter what arguments, privileges and inducements his father might advance, Geoffrey Frost was not meant to participate in the immoral trade of *human beings*.

"We shall repair to my cabin, young Frost. Shame we wus never able to determine who was makin' free with my cane, but there is a new demijohn broached now, and I wish to flavor my coffee. We are bearing down on the port of Cacheu, and south of that the Bissau. But I have some antipathy to dealing with the Portuguese, save in the most dire need—they have cheated me exceedingly in the past. We shall look into the Islands of the Bissagos, where, you will be interested to learn, the majority of trade is conducted with women. On the mainland you will find Betsy Heard at Rio Bereira, just started up these two years past in the trade. Remarkable woman, this Betsy, daughter of a slave woman from this coast and a Liverpool merchant she be. The Mohammedans far inland in the Futa Jallon have been warring against the tribes thereabout and sending down to the coast those who don't accept their religion. Differences in religions be a powerful way to get the losers into a coffle or two."

Wick Nichols yawned and scratched his genitals. "But we must have a cargo soon, because of the rains and fogs along this coast, and the winds we must embrace to hasten us back to Providence, so we must spur on with speed."

Geoffrey waited upon Wick Nichols to his cabin, having first run to the galley and fetched a pot of coffee warming on the bricks of the great stove. In the cabin he dutifully brought up the new demijohn of cane. It was a heavy demijohn, requiring all of Geoffrey's strength to lift it from its locker. He poured the raw spirit into a small tumbler and set the tumbler beside the pot of coffee so Wick Nichols could determine for himself how much spirit to add to it. But Wick Nichols had not emptied the previous demijohn alone. The level in that demijohn had been diminished alarmingly by Jabez McCool. Geoffrey had fearfully, and only after much urgent importuning, shown Jabez the trick of the hair in the neck of the jug, though he trembled still at the displeasure he knew both he and Jabez would incur if Wick Nichols ever learned of the fraud. Geoffrey thought of the woman, Betsy Heard, earning her living from the enslavement of people related to her by blood, just as Wick Nichols was intent upon earning his living from the transportation of people related to him by blood.

But the winds, coming fiercely from east to west off the land, were extremely contrary for closing with the mainland's shore. When the *Bride of Derry* finally managed to crab into a position half a league west of the long sand bar guarding the Bereira River estuary and pointing as high into the wind as ever she could, under half-furled topsails fore and main, a seventy-foot *almadia* canoe hewn out of a single silk-cotton tree and propelled by at least twenty paddlers ventured over the bar. Geoffrey had been keenly observing activities on shore through the *Bride*'s second-best telescope, and he marveled at the ease with which the paddlers propelled the unstable hollowed-out log fiercely upward through the towering surf, the canoe completely obscured in the blowing spume at the top of the wave's deliberate, ominous curl. The long canoe pierced this froth and hurled itself precipitously down the slope behind the great wave, as slick and greasy and lovely as polished obsidian. When the canoe reached the bottom of the wave its bow buried itself into the green, grasping water so deeply that Geoffrey feared the vessel would never appear. But it did, half the paddlers having set their paddles aside to take up calabashes and bail fiercely. Geoffrey saw a rainbow in the water thrown overside so famously by the bailing. The *almadia* stroked masterfully toward the *Bride of Derry*.

A handsome, fair-skinned young mulatto, his wild hair plaited into fearsome dreadlocks, who was standing in the bow of the sixty-odd-foot canoe, shouted out in acceptable English that some sickness of unknown origin had taken away the majority of his mother, Betsy Heard's, stock. Though they were not to worry, there were bracing good wars underway in the interior by the Mohammedans in the Futa Jallon, and the barracoons of the Queen of Rio Bereira, the young man averred, would soon be filled with prime ebony.

"Next voyage, perhaps, depending 'pon your market!" Wick Nichols shouted across the fifty yards separating the Bride from the *almadia,* a decided lack of conviction and commitment in his voice. He turned to Geoffrey, who held chalk and slate to record Nichols' noon sight. "Belay them figures, young Frost. We can cypher plain as day the location of the mouth of the Rio Bereira from the chart. We know to a mortal certainty the distance we stand off the mouth—" Nichols thrust his face a foot from Geoffrey's, so close that Geoffrey was almost overwhelmed by the offensive reek of cane and tooth decay. "How far do we stand off the mouth of the Bereira, young Frost?"

"One league, sir," Geoffrey said quickly. "And we be one-half a sea mile off the bar." Geoffrey fell silent and regarded his captain intently, his lips moving but no words issuing.

"You've something to say, young Frost, then by damn say it!" Nichols demanded.

"Yes, sir," Geoffrey said, not knowing whether his words would be well-received or not, but knowing that he had to say them. "A few minutes ago, as we watched the canoe put out from the shore, we were twice our distance from the bar. I think we have fetched the bar too close by the half. We have been concentrating upon the wind setting off the shore, even with topsails backed, but we have been neglectful of the current's set, which seems to be bearing us into the bar most treacherously uncomfortable, and we have not had a lead going this long while."

"No lead goin'?" Nichols demanded incredulously. "Why, I had instructed Mister Crowninshield to get the lead goin' as soon as we saw the canoe comin' out. Mister Crowninshield, here immediately, sir!"

An ashen-faced Crowninshield appeared as ordered. "Problem getting a lead line unraveled, sir, all gone arsy-versy. Kin't account fer it, no-wise. Got it sorted out now, sir, hand going forward to the weather fore-chains." Crowninshield's voice broke, and he looked deathly pale.

"Less than four fathoms, Crowninshield, and I'll break you! By the Great God Jehovah, I'll break you. Hear me! I'll break you back to a foremast hand if the line trues at four fathoms or less." Nichols heaved his walking cane at Crowninshield, but the shaft was intercepted by a line dangling from the main yard, and it clattered to the deck. Barely containing his fury, Nichols stood, indecisive. Geoffrey sensed the fear and the fury in the man now; Wick Nichols had been distracted, derelict in his duty to his ship. He watched as Nichols hesitated, despairing between decisions less his choice be a wrong one.

A black able seaman named Amos vaulted over the bulwark and scrambled out into the windward foremast chains. Geoffrey dared a glance over the windward side and was alarmed by the sickly greenish-brown and sable color of the water, which was no longer the brilliant bluish-green to which he was accustomed. Crowninshield thrust a tangle of line toward Amos with an urgency that Geoffrey wished could have been the case ten minutes earlier. An interminable minute passed while Amos sorted out the first ten fathoms of line.

"Shoalin' ahead!" shouted a hand, hitching up his trousers as he emerged quickly from the heads. Geoffrey ran to the helm, where a seaman by the name of Pollard with scabrous, crapulous cheeks deeply creased and folded like those of a bulldog gripped the spokes rigidly and stared straight ahead. Geoffrey recalled his earlier observation that Pollard was a conscientious seaman though possessed of a somewhat vacuous air and completely lacking in initiative.

"Pollard!" Geoffrey piped urgently in his prim soprano voice, "The helm down and off the weather for all love, man!"

"Aye," Pollard replied anxiously, "helm down and off the weather it is." But the wheel remained immobile in his grip.

"Let me aid you," Geoffrey said in frustration, jumping to capture in his grasp the king spoke, marked with a bit of gammon, that fortuitously stood at the top of the wheel, indicating a neutral rudder. He let his weight bring the wheel clockwise, to starboard, and then pressed all his strength, hand-over-hand, to turn the *Bride*'s bow seaward, away from the bar. From the corner of his eye Geoffrey saw Amos cast the lead hastily, anxiously.

"By the mark four!" Amos shouted.

Geoffrey, now aided considerably by the mild-mannered Pollard, continued in his effort to turn the *Bride,* first broadside to the harsh breeze off the land, then getting the wind astern to offset the treacherous current hastening the *Bride* toward the bar. "By the mark four!" Amos screamed again. Geoffrey did his best to recall Jabez's comment on the depth of water the *Bride* drew. Twelve feet four inches abaft, half a foot less afore, though the vessel had gone through most of its water and the great majority of its stores, with the barrels having been knocked down to staves and hoops. Surely by now the *Bride*'s draught must be less than twelve feet! But how much less? The *Bride*'s bow was now at an acute angle to the bar, but the current was swinging the vessel's stern in a slow, inexorable arc toward it.

"By the mark—" Amos' voice broke off as the *Bride* juddered; her keel had struck something, and with masts swaying and tackle twanging she was lurching, listing quickly and perceptibly to starboard. The wheel went momentarily slack in Geoffrey's hands, and he was thrown to the deck. Then the wheel thrashed about wildly as the *Bride* swept over what could only be a ridge of sand running off the bar.

"Brace 'round the fore topsail!" Nichols shouted, awakening from his lethargy. "Topsail's all a-shiver! Let go the weather braces! Taut in the lee braces! All weight to the lee!" Men raced to do Nichols' bidding as Geoffrey resumed his desperate tugging on the wheel. The *Bride* was turning to starboard, but at a terrilby ponderous rate. The current had set the *Bride* on an inexorable course toward the long, low bar of sand. But terrified hands had answered Nichols' commands, and bare feet slapped frantically on bare pine planking in a pell-mell race toward the weather braces.

Geoffrey had embraced the wheel again, but the helm was answering torturously slow, the tiller ropes popping and protesting as they reached the limits of their blocks. The bow was tugging round, grudgingly, but coming around nonetheless. The *Bride* surged through the wind's eye and, as with the weather braces were let go, frolicked her bowsprit through an arc of ninety degrees and pointed toward deepening water. "By the mark two!" Amos shouted. The *Bride*'s keel shuddered across another barrow of sand, and the vessel heeled even more sharply to starboard. But the wind filling the fore topsail, now cocked at right angles to the wind off the land, propelled the vessel across the obstruction, though her masts fought it and a deep protest rumbled from the *Bride*'s bowels.

The *Bride* righted herself, rolling first to larboard, then to starboard, steadied, and at last breasted into a foaming roller, bowsprit pointing south by southwest. "Mister Crowninshield, you may account for any water in the cistern," Nichols shouted and stepped to the helm. "That was a close one, young Frost, and I confess, the fault lies with me. Do you ken what I should have done rather than let the current deceive me so severely?" Nichols drew in several deep breaths.

Geoffrey studied his captain carefully before answering. Was Nichols making some sport of him? Or was Nichols actually intent upon fixing blame for the *Bride*'s brush with disaster? "I believe we was all distracted by the approach of the canoe, Captain, to the point we gave low credence to the current's dangerous set. Upon reflection, we should have had the lead going, been more mindful of the current and tide, and anchored in a minimum fifteen fathom of water while waiting to learn the message conveyed out to us by the Queen of Rio Bereira."

Nichols uttered a short laugh. "By the Four Gospels, young Frost, you are not slack in stays, I credit. This is an unfortunate coast, with no slaves to be had, and a dangerous reef all too close by. We vividly attest to the mischief hidden in a moment's inattention, for we were almost brought by the lee." Wick Nichols gestured toward the spume-assailed bar less than half a sea mile behind the *Bride*. "Your alacrity in jumping to the helm is commendable. Do you encounter any slackness in the wheel, any indication that the rudder has been injured? And tell me, had you a plan cyphered to coincide with your recommendation to anchor?"

Geoffrey never had the opportunity to reply, because First Mate Wolcott Crowninshield had emerged from the amidships scuttle, twisting his hands nervously. "If you please, Captain Nichols, there be three feet of water in the hold."

It was very apparent to Geoffrey that this intelligence did not please Wick Nichols. "When the morning watch pumped at first light there was no more than one foot of water a-swill in the cistern, I collect." Nichols' tone was ominous.

"Yes, Captain," the wretched Crowninshield said, perspiration glistening on his forehead and the movement of his hands rapidly increasing in distress.

"If you desire to avoid being turned before the mast, as I earlier indicated in my displeasure, you may work the chain pump until no vestige of water remains in the bilge. Choose not to pump this *Bride* of ours completely dry, and your berth is a hammock in the fo'c'sle from this minute."

"Yes, Captain, very happy, very happy, Captain," Crowninshield stammered, all but collapsing to the deck in relief, though Nichols struck him two heavy blows.

"Get to it, then, and no one is to assist you." Nichols snapped, but Crowninshield was already hurrying toward the chain pump. "'Vast, Mister Mate!" Nichols shouted. "We shall come to short anchor with the best bower—we are safely away from the bar. Then overside with you to survey for stove planking and check the rudder rests securely in its pintles and has not suffered injury."

"But Capt'n Nichols," Crowninshield cried in distress, "sharks be plenteous in these waters—great, vicious, hungry brutes."

Wick Nichols had retrieved his staff and swung the knob, a brass ball the size of a closed fist, with a vicious crack against Crowninshield's ribs that collapsed the first mate to the deck. Nichols rained several whacks, each more vicious than the last, upon the man's defenseless shoulders, then kicked Crownin-shield onto his back and placed the tip of the cane directly on Crowninshield's throat. "We anchor directly, Mister Mate, and you overside for survey."

The press of the cane's tip against his throat prevented Crowninshield from answering, but he blinked his assent. Nichols kicked the man as Crowninshield attempted to gain his feet.

Geoffrey thought that Nichols' treatment of his first mate was cutting it altogether too high, more like a foremast hand than Nichols' premier, and sure a bad thing for the rest of the crew to have witnessed. Granted, the first mate had been negligent in not carrying out the order to have the lead going, but the captain should have noted the absence of a leadsman sooner and inquired as to why his order had not been obeyed, rather than levying all blame upon his hapless mate. However, though Geoffrey was shocked and quite outraged, he was very, very careful to keep these reflections to himself.

oseph Frost laid the adze he was using to shape a gun carriage's axletree from a baulk of oak against the pile of boards that would be sawn into side cheeks, transoms and beds for the carriages and straightened his protesting back. "You ain't real handy with an adze, leavin' a whole lot for me to whittle out," Samuel Stonecypher, his helper, opined, holding out a blistered, bleeding palm and flexing his fingers. "But then I'm no great shakes with this drawknife, seein' I ain't never had a-hold of one until this week." Stonecypher got to his feet as well, spilling a lapful of shavings.

"When we get some canvas you can revert to your trade as a tailor, Sam," Joseph said. "I believe I have some adroit touch with the adze, seeing that only seven months ago I stood in this very spot hacking out runners for sledges for the drayage of cannons taken from yonder." Joseph gestured toward the gray stone walls of the fortress Tyonderoga that had received no care since the year sixty-three. Water seeping between the stones had expanded when it froze and thrown down portions of the walls. Within Joseph's view two bartizans had collapsed, such were the harsh winters on the lands surrounding Lake Champlain. Joseph did not take Stonecypher's remark seriously. "I wish we had elm to fashion into gun carriages. Gunner Rawbone said that elm was better at absorbing the shock of a cannon's recoil than any other wood."

"Be glad we got this oak 'n' not pine," said Stonecypher, a New Yorker sent up from Albany by Major General Schuyler in a draft of men to help build Arnold's fleet. Joseph was extremely glad to have secured the assistance of the balding, pudgy tailor to help with the carriages, though he gathered from some of the man's comments that Stonecypher, who had initially styled himself a shipwright, was glad enough to be away from a domineering wife and a vex of half-a-dozen whining, marriage-age, less-than-beautiful daughters. "Colonel Hartley, General Arnold's aide-de-camp, did a right fair job of bringin' in timbers from sawmills up 'n' down the Lake, 'n' here we sit doin' the light work of whittlin' away to make carriages whilst down at Skenesboro the real hard work of buildin' ships is under way."

"We'll get our chance to build a ship," Joseph said, spitting into his palms and glancing ruefully around at the troops that had flooded into Fort Tyonderoga in the last week. These men were coming from all the New England colonies—states. They were well-clothed and fed and in the main had little desire for the hard work of building fortifications or entrenchments—or, for that matter, gun carriages. Joseph had no idea who commanded these men; well, he supposed Gates commanded them, but it was a mystery how any orders that Gates might promulgate reached the soldiers. The soldiers spent the majority of their time splashing about in the shallow waters or fishing for trout and salmon. These men were far different from the pitiful wrecks of soldiers Joseph had seen less than three weeks earlier at Crown Point. "General Arnold says we're going to build a schooner here 'cause all the stocks at Skenesboro be taken up with gundalos and row gallies. Right now, we've got to build carriages for the guns."

"Be nice to get some bolts to hold these things together," Stonecypher said apologetically. "'N' what do you call them metal pieces that hold the cannon to its carriage? And you had another name for them little wheels, but I plumb forgot."

"The iron straps that fit over the trunnions are cap squares, and the little wheels are called trucks," Joseph said patiently, for perhaps the tenth time that day. "And if we can't get nails or bolts we'll puzzle out a way to use trunnels." Like all Yorkers Joseph had ever met, Samuel liked to talk. He looked at the pile of axletrees and mentally calculated how many more Samuel and he would have to shape. Arnold intended to put a 12-pounder in the bow of every gundalo, if enough 12-pounders and their shot could be had. But the 12-pounders would be mounted on an inclined wooden slide that would absorb the recoil without breeching ropes and let the cannon return to battery. Joseph was not sure he liked the idea, and he was fairly sure that Roderick Rawbone would not care for the concept, but Arnold had told him that it was sound and would allow the gun crew to reload more quickly. The two 9-pounder cannons on either side amidships would be mounted on carriages. Then there were the row galleys and sloops and cutters that had to be armed.

Joseph shook his head in bewilderment. He had no idea how many carriages he should build, but the axletrees, and the transoms, for that matter, could be fairly standard dimensions later sawn to final shape; the cheek pieces, though, would have to be cut for the particular cannon to be mounted. Master Gunner Rawbone had impressed upon him the fact that the overall length of a carriage had to be exactly three-fifths of the length of the cannon's tube.

Each cheek piece would have to be equal to the bore diameter of its cannon in thickness. Well, he would mark out the necessary lengths and thicknesses of cheek pieces for the cannons he had retrieved from their hidden places at Tyonderoga and dray the timbers to the saw pits against the time the cheek pieces would be cut. Taking the dimensions of the cannons' bores would be easy enough, since all the cannons he had retrieved were neatly laid out in three long rows between the lakeshore beside which he and Samuel labored and the rough tent he had fashioned from salvaged hessian—a poor quality jute and hemp that would never do to spread aboard any vessel, regardless of whether it would cruise on fresh water or salt.

Samuel had already seated himself to face the Lake, and Joseph reached for his adze, grateful that a fairly stiff breeze was holding down the mosquitoes and midges.

"Morning, Master Joseph. Reckon I kin get some coffee

goin' for you 'n' the other gentleman if'en you'd kindly show me the pile from whence the wood should be gots."

Joseph whirled around, the adze forgotten, and stared into the dear, kind, concerned and age-lined face of Juby, who stood but ten yards away. "Juby!" Joseph cried delightedly: "Can it really be you standing there in the flesh, and not some apparition?"

"Well, Master Joseph," Juby said with a smile, shaking the lapels of his dusty, faded white linen coverall, "I be me, 'n' I be flesh. Matter of fact I've never been seed without my flesh, comes to ponder upon it."

"But what are you doing in Tyonderoga?" Joseph asked incredulously, advancing the ten yards in a series of bounds to embrace Juby. Then he drew back: had his father dispatched Juby to return him to Portsmouth—to Hannah?

"I be in Tyonderoga 'cause you ain't at Crown Point any more you ain't at Mister Skene's saw mill, places where I was told you might be keepin', which you ain't, 'til I gots here, up to where you really be," Juby said amiably, gently disengaging himself from Joseph's embrace. "Now, 'bout that coffee, I 'pect you ain't had none since you departed Portsmouth 'n such 'n all-powerful hurry, not even givin' me a chance to catch up your coat."

"Well, if you're set on boiling coffee, Juby, you may use any of that thin, slabbed wood with the bark on, and those little blocks and pieces tossed in the pile there. It's all dry and will give a lot of heat." Joseph gestured toward a large pile of culled wood that would not do for gun carriages, or shipbuilding.

Juby turned and walked away on silent boots well-worn-down at the heels, amazing and disturbing Joseph at how silently he had stolen up on Samuel Stonecypher and him. There was not a great bustle about Tyonderoga. Major General Gates and his staff had taken over what passed as the best accommodations in the decrepit fortress itself and were intent upon issuing orders, of every description and in incredible quantity. Orders, so far as Joseph knew, that were addressed to no one, went nowhere, and elicited no response.

The majority of the effort was being expended across the narrow gap of the Lake, atop Rattlesnake Hill, rising some two hundred feet, where a thousand men under the inspired direction of a gifted amateur military engineer, Jeduthan Baldwin, whom Arnold had sent to supervise the works, were building the fortifications of Mount Independence. A few militia from New York drilled desultorily below the fortress, but in the main Joseph and Samuel were left to their own devices to build gun carriages until Arnold had need of them. Juby wearily led back to them a spavined, dun-colored horse of indeterminate age who was heavily laden with panniers and canvas-wrapped parcels haphazardly held together with an amazing lace of rope and crude knots.

"I ain't no sailor-man, but I tied things on so they wouldn't come loose of themselves," Juby said, though not defensively, as he worried at the clumsy knots. "Where you be keepin'? I brought the clothes you would have packed for yourself had you not slipped away so quiet-like. 'N' I've gots some food here that needs eatin', though not by any of the scoundrely army-men pitched up around here."

"Well, Samuel . . . oh, Juby, this is Samuel Stonecypher, he's a Yorker, but you can't hold that against him! He's been helping me make cannon carriages for General Arnold . . . we have a tent yonder." Joseph gestured toward the forlorn scrap of jute and hemp hessian set in a copse of birch trees fifty yards away.

Juby sniffed. "Don't look like no proper place for a Frost to be keepin'. I'll see to it after you've gots some coffee. Reckon you could do with some chowder. That creek gots fishes in it, gots to have. Once I've gots some fried ham into you," Juby shrugged, "might as well feed this Samuel fella, seein' he be a friend of yours, then I'll catch some fishes and makes a proper chowder. I broughts some potatoes from Cinnamon's garden all the way from Portsmouth. Gots some pease, too." Juby wrestled one canvas-wrapped parcel off the placid horse and laid it on the ground. "On thought, salted cod be somewhere in this tackle, 'n' salt cod be better than any style of fish when it comes to a chowder."

Juby paused and eyed Joseph gravely. "Things would goes a lot quicker, Master Joseph, was you 'n' this Samuel fella to make up the fire whilst I gets the pans 'n' proper makin's out of this sack." Joseph whistled as Juby unrolled the canvas to reveal parcels the size of fat sausages neatly wrapped in waxed paper and tied with twine.

"Tea, coffee, sugar, salt, rice, flour, all in these pouches," Juby said proudly. He shrugged out of the dusty coverall, folded it neatly and placed it on the ground. Then he unslung the small musketoon from his shoulder—Joseph had never suspected its presence—and laid it carefully atop the coverall.

"Juby!" Joseph exclaimed. "That's Uncle Pepperrell's old blunderbuss! How came you by it?"

"I borrows it for the occasion," Juby said, "just lacks I borrows the horse 'n' all the provisions. Your Uncle Pepperrell's musketoon comes in handy when men tries to takes the provisions I've fetched along. I jest points the front end of the musketoon in their direction 'n' they finds they's gots business 'n Rumford or Albany or Lake George." Juby shrugged, "'Course, it ain't be loaded, but when the cock, she goes back, she makes a mighty satisfyin' sound, to me at least. Others who hears it don't seems to likes it much. Now, are you goin' to gets me a fire to-goin' or are you 'n' Samuel goin' to stand there bug-eyed as frogs whilst I struggle to feed you white folks?" He knelt stiffly to pull an iron skillet from the welter of neatly wrapped bags.

"Juby," Joseph said haltingly, "you do have Father's permission to be here, do you not? Father did dispatch you to search for me, did he not? You have not run, have you?"

"If you ain't gonna raise a fire, seems I's got to," Juby sighed, deliberately ignoring Joseph's question. "Fryin' hams gots to wait 'til I raises a fire." Juby dropped the skillet with finality.

"Oh Lordy," Stonecypher breathed, coming closer, "he's got a bait of ham! I ain't seen much less had a taste of ham since the moon was last blue! There! Joseph, there be sufficient rocks around, with the both of us scrapping we'll have a fire-ring in two shakes of a dead sheep's tail. Juby, have you steel and flint?

If not, my tools lie in the tent nearby and can be fetched in the instant."

Joseph felt the saliva spurt sharply in his lower jaw. For the past week he and Stonecypher had subsisted on potatoes, potatoes either boiled in a pail of water or tossed into the coals of the fire, then fished out, dusted off and eaten half-raw. He had not eaten a decent meal since he had quitted Portsmouth in such a lather. When was that? A month ago? He had lost count of the days.

"I reckons I gots the fire-makin's, specially with all them woods-shavin's you've planed off them boards," Juby said agreeably and busied himself untying other sausage-shaped bags.

Within two minutes Joseph and Stonecypher had gathered a fire-ring of small granite blocks laying about, making the ring one yard in diameter and throwing handfuls of bone dry shavings into it. "That'll do for kindlin', gentlemens," Juby announced as he picked up the musketoon. From some pocket of his commodious waistcoat he produced a small copper flask of priming powder and sprinkled half a thimbleful of the powder on a mound of shavings. He cocked the musketoon and held it lock down close against the shavings. The cock snapped forward and the flint struck small, bright slivers of steel that burst into sparks and rained down onto the priming powder. The powder ignited in a small blizzard of whitish-yellow smoke, from the base of which flame spurted.

Juby chuckled in satisfaction as he lay the musketoon aside and heaped other shavings onto those already burning merrily. "Gots a good fire beginnin', Master Joseph. Be pleased if you would fetch a piece of bark from one of 'em yonder birch trees sufficient to fashion a bread tray. 'N' while you are trendin' that way, might as well fetch back half-a-dozen of 'em willow branches. Need to peel the bark off 'em."

Joseph did as he was bid with alacrity, then sat on a baulk of oak near the fire-ring and trimmed bark from willow wands with his jack knife. Now that the fire was crackling Juby caught up a tankard from Joseph knew not where and stalked off toward a small coterie of cattle grazing on the lush grass of the foreshore. He returned with the tankard a-brim with frothy milk, some of which dripped down the side. Juby squatted in front of the rectangle of birch bark Joseph had cut for him and carefully unwrapped a parcel. It contained flour and Juby flung several handfuls onto the rectangle of birch bark. He pawed through the flour and in some wise came up with two eggs. Juby cracked the eggs into the mound of flour, rolled up the sleeves of his shirt, poured a generous dollop of milk onto the flour, and began to knead the mixture into dough, judiciously adding more flour and milk from time to time while the fire burned down to coals.

When he was satisfied with the texture of the dough Juby began rolling it into a rope, vigorously shaping the rope by rotations back and forth between his palms. Then he wound the rope halfway around one willow wand, nipped it off, and forced the butt into the soil so the wand, pregnant with raw dough, sagged out over the fiery coals. Juby wound another four wands before the mound of dough was consumed. "You might keeps them branches turnin' ever so often, Master Joseph, so's the dough heats all even." Juby ambled down to the lake's edge with a large copper coffeepot and came back with it half-filled with water. He used the forward edge of the skillet to nudge three rocks into a rough triangle amidst the coals and balanced the coffeepot on those rocks. He did the same with another three rocks, but did not as yet set the skillet on them.

Juby set out two large pewter plates and cups, two knives, spoons and forks, then busied himself with a sack of coffee beans, some of which he carefully poured into a coffee mill. He set the mill aside and addressed a large shoulder of ham he unwrapped from a greased paper, slicing away half a dozen thick pieces before placing the skillet on the rocks. He tested each wand wound with bread dough by thumping it gently with a forefinger. "'Bout be done," he said cheerfully as he raised the lid of the coffee and looked at the boiling water. Satisfied, Juby emptied the ground coffee in the mill's drawer into the pot, then forked the pieces of ham into the skillet, then turned each piece after half a minute. Joseph and Samuel Stonecypher followed Juby's every movement with eager, hungry eyes. Joseph hardly dared breathe.

Juby moved the coffeepot to a flat stone in the fire ring and tossed in the eggshells to settle the grounds. He placed two pieces of ham on each plate, and handed them with a flourish to Joseph and Stonecypher. "Two o' 'em breads goes to each o' you. I'll pours the coffee soon's the grounds all be settled." Juby lifted the skillet onto another flat rock and reached for the fifth wand of fresh bannock bread.

All three men turned toward the sound of approaching horses, though Joseph and Stonecypher continued to eat greedily.

"There is a mighty savory aroma that I verily believe may be the true coffee," Benedict Arnold, Brigadier General of the Continental Army, declared as he and another Continental Army officer drew rein ten yards away from the fire ring.

"General Arnold!" Joseph exclaimed enthusiastically, leaping to his feet: "Please to join us for a slight repast." He held up his plate. "Crisp ham from the best farm in Dur-ham," Joseph exaggerated the name to emphasize the "ham," "and fresh bread from the hands of Juby, principal attendant to my father, Marlborough Frost."

Benedict Arnold, mounted on the golden-bay gelding he had borrowed from Joseph Frost, surveyed the scene with his intelligent eyes and doubtless noted Juby's sour expression. "I thank you, Mister Frost, but for us nutmeggers partaking of ham at midday turns us into logs. Doubtless it is different for those hailing from New Hampshire."

Arnold smiled at Juby as he stepped out of the saddle. "That bacon gives off tantalizing aromas, Juby of Portsmouth, but that coffee has greater fragrance. It is an overlarge pot, and perhaps there can be found a small amount of that sleep-defying beverage for Captain Varick and me."

"If'en you's gots your own mugs, General, there's a-plenty of coffee, 'n' when this be drunk the grounds can be boiled twice." Juby stared defiantly at Benedict Arnold.

"Dick, you should find two cups in my possibles—my saddlebags, and please ease the horses' girths, take off their bridles and tie them near good grass." Arnold tossed his reins to his aide and came forward to shake hands with Juby. "Cooks hailing from the Piscataqua are very welcome on Lake Champlain, Juby of Portsmouth, but can you fetch me shipwrights and carpenters as well?"

Juby shook his head. "Difficult enough it wus to fetches myself, General, Mister Langdon and Mister Lear, they's gots all the carpenters o' any 'count workin' day 'n' night at Langdon's Island to get privateers off the stocks 'n' into the water."

Arnold kicked angrily at a clump of dirt. "Aye, that's what comes of putting profit ahead of one's own country. I need two hundred carpenters to build the ships necessary to deny the turnpike this Lake represents to the British. And more than them, I need a thousand right mariners, men able to reef, hand and steer, and serve a cannon. Men who've hopefully looked a British cannon tube full in the eye from a distance of fifty feet without shitting their britches. Think you, Juby of Portsmouth, you can deliver such men to me?"

Juby shook his head sorrowfully as he reached for the cups the other Continental Army officer extended. "Ever-bodies is all-fired fixed on fittin' out privateers, General. You couldn't get no carpenter knows a bow saw from an auger for borin' trunnel holes here for love ner money. The only man hereabouts I knows who's looked full-square in the mouth o' a British cannon 'n' not run away be Master Joseph." Juby enfolded the cups in his huge black hands. "You're in luck, General, I can offer sugar 'n' milk fer your coffee, 'course it may take a minute to collect the milk, seein's I used all of it in makin' the bannock."

"Lord love you," Arnold exclaimed. "My preference is coffee as sweet as an angel and as hot as the hinges of Hell. Milk be damned as a beverage good only for babes and the doddering." He collected that he had not introduced his colleague. "Gentlemen, this be Captain Richard Varick, aide-de-camp to Major General Schuyler. Captain Varick has just returned from Albany, where he has joyously been relieving shipping stranded at that city's docks of their tackle, sails and other useful appurtenances."

"Now, General Arnold," Captain Richard Varick said uneasily as he joined his general, "I was able to requisition in General Schuyler's name any amount of ships' stores, yes, even strip them of all save masts and yards, but that is because the British have blockaded all commerce on the Hudson. Could in some wise the merchantmen held at Albany gain the sea little assistance would our Continental Army realize from the embargoed fleet."

"Hear him," Arnold said gloomily, squatting close to the fire ring and gratefully, unbelievingly, reaching for the mug of coffee into which Juby was stirring a copious amount of sugar. "Even in the name of General Schuyler, who has given his personal word that the cost of the items taken into the Continental Army's service shall be reimbursed, Captain Varick had to venture as far south along the Hudson as Poughkeepsie and Esopus to gather the all-important tackle we must have to equip our fleet."

Juby, apparently having satisfied himself that Arnold and Varick knew the difference between a bow saw and an auger fit for boring holes for trunnels, had quietly gone off to the nearest copse of birch trees. A few minutes later he handed the Continental Army officers two servings of fried ham on birch bark platters. Arnold and Varick took them eagerly, without any thought of becoming "loggy" later in the day. Seeing that the coffee was all drunk, Juby quietly made another pot, though he had to dig deeper into his precious store of coffee beans than he wished.

"Mister Frost," Captain Richard Varick asked diffidently, "speaking solely for General Arnold and my commanding officer, General Philip Schuyler, second only to His Excellency, General Washington, in understanding and preparing to deal with the critical situation in which our nascent country finds itself—in my humble estimation, I credit you have thrown in your lot with us. But how shall I address you? Do you desire some token or office of rank? A commission signed by General Schuyler shall immediately be forthcoming if that desire be so."

Joseph had quietly commandeered the skillet from Juby and was studiously wiping the skim of grease from the skillet with the final pieces of bannock and thrusting them hurriedly into his mouth. "A commission? No, though I do thank you, Captain Varick." Joseph shrugged his shoulders. "I hope not to live so long as to benefit from a commission. If you refer to me at all in any official dispatch, please refer to me as a 'volunteer.' Samuel Stonecypher here, if he will allow me to speak on his behalf, desires no congressional ordained commission, though he is an excellent tailor and should, by rights, have a warrant as a sailmaker. We, that is, Samuel, undertakes to oversee the sewing of all the sails necessary to propel General Arnold's fleet to victory against the British."

"Mister Frost seeks a glorious death before the enemy," Benedict Arnold said with wry and tolerant amusement, sucking his fingers of ham grease and looking longingly at the birch bark platters Juby was preparing to cast into the fire. "I hope yet to convince him that causing the other fellow to die on behalf of his country is infinitely more satisfying and far more meritorious than dying for one's own." He complimented Juby upon the quality of his coffee as Juby refilled Arnold's cup.

"Messrs. Lawrence and Tudor have been pleased to deliver all the cordage, blocks, riggings and sail cloth possessed in their chandlery in Poughkeepsie," Varick said. "I think the rigging and arming of our ships should take place here, General, that is, across the narrows on the far side yonder. The vessels can lie close against the cliff face and receive their masts, ordnance and stores by tackles suspended from Rattlesnake Hill."

"And how many vessels have slipped down their ways at Skenesboro to join your two schooners and one sloop, General Arnold?" Joseph asked innocently.

Arnold almost choked on a mouthful of coffee. "Not one row gallie is on the stocks, and only two gundalos." Arnold tentatively took another sip. "There had been some unfortunate miscommunication with an officer to whom General Schuyler had earlier given a temporary appointment to supply bateaux for our forces then in Canada. Captain Wynkoop was under the misapprehension that it was better to build barracks first, then our vessels of war, and labor had been concentrated in that endeavour. That has changed, and one hundred and fifty carpenters are less than two days away from Skenesboro, where I expect they shall work double tides."

"Divert some carpenters to Tyonderoga, General, and let us get started on the schooner to be built here." Joseph smiled, "Samuel and I would be powerful grateful to have augers for boring holes, and iron bolts so we can clamp our gun carriages together."

"A blacksmithy is the first order, Volunteer Frost, for there is iron on the way from Albany." Arnold rubbed his temples with a tired hand. "I don't suppose you know anything about running a smithy, do you?"

"Perhaps a little, General," Joseph said bashfully. "It was my father's wish that I involve myself with the casting of cannon balls and other warlike articles of iron. I passed several months observing the iron works at Saugus. My father and brother both thought the husbandry of a foundry would keep me away from cannon fire."

Arnold smote his thigh. "A matross you are confessed, and now I learn you have experience with smelting and forging. Just the man to oversee the smithy we must have here at Tyonderoga. Captain Varick, post back to Skenesboro. Mister Frost will go with you. It is his horse I've been riding. At Skenesboro he will take inventory of the smithy equipment established by Philip Skene and return here with all equipments not absolutely necessary for the maintenance of the smithy at Skenesboro. He may situate the smithy here as he considers will be most efficient for the manufacturing of bolts and nails. Direct sufficient supplies of charcoal and raw iron to be brought up." Arnold nodded toward the soldiers idling on the lake shore. "Canvass among those men. If any man owes to being a blacksmith, or a farrier—anyone who has ever flogged hot metal across an anvil—enlist him as an ironmonger."

Benedict Arnold rose to his feet and thanked Juby for the supper; he had not expected to dine so well. He was now in a proper mood to advise General Gates that he was at the disposal of the Commanding General of the Northern Army. "Take horse and depart directly. I am stiff from so many hours spent in the saddle and fain would use the walk to headquarters to improve my gait." Arnold strode away slowly, up toward the massive fort of Tyonderoga.

Joseph followed Captain Richard Varick to the horses and tightened the girth of the golden-bay gelding. He had held back a small piece of the bannock and let the horse take it from his palm with the wonderfully sensitive, velvety lips that horses have, before slipping the bit into the horse's mouth. "Why does not General Arnold return to Skenesboro directly, Captain Varick? Seemingly there is more immediate work to be done there in getting the hulls off the stocks. Rather than deprive General Arnold of this horse, I can come down tomorrow on a wagon dispatched to fetch supplies."

Varick smiled wanly as he stepped into the stirrup. "I'm sure General Arnold would much prefer that the summons to headquarters had not come, Mister Frost, but he had no choice in the matter." Varick regarded Joseph evenly. "General Arnold, who should be permitted his efforts unhindered, has been summoned to stand trial by court-martial."

❧ IX ❧

THE *Bride of Derry* WAS ANCHORED A FULL SEA-MILE TO THE WESTWARD OF BENCE ISLAND, SWINGING PLACIDLY TO HER BEST BOWER WITHIN PISTOL SHOT OF two other vessels, both brigs of some two hundred and fifty tons burthen, though neither was showing any colors. Geoffrey Frost, togged out and sweating profusely in his green velvet frock coat and white sateen britches, though carrying his silk stockings and shoes in a bread bag after coming ashore in the gig, was walking a wary three paces behind Wick Nichols. His finery, including the black felt tricorne pressing heavily upon his head, had been packed for him by his mother against the day when he would go ashore as an aspiring trader. But Geoffrey had almost outgrown the outfit; the coat's cuffs stopped short of his wrists, and it was tight across the shoulders. The knee buttons on his britches were tripped into their buttonholes with the greatest difficulty, and his feet, callused and hard from climbing rigging, were pinched when he tried to force them into the shoes, which, before he left Newport, had been of a tolerably loose fit. Geoffrey and Nichols were led along a carefully swept sand path, shallow puddles still in places from rain fallen two hours earlier. It wound through a grove of silk-cotton trees resplendent in their thick green leaves. Their guide was a tall, barefooted black man with a kilt of bright tartan wrapped around his waist. Their destination was concealed and unknown to Geoffrey, but he was happily devouring a strange fruit he had never in his young life encountered. Wick Nichols had briefly delayed another black man they had overtaken, long enough for Nichols to wrench several of the elegantly elongated, tapering pieces of fruit with yellowish-orange rinds from the stalk the man balanced on his head. Nichols paid for them with a handful of cowrie shells taken from a pocket of his coat, which he then handed to Geoffrey, along with the strange, new fruit. Geoffrey wondered what he held, and whether it was meant to be eaten, and if so, how to proceed, then emulated Nichols, who split the neck and peeled back the rind in strips.

Geoffrey found the pulpy fruit very much to his taste and consumed both fruits Nichols had purchased him. "Bananas they be called," Nichols said, finishing his second banana and throwing the rind into a bush alongside the path. "They grow in profusion on these coasts, some cultivated, others wild. They take their name from an island immediately to the south of that headland." Nichols gestured vaguely to the south as they broke into a large grassy expanse at the very height of the low island.

On the other side of a magnificent bay that was some miles across, beginning just back from the beaches fringed with palm trees and interspersed here and there with coastal swamps, the whole of which formed an imposing semi-circlular peninsula, was a range of mountains rising to well over twenty-five hundred feet. "The mountains of the lions," Nichols huffed as he sharply ordered the black man to stop while he mopped his face with his kerchief. The heat weighed heavily. "The Portugee who was first to explore hereabouts thought the mountains looked like lions. So they called this place *Serra Leão,* or *Serra Lyoa.* Suffices for the great river that forms this estuary and the country behind." Nichols shrugged. "Kin't say I ken the resemblance myself, but them's see it first have the notion of namin' it. Was always thus, and will always be thus."

They were able to move more quickly on the level path at the height of the island, and Geoffrey could see a massive gray rectangular building constructed of tabby in the distance. The ramparts on the seaward side were pierced for cannons, though they were yet too far from the massive building for Geoffrey to discern if cannons actually stood in the embrasures. Some hundred yards away from them on the greensward a small white ball arched out of the sky, landed on the grass and hopped along merrily like a flat pebble flung across the surface of a lake for a dozen yards or so. Two men, no, three emerged from around a copse of boxwood.

"Pass my coat," Nichols said, stopping to permit Geoffrey to help him into the snuff-colored sateen tunic much stained by seawater. The black man in the party detached himself and ran ahead, passed the ball, coursed in front of it like a hound searching for the scent of a fox, then stopped suddenly. He plucked an ostrich feather from the waistband of his kilt of tartan pattern and pushed the shaft into the grass, then stepped back from the plume of soft frothy feathers as it nodded and ducked in the hot air. Nichols resumed walking, faster this time, and Geoffrey skipped to keep up, turning every third step or so to watch the group.

Two white men approached the place where the ball lay hidden from Geoffrey's view. One man had been carrying a stick jauntily over his shoulder; he paused by the ball, assumed an awkward stance and swung the stick. The white ball hopped from the grass and bounced toward the ostrich feather. A white ball lay just beside the path. Nichols picked it up and tossed it to Geoffrey. "That be a Caledonian ball, or a featherie. Them men be playin' at golf, a game invented, so they claim, by the Scottish, who run this factory for the London Scottish Syndicate."

"Golf!" Geoffrey cried brightly. "I have read of such a game. The early kings of England cried down the games of golf and futball because devotion to those games impinged upon the practice of archery, archery being necessary for the defense of the realm, or so it was thought by the kings." Geoffrey closely examined the compact leather ball, with its intricate, close stitching. It was marvelously light, though very hard and unyielding.

"Leather purse of small compass stuffed with boiled feathers 'til it be burstin', then sewed up and hammered round." Nichols dabbed at his forehead, which was flowing rivulets of perspiration. "Damnable expensive to prepare, those featheries be. Upwards of five shillings for one made proper."

"So you play the golf, sir!" Geoffrey exclaimed. "It must be a capital game."

"No, the game ain't for the likes of Wicked Pythias Nichols," Nichols said bitterly. "It be a game for gentlemen like John Brown, Aaron Lopez, or your father."

"But those men now playing the golf most like be sea captains like yourself, Captain Nichols," Geoffrey remonstrated.

"There be sea captains, and there be Captain Wicked Pythias Nichols," Nichols said with a finality that Geoffrey was astute enough to understand foreclosed further discussion. Their guide led them onto a long gallery that ran around the rectangular tabby building on at least three sides and through a small door, a sally port, cut into a much larger, heavier double door braced all about with iron straps and heavy bolts. Geoffrey prayed his captain pause long enough for him to draw on his stockings, refasten his knee buttons with difficulty, and with greater difficulty torture his feet into the much too small shoes. They proceeded through several unlit passages smelling heavily of mildew and emerged into a pleasant, wooden-paneled though musty long room illuminated with many windows that looked onto a courtyard teeming with brilliant, multicolored flowers. A large parrot, as multihued as the flowers outside the windows but with vivid orange and blue predominating, rose on a perch in a corner of the room, expanded to twice its normal size by rustling its feathers, then shrieked something that mimicked human speech, though in no tongue Geoffrey had ever heard. He covered his ears against the penetrating shrillness of the bird's cackle.

"There, there, my precious," soothed a man of medium height who was dressed in somber black and gray, his neck wrapped in a dirty stock, as he got up from behind a desk hidden in the shadows. The man was stooped, and his face, framed by sparse gray whiskers, was of a grayish-green sallowness that bespoke an immense dislike of the sun. "You shall hae your ground-nuts without resorting to such vexation." The parrot continued its shrieks, and the man muttered something to their guide. The black man picked up the perch and parrot and took them into the courtyard through a large double door set with heavy beveled glass. The parrot continued to shriek for some time yet, but at least its shrieks did not overbear their conversation.

"Do not mind the cully there, and bid you welcome to the London Scottish Syndicate's factory at Bence Island, Captain Nichols," the sallow-faced man simpered, extending a limp hand. "I trust your voyage from the British colonies in North America were a pleasant one, uncomplicated by hurricanes, pirates, French cruisers, or anything o' that like."

"Middlin', Mister Aird," Wick Nichols said shortly. "Middlin', and I wish it would have come to an arrival the fortnight past, for the two Liverpool brigs lying offshore discomfort me that a cargo can be found in this place."

"Aaah, Captain Nichols," Mister Aird responded in a broad Scot's accent that Geoffrey found extremely difficult to comprehend, "you've nae idea the present demand for ebony in the West Indies." Aird moved into the subdued light of the office, surprising Geoffrey with the expanse of his nose, as bulbous and red as a ripe strawberry freshly gathered from the banks of the Piscataqua River, standing out startlingly from his sallow face. The thought of that great river upon which he had learned to swim and dive and row brought on a miasma of yearning for home so poignant that Geoffrey had to bite his lower lip to keep a tear from starting.

"The last sugar harvest sadly diminished because of hands lackin'," continued Aird. "Saints take pity over our frailties. Had there been more black hands to gather in the harvest, sugar would hae been less than twenty guineas the hogshead the year past, 'n' any mistress o' house anywhere in the kingdom could hae indulged in marzipan, ruinous rents o' naught. Indeed, the surfeit of marzipan would hae stifled dissent. But nae! There warn't sufficient hands descended from Ezri for the tillage of the crop, not by a damn sight! So Jane Hames goes a-snufflin' for her sugar at impossible tariffs, and lays her mate by the ear 'til he howls the meek, 'n' the kingdom be all in a broth because the marzipan be out."

As the man drew nearer Geoffrey made a decent leg and swept the hat he had carried across his chest. Mister Aird reached into a heavy glass canister on a corner of his desk and brought out a hard candy. "'N' who be this lad accompanin' you, Captain Nichols? A likely bairn, payin' proper attention to his elders, I specifically warrant." Aird extended the piece of candy to Geoffrey, who took the sweet, meaning to render no offense, but as soon as the occasion offered tucked it into his pocket.

"Be my squeaker 'n' supernumerary for this voyage," Wick Nichols grunted. "His pater and associated men-o'-business in Rhode Island and the Providence Plantations insist he learn the trade in one voyage."

Mister Aird spread his hands helplessly. "Would that I could aid your distresses, Captain Nichols, but the two Liverpool brigs preceded you to this factory and be first in right. Between the two our barracoons are bein' emptied. Indeed, I fear the cargo o' one brig must be slightly abbreviated, unless we reach agreement on the discount fer children, in which event I can tip in a lot of girls and bairns from Port Loko. Both brigs hope to weigh by the end o' the month, provision in Fernado Po, 'n' arrive in the Barbados in time for the cane harvesting season, when their ebony will command the best prices."

Mister Aird fished a pouch of tanned leather with an elaborate silver clasp from his waistcoat and treated himself to a copious pinch of snuff, which resulted in several compulsive sneezes. He wiped his rheumy, watering eyes with a large cambric handkerchief with lace edges. "The wars between the Mohammedans in the north 'n' the simple *cultivateurs* o' the immediate interior go well, that is, with the Mohammedans sendin' the *cultivateurs* fleein' southard. That is, I am definitely assured the interior wars go to our benefit by the Sherbros in Port Loko and Pepel who organize the outposts to bring in the stock. But I nae kinna, in good conscience, predict replenishment o' our barracoons sufficient to requite your needs until mid-September at the optimal."

Aird reached across his desk for a small silver bell and shook from it a single soft, pleasing musical chime. A woman, no, a girl no more than two years older than Geoffrey appeared through a door in the further wall that had opened noiselessly. She wore a single wide strip of gaudily dyed, multihued cotton fabric wrapped around her waist and tucked into itself, then thrown over her shoulders, and a large mobcap of the same brilliant cloth. "Verily, the girl wears cloth that Joseph, son of Jacob, would have envied," Geoffrey thought. The girl approached silently on bare feet and stood, her hands held motionless against the sides of her small body, her eyes downcast and demure but not submissive. Her features were regular and fine and could have been delicately sculpted from a block of the hardest and purest anthracite, though her face was disfigured by a large knot, just healing, on the point of her chin. Her left eye, reddened as from a blow, was a blood-red coal set in the anthracite.

"Gentlemen, I forget my manners. We must refresh ourselves, and since the sun be not directly overhead, chairs in the courtyard outside beckon. Captain Nichols, I hae yet some brandywine in a small cask with the bung still sealed gifted me by a French *négrier* the year afore this cursed war broke out between our respective empires—wars are always such disruptions to our trade! I would value your comments upon its qualities. 'N' you, young sir, pardon, but your name was nae given me—see what lassitude affects one's brain in a climate such as this—I should hae inquired directly. What refreshment kin I offer you?"

"Geoffrey Frost, sir, from Portsmouth, in the colony of New Hampshire." Geoffrey bowed slightly. "If you please, sir, I would be most grateful for a cup of milk, either that of the kine or that of the goat." From the corner of his eye he glimpsed the lithe young girl, who had advanced two paces, and coloring hugely he averted his eyes.

"'Pon my word, I nae collect ever such a request from a visitor off a *négrier*, 'n' I be a-feared this factory can offer nae such. Perhaps a mango punch? You may hae it flavored with cane, or brandywine."

"Please, sir. A cup of tea would bear marvelously." Geoffrey had no idea what a mango punch might be, but he opined his mother would be highly offended at its being offered him. "Tea! Of course! The very item! I am possessed o' some capital tea, a chest from an East Indiaman on its return voyage to England that sought shelter from a cyclone behind this island the year past. Some people nae can tolerate a steeped beverage in such a torrid climate as ours on Bence Island, but embarrassed as I am at the regrettable lack of milk, I do believe you will find the tea delectable." Mister Aird spoke simply to the girl in a sing-song dialect from which Geoffrey could identify only a word or two. The girl turned and walked toward the door through which she had appeared.

"It is Creole that I spoke, a contrived language, sometimes called *gullah,* that is used in this coast by the various tribes as a common tongue for rudimentary communication." Mister Aird ushered Nichols and Geoffrey into the large courtyard and motioned them into chairs around a table under an awning of stripped canvas. The parrot was contentedly burrowing in a cup attached to the end of his perch, winkling out groundnuts and cracking them in its massive beak.

"Tribalism, Captain Nichols, as you well know, be the source of all frictions among these native people, some slight, imagined or real, always settin' one tribe agin another, leadin' to brawls over cropland er fishin' rights to a portion o' river." Aird sighed. "Faith, in the year fifty-eight two tribes argued over the fruits o' one palm tree thirty leagues up the Rio Sierra Leone. The palm tree was the mark o' boundary 'tween their respective tribes. All the coconuts fallin' to the north side belonged to one tribe, 'n' all the coconuts fallin' to the south side belonged to the second tribe. But, you ken, a horrendous great wind arose from the south, 'n' all the coconuts went spinnin' across the northern keep. The two tribes went at each other tongs 'n' hammers, 'n' whilst they were brawlin' the Mohammedans came in behind 'n' took all captive, includin' that child there, standin' so statuesque."

Aird sighed again. "Thankfully, the end o' the wet season

finally be upon us." Aird picked up a fan woven from palm fronds that lay on the table and fanned himself energetically. "Now all we hae to contend with be heat and mosquitoes, and nae longer the infernal wet." Nichols and Aird talked desultorily about the affairs of the London Scottish Syndicate, and the last time the proprietors of Bence Island, Mister Oswald and Sir Alexander Grant, had been out to inspect their property in the estuary of the Sierra Leone River.

The young girl came up, demurely bearing a tray woven of palm fronds similar to the fan Aird was plying so industriously. The tray bore a small wooden cask capable of holding near onto a gallon, stood on its end, two glasses of delicate stemware, a teapot with a hint of vapor escaping from its spout, and one delicate cup. The girl placed the tray on the table with great care. She set the silver strainer atop the cup and poured the tea with great studiousness. When the saucered cup was full she placed the cup with equal care before Geoffrey, who could not help but note that she had been biting her tongue with fierce concentration.

"My thanks," Geoffrey said, but the girl's face was an inscrutable mask. She placed the teapot on the table, then the two delicate goblets and the small cask, and withdrew.

Mister Aird picked with a dirty forefinger at the freckled and chipped burgundy-colored wax sealed over the cork plugging the bung. Then he drew the bung with his teeth, spat it out, and brushing the chips of wax away poured both goblets brimful. "A most pleasant sound, think you not, Captain Nichols," Aird said enthusiastically, "this gurgle as the brandywine floods from the cask. Mind, it is not the *uisge beathe* distilled in my native highlands from the barley grain, but the French ain't too shabby by half when it comes to putterin' about with the grape."

"Speakin' o' the French," Nichols said gravely, as he lifted his glass in a brief salute to Aird, "but I spied out a large sloop carryin' the lilies flag at first light this morning, standin' well to the south."

"Yes," Aird agreed readily, "there be several French *négriers* about, despite our nations be officially at war. No mutton to my beef so long as they nae be warships. Thank goodness, Admiral Hawke's lesson to the French at Quiberon Bay in November last was a sound one 'n' left no fleet capable of descending upon this coast. The sloop you saw be out of Honfleur, destined for the Banana Islands and, I nae misdoubt, a fine cargo of ebony at the out-factory there sponsored by English *lançados* such as Mister Cleveland, who hae grown up in that place. A good round four hundred they did nae deign to consign to my barracoons, though the French will pay a premium for that stock. Aye, 'n' they'll be payin' with gold guineas, not trade goods."

"But you need the trade goods the *négriers* bring, Mister Aird, to pay your flesh-peddlers on the mainland. The French shall have their stock, Mister Aird," Wick Nichols said ominously, "and the two slavers out of Liverpool shall have their cargoes, and why should I languish?"

Aird drank off the majority of his glass at one toss and dabbed at his lips with the handkerchief much edged with lace. "Your tea, lad, it be untouched," Aird cried. "If that wench nae has brewed it to your taste she shall be thrashed."

"Oh, no, sir!" Geoffrey said quickly. "The tea be capital. My mother taught me that a burned tongue would result from addressing the tea too quickly. For proper enjoyment the tea must give up some of its heat before quaffing." Indeed, the first sip of the tea had been quite pleasurable, the first tea Geoffrey had drunk since immediately before his departure from Newport. But he most desperately did not wish the young girl—or anyone, for that matter—to be thrashed on his account, ever.

"Very good then. I am happy to see that since you be possessed of two eyes and two ears but only one tongue, you devote more time to observation."

"Yes, sir," Geoffrey said miserably, heartily wishing himself rid of his constricting, stuporific clothing, so ridiculous to him now when he could be ranging lightheartedly about the *Bride of Derry* barefooted, garbed only in trousers of light duck, a shirt of worn linen, and yes, a sennit hat cleverly woven by Jabez as a guard against the sun. Bence Island depressed him mightily.

"Allow me to refill your glass, Captain Nichols," Aird said, suiting his action to his words and tipping the bunghole of the small cask over Nichols' goblet, being careful to balance the small cask in both hands. "Now, please share with me your desires. I do hope it is your wish to await a cargo here at Bence Island. I assure you, while I can nae foretell the delay, it will be time well spent. In the fullness of time my barracoons shall be burstin' with the children cursed by Noah."

Nichols tossed off his brandywine appreciatively. "I agree the French ain't shy by half when it comes to chivyin' the goodness out of the grape." He placed the goblet carefully on the table. "Tell me, Mister Aird, was I to stay here, think you I could play your game of golf?"

Aird hesitated for a long moment. "You are perfectly free to play golf as much as you like, Captain Nichols," Aird answered brightly. "Yes, as much as you like."

"But no one here will play with me." Nichols' tone made the words a statement, not a question.

"My dear fellow," Aird responded, somewhat flustered, "I play the game, but very poorly, if you must know, and I hae a power of work, 'n' little time, the Dear knows, to accomplish it to the satisfaction of the London Scottish Syndicate."

"And no captain out of any *négrier* that ever calls at this factory will unbend to play golf with me," Nichols said, his voice smoldering with sarcasm.

"The choosin' o' one's golf partners be left to the choosin' o' one's golf partners," Aird said pleasantly. "But 'tis the end o' the wet, 'n' the links be available to one 'n' all who call here. The wee bairn likely will take to the game. I hae available any number of sticks with which to mangle the Caledonian ball, 'n' for a few cowries the caddies will share with you the much they know."

"But you ain't goin' to play golf with me, are you, Mister Aird?" Wick Nichols slapped the table an ominous blow with his fist.

"Gracious goodness, Captain Nichols, I've told you my duty demands the majority o' my time, and what precious few hours

I am able to claim as my own, my preference is toward other pursuits." Aird's gaze turned toward the young girl, who stood submissively near the parrot's perch.

"I must careen my ship and come at a monstrous leak," Wick Nichols said and attempted to get to his feet, but unsteadiness sent him back to his chair. "I intend to look into Cape Mesurado and Grand Bassa for ebony, perhaps even Cape Coast. But I believe this entire coast be cursed until I progress as far as the Dan-Home."

"The Dan-Home is a good three hundred leagues away, Captain Nichols," Aird said smoothly. "A long way to drive a vessel which you say took a prodigious shock below the water. We offer no dockyard, the pity—we hae an excellent location for a dockyard to effect repairs, but we do hae slopin' beaches 'n' trees nearby where hawsers kin be triced handily. 'N' o' course you will careen under the care o' the cannon we mount." Aird cocked an eye at Geoffrey. "You seem fair burstin' to ask a question, Mister Supernumerary, but politeness 'n' respect for your elders and betters keeps your tongue silent. But speak! If you frequent these coasts much in future you'll find those who mind the shop year-in, year-out always charmed to hear a Christian voice."

"Well, sir," Geoffrey said, choosing his words with great care, "it would be most kind of you to explain the curse of Noah, for I have no knowledge of it."

Aird laughed. "Art a scholar o' the Bible, lad?"

"Not a student, sir," Geoffrey replied respectfully, "though I enjoy the reading of the Bible in French and English versions— I be particularly fond of the language of the book King James authorized—the verses fair soar! And of course I have spent much time in the Torah."

"The Torah!" Aird exclaimed. "Art Jewish?"

Geoffrey paused, seeking the answer to a question he had never asked himself. "I can't rightly say, sir. No more that I can rightly call myself a Catholic. My mother is a stout Catholic of the particular French persuasion, being that she comes from the Island of Martinico. My father is equally devout in his Judaism.

But my father insists that I learn the why of Catholicism, and my mother is equally insistent that I be as precise in my study of the religion professed by the Jews."

"'N which religion do you identify?" Aird asked expectantly.

"With neither and all, sir," Geoffrey said firmly.

"All, Master Frost?"

"Yes, sir, all, for there be bounteous religions, though I be familiar only with the Catholic, the Jewish, and some of the Protestant religions resident in the northern colonies. Master Graham, the pedagogue, is a Quaker, and we conversed frequently about religion. Our consensus is that religions are akin to mathematics, which teaches that parallel paths converge ultimately at infinity."

"And infinity is where God resides, eh, Master Frost the papist?" Aird said smugly.

"I do not presume to know where God resides, sir, though I always find God but a thought away. And neither my mother nor I are what you would call right papists, since we do not ascribe to the theory that a human, though he be much learned and all, and proclaimed a veritable descendant of the Great Fisherman, is infallible. Indeed, as our dear Rabbi Amos instructs, for every biblical allegory there be many legitimate explanations, though there be a thousand lurid explanations with no foundations."

"Well then," Aird said, with an inordinate amount of smugness, "with all your learnin' you no doubt be familiar with the tale o' Noah and his vessel, as described 'n the Book of Genesis."

"Aye, sir," Geoffrey said diffidently, for by his lights he should be speaking far less and listening far more. "Noah went into the great ark of gopher wood he was commanded to build, together with his wife and his sons Shem, Ham and Japheth, and their wives. I believe it be chapter nine or thereabouts where God speaks of His covenant with mankind after the ark had regained the ground."

"And you doubtless recall that old Noah got low on wine

after the ark came to ground, and his son Ham was gravely shamed to see Noah wallowin' 'n filth and nakedness. So Ham sent in his brothers to cover their father's nakedness, and when old Noah came out o' the wine, he was fearsome raged at Ham because that son had seen him wretched, and he placed a curse on Ham. Now," Aird said, lifting his glass to his lips and draining off the brandywine remaining in one toss, "the entire Christian world knows that Ham was black, 'n' his own father cursed that he would always be a servant of servants upon his brothers."

Geoffrey's distress was apparent to Wick Nichols, as well as Mister Aird. "Well, youngster," Wick Nichols said, "your face recommends your disagreement with the Biblical truth revealed. How be it that you disagree with Holy Writ?"

Geoffrey had no wish to be arguing with his elders, but their knowledge of the Old Testament—he recalled the well-worn Bible in Wick Nichols' cabin, and he had no doubt that both Wick Nichols and Mister Aird were well-read in the Old Testament—was deficient. "Noah did not curse his son Ham," Geoffrey said in a very low, respectful voice. "The curse of Noah fell upon Canaan, the oldest son of Ham. It is then true that the Canaanites were once slaves of the Hebrews, and the Hebrews were later themselves slaves of the Egyptians, so there you see the fulfillment of servant of servants. And, I believe myself certain of the facts, the Hebrews who were slaves of the Egyptians were so heartily sorry of that situation that once shut of it and across the Red Sea they abjured slavery. And I am perplexed why the Scriptures never clearly explained why the son, Canaan, was punished for the sin of his father, Ham, whose sin, if sin indeed it was, consisted only of having seen his father naked, and wishing to have him covered, and all. Seems most like Noah should have been rebuked for allowing himself to get so low."

"And you be how old, young sir," Aird demanded frostily, "to speculate upon such weighty matters, when all the world knows the right o' holdin' slaves is firmly grounded in the Holy Scriptures." Then to Wick Nichols: "Please permit me to serve your glass again. It seems this small cask hae taken on a surprisin' lightness, and if that be so, we should hasten to relieve it of all possible weight so it might be used again."

"Rising ten, sir," Geoffrey said in a contrite, hardly audible voice. "And I apologize that my manners have been so froward as to remonstrate with you. 'Twas meant as no disrespect, please ken. I only responded as Mister Graham would desire was we engaged in Socratic discourse." He took refuge in his cup of tea.

"Well, it be good for us engaged in the ebony trade, whether we be Jew or Christian, that another religion claimin' kinship with the Almighty is ascendant in the north of Africa," Wick Nichols said, just a bit unsteadily. Geoffrey quickly calculated the amount of brandy Wick Nichols had drunk: the master of the *Bride of Derry* had to have imbibed close to a quart of liquor. "The Mohammedan bestirs and afflicts those who in his image is cast in all save their allegiance to his peculiar religion."

Geoffrey prudently said nothing, and Mister Aird nodded approvingly.

Wick Nichols fetched the featherie from his waistcoat pocket and laid it carefully on the table before Aird. "Your kind offer I must decline. None of us knows but what a French squadron, Admiral Hawke's great victory off the Brittany coast notwithstandin', might appear over the horizon before dawn the morrow, Mister Aird. Your cannons, such as they might be, stand only for appearance, for there be none to serve them. Even if the gentlemen-captains out of Liverpool would deign to play golf with a white nigger I would be far closer to a profit of twenty-five percent by delivery of as much stock as I can stow in the *Bride of Derry*'s holds to the Carolina by November. Careening the *Bride* 'n' roustin' out a spoiled plank or two behind one of the Banana Islands be far more in my line than swingin' sticks at Caledonian balls with captains out of time for their vessels."

Aird spread his hands deprecatingly. "Bence Island has ample godowns where you may store your trade goods with nae worry, Captain Nichols, rather than chance your goods twice across the beaches. The Banana Isles lie close, 'tis true, but twixt there 'n' here be sufficient water to cover a fleet o' ships with tender parts."

"Thankee, Mister Aird, but was I to unlade here to come against the tender planks, the sight of ebony enterin' a ship other than my own would prey so mightily upon my mind that I would be thrown altogether out of spirit, and likely quarrelsome with the Liverpool captains." Wick Nichols helped himself to a healthy tot of Mister Aird's French brandywine, then said speculatively, as he swilled it, "The girl there, has she been taught any tricks, other than servin' at table?"

"The child yonder?" Mister Aird studied the girl standing near the now silent parrot through his rheumy eyes and smiled slyly. "Why no, though I hae been bringin' her along myself, the slow kind you understand. Now, I certainly understand you hae been long at sea without the comfort that only a woman brings, so if it be tricks you want, I hae a round dozen o' comely wenches who've been thoroughly acquainted with all modes of lechery, both ancient 'n' modern. Two of 'em, I warrant, kin perform more tricks on a six-inch dick than one o' the monkeys dwellin' in the forests on the mainland kin perform swingin' on a thousand-foot vine. 'N' one or all at a very fair price."

Geoffrey lowered his eyes to the table and knew his face was flame red. The men in the fo'c'sle had been quite ribald and explicit in their descriptions of their methods of wresting temporary carnal pleasures from a woman's body and all the more boisterous to discomfit him, though he did not know it. "Mister Aird must have no mother or sister, else how can he speak of a woman so?" Geoffrey asked himself fiercely, thinking of his own mother and sister, and the thought of such offensive language reaching the ears of the women dear to him brought on even more aggravations of discomfort.

"'Tis true my men be like rams, sore restive for bein' held so long from the ewes, but they are some time away from their allotment of privilege women, and I was lookin' for a woman to share out while we careen."

"Was you to careen here, Captain Nichols, comfort women

would be included in the exceedingly small duty I must assess for securin' your trade goods in my godowns."

"'N' I've represented to you how I would prickle with righteous jealousy at the sight of ebony entering any ship but my own, Mister Aird, so I must be away, you ken. I have a particular island in mind, and I prefer to keep my men's attention centered on their work. A share-out woman would be most welcome." Wick Nichols snapped his fingers. Startled, but knowing what Nichols wanted, Geoffrey dutifully and quickly drew the small purse that Nichols had entrusted to him from his waistcoat. Nichols shook two guineas out of the purse and pushed the heavy gold coins across the table to Aird.

"Alas, any of the experienced women at my disposal command a price of three guineas, with selection left to my discretion, you agree."

"The girl yonder," Nichols said, his tongue passing furtively, snake-like, over his lips. "My men would appreciate a young 'un."

Aird pushed the two coins back across the table, his face tightly smug. "You mean *you* prefer young 'uns, Captain Nichols. I doubt not you would bring any woman first under your lee before sendin' her forward."

"Three guineas then, the same price as one o' your experienced 'uns." Nichols added a third coin from the purse.

Geoffrey watched the Scot's mouth twitch with avarice, then shot a quick glance at the girl. She was standing as still as a monument, expressionless, but Geoffrey knew she was well aware the men's conversation involved her.

"Doubtless she be one of the privilege women you are allotted, so her price be aught but profit for you, Mister Aird," Wick Nichols said as he pushed the three guineas back across the table.

Mister Aird made no move toward the coins but said disapprovingly, "Your actions signal you hae a great desire to possess that particular woman, Captain Nichols, 'n' such signals should be eschewed by traders, since they attach greater value to the property than otherwise warranted, always to the detriment o' the purse."

"You rightly remind me so, thankee, Mister Aird." Wick Nichols reached to retrieve the guineas.

"Nay, Captain Nichols." Aird placed a hand protectively over the coins. "It happens I be especially fond of guineas, the name given by Charles the Second, when he came to the throne, for the gold came from this wild Guinea Coast. Every guinea won signifies a week of comfort when I return to Dundee, and a snug little cottage lookin' out on the Tay. Each guinea won signifies a fortnight closer to the happy day when I can visit St. Andrews at my leisure." Aird picked up the featherie and slipped it into a pocket of his somber coat. "When I hae the pleasure of snappin' this fine Caledonian ball, I shall recall with special fondness its giver."

"Then we've struck a deal," Nichols grunted.

"We hae a deal when the pieces o' 'em beautiful guineas tote four, Captain Nichols," Aird said with a smile. "For the comely woman ships with a child. It would uncommon cruel to separate a child o' tender age from its mother, so if you be determined to hae the woman, you must take the child as part o' the bargain. Dinna fret so, Captain Nichols, the child be weaned." Aird's smile broadened as Nichols winkled another guinea from the purse. "We must drink to our mutual bargain!" Aird snatched up the brandy cask but, unsteady from all that he had drunk, fumbled it, sending it crashing across the table and splintering both glasses. Geoffrey was able to snatch up cup and tea service as the cask rolled in an erratic ellipse before Aird pinned it, quickly plugging the bung with his forefinger.

"Ah, well," Aird said, as Geoffrey handed him the cork. "This be the Almighty's way o' tellin' us to foreswear drink for the moment, alas upon us with the brandywine only half gone." Aird made a half bow in Wick Nichols' general direction, though no more than a half bow, as if Aird were afraid he might fall.

Wick Nichols clinked the four guineas into a small pile and tucked the coins into a pocket in Aird's waistcoat. "The squeaker 'n' I be on the return to our ship this moment, and you'll understand, Mister Aird, that I'm exceedin' anxious to march along the wench and her spawn."

"Quite understandable, Captain Nichols," Aird said in the querulous, slurred voice of one descending into drink. "And her bairn shall be fetched on the instant. But her finery she's obliged to leave behind. I have half a dozen wenches who can shape their forms into its folds—it be but a strip of cloth, nothin' more. But her finery be not part o' our struck bargain, havin' cost me two and tuppence the yard."

Wick Nichols rested his knuckles on the table, its white cloth dazzling in the noonday sun, and stared unsteadily into Aird's small, pig-like eyes: "Don't have no need for such foofaw in the *Bride,* as you well know, Mister Aird. Most dress be affectation here in the tropics, you'll agree." Wick Nichols slipped the leather purse into his coat pocket. "Good day to you, Mister Aird, and if an unexpected consignment of ebony should come your way by virtue of the Mohammedan wars, do send a boat with such adviso. I don't expect to be hard to find in the Bananas, though my careen will take no more than ten days. I must be on the step for the ports on the Bight of Benin."

Geoffrey was glad enough to relieve himself of his restrictive shoes and peel off his stockings once Wick Nichols and he were outside the tabby fort. But he was greatly dismayed when a black man appeared leading the woman by a rope around her neck. The woman no longer wore the brilliantly hued dress and mob cap but was garbed in a strip of cloth passed once or twice around her waist, and another passed over her shoulders and tied between her breasts to restrain a youngster snuggled close against her back in the same wise Geoffrey had once seen a Narragansett woman pack a youngster on an Indian cradleboard. Both strips of cloth were exceedingly nondescript and worn.

"What ho!" Nichols shouted in delight, clutching up the rope from the man and cavorting around the woman. "A bargain fer sure, fer it has been much a long, spavined time since I've had the comfort of a woman." He leered at Geoffrey. "Bein' my squeaker 'n' supernumerary 'n' all, you can claim dibs on her ahead o' the men."

Geoffrey's response was his immediate and fierce coloring and looking away so as not to see his captain's drunkenness or the woman's shame. "Here," Nichols said, thrusting out the rope, "hold her while I go ahead. If she tries to turn aside, belay. If she fails to keep pace, start her with a blow across her buttocks. We must win the ship ever as fast as we can."

Geoffrey tried to refuse the rope, but Nichols looped the end around his fist and started down the sandy path at a near trot. Feeling more wretched than he had ever felt in his young life, Geoffrey started after his captain, glad that the woman was walking determinedly, and on her own volition, for he could never have struck her, even though it would have meant his own life forfeit. Geoffrey kept pace with the woman, though she carefully avoided his eyes, and from time to time he looked at the baby slung on the woman's back. He was no expert at guessing the age of a child, but surely this one—he could not tell if it were a male or a female—had to be passing one year. The child, a light coffee color with reddish-blonde kinked hair, sucked a thumb as it slept contentedly, pulled tightly against its mother's back by the strip of cloth binding it securely.

Geoffrey said nothing as he stretched out to keep pace with Wick Nichols and the woman, but his mind was working furiously, turning over and reflecting on the parable of Joseph being sold by his brothers to the Ishmaelites—a slave to the Ishmaelites, for twenty pieces of silver. And that beautiful coat of many colors had been besmeared with the blood of a kid so that Jacob could be deceived into believing that an evil beast had devoured the son of his old age. "I reckon twenty pieces of silver cyphers to four guineas of gold, today's value," Geoffrey reflected bitterly. "All the coinage necessary to exchange for a human life."

He desperately wanted this voyage over; he desperately wanted to talk directly and earnestly with his father. Surely his father could not know the truth about the debased trade in human life. Others, men of mean intent, were concealing the horrors of the slave trade from his father. The gentle, kind Marlborough Frost he knew could never have indented his oldest son into this trade were he aware of the soul-robbing abomination that for the simple passage of four gold guineas all right, title, interest and fee simple absolute in a living human being had been transferred from one person to another. It *was* an abomination! His father would set all to rights, reorder the universe immediately, of that Geoffrey Frost was sure. But all the same Geoffrey was painfully aware that it would be at least six months before he would see his father and mother, and the immense breadth of the Atlantic Ocean, with its attendant storms and vicissitudes, separated him from his beloved family in New Hampshire.

They emerged upon the broad beach of dazzling white sand where the gig lay. The tide, modest in extent, so unlike the seven- and eight-foot mean variances to which Geoffrey was accustomed in the Piscataqua's run, and incoming now had brought the changeable sea's edge lapping to the gig's hull. It took less than a minute to run the gig into water deep enough to float her, and Geoffrey handed the woman into the gig with all the dignity he could muster. He settled into the stern sheets, the woman between him and Wick Nichols, and the four men at the oars, all grinning and smirking hugely, pulled enthusiastically for the *Bride of Derry,* anchored sedately a good sea mile off the westernmost shore of Bence Island.

The woman was pressed tightly between Geoffrey and Wick Nichols on the narrow bench. Nichols had the tiller tucked under his left arm, and his right hand was resting familiarly upon the woman's knee. Geoffrey stole a glance at the baby—it was sleeping still—but he could not bear to look at the woman, though she made no sound as Nichols' hand left her knee and roved along her thigh. The woman spread her legs and permitted Nichols' hand to quest higher.

"Hoot, Captain! She be hot fer ye!" one of the rowers exclaimed.

"Mind your stroke, Farmington," Nichols grunted. "She ain't no normal comfort woman. She be a queen from some tribe far to the north, who, through a series of misfortunes, and the misalignment of planets, I'll warrant, found herself on this coast 'n' throwed herself upon our protection."

"Hoot, Captain," Farmington exclaimed again, "'n' judgin'

by the mulatto slung a-back she's helped the Scot's trader polish his pole more'n once, belike."

"Stow your gob, Farmington," Nichols said, voice rising menacingly. "This be a proper lady out of a good family, though brought low by misfortune, as could any of you be, the moment's notice. I've bought her out of the Scot's clutches, 'n' she wishes to entertain us, civil like, perhaps with some heathen dances as she may elect to display."

"I'll await my turn, Captain, no one's ever said ol' Haynes don't know how to wait his turn. But she appears right choice, 'n' I hope us fo'c'sle hands don't have to wait our turn overly long, if ye ken our drift—I speak fer my mates," Farmington said.

"Stretch out then, Topman Farmington, you and your mates are laggin' sadly. Sooner aboard, sooner comfortably ensconced 'n your hammock with comfort 'n your arms." Nichols grinned at his crewmen as he probed the woman's groin familiarly. "Backs into your task, for I be fatigued and fain must seek my cot immediately aboard our *Bride*."

The gig fairly flew over the surface of the calm sea while Geoffrey retreated deeper into his embarrassment and sought to block out the jeers and ribald comments of the gig's crew. The gig appeared on the *Bride*'s larboard side in astonishing course, but the waist entry was blocked by Hector Grumman, the sailmaker, who had stretched and was inspecting a great length of heavy-weather duck intended for the foretop gallant sail. "Ease around the bow, 'n' come in from starboard," Nichols commanded, and the stroke, obedient to his order, changed course. Nichols was no longer tending the rope around the woman's neck but was pawing the cleft between her legs. The gig passed beneath the bowsprit and instantly the woman stood up, arched her back, whipped the rope out of Nichols' grasp, and was overside in one smooth, fluid motion. The gig rocked precipitously, shipping water over the gunwales in immense quantities, bringing the gig to a confused halt, almost at the point of sinking. Geoffrey, throwing off his coat, dived overside. Eyes stinging from the salt, he glimpsed the woman pulling herself strongly down the anchor cable.

From the disjointed way she fought along the cable Geoffrey knew the woman had never swum a stroke in her life. He surfaced, drew air into his lungs, and, exhaling half, dove again and stroked fiercely after the woman. His ears popped alarmingly from the pressure, then abruptly cleared, and he followed the woman as she clawed her way, hand over hand, down the anchor rode. The woman reached the anchor, the *Bride*'s best bower, its fluke dug well into the sand on the clear bottom. She grasped the anchor's shank, clutched it with both hands, rolled over and kicked viciously at Geoffrey as he swam down to her. A foot struck his nose, a numbing blow, and a moment later blood began to stain the water. Geoffrey blinked his eyes against the pressure and the salt and grasped a leg, attempting to break her limpet-like embrace of the anchor. The woman kicked her legs violently, and Geoffrey abandoned the effort.

Immediately he swam around the anchor stock and reached out for the child. The woman turned on her side and foiled Geoffrey's grasp. His lungs were bursting for want of air, but still he sought the child. The woman thrust a leg triumphantly through the anchor ring, jamming in her leg as far as she could force it, then shuddered and lay on her back, losing buoyancy, a tendril of air escaping from her mouth. Geoffrey could no longer see the child, but he knew, he knew it was already too late. Despairing, he grasped the anchor cable and kicked upward in desperate ascent. How deep did the anchor lie? Perhaps ten fathoms. He rose in a welter of foam just beside the gig, shaking his head for breath but unable to block from his mind the beatific, enigmatic smile wreathing the face of the woman who had so gladly embraced death some sixty feet beneath him.

Wick Nichols caught Geoffrey by the hair, pulled him half out of the water and glared into his face. Abruptly he let Geoffrey go. "Piddlin' waste of four guineas," he said irritably, and spat. "Made a fool o' me, she did. Clap onto the gig's stern 'n' we'll tow round to the starboard entry. Lest you want to come into the gig now, your blood will draw all the sharks of the Guinea Coast."

Once on deck Nichols ordered the gig tied off astern and

snarled: "Weigh the anchor. Raise jibsail. Ready fore top sail. Sheet home fore top sail when we pick up the anchor." Nichols turned. "Course due south," he shouted at the men running to the helm and kicked viciously at a hand running toward the capstern, hitting the man in the left thigh and tumbling him into the scuppers.

Geoffrey ran to the capstern, where the frightened men collected there had already shipped the bars, and jumped onto a bar immediately behind Holly, the cook.

"Lord, don't let that man get no staff er rope," Holly said softly, so that only Geoffrey heard. "Least o' all, don't let Wick Nichols get no axe nor knife." The cook's nostrils were tightly pinched, and he was perspiring profusely.

"Heave down," someone at the capstern ordered: "Heave and stamp, hearty now!" The men at the capstern leaned into their work and the endless messenger cable began its twang. Geoffrey pushed against the heavy oak bar and moved in the circular rhythm demanded if the *Bride of Derry* was to win her anchor. "Heave and stamp, way on!" the man cried, suiting his actions to his word and stamping a sharp blow onto the deck with his left foot every time the hinged metal bar that was the pawl head at the base of the capstern drum dropped into the pawl rim. The men walked the capstern briskly round, the messenger running effortlessly, until strain came on the anchor cable and the clicks of the pawl were less frequent and more measured. But with each click of the pawl Geoffrey Frost, his face lowered so no one could see his wretched tears as they mixed with the saltwater running from his hair and the blood from his nose, all spattering onto the deck, sent first a Christian prayer, followed closely by a Jewish prayer, for the repose of the souls of the young woman and her child, newly released from their sad imprisonments these last five minutes.

～〆 X 〆～

oseph Frost did not want to leave the comfort of the
bed of fragrant balsam fir branch tips that Juby had
made by pushing the ends into the ground, closely
packed, and thereby fashioning a delightfully light
and springy mattress. He did not want to surrender his hold on
sleep, for he was fatigued beyond all belief. But Juby persisted
in his urgent coaxing. "Gots coffee a-bile, Master Joseph. If you
don't be up 'n' about in the minute, likely Samuel be drunk it
all hisself."

The prospect of coffee brought Joseph instantly awake. It
had been weeks since he had a cup of coffee. Fully dressed
except for his shoes, he threw off the light sheet that served as
some protection against the everpresent, ever voracious mosquitoes while he slept, and puffy-eyed from want of sleep and
from mosquito bites he sought them in the fitful light from the
fire pit fifty yards away. Finding his shoes, Joseph pulled them
on with hands painful and stiff from raw open cuts and vast
blisters broken open. Joseph shambled after Juby as quickly
as he could and collapsed to his knees at the edge of the fire.
"Morning, Joseph," Samuel Stonecypher said by way of greeting. "Reckon we launch the *Revenge* today."

"May do that," Joseph agreed, reaching eagerly for the steaming cup of coffee that Juby held out. "Depends on whether we
can get all the oakum seamed in as it should be." He perked
his ears to the clang and ring of hammers on anvils from the
blacksmith shop. He could even hear the *whoosh* of air being

compressed by the bellows. The men from Continental Army units who had been so injudicious as to identify themselves as wheelwrights, or iron mongers, or farriers, or any variant of the blacksmith's craft had been plucked from their units and set upon the serious tasks of fashioning metal implements of war. And they were working double tides. "We've finally brought the smiths to the point they can fashion acceptable caulking irons, though should any shipwright working for my cousin John Langdon see such laughable lumps and chisels wrought from iron they would be fair amazed that such implements can, in fact, introduce spun oakum into a vessel's seams."

Joseph struggled closer to the fire ring in hopes the mosquitoes would not intrude into its shield of heat. A hundred yards away the hull of the schooner that had been given the warlike and daunting name *Revenge* stood in rough outline only against the first discernible hint of magenta, cobalt and salmon colors skittering on the eastern horizon. Wordlessly, Juby held out a plate of fish chowder. Joseph took a tentative sip of his coffee. "Why, Juby! This is real coffee! I conceit your promise of coffee this morn would prove to be only the false parched corn." He eagerly drank off half the cup and held it out for more. The cup was stuck in his claw-like hand from the dried blood, serum from his blisters, and pitch, so he had difficulty in releasing it. Instead, Joseph rested it on a rock of the fire ring and Juby filled the cup from the steaming coffeepot.

"Man from Portsmouth brought it durin' the night," Juby said off-handedly as he returned the coffeepot to its trivet of stone.

"A man from Portsmouth, Juby!" Joseph cried eagerly. "Who? What was his name? Did he bring items more important than coffee, news of Maman, Father, Charity and Marcus and the children, and Geoffrey? Is there news of Geoffrey?" Joseph swallowed. "Was other news borne by this mysterious man from Portsmouth?"

"The Tai-Pan, your brother, fetched in a clutch of British vessels as prizes but didn't tarry long and was quickly away to sea, to the mortification of his crew, who already had cyphered how their prize money would be spent." Juby sniffed virtuously. "Most like in riotous and licentious behavior, with never a thought for their families. Master Marcus continues to better his walkin' under Mistress Charity's carin'. Your father be troubled much with the pains in his legs and was greatly dismayed that the Chinee who attends Master Geoffrey was unable to employ the healin' needles." Almost as an afterthought Juby said, "Coffee be from the Lady Thérèse on account of your birthday two weeks ago."

"Aah!" Joseph exclaimed. Great fatigue had caused him to neglect the day, but yes, he was at least two weeks past his eighteenth birthday. But his mother had remembered. His dear, dear mother! Did Maman know all the embarrassing, painful and sordid details of his flight from Portsmouth? In her state of mind, could she know? If the Lady Thérèse could remember his birthday, she was capable of understanding other things. At least his brother-in-law who had been so hideously maimed within Louisbourg gaol was convalescing in the love of his family. Joseph prised his fingers from the cup and seized the plate of fish chowder. He ate because he knew he must, but he could taste nothing that he mechanically spooned into his mouth, so heavy was the sense of shame and disgrace that welled up in him. Hard, long hours of heavy work and a goal to work toward had submerged those sensibilities, but the gift of coffee from his mother had summoned them again, all the more bitter because Maman had to know how gravely her last born had besmirched the family's honor. Joseph got to his feet and started toward the bare hull of *Revenge.*

"Hey! That caulkin' ain't so important you can't finish your coffee," Stonecypher said.

Joseph made no reply but stumbled through the darkness until he fetched up at the hull and by touch and feel located the tub of picked oakum under its larboard counter. There was a betty lamp somewhere that he could light if he wished; it would be some minutes yet before there would be light enough to caulk, but at least for the nonce he could spin the oakum into the long coil that would be inserted in the seams. Sitting on a stack of rough-sawn boards in the darkness, Joseph could still roll the strands of hemp picked out of short pieces of ropes and cables between his palms, spinning the strands into a coil of oakum in much the same fashion that Juby had rolled out the dough for the bannock bread. When there was light enough he reached for his caulking mallet.

"Hey, you up there on the ladder, you be the matross?"

Joseph had been concentrating on running a good seam with his iron and caulking mallet; the voice startled him, and he just managed to avoid smashing his thumb. "You shouldn't slip up on a fellow like that," he said crossly. "You might get a caulking iron dropped on you." Joseph looked down at a cheerful, ruddy-faced man of about his brother's age peering up at him with a lean, satirical look.

The man was dressed in duck trousers, a shirt of fine white but unadorned cambric and a well-made tricorne of dark brown felt. His shoes were no-nonsense sturdy cloggers with tarnished pewter buckles. A business-like seaman's cutlass was belted around his waist. "Name's Rue, Benjamin Rue. I've got command of the *Philadelphia* gundalo yonder." He pointed toward a gundalo with a red-painted hull but no mast or armaments, its bows nudged up on the beach.

Joseph finished paying the seam he was on, then descended the ladder. "You look like more of a sailor than anyone I've seen at Tyonderoga excepting General Arnold," he said, trying to rub pitch from his crabbed and blistered hands with a mop of oakum.

Benjamin Rue laughed, his eyes disappearing in squints. "There be three o' us all told. General Arnold, as you say, and Seth Warner's come up from Connecticut. He'll get the next row gallie to come off the stocks at Skenesboro. He'll be lookin' for a matross as soon as he's got sweeps in the water and hands enough. I got to the matross first."

Joseph looked at the sun. Almost noon, and Juby was coming toward him with a pail of water. Joseph was suddenly conscious of his extreme thirst, having tasted nothing liquid since breakfast. "I don't hold myself out as a matross, but I'm not so dense I couldn't learn how to point and serve a cannon from a master gunner, name of Rawbone."

Rue nodded. "Arnold's goin' to lead us into one hell o' a dust-up with the British any day now, and I want my vessel outfitted with the pick o' the cannons Tyonderoga can disgorge, and I want my crew to be able to give fair account o' themselves."

"Can you tell me anything of General Arnold? There was this talk of a court-martial," Joseph asked anxiously, grateful for the gourd of cool water Juby held out to him, drinking deeply, and then offering the gourd to Rue, who was obviously wilting in the haze of brass-colored midday heat.

"Aye, a court-martial brought on by as sorry a cabal o' blatherskates as ever assembled under one roof." Rue grimaced as he accepted the gourd. "Cowards like Roger Enos, who treacherously deserted Arnold on the Kennebec with all the expedition's medicines and most o' the rations. Our General Washington ordered a court-martial o' Enos soon as he showed his weasel nose in Cambridge, but didn't do no good, seein' as how Sullivan was president o' the court, and even though the charge was 'quittin' his commandin' officer without leave,' Enos was congratulated that his cowardice was 'prudent and reasonable.'" Rue spat. "Now another New Hampshire officer got appointed as president o' Arnold's court, Enoch Poor—imagine, a colonel presidin' over the court-martial of a brigadier general, who spent days . . ."

"For God's sakes, man!" Joseph cried in exasperation. "What are the charges laid against General Arnold?"

"Near as I can make out, General Arnold be charged with robbin' merchants in Montreal and enrichin' himself off the plunder. A pissant name o' John Brown and another name o' Moses Hazen—the fact they be appointed colonels in this Continental Army shows just how free them Congress fellas be with their commission papers, handin' 'em out top, bottom and sides—they took tales to Congress, which be lookin' for someone to blame for the failure to hold on to Canada."

"Those charges are ludicrous," Joseph said indignantly. "I've met General Arnold on two occasions only, but since coming to Tyonderoga I've talked with any number of men who've served under him. They all say he's a right tartar in battle, and how he kept fighting in front of Quebec even with a bullet in his leg." He sat down on the pile of rough-sawn lumber and, to occupy his hands and thoughts, reached into the barrel of oakum and began spinning a coil. "Any of these people accusing General Arnold got bullets poked through them?"

"No, of course not," Rue said. "Though the surgeon to Poor's brigade, Doctor Lewis Beebe, wants to make the sun shine through General Arnold's head with a musket ball. All his accusers got 'cross the breakers with General Arnold 'cause he be a fightin' general, like Montgomery was. These *officers*," Benjamin Rue fairly spat the word, "always skulked 'round safe behind the lines held by better men then they. Perfumed and pampered princes o' the Continental Army, they be. Not a one can be trusted in a sheep cote at night. United in nothing but their hatred o' a far better man and leader, the man they'd like to be, but ain't likely 'cause they don't know that leadership is a process, not just the shoutin' o' orders that make no sense. No muddy boots for them."

"And what's General Arnold done in his defense? Surely he is able to marshal facts and figures to refute those base charges?" Joseph kept rolling the oakum into a coil between his palms.

"Kinda hard to get witnesses fled to Canada, and witnesses such as Major Scott who be willin' to testify for the general be disqualified by Poor as bein' too far interested. So General Arnold challenged all the bastards on the court to duels, separate or individual, he don't care which." Rue dusted his hands in satisfaction. "All the New Hampshire officers be blatherskates who hate Schuyler and Arnold because they are aristocrats, while Gates, the Windy Wonder, manipulates everything to his advantage 'cause he considers he should have been picked to command the Continental Army rather than that Virginian, our General Washington. Tripes, but General Arnold never had no call to steal anything from nobody because he's got his own money, and plenty o' it. And he's spent a lot o' coin out o' his own pocket seein' to the construction o' this fleet."

"Well, I know nothing of these political things, but seemingly we'd better emulate the gods' messenger and sprout wings from our ankles," Joseph said irritably, "because we are a long way from having any sort of fleet."

"Well, I'm glad you ain't been sittin' here waitin' for no court-martial to make up its mind, but you've been buildin' warships to General Arnold's patterns. Now all we needs is to get cannons and sticks into my gundalo, and get somebody knows which end o' the cannon faces toward the enemy to train my crew."

Joseph looked sharply at Rue and then at the *Philadelphia* gundalo. "General Arnold prescribed the crew of a gundalo at forty-five men. How many men you actually got?"

"Well, not forty-five," Benjamin Rue admitted warily.

"Then here's the trick you're dealt, Captain Rue," Joseph said. "Trot your crew up here to give us a hand trimming this schooner to shape. If you can bring up even twenty men who can saw a board and keep the corners moderately square, or daub on paint, we can get *Revenge* into the Lake before nightfall. Then we'll go rummaging around in the cannons laid out in the park. I confess to having my eye on a Swedish-cast 12-pounder, she's more robust than the British or the French cannons, and there's a pair of long 9-pounders that would complement your *Philadelphia* admirable. We can get some parbuckles around them and have the cannons down to water's edge, ready to go over to the sheers at Rattlesnake Hill first thing tomorrow."

"Done!" Benjamin Rue said, grasping Joseph's hand and shaking it much like a pump handle.

The next morning, as Joseph, Juby, Samuel Stonecypher and half a dozen crewmen from the *Philadelphia* were grunting the first of the pair of long 9-pounders onto a carriage assembled from the pieces of oak Joseph and Stonecypher had so laboriously sawn and adzed out, Benedict Arnold strode toward their small group. Arnold whistled a chipper tune as he walked, picking his way through the militia units muddling through maneuver and drill on the foreshore, seemingly without a care in the world and accompanied by a tall, muscular, flat-faced Indian dressed in seaman's pantaloons, jersey, and old frock coat. The Indian was chewing placidly on a twig of maple.

"This is Broadhead," Arnold said in his shrill voice by way of introduction. "He's a Pequot from down my part of Connecticut. You can't pronounce his Pequot name, but he's sailed with me on half a dozen voyages to the Dutch and Danish isles in the Caribbean. He don't talk much, but when he does, listen to what he says. He's as good a bosun as ever been to sea and volunteered to make himself useful to our Army." Arnold turned to Benjamin Rue. "You're Rue from Pennsylvania, ain't you? Got an eye for cannons, and an eye for my matross, I ken." The two Continental Army officers returned each other's salutes.

"Well, General Arnold, I intend to take the *Philadelphia* gundalo right into the midst o' the British fleet and spit Governor Carleton square in the eye. Then I intend to cannon his vessel into pick tooths."

"A proper fighting spirit, yes, sir, a proper fighting spirit, and I admire that in a commander, Captain Rue. It's a great comfort to know that I have men under me who are all meat and very little rind, unlike some of the officers of this Continental Army with whom I be intimately acquainted, who are exactly the opposite, I tell you in all candor, to the mutual displeasure of those officers and myself." Benedict Arnold turned to Joseph. "Mister Volunteer Matross, how soon can mast be stepped and the rest of *Philadelphia*'s armament brought aboard?"

"Well, General, it was my thought to get the two long 9-pounders aboard with their carriages—as you can see, we have a bridge of planks laid from the shore to the deck for that purpose." Joseph pointed toward the run of planks leading from the shore to the top of the gunwales, some three feet above the water. "We would then sweep *Philadelphia* over to the sheers under Rattlesnake Hill, while bringing the 12-pounder along on a raft. I believe I understand how the wooden slider for the fore-cannon is to be constructed, but having never done such, of necessity it will take some cut and try, and of course the more men allocated into Captain Rue's crew, the greater rapidity with which the undertaking may progress."

"A trifling matter, Mister Frost, easily accomplished well within two days. I must have a vessel to send down the Lake, all the way to the head of Richelieu. A dual mission to show the British what will challenge their passage and to gather intelligence of British, Canadian and Indian forces. I also need soundings around the bays and islands to supplement information already garnered. I think to employ the first vessel got up to fighting trim on this enterprise, a vessel able to sail well with the wind from aft, well-manned but able to run away handily from anything the British can dispatch in pursuit, depending on sail or sweeps." Arnold smiled thinly. "Of course, this may not be the vessel to undertake such a mission, and perhaps I would be better advised to await Seth Warner's arrival in a proper row gallie that can accommodate twice the force. Yes, a larger vessel will show more to advantage . . ." Arnold broke off. "Mister Broadhead, I'd be obliged if you would give those lads a hand getting that cannon aboard. They're having a hard time of it."

The Pequot Indian stalked over to the bridge of planks, which was sagging and dangerously close to breaking under the weight of the long 9-pounder that was being inched up the incline by double blocks and tackle. Broadhead barked a few short commands in a guttural voice, then crawled beneath the drooping boards, rested his hands upon his thighs, flexed his shoulders, and strained his back partially upright, taking the sag of boards squarely upon himself. A disbelieving Benjamin Rue still had presence of mind sufficient to bawl out as he ran toward the *Philadelphia:* "All you men on the tackles, haul away smartly! You, Barney and Chichester, set your push-poles against the carriage, and the rest of you idlers, clamp onto the push-poles and push your guts out!"

Rue reached the knot of sweating, swearing men and grabbed a push-pole, adding all his strength to the energies of the men on the push-poles and the deck gang hauling briskly on the tackle lines. The two thousand, five hundred pounds of iron and oak inched slowly up the now straight incline of planks. Joseph, his mouth still agape, ran to add his effort, but the cannon was already trebling over the bulwark and onto a shorter plank that led to the deck.

"Admirable, Broadhead, admirable," Benedict Arnold said as the Indian crawled from beneath the inclined boards, "but there is no need for your back to serve in place of proper reinforcement. Captain Rue, if you are insistent upon taking the other cannon aboard your vessel in such wise, though the run not be overlong, you may wish to keep the span from sagging under weight by using some baulks as a buttress at the mid-point."

"Yes sir," Benjamin Rue said, red-faced. "These men had no idea the amount of a cannon's weight, and I was not as vigilant as I should have been in supervisin' the *Philadelphia*'s loadin'."

Broadhead snapped open the lid of a large silver box that he produced from an inner pocket of his coat. With an elaborate flourish he offered the box around. There were no takers, so Broadhead dipped a twig he produced from his hat, its end now much frayed into a rude brush, into the fine brownish powder the silver box contained. He rubbed the powder—snuff, Joseph surmised—vigorously against his lower gums, smiling happily at the tobacco's bite.

"Get me a score more men, General Arnold," Benjamin Rue said earnestly, "and this *Philadelphia* gundalo will pull the tail of the British lion by parading the colours of our confederation of states between Mound Island and the Nut Island. Though that will be after observing your orders to sound and survey."

Arnold thoughtfully rasped the bluish-black stubble on his jaw with a blunt thumb. "No one has yet put much thought to a scheme for a common standard symbolizing our independent states, Captain Rue. I've seen a power of designs—pine trees, snakes, why the Green Mountain Boys even have a standard. The flag of the Second New Hampshire with the names of the thirteen states declared independent in interlocking circles, surrounding a sunburst announcing 'we are one,' is a right comely standard. But for the nonce we should settle on the Flag of Grand Union that was flying at General Washington's headquarters in Cambridge the third of September last, when I was given my orders to lead a force to capture Quebec."

Arnold's slate-gray eyes regarded Joseph and Rue thoughtfully. "I confess I have not studied the matter of an encompassing emblem over much, being occupied with other things. However, if you can find someone to stitch together some bunting into a Flag of Grand Union you may display it on your cruize."

"Samuel Stonecypher is a capital tailor, General Arnold," Joseph said, indicating a reticent Samuel with the sweep of an arm, "and I know the arrangement of the Flag of Grand Union. Samuel can run up a capital flag once we have discovered some bunting of blue, white and red. But first I believe Samuel hankers to begin cutting and sewing the sails for Captain Rue's *Philadelphia* gundalo. How is this first gundalo to be rigged? With the lateen sails of our Piscataqua gundalo?"

Arnold stepped onto the plank incline, followed quickly by Benjamin Rue and Joseph Frost, and made his way aboard the *Philadelphia*. He walked around the rough interior wales, much cluttered with cordage and much in need of a thorough cleaning of sawdust and shavings, examining everything critically. "When I designed the gundalo, I had in mind a vessel low to the water that would be maneuvered primarily by rowing. My original draught calls for a length between perpendiculars of fifty-one and one-half feet, with a keel length of forty-eight feet. Standard breadth would be sixteen feet, and with a depth of three and one-half feet each gundalo would draw one and one-half feet when equipped with armaments and crew complement."

Arnold stopped at the tiller and worked it back and forth vigorously. Satisfied, he continued: "My draught specified a small keel as an aid to steering, though I verily believe, Captain Rue, that the carpenters at Skenesboro neglected to fix this *Philadelphia* of yours with such a valued aid to steering. In the press of construction, with men laboring to get lumber into water as quickly as possible, some dimensions are not fastidiously measured and sawn. Still, she will do, she will do." Arnold fastened on Joseph. "I know the Piscataqua lateen sail and had considered lateen sails for the gundalos, and row gallies—definitely for the row gallies—but I think the proper rig for the gundalo is square topsail above a square course. Such sail plan will only be useful when the wind is astern, so Captain Rue, my advice to you is to recruit brawny men with strong arms, because that is how your *Philadelphia* in the main will be maneuvered."

Benjamin Rue cleared his throat. "Yes, General Arnold, the subject of men to augment the crew presently aboard."

Arnold sighed. "There are many men flocking to Tyonderoga, over twelve thousand at last count, but the vast majority of them would rather await the British in defence behind stone walls or in deep entrenchments. There are precious few who wish to perch two feet above the iron-gray waters of Lake Champlain, sheltered behind two inches of puny planks, when we take the fight to the British." He smiled a bleak smile that reminded Joseph so very much of his brother, Geoffrey. "So I plan to draft Continental Army men born within the sniff of ocean, and do so this week." Arnold grinned wolfishly, and for a moment Joseph could have sworn that it was Geoffrey grinning at him. "I have it on good authority that virtually all the men enlisted in the New Hampshire regiments have some salt water in their veins."

Arnold slapped his thigh, and favoring his right leg slightly he walked toward the plank incline. "Captain Rue, I'll see what can be done to augment your crew, but in the meantime your own recruitment should show increase. I shall deliver your orders this hour two days hence at this very place, with you expectant to cruize against our enemies. Armaments aboard, course and topsail hanging from their yards, and forty-five men enumerated in your crew. Mister Broadhead, if invited properly, may be coaxed into joining this cruize. You will cruize into the lair of the enemy to convince him more time must be invested in building ships to oppose us, though astutely refuse battle. I tell you truly, all of you, every day that dawns without a British sail in prospect is a day of grace for our nascent nation." He tipped his tricorne toward Joseph, though Arnold's eyes were suddenly veiled. "Mister Frost may accompany you on this cruize, but upon return he shall find a great number of aspirant matrosses, and it will be his duty to make them so."

Benedict Arnold paused and beckoned Joseph imperiously to him. When Joseph stood close Arnold whispered so that only Joseph could hear. "You seek a glorious death on this Lake, Volunteer Gentleman Frost. Aye, and chances are you will surely find death seeking you. But you won't die until I'm through with you and tell you that it's alright to die, and I'm nowise through with you. Do you hear me, *Mister* Frost?" Arnold's eyes, suddenly unhooded, seemed to peer into Joseph's soul.

"Yes, s-s-sir," Joseph stuttered.

"Good!" Benedict Arnold said and reached out to pat Joseph's cheek affectionately. Then he was gone.

ISTER CROWNINSHIELD, SWEATING AND
TOSSING IN THE HAMMOCK SUSPENDED
BENEATH THE MAKESHIFT TENT, WAS
NEAR DEATH, SO NEAR THAT HE HAD PIT-
eously asked that young Geoffrey Frost and Jabez McCool
shrive his burdened soul. Geoffrey had long before abandoned
any faith in Damon Nichols' powers as a physician, and so obviously had First Mate Crowninshield, for he called out specifically and loudly for Jabez and Geoffrey. "Don't let that devil o' a
drunk nigger near me!" the mate had rasped through clenched
lips when the spasms first wracked him. "I'm kilt already, but
he's kilt a power o' his own kind, 'n' I don't want no unclean
hands o' hissen tryin' to physic me!"

Crowninshield repeated the words again in a hoarse, ragged
whisper as he lay in his sweat-besotted hammock and spat a
great gout of bright, foamy blood into a wad of wetted tow
that Geoffrey had been using to sponge the man's forehead.
And Crowninshield, ranting helplessly, was equally adamant
that it was Wick Nichols who had killed him and cursed the
man roundly, though not loudly.

Geoffrey carefully wrung out the wad of tow in a pannikin
of water, now pinkish, and shifted it for another, methodically
mopping at the heavy perspiration beading on the mate's forehead. Geoffrey rocked forward on his knees, completely overwhelmed that he, not having yet attained ten years of age until
this September coming, now found himself charged with the

care and nourishment, yes, the life itself, of the *Bride of Derry*'s first mate. The mate lapsed into a troubled sleep, punctuated by spells of heavy coughing. Geoffrey got slowly to his feet and steadied himself against the spar holding up the makeshift tent—actually the mizzen topmast yard, spreading the canvas that ordinarily did duty as the mizzen topsail. He looked across the eye-searing, dazzlingly white sand to the tide's edge, where the *Bride* lay all a-hoe at the edge of the out-tide, a pregnant hull only, spars and stores, not to mention her popguns of cannons, all out of her on this protected lee side of the island.

The *Bride* lay completely and ignominiously hove down on her starboard side, and men with adzes and drawknives were working to hack and scrape away the flourishing animal and plant life that had attached itself tenaciously to the ship's hull. Long, taut cables and doubled tackle-falls and parbuckles that had trundled and triced the *Bride* into such a painfully awkward position led from the beached hull to the butts of palm trees and anchors dragged inland on the fringe of sand where the true beach ended and the true island itself began. Mate Crowninshield's injury had turned serious after the *Bride* had been hove and laid down on her starboard side so the carpenter and his mate could come at the tender planks that had been so sorely bruised when the hull had dragged over the hillock of sand running off the bar at the mouth of the Bereira River.

Mate Crowninshield had been inspecting the barnacles and weeds flourishing beneath the waterline on the larboard side of the exposed hull when he took faint and tumbled with a heavy thud, like that of a mallet strike, onto the wet sand just beneath the bows. He had appeared none the worse from the experience for the remainder of the day but had complained during the night of a constriction in his chest, difficulty in breathing, lightness in the head, a taste of bile in the throat. Then, two days ago, he had collapsed in a miserable heap of piss and frothy blood. A very agitated Wick Nichols ordered Geoffrey to take Crowninshield to the bare canvas rigged to cover the galley stores, hard by the 4-pounder cannons thrown down in a thoroughly haphazard manner that totally lacked any notion of a defensive placement. Nichols charged Geoffrey to "by damn cure him or kill him." Having listened to his mate's coughs for two days, something that evidently grated upon his nerves, Wick Nichols gave Geoffrey to understand in no uncertain terms that he did not care whether the mate was cured or died.

"Jabez," Geoffrey said in a low voice, "I be youth at its most callow and unknowing, and you ken I clearly be no physician. But Mate Crowninshield shall surely depart this life, to our misfortune as a ship's community, 'less we cypher something that augers health's increase."

Jabez McCool was calmly swilling a large calabash of cane diluted by half with water from a tepid creek snaking from the true island to dissipate its fetid contents into the dazzling sand. "Mate, he spoke proper 'n keepin' Damon away from him. Damon would love nothin' more 'n this life than to do the venesection, spill out a quart o' blood, er give an emetic, er perhaps pound up the asshole a great, grand bolus to cause the profound sweats 'n' bring on the coolin' fever." Jabez spat to show his opinion of Damon's medical prowess but repeated the medical word for opening a vein, taking evident satisfaction in knowing its meaning. He resumed sipping his diluted cane appreciatively and cocked a speculative eye at Geoffrey. "Damon aspires to be a medico, 'n' failin' that he aspires to be took as one, which he ain't 'n' never be." Jabez raised the calabash in half salute. "I could be easy persuaded that Mate's death be a good thing, 'cause ye would definitely advance to his place."

"Lo!" Geoffrey said in exasperation, with derision and fear: "Jabez, you be a jack-pudding indeed! Mate be dear to me. He ain't no hard-horse and stands well with the men. I have little learning—nor have I the age, as you well ken—and I certainly am not tinged with any desire to supplant Mister Mate."

"Be only three people on our barky kin navigate, laddie," Jabez said, smacking his lips. "Capt'n, Mate 'n' yereself. Mate loses his place 'n the mess, 'n' Beelzebub must come to ye, despite yere age 'n' experience. 'N' it won't be 'cause he owes yere father or the owners o' this barky any favors, but 'cause ye can keep him off'n a lee shore."

"Mate Crowninshield must not die!" Geoffrey said fiercely. "He is a good man, and I am nowise more than novitiate in the science of navigation. Lo, Captain Nichols had bade me cypher a noon sight with his quadrant. He has given me to understand that navigation in these waters requires the precise nicety. Though notwithstanding the necessity for a precise computational mark, in some way we must come to a theory for Mate's relief."

"Be better far for ye, laddie, was ye to let Mate die," Jabez repeated, regarding Geoffrey evenly over the rim of the calabash and taking small sips to make the liquor last longer. "Death be our destination all, no deviatin', ye ken. Faith, out o' this vale o' woe this year, whatever the cause, 'n' no worries about the next. But Beelzebub now, he'd have to go easy with ye. Truth, he would in no wise dare drub ye, for he fears to lose ye. 'N' ye must know, Mate's malady—though it causes death certain—be nothin' more than a rib bone stove by Beelzebub's cudgel. Ken ye how that staff was so industriously 'n' indignantly plied when he accused Mate o' inattention to our set 'n' distance whilst we was before the bar at the mouth o' the Rio Bereira. Bone's broke 'n' diggin' into Mate's breathin' box, most like. Saw the same once afore I took to the sea; happened on a horse o' my grandpa's who rode post throughout Poole. A stove rib into the breathin' box certain shows itself with the red blood, all foamed-up like."

"Jabez," Geoffrey demanded, "I conceit myself confounded with your intellect, but pray, with what brilliant diagnosis be the course of physic for the mate?"

"Waal," Jabez said dubiously, "Mate ain't no post horse, but assumin' he wus, which we got to pretend like he be a horse—physic be to get him on his pins 'n' not let him lie on his back where the vicious humors kin collect. 'N' cosset him prettily with a garland snugged tight 'round his chest to prevent the rib's cuttin' into the breathin' box."

"You are the true wizard!" Geoffrey exclaimed joyfully, seizing the calabash from Jabez and applying it immediately to the mate's lips. "We must induce a most wholesome slumber for the mate. Then when he is immune to pain ordinary, we must constrict him tightly and then keep him upright, so the bloody humors may be expelled from his lungs. For that be the proper term for his breathing box, Jabez McCool."

"Waal, the post horse did die, withal," Jabez reflected somberly, then remonstrated, snatching too late for his calabash, "laddie, that be all my allowance o' spirit for dinner, 'n' ye know Beelzebub don't issue on land but at dinner 'n' supper, 'n' that be with powerful grudgin'."

"Withal, we have abundance of spirits in these casks and demijohns," Geoffrey said. "We may survey the spirits without qualm, for certainly we have Captain Nichols' charge to restore Mate to health. Betimes, Mate has not had his ration of spirits since he took his tumble, so he be vast overdue."

"Waal," Jabez said with a wry face, wincing at the sight of good cane going down the throat of another, "that be true, but now that we touch Africa Beelzebub looks upon all the barky's spirits as trade goods 'n' does issue powerful grudgin', ye ken."

"There!" Geoffrey said triumphantly, as he upended the calabash into Crowninshield's gasping mouth, tendrils of liquor coursing down the man's chin. "Jabez, is it possible for this cane to be drunk neat without killing a man, or must it always be mixed with equal parts of water?"

"Waal, most jack-tars reckon for the mix with their ration, 'cause that doubles the amount, prolongs the drinkin', 'n' makes the drink lie more comfortable in the belly. But sure, no man grown to his likker ever turned away pure spirit when he kin have it in full measure."

"I can draw upon Captain Nichols' private demijohns, then, without qualm," Geoffrey cried with delight and immediately began a search through the stores the crew had deposited quickly and in no particular order beneath the sailcloth. At length he triumphantly raised up a demijohn, drew the cob stopper and splashed undiluted cane spirit into the calabash with abandon.

"Now, laddie," Jabez said, looking longingly at the demijohn, "mighty hard it be on ol' Jabez to see that best cane follow down the gullet, even o' the mate, what us foremast hands draw as sole ration."

"Why, Jabez," Geoffrey said innocently, "there is only one calabash, and presently it is in use."

"Waal, nip it to the mate slow 'n' every now 'n' again pause to let me refill the calabash," Jabez remonstrated. "Matter o' fact, best I take a taste o' that cane now. The great Jehovah forbid, but supposin' somebody been dilutin' the capt'n's private store o' likker? Be more than merry hell to pay, that be the case, so best I ship a bit now 'n' again to see how it stands."

Geoffrey reluctantly extended the calabash but did not relinquish his grip, and he drew back the calabash once Jabez had put away two great gulps. "Someone during the voyage out did slip into Captain Nichols' private demijohns and replace the vanished spirit with waters. Captain Nichols propounds that you were the culprit."

Geoffrey continued to trickle cane into the mate's mouth; at first the man would not swallow, but Geoffrey hit by chance upon stroking the mate's throat just beneath his heavy jowls. The mate swallowed reflexively as long as Geoffrey continued the stroking. "Jabez," Geoffrey said at length, "does it appear seemly to you to restrict Mate's breathing with a tight wrap? Should not the curative be the encouragement of breathing? I fear swaddling him in a band of rumbowline canvas would inhibit proper respiration. For surely if the lung was greatly injured it would saturate so completely with blood no breath could be drawn. Might not Mate be distressed only by great pain caused by abrasion of a broken rib against the lung, a pain refreshed with each respiration?"

Jabez picked reflectively at a tooth with a dirty, broken fingernail. "Waal, certain that is one way to account fer Mate's pains, but Mate does bellow overmuch from the pain, ye will grant, 'n' be that bellowin' that grates so fierce-like with Beelzebub." Jabez sucked at the tooth, one of the few still resident in his gums. "So, grantin' ye don't band Mate tightly, ye'll still have to keep him awash 'n' spirit to keep him from the cryin' 'n' bellowin' that torments our capt'n so."

Geoffrey glanced at the mate as a long tendril of cane-tempered drool lengthened, a brilliant ruby of blood glowing at the pendulous tip. The mate began to snore loudly. Geoffrey hammered home the cob stopper of the demijohn. "No, Jabez," he said firmly and somewhat accusingly. "No, Jabez, that doesn't answer. While the cane spirit can provide comfort in moderation, illiberal use can bring depression of breathing—as you well know," Geoffrey finished mildly.

Geoffrey, first taking the precaution of shifting the demijohn and the calabash out of temptation's reach behind a trove of hogsheads, burrowed about in the stores for the better part of ten minutes, then emerged with a double armful of rumbowline canvas. "Ha ha," he exclaimed, holding up the worn and grubby canvas triumphantly. "Wondrous soft these sheets be after thousands of miles attempting to contain the wind. But first, Jabez, kindly assist me in sliding Mate out of the hammock and propping him against yonder stack of pipes. We shall endeavour to fashion a hammock chair for Mate out of this rumbowline." The mate was a large and heavy man, but at last the two of them contrived to remove him from the hammock, and Geoffrey patiently removed the mate's tattered shirt so as not to provoke further injury as they carefully tugged and totted him so he would recline against the pipes containing trade spirits.

"Lo!" Geoffrey exclaimed, examining Crowninshield's exposed torso. "Mate be all ate up with fleas, or some other vermin. Jabez, think you the spirit may suffice to scour away these scabies?"

"Prodigious waste o' good cane," Jabez sniffed. "Once Mate breaks out in a proper sweat, them buggers will die joyous 'n' offend no man further."

"I think to apply cane as an anti-pestilence," Geoffrey announced, drawing out the demijohn again and half filling the calabash. He plunged the wad of tow into the calabash, squeezed out the excess, and began to sponge the mate's chest. "Jabez, be so kind as to assist in turning Mate so I may cleanse his back—what is this? A great lesion, no, great bruises . . ."

Geoffrey stared at the bruises, monstrous black scabrous things shot through with tentacles of noxious greens and poisonous yellows and reds, though the skin was apparently unbroken, for there were no scabs or open, running sores.

Jabez sighed and pointed to the largest, most colorful bruise. "That be most likely the place Beelzebub's staff broke a rib." Jabez twitched himself over to Geoffrey and turned his back. "Here, put yere ear 'gin my back, 'n' listen quiet. Taken yere time, then tell me what ye hear."

Geoffrey did as he was bade, pressing his left ear close against Jabez's back for a good minute. "I hear only what I take to be normal respiration," he said finally, "the subdued expiration and inhalation of breath."

"Now listen the same for Mate," Jabez grunted, looking longingly at the calabash.

Geoffrey applied his ear similarly. "There be confusion in Mate's breathing out and breathing in," he said after a moment.

"Plenty o' cane left 'n that tow to swab Mate," Jabez expostulated as Geoffrey thrust the wad of tow into the calabash. "Be we conserve the actual."

Geoffrey swabbed carefully around the great bruises. "Jabez, in nowise will this cane be returned to the jug, nor drunk, mind. Mate has missed a tide of baths, and the cane be fearsomely discolored—nay, sand comes off the skin. Here, please bear a hand to rig a hammock chair."

"There!" Geoffrey declared with satisfaction, sitting back on his haunches to survey his handiwork. "We shall rig it against the spar, to hold Mate upright." He leaned forward to place an ear against Mate's back, then shook his head doubtfully. "I detect no change in the respiration."

"Doubt it would come so soon, if indeed it comes a-tall," Jabez said soberly, even though he was fairly reeling from the quantity of cane he had consumed. "Done all we kin for Mate. Keep him from tossin' about, keep him quiet, keep him sittin' upwards, that be the cure ye ken. Though wus it left to me I would strap him good about the body 'n' keep him soused."

"I shall pray for him, Jabez," Geoffrey Frost vowed solemnly. "But first, let us assist Mate into the hammock chair so he can be sat upright and avoid lying in his own humours. Then you must attend Mate for a watch while I take the noon sight Captain Nichols wishes. At the end of the watch we shall exchange places. But mind, Jabez, I cannot recommend you administer the draught of cane to keep Mate's wits confused. For Jabez, while I love you dearly, your wits, was you in a condition to admit, be almost as addled as poor Mate's."

Marveling at how steady this small islet just south of the much larger Banana Island was, how unlike a vessel pitching and tossing in a seaway, Geoffrey achieved an excellent noon sight. Wick Nichols' clock was notoriously befuddled in the matter of accurate time-keeping, but Wick Nichols had at least taken advantage of the opportunity to compare his piece against the accurate repeater in Mister Aird's office when he counted out the guineas for the young slave's purchase. That was the only consolation Geoffrey could glean from that altogether barbarous and evil transaction. And the evening before Geoffrey had scored an accurate transect of the moon, as well as obtained a tolerably good azimuth of Venus. He retired to the shade of mainsail thrown over a cable taut between two palm trees that constituted Wick Nichols' commodious quarters, took up the somewhat tattered and frayed Scotsman Napier's tables of astronomical observations and reductions, and meticulously compared his results against the Frenchman Berthier's computations. Geoffrey sharpened his nub of chalk, rigorously cleaned his slate, and began the tedious tasks of ciphering the numerous measurements to something that would equate longitude and latitude.

Geoffrey transferred his initial computations in his finest cursive, using a herring gull's quill and best India ink, to a scrap of paper torn from a ledger, and cast his accounts with chalk and slate again. He made several minor adjustments, correcting for the earth's less than spherical diameter, but he was inordinately pleased that the averaged results varied less than half a degree.

Once again he copied the coordinates, assured of their accuracy, onto a strip of paper and went in search of Wick Nichols. Nichols was standing beneath the loom of the *Bride*'s hull and berating the carpenter.

"Mister Chips, a one-armed, one-eyed carpenter with a cast in his remainin' eye, usin' naught by a rusty drawknife 'n' a mallet, would have achieved a proper scarph joint on the stove plank within one hour o' the tender point bein' exposed!" Wick Nichols thundered, his swarthy face suffused with dark blood. The carpenter was a compact, red-complexioned man with gold earrings in both ears and a thick goiter surrounding his neck, from Dartmouth, Massachusetts. Willis Bruce was one of the few men shipped aboard the *Bride of Derry* whose occupation was absolutely vital to the husbandry of the ship. He was thus able to stand up to Wick Nichols, countering him on his own terms, and Bruce answered stoutly enough.

"You ain't shipped no one-armed, one-gimlet carpenter this cruize but a man possessed o' both, 'n' right good tools as well. 'N' I tell you, Captain Nichols, we be lucky to the extreme our barky swam this far after takin' such unkind treatment off the Bereira. The plank was started a good inch from its butt, with all the oakum gushed out. Only by the commodious assistance o' all the apostles 'n' boundless appeals to all the saints wus I able to come at the sprain in the hold 'n' give it a mighty seatin' thump with a mallet, followed by a jack-screw budgeted against the butt o' mainmast."

Wick Nichols turned. "What is it, youngster," he said irritably.

"Our position, sir, with all duty," Geoffrey said respectfully, holding out the scrap of paper.

Wick Nichols examined the figures for a long moment. "I make our present whereabouts thusly," he growled, scuffing clear a space in the sand with the side of his boot. He used the tip of his staff to trace in the moist sand. "There!" Wick Nichols shouted triumphantly, staring down at the figures he had scratched. "I fixed our position yesterday at nine degrees and forty-five minutes north of the Equator, 'n' touchin' thirteen degrees west o' the meridian passin' through Greenwich. What have you to say on that!"

"I shall cypher my numbers again, Captain," Geoffrey said miserably, "but I conceit us to be precise on the eighth degree of latitude north of the Equator, with a longitude, adjusted for refraction error, of twelve degrees and ten minutes west of the English meridian."

Nichols threw the scrap of paper at Geoffrey. "We are shoals apart in our cyphers, youngster! Assumin' we navigated with your calculations, we would be cast ashore on the Isle of Sherbro when we take our southin' followin' careen." Nichols freighted his voice with even more sarcasm. "That is, should our indefatigable Chips deign to put our *Bride of Derry* aright with a proper scarph joint, 'n' seal it with sufficient oakum driven in 'n' sealed proper with hot pitch." Wick Nichols glared at Carpenter Bruce. "We ain't got no year to spend lollygaggin' 'n' takin' our ease on this island 'til we get the strake set right, Mister Chips. We've got to ship cargo 'n' make our westerin' before the hurricane season. 'N' we need a tight ship to see us true across the middle passage."

"We ain't lollygaggin', Capt'n," Bruce said stiffly. "Our old *Bride* be on her tenth robin-round, 'n' she's been pushed hard-by-God-hard by the Jews of Newport. Ain't sayin' who's got the fault fer her groundin'. Fact be she grounded, 'n' was wounded sore. We've come at the tender spot, 'n' there be a passel o' scarphin' to win, praise be. But me 'n' my mate, workin' double tides, won't have our *Bride* ready to receive stores fer another six days. 'N' by the Four Gospels, what I would not give fer a baulk o' well-seasoned timber six inches in width, ten inches in height, 'n' twenty feet long. Present me that, Capt'n Nichols, 'n' I warrant our *Bride* will convey us 'n' all we can fit inside her safely to the Carolina colony. But even so, her lower futtocks be all punky. 'N' after this voyage she'll either go to the ship breakers or will have to be rebuilt complete. 'N' there you have the benefit of the full situation, sir."

"Better press on with it, then," Wick Nichols snarled, turning away. "When I ease myself 'n the thicket yonder I shall search earnestly for such princely a length of wood as you describe, Mister Chips, though I much doubt it possible to stumble across such a baulk of wood amidst these palms."

"⁂⁂⁂⁂⁂ *uby! I cannot for the briefest instant credit what you*
⁂ *J* ⁂ *are telling me! It is nonsensical and flies in the face of*
⁂ ⁂ *all reason! You have pinked this yarn from whole cloth!*
⁂⁂⁂⁂⁂ *You should apprentice to Samuel Stonecypher as a tailor*
—no! You should hie off to the weavers in Exeter and ply
there your shuttle to fabricate even more improbable cloth!"
Joseph Frost frantically paced in front of the makeshift tent he
shared with Juby and Samuel Stonecypher beneath the loom of
Fort Ticonderoga's battlements and two hundred yards from
the shore of Lake Champlain. His excited pacing was due as
much to the pronounced chill in the air as to the momentous
import of the words Juby had just uttered. He held in his hands
a packet of various white, blue and red bunting just given him
by Juby from some secret source, and Juby was placidly tending a boiling pot of coffee, the beans for which had come from
the same recent source.

"Banns of marriage a-tween Mister Lancelot Duford and
Mistress Hannah Devon was read out in Mister Parson Devon's church, with Missus Devon 'n' all Mistress Hannah's sisters, the Mistress Deborah 'n' the Mistress Mariah cryin' 'n'
takin' on somethin' fierce," Juby repeated patiently, even dole-
fully. "The banns was read out the first Sunday of July, 'n' at
the end of September Reverend 'n' Missus Devon pronounced
to all Portsmouth 'n' sundry that Missus Hannah Duford 'n'
her husband was travelin' to Mister Duford's relatives in Cambridge to await until her confinement be accomplished. Says so,

'n' more, right there in that paper torn from the *New Hampshire Gazette* came with the buntin.'"

"Juby, that is absolute gibberish," Joseph repeated petulantly, desperately, his mind reeling. Hannah . . . married to Lancelot Duford, the Harvard matriculate who assisted the Reverend Devon with his public services and was cited by all for his rectitude and saintly demeanour. "Your tale is as fanciful as anything spun by Scheherazade! I rue the months Maman spent teaching you and Cinnamon to read!" Joseph paused in his frenzied pacing. "Juby, please name me the day. I conceit the days we have laboured here beneath Fort Tyonderoga and on the far shore beneath Mount Independence are indistinguishable one from another."

Juby tapped his forehead thoughtfully with a forefinger for a moment, then replied: "Today be the first of October, a Tuesday, I collect."

Joseph's mental computations were painfully transparent. "I arrived at Crown Point seeking General Sullivan on the seventh of July, and that was a Sunday. So that means . . . the last Sunday in June was the thirtieth."

"Yes, Master Joseph, 'n' you left Portsmouth in an all-mighty hurry on Sunday, the thirtieth of June."

Joseph sat down abruptly on the frost-rimed grass and turned disbelieving, glassy eyes on Juby. "It cannot be . . ." he blushed fiercely. "Hannah's child by me could not be born until well after the turn of the year. February, I cypher."

"Oh, it be only the second chile's need nine months, Master Joseph," Juby said affably. "The first, now that chile's liable to come along any time." He poured a cup of coffee that sent tendrils of steam into the chill air and set the cup on a stone within Joseph's easy reach. All around them on the foreshore Continental Army and militia units were being drilled by their sergeants to a cacophony of ribald shouted orders, the shrill of the fife and a brisk tattoo of drums. The smell of dry, bruised grass hung in the air.

"The banns were published one week after I departed Portsmouth in such a swivet," Joseph said dully. "Hannah has removed to Cambridge to await the birth of a child, a blessed event, to be sure." Unexpectedly, he began to cry.

"Well, I don't know much about birthin' seein', as how such belike left to the women, but Cinnamon, now she's right pert in figurin' such things, 'cause she's helped out at a power of birthin's. Lot o' white folks in Portsmouth, Dover 'n' Durham send for Cinnamon rather than ol' Doctor Merrill when they feel a birthin' comin' on. Now, bless him, Doctor Merrill done seed a power of chiles into this world, but there be some who says he rightly deserves his name of Three Bottle Merrill and don't want no truck with his docterin'." Juby walked over to Joseph and from some secret place miraculously produced a well worn but clean kerchief. "Now, Master Joseph, you jest cry it out, cry it all out, 'n' you'll feel the better for it." He self-consciously pressed the clean kerchief into Joseph's hand. "Now, Cinnamon, and she had a good close look at Missus Hannah before I came lookin' for you, 'n' she cyphers Missus Hannah be brought to bed in November."

"So you knew all along, Juby!" A blubbering Joseph blew his nose noisily. "You knew since you came looking for me—you knew before you came looking for me. You knew Hannah's child could not be mine!"

"Well, reposin' the confidence I have in Cinnamon, who your father agreed should be my woman, 'n' for that I eternally thank Master Marlborough—she reckoned that you and Mister Knox was just about drayin' them cannons into Boston at the time Missus Hannah decided it was high time she wanted to get a chile." Juby knelt down and awkwardly patted Joseph on the shoulder.

"Juby," Joseph said, looking up at Juby through his tears, "why did you not tell me sooner? People in Portsmouth must think of me with the deepest loathing."

"Well, I don't rightly know what people in Portsmouth think of you, Master Joseph, the which in any event shouldn't give you no concern." Juby continued to pat Joseph's shoulder as one would comfort a child. "I's heard that some of the quality was scandalized you up and went off, leavin' your poor mother without a son to care for her. But others of quality said you was doin' what you felt was right to help your country win this war between cousins, like as when you took off with Colonel Knox to come up here to Tyonderoga to prospect for cannons."

"Juby, I've been a fool," Joseph said, blowing him nose mightily and pocketing the kerchief. He got to his feet and hugged Juby affectionately, smelling the woodsmoke that permeated the man's clothes, and realizing that the same pungent smell reeked from his own garments. "But what word have you of my mother?"

"Well, most peoples be fools various times in their lives, Master Joseph. Trick to it bein' knowin' when you be the fool, and thus leave off. As far as word of the Lady Thérèse," Juby shrugged, "she spins, she weaves as ever the same, though Cinnamon is always no further than one word away."

"I see," Joseph said, dejectedly, then added exuberantly: "I didn't have to leave Portsmouth! I was a fool to leave Portsmouth! I can return there now! To Father and Maman!" He looked Juby full in the face and saw there all the reasons he could not possibly return to Portsmouth at this time. "Yes, Juby," Joseph said hastily, "your deportment bears reproachful though silent witness to my foolishness, and my engagements. I have exchanged one burden for another, and I, in all honour, am precluded from setting aside the burden I have willing assumed."

"Master Joseph," Juby said urgently, "I just be a slave, property, I know, of your father—though I thinks I can go so far as to say I loves you as much as I would my own son. So hear me now. It not be fittin' for you to go searchin' for some glorious death. It has been most disagreeable for me to hear talk about your comin' to this here Lake in search of such. That be stuff 'n' nonsense, Master Joseph, 'n' you know it. Death for sure ain't no glorious thing, 'n' what your pore mother, the Lady Thérèse, goin' to do for a son if'en you throws yourself in front of some cannon? Peers to me you've been thinkin', no, you've been mopin', feelin' right sorry about yourself, 'n' not thinkin' of nobody *but* yourself."

Joseph clapped Juby on the shoulder happily. "Yes, Juby!

You are on the mark! I happily owe allegiance to Marlborough Frost and you as my dual patrimony. Though, you ken, I have learned far more under your tutelage than I ever learned in my father's counting house. You have in the last ten minutes given me much to meditate upon. And you revealed it at the proper time. I would not have conceited it had you divulged your intelligence sooner. I confess my wits are still much in a stir. But come, General Arnold shall address us in a few minutes, so we must make our way to the shore. And then, since we lack swan shot for the swivel guns, I am of a mind to chop some gunner's dice from those lumps of iron left as dregs by the smithy. But first, since by some mysterious agency vittles, like manna, fall into your lap from the heavens, I shall happily drink off this coffee and savor a second cup while I await with all serenity whatever marvelous breakfast you are able to concoct."

"I done singed the quills offen the porcupine, Master Joseph," Juby said, throwing something into a skillet, "'n' just think of these cut-up pieces of rattlesnake like so much sausage."

Samuel Stonecypher, his eyes puffed from sleep, but not the poison of mosquitoes now that the frosts of autumn had arrived, stumbled out of the communal tent, vainly attempting to stuff his ragged shirt into his equally ragged breeches. "Oh my soul, oh my soul! Is that indeed coffee that I smell? Oh, Juby, have you conjured yet another miracle?"

"Souse cheese 'n' trotters," Juby declared happily, "all the long way from Portsmouth, with bean of the coffee. Speakin' of which, if'en you can fetch me your cup I'll pour you a measure. 'N', if'en you'll look in that sack hangin' from the tent post, Mister Samuel, you'll like to find a loaf of bread from the commissary bakers, go mighty well for soppin' up the grease from the skillet. Gots to have a full belly in order to pay attention to Gener'l Arnold, just back from what he calls a re-cog-norter down the Lake."

"Gentlemen," Brigadier General Benedict Arnold intoned solemnly, "I'm just back from the base we established at Isle La

Motte. Our two small schooners are keeping up a constant blockade," he smiled wryly at the term, "that is, they are maintaining a vigilant watch for the British to sortie and serving as advisement that their passage will be contested strongly. I am returned here for such supplies as may have arrived, and to take all vessels such as are ready to sail northward to await the British sortie." He was interrupted by Juby, who approached with a cup of coffee that he gave to Arnold.

"Lots of sugar, Gener'l, 'n' coffee be hotter'n the hinges of the place where the bad peoples go when they depart this life."

"God's teeth!" Arnold exclaimed. "I haven't tasted coffee since the cup you last so kindly prepared for me." He smiled his thanks as he took the cup and drank down a huge swallow. "Elegant, simply elegant," Arnold said, then sipped the coffee slowly. "Gentlemen, if you please I shall read from my most recent supply requisition." He took a sheet of foolscap from his portable writing desk. "And ken, this be articles which have been repeatedly wrote for, and which we are in the extremist want of. Vizy: ten double-headed shot, ten grape shot and ten chain shot for each of the following poundages, from 18-pounders ranging down to 4-pounders, to the sum of one thousand seven hundred and forty individual balls of shot. Three hundred pounds musket balls. All the useless old iron that will do for langridge. Two hundred pounds buckshot. A sufficient quantity slow match for the fleet, being what is on hand is very little, and that exceedingly bad. Twelve horned tin lanthorns. Fifty swivels with monkey tails. Three anchors, one hundred and fifty pounds, two hundred pounds and two hundred and fifty pounds." Arnold looked up from his list sharply. "Gentlemen, there is not a spare anchor for any vessel of our fleet, and as you all know September was a stormy month on the Lake, and this October bids fair to offer even more."

Arnold shrugged and resumed reading. "Three cables for ditto. Rum, as much as you please. Clothing for at least half the men in the Fleet, who are naked. One hundred seamen (no land lubbers)."

Benedict Arnold glanced archly around the officers of his

various vessels, who were gathered in a tight knot around where he perched on a pile of lumber on the shore. His flagship, *Royal Savage,* rode at short anchor fifty yards away. "That's the short version. I asked for a lot more. All the old junk that can be spared, ratlines, casks of nails, barrels of pitch." Arnold's voice rose: "I asked, most politely asked, these items of warlike gear from our Congress!" His gaze darted from officer to officer. "Does a man of you ken what the Congress and the officers that body has appointed have to say regarding this very mild requisition of the barest materiél we must possess as we sortie against Carleton?" Arnold's neck swiveled angrily from face to face.

"We have sent you every article that you demanded, except what is not to be had here. Where it is not to be had, you and the Princes of the Earth must go unfurnished! Can you ken that? You and the Princes of the Earth must go unfurnished!" Arnold sought out Joseph. "Mister Frost, I am in particular need of a surgeon to accompany our fleet. I know that Doctor Ezrah Green, who accompanied you and your brother on the foray to Louisbourg, is come to Tyonderoga to serve in our Army. Think you it is possible to persuade the doctor to accompany our fleet?"

"Doctor Green would listen to the entreaty of an officer wearing a general's epaulet far more willingly than he would listen to a former shipmate," Joseph said, feeling his neck redden. He knew that Ezrah Green had arrived at Ticonderoga early in August but had been fully occupied all of the time since at Mount Independence, seeing to the health of the thousands of Continental soldiers and militia, an overwhelming and thankless task. Joseph, not knowing what Ezrah Green knew of his reason for departing Portsmouth so hurriedly, had not sought out the physician. On the two occasions when Ezrah Green had briefly stopped by the tent he shared with Juby and Samuel he fortunately had been away to Skenesboro.

"I see," Arnold said flatly, thrusting out his heavy lower lip. He was obviously disappointed that there was yet one more inquiry for him to make, in addition to the myriad inquiries into the lack of blocks for gun tackles, cordage, sail needles, canvas, and clothing for the nearly naked crews of his fleet. "I shall call upon the good doctor presently. I am down the Lake in *Royal Savage* tomorrow at first light, bearing in train all the vessels able to take the water. The rest shall follow as they are fitted out. I shall appoint our rendezvous presently." Arnold addressed John Thatcher of the row galley *Washington* and James Arnold of the row galley *Congress.* "When do you gentlemen reckon you will complete your crews?"

Captain Thatcher spoke first. "I reckon to have the thirty men I need to fill my complement within two days, General. I'll put aboard what stores can be found, and if Mister Frost will oblige I intend to run all my crew through the matross drill he has devised."

"Same with my *Congress,* General," young Captain Arnold, no relation to the general, said resolutely. "I've less men to entice aboard, but the two 18-pounders have yet to be mounted. And I cannot in good conscience ask men to follow me into a battle with well-drilled Royal Navy gun crews until my men know the difference between a sponge and a rammer, between solid shot and grape."

"General," Captain Seth Warner said in a barely audible voice, for he was suffering mightily from a tearing head cold, "I ain't got but the one 18-pounder 'n' a pair o' 9-pounders aboard the *Trumbull* galley as ordnance yet. I stand in mighty need o' oakum to complete her seams. In addition to needin' instruction in rammin' home cartridge 'n' ball, then applyin' fire to the touch-hole 'n' swabbin' out, my crew don't know the difference a-tween larboard 'n' starboard, bow 'n' stern, sheets from stays . . ." Warner's raspy voice was lost in the rustle and caw of a massive echelon of heavy birds almost the size of crows, pinkish and gray in color, that suddenly flowed steadily from the north. The first echelon was followed by another, and then another, and then another, layers and layers of birds, until the sun could scarcely penetrate through their massed flights extending to all horizons in a vast cacophony of wings relentlessly rustling, beating the air. Joseph's ears drummed and ached from the rush of sounds.

"Passenger pigeons!" several men shouted at the same time.

"Oh, my yes, passenger pigeons," Benedict Arnold shouted above the din. "When they start to settle down for the night we can send out scores of men to knock them off the branches where they alight. We can, at least, provide our crews a bait of meat this night." He addressed Seth Warner. "Save your voice, Captain Warner, I ken you well enough. Instruct your men in the differences between bow and stern, larboard and starboard. Sail to the rendezvous as quickly as you have pricked your seams with oakum. I am of a mind to make the *Liberty* schooner—she is of a fast turn of speed and a handy sailor—into a hospital ship and victualer. We can change her cannons into your *Trumbull* at the rendezvous."

Arnold turned to face Joseph, shouting to be heard above the heavy, roaring cataracts of wingbeats. "Mister Frost, while the crews of *Washington, Congress* and *Trumbull* are making up, will you continue the matross drill, and then will you journey down the Lake, exchanging among the various vessels to drill their crews as realistically as possible?"

Joseph was unable to speak for several moments while he struggled to pull the one thread from the skein of tangled emotions flushing through him that would sort out everything as logically as the neat lines cast in his father's account books. He was patently guilty of the unacceptable licentious behavior of fornication, and Joseph felt his neck flame with the consciousness of his carnality. He had not succumbed to *carpe diem,* he had enthusiastically sought out the transient, illicit pleasures and embraced them, to his everlasting shame and sorrow. But he had not brought true or permanent disgrace to his house or to his name, and Joseph realized with exhilaration that he now had every reason to live, that there was no reason—never had been—to seek death in some glorious *dénouement.*

What was more, he had volunteered his services to the Continental Army and Brigadier General Benedict Arnold. As a volunteer *he* formulated the terms and conditions of his voluntary association, and Joseph was free to abjure those terms and conditions whenever he pleased and as it suited him. What was more, he owed no explanation to anyone. Joseph looked directly at Benedict Arnold and smiled. "Willingly, General Arnold," he said loudly enough to be heard over the concussive thunder of hundreds of thousands, no, millions of wings drumming in the air, "and Samuel Stonecypher will have sewn up sufficient of the Grand Union banners to afford one to each of the vessels under your command."

"Well said! By God's eyebrows!" Benedict Arnold slapped his thigh in delight. "I must be off in pursuit of Doctor Green, and cordage and pitch and blocks and powder—mind! You're not to shoot away any powder in your drill, Mister Frost! The Dear knows what scarcity of that sovereign and specific antidote to tyranny we endure." Arnold jumped to his feet as if he had never in his life known fatigue, despair or defeat. "Captain Warner, if you'll be good enough to step aboard the *Royal Savage* you'll likely find a cask of pear cyder. I conceit a hearty draught will do your throat a power of good, and I encourage my other officers to quaff it as an anodyne to the croup and cough." Arnold bustled away, then arrested by thought, he turned and shouted above the tumult of passenger pigeon wings: "Gentlemen, your rendezvous with me is south of the Isle of Valcouer, which itself lies south of Cumberland Head." With a wave of his hat Benedict Arnold was gone.

◈ XIII ◈

G EOFFREY FROST DROVE HIMSELF RE-LENTLESSLY. HE HAD WORKED AND BEEN WORKED HARD, VERY HARD, THE THREE MONTHS HE HAD BEEN aboard the *Bride of Derry,* but now there was so much more to be done, so many more cares and responsibilities. He had to nurse First Mate Wolcott Crowninshield, for Jabez was less than an indifferent nurse when in the vicinity of an unbounded supply of liquor, so Geoffrey had tactfully returned Jabez to duty with the carpenter and kept vigil with Crowninshield by himself. But of course the luxury of devoting his time entirely to Crowninshield's welfare was denied him. Wick Nichols reluctantly begrudged Geoffrey one hour out of every watch during daylight to tend Crowninshield, see to his ease, bathe him with cool water, feed him, and keep him sufficiently inebriated that he could not stir overly much. But not so inebriated that breathing was at risk. Above all, he had to keep Crowninshield sitting upright, for Geoffrey greatly feared that lung fever would set in if the mate were to recline. Thankfully, Wick Nichols did not require Geoffrey to stand night duty but permitted him only the mid-watch to sleep.

Then there was the tedious paying of oakum into the seams above and below the newly scarphed pair of planks, balancing on the awkward rough staging and then carefully plying mallet and caulking iron. Not too lightly driven or the oakum would speedily work itself out of the seams, and not too heavily driven, either, else the oakum would force the planks too far apart, stressing the planks and the entire hull. At least Geoffrey did not have the onerous task of picking oakum. And he did not have to work inside the *Bride*'s hull; he did not like the air, the stench captive inside the hull everywhere pervasive, and he was very glad to be caulking oakum from the outside. Jabez's failing eyesight had caused him to smash one finger almost to jelly with a caulking mallet. So he had been relegated to the laborious task of picking apart the odds and ends of cables to separate the strands of hemp, then tediously spinning the strands into a continuous skein by rolling them between his arthritic palms.

"Same way that *cigarros* be made in the Habana," Jabez volunteered once as he stiffly but gamely made his way up the rickety ladder to replenish Geoffrey's store of oakum. "Savin' this oakum can't be smoked," he wheezed. "Sure wish Beelzebub would serve out some o' the baccy from stores."

"Arthur McCoy was apprehended by Captain Nichols trying to winkle a twist from a barrel of tobacco, and he shows the bruises for it," Geoffrey commented dryly. "Captain says all stores be preserved for trade."

"Ye pay a tolerable proud seam," Jabez said grudgingly, "'course, not so good as old Jabez in his prime wus able to do, when he didn't have to squint so to see." Jabez dropped the loose coil of unevenly spun oakum on the hull and peered anxiously at Geoffrey. "Ye don't think I'm overly much past my prime, do ye, laddie? I ain't touched forty years yet, but movin' 'bout with any handiness 'tall takes some doin', the old bones do cry so. 'N' after all these years at sea my eyes ain't what they once wus, 'n' I find myself fearsome mortal like, dwellin' overmuch on the horrors of old age."

Geoffrey carefully scanned around for sight of Wick Nichols, then gratefully laid down his caulking iron and massaged the small of his back. "Jabez," he said kindly, "age does bring many changes, it seems, though pardon my youth with its hopes to be spared. My father, though not yet your age, strains his eyes over accounts and ledgers, whereas you have strained your eyes in the glare of sun off the sea. My father reads perfectly well with the use of spectacles. He has two pair, one he leaves at the counting house, and the other, which folds into a small case, he carries with him in the pocket of a coat. Doubtless a visit to an oculist when we return to Newport will set all aright with your vision."

"All very well for the folks of quality," Jabez said gloomily, "but I ain't possessed o' no pound nor pence either to purchase such an implement."

"Then, Jabez," Geoffrey said lightly, "you must repair home to Portsmouth with me at voyage's end, and I shall have father pay for your visit to Mister Harland, the oculist who serves all Portsmouth, a capital fellow . . ."

"Youngster!" Wick Nichols roared, appearing unexpectedly like an apparition at the foot of the stage and slashing fiercely at the ladder with his staff. "You 'n' McCool have been lolly-gaggin' this hour past, to the detriment of the ship 'n' our trade. I've a mind to make you take a strip o' hide off McCool, then have him serve you in the same manner. Only, havin' recently had my dinner, I am so indulgent as to overlook your indolence—this once!"

Geoffrey hurriedly picked up his caulking iron while Jabez fed the oakum into the seam between planks. Geoffrey resumed the careful push with the caulking iron, then the carefully measured tap-tap-tap against the iron with the caulking mallet.

And then the caulking was done, and the seams sealed with tar heated to boiling and poured carefully from a can with a long spout. All the while the luxuriant marine growth on the hull had been scraped off and scrubbed with mats made from dried palm fonds, until the entire hull was sweet and dressed with tar. Then the anchors had to be moved on rollers from where they lay kedged ashore, back-breaking labor though it was, and wrestled into the boats. Cables were newly rove, and the anchors were taken out to the full scope of the cables, then carefully tripped overboard. As soon as his boat had pulled back to shore, Geoffrey, arms and legs utterly fatigued from the long, heavy pull on the oars, staggered to the rude tent as fast as ever he could to see how Mate fared.

The mate breathed comfortably, even snored. He no longer spat up blood. Geoffrey ran off to the cooking fire to help Holly prepare the evening meal. On most occasions this meal consisted of rice mixed with dried beans long soaked in brackish water and then boiled, and small fish netted in the lagoon and fried in a spider greased with slush directly over the coals. Geoffrey returned to the shelter with a heavy pewter plate of boiled rice and beans and a fried fish. He stripped the flesh off the bones with his fingers and mixed the fish with the rice, roused Mate Crowninshield long enough to feed him, and then led him, wheezing mightily, to the latrine pit Geoffrey had dug fifty feet away from the shelter to ease himself. Then they went back to the tent, where Geoffrey worked the mate's heavy bulk into the hammock chair and patiently held a calabash of well-watered cane until the mate had swigged it all. The mate fell asleep, and so did Geoffrey, curling up on the rectangle of rumbowline canvas spread on the warm sand only for a moment before plunging headlong into a deep well of darkness that tempered, but did nothing to relieve, his exhaustion.

Awake in the morning one hour before first light, Geoffrey trotted off to rekindle the fire for breakfast cooking, gently awoke Holly—unwrapped him, rather, perspiring heavily, from the cocoon of canvas in which the cook sheltered himself against the "mortal, pervasive vapors 'n' the skeetos"—and heaped on the firewood gathered by other watches, augmented with a few punky carlings and futtocks taken out of the *Bride*. Then his own ablutions: a quick rubdown with a small square of soft canvas splashed with lukewarm water from the kettle half-buried in old coals and ash that were nourished into new life with fresh billets of wood; a vigorous brushing of his teeth with soda; and a gargle of salt water. When the kettle threw out its whistle Geoffrey poured a mug in which to steep his tea leaves or tossed a handful of cracked coffee beans into the kettle and stirred the boiling water briskly.

Once roused from his cocoon and fully awake, Holly drew the pieces of salt-preserved pork, cut fine, out of the half-barrels where they had been soaking in what passed for fresh water on this islet and threw them onto large shallow spiders atop the coals Geoffrey had raked aside. The meat splattered and crackled while with a giant cleaver Holly split two coconuts and threw the milk onto the pork. Geoffrey hastily dug out the white coconut meat and threw pieces into the spiders. He saved the last piece for himself and found great contentment in the chewing of the crisp coconut meat.

In a large copper saucepan Holly stirred corn meal and fragments of ship's biscuit into a preparation of slush thickened with crude brown sugar to make a thick gruel. Periodically Holly threw a piece of fat onto another shallow spider, and when the fat was sizzling properly he ladled a spoonful of the gruel atop it, and once it solidified from the heat, he flipped the cake with an iron spatula. "Here be two slush cakes for Mate, Geefroy." Holly said happily. "Tell him cracklin's be insides." Holly dropped the slush cakes onto a palm fond to cool and flipped a third cake to Geoffrey, laughing aloud when he caught it. It was hot and Geoffrey immediately set it down on the palm fond and blew on his fingers. "Cake be for you, Geef-roy. Another be done by time you feed Mate his vittles."

"Oh my!" Geoffrey peered anxiously at the piece of coconut meat from which one of his deciduous teeth, an upper incisor, protruded, and said rather unnecessarily: "I have lost another tooth."

"Let me see in your mouth, Geef-roy." Holly lifted a brand from the fire and probed inside Geoffrey's mouth with a thick greasy forefinger. "Lordy, you've got another 'un all skewed. Wider now!" Holly's even thicker thumb closed on his forefinger and he moved the brand closer; Geoffrey instinctively drew back. Holly triumphantly held out a second primary tooth, which he dropped into Geoffrey's hand, then patted Geoffrey's cheek. "New teeth sproutin' out fine as could be asked, Geefroy. You've got the best teeths of anyone in the crew, exceptin' me!" Holly threw back his head, laughing, mouth opened wide to display his dentition. "I brush my teeths religious. You do the same 'n' you'll have good teeths."

An image of dear kind Jabez's face floated before Geoffrey; he certainly did not want his mouth to resemble Jabez's when he reached his growth. Geoffrey picked the tooth out of the coconut meat and put both abbreviated primary teeth into the only pocket of his breeches. His Maman had charged him strictly to bring back to her any deciduous teeth shed during this voyage, though he had not a clew why Thérèse Maria de Villette Frost had so charged him. His gums were tender, so Geoffrey contented himself with eating, gnawing really, the softest slush cake he could find on the palm fond where Holly had spooned them to cool. Then it was off to feed Mate, and then came the call from Wick Nichols to all the crew to gather at water's edge, for the ballast had to be got back in.

It was cruel work. All the slabs of stone that had been taken out, and the rounded river stones, like misshapen cannon balls, into the spaces between; then the multi-sized shingle placed atop to hub and keep the larger, heavier stones in place and prevent movement, all swept up into barrels, some twenty-five tons of stone, had to be put back. The stone and shingle was rowed out in the two ship's boats in thin showers of warm rain that turned violent and crushing in the early afternoon, to where the hull of the *Bride* lay anchored with a bare five feet of water beneath her keel at mean low tide, though this close to the equator the tidal change was negligible. The larger stones were handed through the ballast ports to men standing in the interior, who passed them hand-to-hand to others who paved the stone along the keel. When all the large slabs and rounded river stones were laid, the shingle, hoisted laboriously in barrels to the deck with a double whip, was spread on the slabs to hub them. The shingle was first meticulously sieved to separate out any sand, for sand could easily work through to the lowest bilge and stop the pumps.

But the cruel work of getting in the ballast was no more than fret work when it came to getting in the masts. There was not the luxury of actual sheer-legs, so the foremast and mizzenmast formed two legs of the sheers held together at their tops with a sheer-head lashing, with a double block luff-tackle suspended. One sheer-leg was positioned against the bulwark inside the larboard main chains, with the other sheer-leg positioned exactly opposite. A three-inch cable of the best hemp the *Bride* could muster ran through a heavy block attached to the sheer-head lashing, then through a jeer-block attached to a ring-bolt in the deck halfway to the capstern. The mainmast to be stepped was fastened to the luff-tackle hook just above mid-length with a selvagee stop. "Hoist away there!" shouted Wick Nichols to the capstern crew, which included Geoffrey Frost.

Slowly the capstern crew stamped around the drum, causing the sheer legs to rise slowly, cumbersomely lifting the mainmast, a heavy canvas pad seized around the butt to keep it from gouging the deck, while another crew tailed onto guy ropes running fore-and-aft and sideways to keep the derrick-rig steady and prevent movement except in the vertical plane. When the sheer-legs were raised to the absolute vertical by the cable running through the jeer-block, Nichols called them to belay. The capstern was securely pawled against rotation, and Geoffrey joined the crew hauling on the luff-tackle to raise the mainmast sufficiently high and vertical to permit the butt of the mast, its padding stripped away, to be guided into the round opening of the partner plate.

Nichols hovered about, anxiously scrutinizing every maneuver and cautioning "Easy, easy now." Everyone on deck was acutely aware of the gnarled staff in his hand, but Nichols wisely refrained from menacing anyone with it during this most delicate of maneuvers. Should the mast lip off the luff-tackle, should a weak strand of the three-inch cable, stretched taut as a fiddle string, betray itself, should one sheer-leg suddenly shift out of its pins, the heavy mast would fall straight down. Likely the blunt quarrel of the mast would not break the keelson but would pierce the hull, pinning the *Bride of Derry* to the sandy bottom of the small bay—a fish impaled on a trident. The wound would not be mortal, but all the crew's drudgery of emptying out the hull, warping the hull inshore, and careening her again to get at the splintered planking would have to be repeated. And the carpenter had earlier confessed the *Bride* as being perilously short of repair timber.

The mainmast butt was carefully guided over the mast hole, and slowly under the critical eye of Jabez McCool the luff-tackle was slacked off to permit the mast to be lowered inch by crucial inch through all the partners of the decks below until the butt was guided into its step on the keelson. Geoffrey Frost was keenly aware that by all rights he should find himself exceedingly fatigued—if he were to permit himself to dwell upon the matter. Which he did not, for already Wick Nichols was impatiently bawling out for the mainmast stuffing, stamping his staff against the deck for emphasis. Geoffrey was part of the crew that moved with all possible speed to let down the sheer-legs and undo the sheer-head lashing, for a third sheer-leg had to be rigged to make a true derrick. This third leg was the main topmast, and they pinned the derrick abaft the foremast hole. The lever arm of the derrick, raised and lowered by a double whip seized at the distaff end and working through another block secured to a ring-bolt on the deck, was the fore yard spar. The crew, Geoffrey and Jabez among them, went to work with a right good will fishing the raft of spars floating alongside up onto the deck.

The spars were brought aboard, and before the coming of night forestalled further work on the *Bride* the foremast and mizzenmast had joined the mainmast on their steps. Being dismissed by Wick Nichols, Geoffrey dived from the waist entry the eighteen feet down to the warm sea water, arcing down from the force of his plunge until his chest was just inches above the bottom of fine whitish sand turning golden as the sun fled, then bluish-green. Geoffrey propelled himself along the bottom with long, powerful kicks, the locomotion coming from his hips so his legs and feet synchronized together. His ears popped and his lungs were on fire, though not an unpleasant fire, actually a constriction of the chest that forced an amazing amount of blood into his brain, enough to sustain him for near on to one hundred yards. He surfaced seventy-five feet from shore in a depth that permitted him to splash the rest of the way, leaping high with boyish enthusiasm through the nonexistent surf, hair streaming copious amounts of water, heedless, grinning, his tongue tentatively exploring the gaps in his gums where his newly surrendered primary teeth had been. Then Geoffrey remembered the young woman and her child, and he sobered instantly. He rinsed his mouth with warm salt water, shot onto the sand, and made for Mate Crowninshield's awning with all possible speed to attend that worthy, though yet with a pause to breathe a prayer for the peaceful repose of their souls. For never in all under God's great heaven spread had there been such innocence or complete lack of guile.

Mate Crowninshield was healing nicely; his cough was gone, he no longer complained of pain in his ribs or chest, his appetite was back in full force, and the only difficulty lay in weaning him away from the copious amounts of watered cane to which he had become habituated. After he brought the mate his food from the galley overseen by Holly, and Crowninshield had consumed it with gusto, Geoffrey walked the mate on the foreshore, phosphorescent in the light of a quarter moon and a myriad of stars in air so clear the stars blazed steadily, unblinking, only a little less bright than Mars, just appearing in the eastern sky.

Mate Crowninshield devoted the better part of an hour to pointing out and commenting with surprising knowledge and appreciation upon the equatorial constellations, particularly Crux or the Southern Cross, which was visible in its entirety though very low to the southward. "Old Crux now, some would have it that Crux can be observed only when well south of the Line, though that ain't true, for Crux be visible from as northward as thirty degrees, if'en you know where to look 'n' don't expect much in the way of a cross-look." Then he abruptly changed the subject. "Beelzebub hates my tripes," Crowninshield confessed fearfully, as Geoffrey led him along the sand in a direction away from the main encampment. "He will dish me directly, I know it; he won't need no reason. Just bang me on the backside o' my skull with that great orb o' brass when I'm not looking, and then tip me overside to feed the sharks. It will be easily enough done."

"Hush, Mate," Geoffrey said placatingly, finding it extremely awkward that he was cast in the rôle of soothing a man almost four times his age. "Captain Nichols knows your true worth. He depends entirely upon you for navigation and the management of the men." Geoffrey hesitated to say more, but he had been somewhat exercised at Wick Nichols' treatment of his solution to their vessel's present position. He had given his quadrant, which was actually Crowninshield's, back into its owner's hands with the mild suggestion to engage his time and mind by cyphering to a nicety the latitude and longitude of the island in the Bananas Archipelago where the *Bride of Derry* was refitting. To Geoffrey's certain knowledge Mate had cogitated over the figures after making his observations painstakingly for a good five hours. Once Geoffrey was certain Mate had cast his final cyphers he showed the mate his own final calculations, and the position Wick Nichols had derived.

"Well, it's as plain as the nose on your face, laddie," Crowninshield said, a trifle unctuously: "Once you've done the cypherin' proper, we be square on eight north 'n' twelve west. Well, perhaps as much as another eight or nine minutes west. Ain't no two ways 'bout it. No way in this life we can be thirteen degrees west as Beelzebub says. Twelve and nine it be for my cyphers all square. Why, wus we to leave this anchorage 'n' take up that southin' as our line o' departure, runnin' through the night, full courses and no lookout, we would find ourselves sittin' right pretty on the shoals of Sherbro Island. Wait!" Mate Crowninshield smote his forehead with a great palm. "It be as plain now as Mars just a-peepin' over the horizon just shy o' where the Line would be: the captain did not account for the moon's parallax. That omission be good for a solid degree o' difference, 'n' sixty sea-mile east o' where your best twig pricked you on the chart," Crowninshield finished ominously. "Sixty mile encompass a terror o' shoals mayhap avoided with a staunch regard to the vicissitudes o' parallax o' the moon."

"See! You confirm that Captain Nichols requires your attention to navigation. I am certain he is truly appalled that he mistreated you so—sure it was but a fit of bad temper brought about by distress that our hull had touched a barrow of sand beneath the water. You could not have foreseen it, much less take the onus for it." Geoffrey spoke jocularly, but desperately. With a youth's keen insight he had come to a grudging acknowledgment of the intoxication wrought by the unrestrained exercise of power at sea. He kenned that the wielder of unchecked power, absent a moral sheet anchor to windward, would always be a petty tyrant joyous in the ability to consign normal life to the suburbs of hell.

"I should get myself down to the strand and help with the refittin' best as I can," Crowninshield said morosely. "Beelzebub will take it greatly amiss if I do not appear until the barky be ready to unmoor."

"Appear at your leisure," Geoffrey soothed, "though please to remember that as soon as you appear, you shall be set immediately to work. And we have three days yet until all the stores be got in, the rigging newly rove, the ballast adjusted to trim the *Bride* exactly so. Captain Nichols has set our departure Monday next, just as the tide makes, what little there may be. Another three days to contribute to your ribs' healing. My troth, you should just go aboard the *Bride* and take your cabin like it were the most natural occurrence in the world."

"I should go now," Crowninshield said hesitantly. "Do I not herald my presence on the strand, Beelzebub will maroon me here, sure."

"I am certain Captain Nichols has berated himself many times over your harsh treatment and would give mountains of gold to make amends. Though as you ken, command of any kind, particularly at sea, is a singular affair of great solitude, and Captain Nichols for one cannot make much of your appearance for fear of appearing diminished in the eyes of the crew." Geoffrey paused, his voice breaking, for he had become deeply attached to Mate Crowninshield, as much so as he had become attached to Jabez and Holly.

"I be a dead man, laddie," Crowninshield said with a sad

finality. "Beelzebub will dish me sure this voyage. He set about with a vengeance to punish me for hazardin' the *Bride,* which, Lord above knows, I did," Crowninshield admitted sheepishly, "for now he sets such great store by your navigation that he don't need mine, and once I'm overside my share o' the voyage becomes his'n."

"Mate, Mate! You do take on ever so wrought," Geoffrey admonished his elder. "Captain Nichols in no wise intends your maroon here, nor your death during our return voyage to the Rhode Island Plantations."

"All the same, laddie," Crowninshield said lugubriously, hopelessly, "these old eyes ain't to behold Point Judith again, nor the snug little cottage my wife keeps a mile behind, over-lookin' a bog o' the cranberry that I dote on. It was my thinkin' to retire from this venal trade after this voyage."

"So you shall! So you shall!" Geoffrey cried. "Two nights hence we shall strike this shelter and bring you aboard directly to your own cabin, all set up proper. And on the third morning you shall ascend to the quarterdeck to take your watch, with a look of gratitude from Captain Nichols to see you restored so."

"'N' where does Beelzebub shape a course from here?" Crowninshield inquired, having walked as far as a small half-sand, half-rock promontory to the westward where a great tangle of palm trunks had washed up during some terrible storm within the last year, which marked the limit of the ship's company's westward search.

"Captain Nichols," Geoffrey said precisely, always giving his captain his proper due, "speaks of the Grand Popo as being our destination."

"The Dan-Home, then," Crowninshield said with grudging approval: "We be chasin' the rains southeast along the coast. Doubtless Beelzebub intends the voyage as a test of the *Bride*'s repairs, for it will be a run through more than sixteen degrees of longitude and some thousand sea-miles. There are a dozen slave ports between these Banana Islands and Grand Popo. Cape Mount, Cape Mesurado, Grand Bassa, Cape Palmas,

Cape Three Points, Cape Coast, Accra. 'N' visitin' them as lies between would just keep us on the hind tit, behind the other slavers out o' Liverpool, France, the Dutchies, the Danes, 'n' our own fierce competition. Beelzebub intends to leap ahead o' all to reach a prime cruisin' ground. Yet, if mischance comes aboard through the hawseholes, we'll have the land directly under our lee where we can repair should need arise."

"Mate, surely you'll collect to address Captain Nichols by his proper and respectful title and not Beelzebub," Geoffrey said anxiously. "I ken Captain Nichols would remark your special name for him, which between us we acknowledge as a term of endearment only, with some hint of dudgeon. We both must court Captain Nichols' better muse with the greatest assiduousness."

"Said well, laddie," the huge mate Crowninshield exclaimed, reaching out to pat Geoffrey affectionately on the shoulder. "I be mortal a-feared o' the man, 'n' I've shipped with him these five voyages past, beginnin' as an able-body, then third mate, 'n' on to first mate the last voyage and now this 'un. No man knows him better. Doubtless he knows the private name I be given him, but as you assert, no good would come o' remindin' him public-like that not everyone under his dominion looks upon him as a god-like figger."

Two hard, hard days of work followed, begun before daybreak and extending long past the sun's vanishing behind the palm trees. Two hard days, but in the end all the masts were stepped and the yards were hanging from their slings and parrels. The riggings were all rove, and the sails newly bent, fresh ropes stretched taut, then stretched again, before being attached to the yoke of the rudder and led through blocks and wound around the helm's drum. The stores, barrels, bales and chests, rowed out from shore in the ship's boats, were lifted aboard via fish davits rigged larboard and starboard just aft of the main chains. And last, contained in frayed bags of canvas fit for no other purpose, came the chains and U-shaped shackles with their connecting pins of iron, all heavy with scales of rust. A bag burst just as the topping lift swung the starboard fish davit aboard. The chains and shackles gouged and scoured the newly flogged clean deck, and flakes of rust the size of Portuguese joes scattered about.

"Christ's Holy Mother and her spawn," Wick Nichols swore, seeing his deck defiled so, "strike down those irons into the forward hold for now, but no further. The rust must be hammered away and the iron coated with slush against the iron's comin' use. Useful employment for hands otherwise not engaged during the run down to the Grand Popo." Geoffrey Frost, who had been tailing onto the fall of the topping lift with a great deal of enthusiasm, for he was keen to get underweigh, saw those horrific tools of the slaver's trade for the first time, and his stomach churned in distress. Geoffrey intended that his hands would otherwise be employed during the ensuing days, at anything, even the most objectionable of tasks, gladly swabbing and flogging the heads, anything not to touch those devices designed to lock humans ankle to ankle.

First Mate Crowninshield deliberately chose this time to good advantage to appear on deck. "Wilkes, McCool, Teague," he ordered the men unloosing a barrel from the larboard fish tackle's cant-hooks, "below with this gear! Forward hold, as the captain says. Lively now!"

The hairs on the back of Geoffrey's neck prickled as he watched Wick Nichols saunter over to Wolcott Crowninshield. Holly, just clambering aboard and hauling up a great fish harpooned ten minutes earlier, exchanged wide-eyed glances with Geoffrey as they watched the two men circle each other like dogs sniffing for advantage.

"Lordy, Geef-roy," Holly breathed, "the capt'n gonna kill the mate, er the mate's gonna kill the capt'n. Which do you think it'll be?"

"Neither, Holly," Geoffrey said with far greater conviction than he felt. "Both are in need of the other. We are many thousands of sea-miles away from our harbour at Newport, and this barky's husbandry requires every hand."

Indeed, Wick Nichols had approached Mate Crowninshield menacingly until less than one foot of distance separated them. Nichols grounded his staff on the deck and stood, tossing it idly, oscillating, back and forth between his hands. "You've been absent the past two weeks," he said accusingly.

"Recoverin' my strength with a run ashore, duly seekin' yere pardon, sir," Crowninshield said diffidently. "'N' I be morbidly conscious o' the fact the groundin' o' our poor vessel resulted from my error."

"No pleurisy, no lung fever, then?" Nichols demanded.

"I had a tussle with the lung fever, Capt'n, but the tussle, bad though it was, be behind me, 'n' I be recovered to duty."

"You have avoided duty these two weeks past, Mister Mate," Wick Nichols said in a low, threatening voice as he advanced menacingly toward Crowninshield, "while your mates have worked double tides to compensate for your sloth." Then, incredibly, Wick Nichols smiled. "You have been shrived of your sins, of which you possessed an inordinate proud-necked amount, Mister Mate, as you cannot but agree. But havin' been shrived you are returned to life on our *Bride*. She has need o' you, for I am weary, truly." Nichols thrust his face almost against Crowninshield's: "I trust you have observed from the distance 'n' acknowledged our progress, and be ready now to bear a proper hand."

Crowninshield stiffened: "I have marked all goin' on aboard our barky since I awoke from the lung fever, thanks to our supernumerary, Master Frost. You may repair to your cabin 'n' rest comfortable knowin' I can see over the bringin' aboard the remainin' stores, and bendin' on the proper sails to have all in readiness for a departure on the morrow's first light."

XIV

J oseph Frost, his way blocked at every turn by shouting, sweating Continental Army and militia troops drilling on the foreshore beneath Fort Ticonderoga in the dank air of morning, managed to carry his worldly possessions down to the shore, where the row galley *Washington,* bow-on to the shore, lateen sails gathered in their bunts, and sweeps run out, awaited him. His personal belongings were scanty enough to fit comfortably into the pockets of the worn greatcoat he wore against the chill and flurry of snow. Toothbrush, with a paper spill containing a dentifrice of salt and soda, a razor to which he resorted every third day, though as yet without actual need, one extra pair of stockings, and two kerchiefs. Whatever else remained of his worldly estate he had gladly disposed to Samuel Stonecypher, who remained behind to sew sails, even his horse, with the proviso that General Arnold could have the use of the animal whenever needed. In his arms Joseph carried the massive bundle of bunting, neatly rolled and tied, that Samuel had so proudly sewed into Grand Union flags, sixteen of them.

Joseph stepped aboard the *Washington* in time to see Juby tying the painter of a small birchbark canoe to the railing on the larboard side of the row galley, just forward of the tiller. "Juby!" Joseph said in disbelief. "You have no business here. It is time for you to begin your return to Portsmouth and the comforts of Cinnamon that you have so long denied yourself." Joseph put down his bundle of bunting and seized Juby by the arm.

"You must go ashore this instant. Captain Thatcher is preparing to give the order to sweep off."

With great dignity Juby removed Joseph's hand from his arm and nodded to Broadhead, who had just joined them on the crowded, raw quarterdeck: "A power o' a good morning to you, Mister Broadhead. Looks to be a fine day, it sure does."

Broadhead peered curiously overside at the birchbark canoe as he stirred his brush in the silver snuffbox. "So that is a canoe," Broadhead said with some wonderment, transferring the dip to his gums. "I have never been in one, and it looks so very awkward. Would you consider taking me into your canoe, Mister Juby, for a few minutes only, so that I may acquaint myself with this most unique form of waterborne transportation?"

"It will be my pleasure, Mister Broadhead. Nothin' to the use o' the canoe, goes by itself it does, and its peculiarities of balance be quickly learned." Juby glanced slyly at Joseph. "The canoe o' birchbark be a favorite conveyance of Master Joseph."

Just then Captain Thatcher shouted: "Sweeps out! Ready a-stern all! Smartly now! The stroke on both sides even!" Men who had quietly gathered at their places on the sweeps dipped their long oars into the shallow water.

"Juby! Get yourself ashore this instant!" Joseph demanded. "Where this row gallie be bound there's surely going to be a lot of fighting, and you've got no business in such a strait."

"'N' just why don't I have no business in such a strait, Master Joseph?" Juby asked with infinite sorrow, gazing directly at Joseph with his deep, chocolate-colored eyes showing profound hurt.

"Because . . . because this is a business of winning freedom for Americans from the British overlord that seeks to bend us to his will in all matters," Joseph said, knowing his response was exceedingly lame.

"'N' I ain't no American 'cause I be a slave, 'n' slaves don't go knowin' nothin' about freedoms 'n' such," Juby returned the salute of a smiling Samuel Stonecypher, his face pinched blue with cold, who had made his way to the lake shore to see them off. "Thereof, I ain't got no dog in this fight."

"Damn it, Juby, you're taking everything I say and twisting it against me," Joseph said desperately. "I'm just saying that there's likely going to be a lot of fighting and hard knocks, and some people inevitably are going to be killed. I'd rather you be spared such horrors."

"You mean you don't want your father's property bein' put in the way o' harm, 'n' 'cause it ain't fittin' that a slave who's got no rights to hisself ner anythin' else help out in the cause o' winnin' liberty." Juby smiled and stepped closer to Joseph as they huddled on the confined quarterdeck of *Washington*. "Master Joseph, I's done got my freedom. Master Marlborough, he didn't tell me to come after you, 'n' I didn't run, either. I told Master Marlborough that I wus comin' after you, 'n' whenever I sent back to Portsmouth fer somethin' he always found a way o' sendin' it.

"Master Joseph," Juby continued urgently, but in a low voice that only Joseph could hear. "I's done as much work gettin' Gener'l Arnold and his fleet put together as any man here. When I wusn't cookin' fer you 'n' Samuel, I wus drayin' planks 'n' boards, seamin' oakum, loadin' stores. I's as good as any mans who laboured a-buildin' Gener'l Arnold's fleet. 'N' that means if'en these other mans be free, then I be free same as them."

Joseph moved out of the way as an obviously fatigued Captain John Thatcher came aft to take the tiller. Thatcher smiled at Joseph through his fatigue. "Wind can't make up her mind which way she'll blow. She's directly out of the north now, but she's likely to veer one side or the other, and when she veers we'll see how she does with these lateen sails. Until then, we'll sweep." Thatcher put his weight on the tiller to nudge the bows of *Washington* more toward the western shore of Lake Champlain as the men at the sweeps changed from rowing a-stern all to propelling the vessel forward. "Reckon this gallie will handle like one of your Piscataqua gundalos, Mister Frost?"

"Alas, Captain Thatcher, while I have frequently observed the gundalos in commerce on the Piscataqua and her tributaries, I have never been aboard one under sail." Joseph was struck with the sudden realization that while Thatcher, like all the other captains of this cobbled-together, tatterdemalion fleet, had been Arnold's choice for command, only Arnold, David Hawley, who was commanding the largest American vessel, *Royal Savage,* and Seth Warner had any sea-going experience. For John Thatcher and the entire eighty men of *Washington*'s crew, sailing and fighting their unwieldy row galley was an alien experience. He knew why Arnold had put the Pequot Indian bosun aboard *Washington.* "I reckon I can assist your men in pointing cannons, but Mister Broadhead is the person to whom application in the handling of sails must be made." Joseph had absorbed enough of the etiquette of shipboard life during his cruise to Louisbourg with Geoffrey to defer to the captain. "With your permission, Captain Thatcher, I'll see to the cannons' tackles and accoutrements. I warrant I'll in no way interfere with the men at the sweeps."

Taking Thatcher's weak grin as granting permission, Joseph grasped Juby's arm and tugged him down the short ladder to the main deck. A glance southward showed the *Congress* row galley, her red-painted sides as gaudy as the autumnal colors of red, orange, tawny-gold, and burnt-brown blazing brilliantly from the forests on either side of Lake Champlain, just getting underweigh under sweeps.

"Juby, you are entirely in the right," Joseph whispered earnestly as the youth and the man made their way down the length of the gun deck, cluttered and piled with equipments not properly stowed, avoiding as best they could the men, most now stripped to the waist despite the chill wind, who toiled at the sweeps run out through their ports between the bowsed cannons. "I know so little and have so much to learn about this world into which white and black and red and brown people are born in varying degrees of equality. I know how violently opposed to the ownership of one human by another my brother is, and how slavery is everywhere accepted without question by upright and God-fearing men such as my father and John Langdon. It is true I have much to sort out, but you are right entirely that you are a free man."

Joseph stopped halfway between main and fore masts. "This I ken, Juby—you are a free man not because you have toiled equally with any other man in building this fleet with which General Arnold intends to engage the British, but because like any human being freedom is your natural birthright." Joseph Frost saw clearly that Juby was exuberantly more free than he was, and he also realized that Juby was a saintly man, far, far more attuned to whatever God there was and vastly more meritorious in God's sight than the avariciously pious Reverend Devon. Joseph impulsively threw his arms around the shorter, much stouter black man and hugged him as he would have hugged his own father, Marlborough Frost. "Juby," he said, "you have always referred to my brother as Tai-Pan, a person engaged in the China trade, and he has always called you *Baba,* though neither you nor Geoffrey have ever divulged the meaning of that term."

"Master Joseph, you ain't never asked!" Juby said, his face crinkling into laugh-lines that hid his eyes in folds of flesh. "Baba, now it have several meanin's, but the way it be used a-tween Tai-Pan 'n' me is *little father,* or *elder brother,* or even *uncle.* Tai-Pan, he done be callin' me Baba since the day Master Marlborough bought me at the slave market in Portsmouth. Tai-Pan, when he calls me Baba he means that I be a respected elder."

"A sage! A wise man!" Joseph exclaimed. "Of course! Geoffrey will always pierce straight to the kernel." He sighed. "I believe Father would attach greater worth to me were I more like Geoffrey." They had paced to the bows of the *Washington* row galley, and they both sat down on a haphazard snarl of cordage in order to be out of the way of the men lugubriously tugging at the sweeps.

"Don't go thinkin' your father prefers one o' his sons over the other; he loves you both atter his own way. You 'n' Tai-Pan, you be vastly different, Master Joseph, 'n' your father sorta held onto you closer 'cause o' what the loss of Master Jonathan meant to the Lady Thérèse, 'n' you bein' the youngest 'n' all." Juby shivered violently and hitched up the collar of his frayed greatcoat. "Somebody just walked across my grave, Master Joseph," Juby said quietly.

"Superstitious nonsense, Juby!" Joseph declared. "It's the chill air, is all. There's snow newly fallen on the mountains of the Adirondacks. Snow this early in the season portends a wretched winter. I'll be glad when the two of us be returned to Portsmouth after throwing British arms into consternation, turmoil and defeat!" Joseph beat his arms about his torso to flay some warmth into his body. He marveled at how swiftly the row galley pushed through the water. They had entered a broader expanse of the Lake now, and the water was confused and choppy. The wind continued from dead ahead, and though the lateen rig of the row galley would permit sailing much closer into the wind than a square-rigged vessel, still, no sail plan ever devised could sail directly into the wind.

"Juby, what will you do once we are returned to Portsmouth, after having savored such liberty as we have known on this Lake?"

"Well, Master Joseph, betimes I'm goin' to throw a bait overside 'n' hook us a bait o' trout sufficient I hopes to feed this whole crew, seein' they ain't got no cook. 'N' as to what I'll do once we gets back to Portsmouth 'n' thaws out our bones, why, I'll do what I be doin' these past twenty year, lookin' atter your father 'n' your mother. 'Cept this time I'll ask for, 'n' I'll get, some wages to go along with the boardin' 'n' the food." A brisk wind whisked away most of the clouds from which small, hard pellets of snow had been falling and revealed the ghostly image of a wolf moon low on the horizon. Juby threw back his head and laughed, again and again, and a delighted, relieved Joseph Frost laughed with him.

❦ X V ❧

❀❀❀❀❀ S GEOFFREY FROST STOOD TWENTY-
❀ A ❀ FIVE FEET ABOVE THE DECK IN THE
❀ ❀ LARBOARD RATLINES OF THE FORE-
❀❀❀❀❀ MAST WHILE JABEZ MCCOOL STOOD AT
the same height in the starboard ratlines, both of them peering anxiously down and ahead into the waters through which
the *Bride of Derry* was slowly moving under single-reefed topsail and partially furled fore staysail, Geoffrey reflected on Mate
Crowninshield's earlier observations during their careen about
leadership and loyalty.

"There be some captains ye follow because of loyalty," Mate
Crowninshield had confided as he quaffed cane that Geoffrey
had ensured was cut extremely with water. "That is, there be
loyalty up 'n' there be loyalty down. Follow ye?"

"I ken your logic be that the subordinates freely owe their
loyalties to their captain because they know their captain reciprocates the loyalties of his men in full measure, and shall do
all to merit that loyalty," Geoffrey had said. He moved about
a standing Mate Crowninshield, who was hooked onto the
spar supporting their pavilion with a stout grip while Geoffrey
sponged his sweating body from a calabash of sweet water.

"I admits to some confusion as to the meanin' o' *reciprocates*,
but ye have the nub o' it right enough," Crowninshield said
gruffly. "A loyal captain knows his commands be given flesh
'n' obeyed on the instant because his men trust him. Ye will
always obey a captain who abuses ye, who drives ye with fear.

But ye do so grudgingly, with one eye to leeward, 'n' the first chance ye get ye skip."

"Come, Mate, I must wash your hair in this sweet water, and plait your hair anew." Geoffrey had dashed out the bath water in the calabash and dipped fresh water, though more than a trifle brackish, from a tub formed from the carapace of a giant sea turtle that had long since made a meal for the entire crew of the *Bride*.

Mate Crowninshield, whose torso was still over-much tender from the broken rib that could have abraded his life into one long, dolorous cough, sank down onto the fine white sand that was the pavilion's floor and unbound his long queue. "Aye, laddie, sweet water my hair fairly demands after all these months denied an allowance of sweet water at sea for washin'. I had caught sweet water in a canvas rig durin' one o' the tempests we passed through off the Green Isles, but Beelzebub copped it for hisself."

Geoffrey drew the mate near the turtle's carapace, dipped water over Crowninshield's hair, fished a bar of lye soap made by Holly from slush and wood ash from beneath the carapace, and began to shampoo Crowninshield's hair. "Aaah, laddie, that treats, that treats it rightly does," Mate moaned in satisfaction, as Geoffrey worked the soap into lather in double-handfuls of Mate's thick hair as his head bowed over the carapace. "Now, there be wretched captains, but captains nevertheless because God er some owner never been to sea give 'em a ship, 'n' made 'em so. 'N' men follow because those captains be so arch 'n' askew that men follow just to see what devilment will fall out. Then when their sides be tender-sore from laughin' at the devilment, they steal away to find a better captain, 'cause they know what they need avoid."

"So you tell me that as much can be learned from a bad captain as a good captain," Geoffrey said, somewhat doubtfully. Mindful of Holly's charge about the use of the caustic lye soap, "one rub, no dirts, two rubs, no skin," he reached quickly for the calabash to rinse Mate's hair.

"Well, belike most hands find there be more advantage

to shippin' with a captain knows his onions afore the barky unmoors 'n' the hands find the land sunk a-hind them. But I tell ye true, laddie, be far more captains afloat in this trade who'd nae hesitate one dram to swat the hide from abaft yere ribs for crossin' his hawse, than those captains see to the comfort o' their men afore their own." Crowninshield seized his massive length of hair and began to wring the water from its coils.

"But there be commerce as well, other than in this selfish trade in lives," Geoffrey said stoutly. "Commerce for spices, foodstuffs, cloths, finished goods such as furniture, bulk goods such as clapboards and tall trees cut for masts. Just up from the Pool in Portsmouth where the ships from the West Indies and England lie is the pond where the great pine trees marked with the King's broad arrow are brought by oxen during the winter snows to await the arrival of the mast ships. My parents' house overlooks the Pool," Geoffrey finished proudly, then shook his head doggedly, thinking of the young woman who had willingly drowned herself and her babe. "Surely this blighted trade for people exceedingly reluctant to be parted from their native lands is a minute portion of the trade of civilized nations and shall soon cease."

"Fetch me the rumbowline, laddie," Crowninshield said, not unkindly, splashing water in his face but careful to keep his eyes closed against the lye soap's bite, blowing like a breaching whale, with tepid, soapy water thrown up from the turtle's carapace. "'N' no, this trade's not likely to go by the scuppers any time soon. Demand for sugar from the islands be so great, 'n' there be the cotton 'n' tobacca grown in Mister Lauren's country. Hands for the hard work in the fields ensure the women in their kitchens back in England get their flavourin', the men at the coffee houses in London 'n' Liverpool 'n' Bath get their tobacca, 'n' the cotton be delivered to the mills in the Midlands for weavin' into small clothes. Also got the corn 'n' rice to get in." Crowninshield shook his head knowingly as he toweled his hair: "Nothin' gonna change on this coast for a thousand year."

. . .

A light rain was pitting the surface of the sea, making it difficult to peer down into the waters to spy out the colors that marked changes in the depths into which the *Bride* was slowly advancing. Below them in the foremast chains leadsmen were heaving their sounding lines on both sides. Geoffrey kept one knee hooked securely through a ratline and maintained a tight grip on the shroud, for he was curiously light-headed, and a fire had been kindled behind his eyes. He was quite giddy and his teeth, such as he still retained, chattered uncontrollably. Geoffrey concentrated on studying the waters ahead and glanced only occasionally at the low sandy dunes spread haphazardly on either side of the channel into the lagoon toward which the *Bride* was making her way, though ever so slowly.

"By the mark ten with this larboard line," chanted the leadsman, Black Amos, in the chains beneath Geoffrey.

"By the mark ten with this starboard line," trilled the leadsman, Wallace Harper, beneath Jabez.

A few rays of sunlight momentarily shot down from a rent in the gray overcast, being absorbed into the water directly in front of the *Bride* but reflected dully off a ridge of whitish-brown sand underwater at no great distance to the west. "Water shoaling two points off the larboard bow!" Geoffrey shouted.

"Water shoalin' two points off the larboard bow!" Mate Crowninshield bawled, standing ten feet in front of the mainmast, turning his head so that Captain Wick Nichols and the helmsmen on the quarterdeck could definitely hear the repeated cry. After having injudiciously run the *Bride* too close inshore at Rio Bereira and brought her keel over a hidden bar of sand, with the resultant loss of two weeks' trading time while the *Bride* was careened to repair the ruptured planks, Wolcott Crowninshield was mortal skittish to have the *Bride's* keel within half a league of shoal water.

Wick Nichols ordered the helmsmen to alter course one point to starboard, and the *Bride* continued her cautious entry into the circuitous channel. So hot was the fire behind his eyes that Geoffrey had difficulty focusing. Even though the *Bride* was entering on the highest of the negligible tides at this latitude he personally thought it would have been more prudent to lay off beyond the bar and send in a ship's boat to sound and buoy the channel. Nichols earlier had iterated that he had negotiated this channel into the lagoons fed by the Glewe River two years before. And Nichols had found his way safely into the port of Quidah some five leagues to the east the year before that.

But the channel unobstructed two years ago could easily have silted, and if, heaven fore-fend, the *Bride* were to perch ignominiously on an unexpected patch of sand, she would do so on a falling tide with night approaching on a strange coast. At least Nichols had ordered the larboard bower anchor got over the side, suspended directly beneath the cat-head, and the cable stoppered immediately before the bitts with its bight put over the bitt-head and ready to be let go. Geoffrey Frost was learning a lot about what he would do in the unlikely event that he would ever have command of his own vessel by weighing what Wick Nichols was doing.

Now Geoffrey was battling fevers and chills that rattled his teeth and squeezed eyesight with a tourniquet of pain tightening just behind his eye sockets. But he gripped the shroud-line more closely and forced his eyes to remain open as he helped con the *Bride of Derry* through the narrow cut between the low, seemingly endless dunes of sand stretching away monotonously to the west and east as far as eyes could see. Nichols called for the sail trimmers to brace the main topsail yard half a point to windward because the sea breeze was beginning its late afternoon increase.

"Water's shoalin' one point off the starboard bow!" Jabez cried, his call being taken up and repeated by Crowninshield.

"By the mark seven with this line," Wallace Harper called out.

The *Bride* pivoted slightly around her rudder, and her bowsprit slowly moved a point to larboard.

"Water's shoaling one point off the larboard bow!" Geoffrey shouted.

"By the mark six with this line," Black Amos chanted.

Geoffrey could see the course of the cut trending to starboard, and narrowing. He reported his observations.

"By the mark five with this line," said Black Amos, his voice unchanging and calm, though sufficiently loud to carry to the quarterdeck without need of Mate Crowninshield's amplification.

"Starboard your helm one point," Wick Nichols commanded.

Both Geoffrey and Jabez watched the ominous change of color in the water to starboard, from a dirty green to a pale yellowish-green. "We be about as much tonnage as kin win this passage," Jabez said just loudly enough for Geoffrey to hear. "Bigger vessels, general-speakin', tend eastward three leagues 'n' anchor off the bar at Quidah Road. There be a triple surf there, but mayhap better'n gettin' caught in this devil's gullet."

Geoffrey was too ill to speak unless it would be to warn of shoal water. The *Bride* was at the narrowest constriction of the channel now, and the distance between the low hillocks of sand on either side was less than the length of the *Bride*. It was an eternity aboard the *Bride* before the bows nudged into more open water.

"By the mark seven with this line," Black Amos chanted.

"By the mark eight with this line," Wallace Harper replied.

Geoffrey said nothing, willing his eyes to focus, willing himself not to vomit. He could see a promontory of sand in the distance, slightly higher than the bar stretching away on either side. The promontory appeared to be little more than a sea-mile away, and there were some scraggly trees—he could not tell if the trees were palms, and there was a glimmer of broader water. The *Bride* slowly emerged from the cut into a long, narrow lagoon, a few small, low islets of sand far to larboard. The low shore of the mainland was a continuous fringe of marsh. The rain came on heavily now, and Geoffrey opened his mouth gratefully. He felt his grip on the shroud slipping as blood pounded in his ears.

"Amos," he cried weakly, "I must come down to the deck. Will you help me down?"

Amos, still sounding from the larboard fore-chains, had just heaved in his lead-line. He looked up, eyes blinking against the sting of rain, then threw his line inboard and jumped into the ratlines, running upward as agilely as a cat. "Hold on, Geoffrey, don't let go, boy! Hold on, boy! Jabez! Wallace! Bestir yere fat asses!" Black Amos reached Geoffrey's side just as Geoffrey's hand opened against his will and he lost consciousness, though his arms were tightly hooked and wove in the ratlines and prevented his fall.

Black Amos plucked Geoffrey out of the rigging as a gigantic spider would pluck a fly caught in its web. He touched a tentative palm to Geoffrey's brow. "Come by here, Jesus, the boy's burnin' with fever! He's got the yellow jack, most like!" Black Amos threw Geoffrey over his shoulder as casually as a farmer would throw a sack of oats, though Geoffrey weighed far less than a hundredweight. Black Amos and his sad burden were on the fore deck of the *Bride of Derry* in less than ten seconds as the rain started down in blinding sheets.

Jabez McCool possessively seized Geoffrey's slight form from Black Amos but then stared around in bewilderment. "Git him below, Jabez!" Black Amos shouted. "We've got to git those wet rags off'n him, then git him sponged dry 'n' into his hammock, no sleepin' on the floor outside Beelzebub's cabin. 'N' whatever we do we kin't let Damon touch him."

Two other hands were stricken that day, though Geoffrey Frost did not know it. He was far from knowing anything for the following three days, so far had malaria gripped him in the disease's deadly vise. At odd times he heard voices, though he could hear them only indistinctly. "But I've got to cup him," Damon Nichols cried in shrill desperation. "I've cupped the other two, relieved them o' cups 'n' cups o' unwholesome blood, same as Charles says to treat the jack, 'n' they be the better for it. God strike me down if'en they not be the better, 'n' I've got to do the same by the boy!"

"God strike ye down, is it?" some nearby voice replied. "Well, Damon, bugger off to the main deck, 'n' practice fallin' down 'n' gettin' up, 'n' presently we'll all have a turn at dischargin' God's work on you. Bugger off with that bowl 'n' lancet, 'n' don't come back unless yere able to locate some o' that Peruvian bark amongst yere stores."

But there was no Peruvian bark in the medical chest that John Brown of Rhode Island and Providence Plantations had grudgingly allowed to be shipped aboard the *Bride of Derry.* Everyone knew that the blacks of Africa's West Coast were proof against the yellow jack, the yellow fever, the black water fever, the malaria; they never came down with those maladies. The medical supplies were better reserved to physic against a host of other ailments the slaves might bring aboard. And as for ailments that might befall the crew of the *Bride,* they were all right men breached in the northern colonies, the majority of them anyway, and sturdy of disposition. A broken bone or two, if they were particularly unhandy aboard ship, well, they would have only themselves to blame, of course. But the own-ers would not want themselves inconvenienced or their hands laid up overly long for all that, so the medical supplies were long on physic and bandages but woefully short on curatives for the maladies of the Slave Coast.

And Geoffrey Frost came very, very close to dying of malaria. He did not really mind dying, for at various times during his deliriums he saw—though from a great distance—a beautiful woman beckoning to him. The woman was standing on a gen-tle promontory amidst vivid emerald green grass, all warmly illuminated by a sun sending its streams of multi-hued radiance through a bank of low clouds, puffy white, on the other side of a large brook. The brook was still, unruffled by wind, and show-ing no stones, quite unlike the swift brooks Geoffrey remem-bered from his forays along the shores of the Great and Little Bays and the Piscataqua under the studious tutelage of Juby.

The woman's hair, waist-length and luxuriously golden with highlights of red, floated in gossamer strands about her face, and she brushed it back from her radiant face with a languid hand. To a degree the woman resembled Thérèse Frost, though Geoffrey knew the woman could not possibly be his mother. The woman was looking at him with yearning, one hand resting placidly on her bosom, her dress of simple design, gathered and caught by a doubled golden sash just beneath her bodice and woven of some marvelous cloth that shimmered and caught and reflected the warm, enchanted light.

The woman stretched out her right hand, her fingers, long and shapely, summoning him in a most beguiling manner. Geoffrey had no feeling in his legs or feet—or anywhere in his body—but that did not matter. He knew that even in his drowsy state he could walk the few short steps to the edge of the brook. And he knew there were stones just beneath the surface of the smooth water, stones that would raise themselves even with the surface exactly where he would expect to find them, so that he could step across the brook without getting his feet wet. Maman was always cautioning him about walking in wet shoes. The woman smiled, a smile that was at once sad and beatific, and at her side appeared the young black girl he had seen in Mister Aird's office in the London Scottish Syndicate's factory at Bence Island. She was clad in the single wide strip of multi-hued cotton and bore her child in a sling crossing her breasts so that only the child's reddish-blonde kinked hair was visible.

Geoffrey Frost stumbled down the short slope of greensward that separated him from the brook's margin.

"Reckon we should hae ground the bark a mite finer?" a voice nearby queried. A gentle voice brought Geoffrey up short.

"Holly shredded it sommers good 'n the pepper mill."

"But what be th' right douse?" Another voice. "Tea or a pill made up from th' powder? Them niggers at the Portuguese fort had no idee what th' right douse be. Willin' to sell th' bark to us while th' factors wus off lookin' fer slaves followin' them wars up country, but wusn't no use fer calculatin' th' douse."

Geoffrey drowsily noted the first voice was that of Jabez McCool and the second Black Amos. He was impatient to resume his journey to the other side of the brook. Only a few steps separated him from the brook's edge.

"Holly poured a mug o' boilin' water over th' chopped-up bark, so we'se got a tea decoction, 'n' we ain't got no time to be rollin' pills, as if we knew how."

"Guess th' tea's steeped enough to be handy. Get his mouth open. He ain't gonna like this."

Geoffrey was convulsing violently, but he attempted to lift his arms in protest as strong fingers pushed inward at the corners of his set jaws and the vilest, most astringent liquid he had ever experienced was forced into his mouth from a teapot's spout thrust between his lips. He was too feeble even to raise his arms, but he tried to avert his head, to no avail, and then tried to spit out the vile liquid. But a hand was holding his mouth closed and also pinching off his nose so that he could not breathe. He swallowed involuntarily, almost threw up, and the teapot tilted again. "I cross the riber," Geoffrey said, managing to turn his head just enough to dislodge the teapot's spout. "I cross the riber. Let me cross the riber . . . she's so beautiful."

"What's that boy goin' on about?" Amos said querulously. "Ain't no woman here, or we'd know it."

"Holly said we'se ought to get th' entire pot into him, and th' same beginnin' next watch. Clap off his mouth 'n' stroke his guzzle, 'n' this syrup will slide right down slick as a whale's dick."

"She's so beautiful," Geoffrey whimpered, then retched as the foul-tasting, foul-smelling liquid was tipped through the spout. His struggles were for naught as one hand easily held his mouth closed while the fingers of the other hand gently stroked his throat. Then the last of the tea was down, and Geoffrey gritted and chewed against the few minute pieces of bark that had settled on his tongue. "She's so beautiful," he whimpered again. "She wants me to go to her." But Amos was gently massaging Geoffrey's temples, and Jabez was patiently restraining Geoffrey's feeble attempts to raise his arms in protest, one man kneeling on either side of his hammock.

There was the sound of a sponge being daubed in a bucket of water and then the blessed stroke of dampness against his perspiring forehead, and then again on his shriveled chest. And then another voice, anxious, familiar. "How does the laddie?"

"On th' cusp, Mister Mate, on th' cusp. He kin slip either side. Seems he's got us this side tuggin' to keep him in this life, 'n' there be a woman t'other side wants him equal bad."

"Kin either of ye coves pray?" the voice of Mate Wolcott Crowninshield demanded.

"Now, Mate, don't take on so. Both Jabez 'n' I ken pray a dead man straight into th' right kingdom, gives we knows th' cove well enough, 'n' he weighs anchor with all his debts settled."

"But kin ye pray for the boy?" Crowninshield demanded. "God's life, he don't owe none o' ye no money."

"Aye, we kin pray fer th' boy, Mate, 'n' sure, that be only a Christian's duty. But we'd rather put our trust in this here bit o' stem 'n' bark we got in the Grand Popo." Through the fog of his intense and debilitating nausea Geoffrey heard Jabez's voice just a trifle more clearly. "She's so beautiful," Geoffrey repeated forlornly through violently chattering teeth. Jabez held his head immobile for a moment, forced his mouth open and pulled out a deciduous tooth that had chosen to detach itself from Geoffrey's gum.

"I've been salted agin th' yellow jack," Geoffrey heard Crowninshield say in a distant, dreamlike voice. He clenched his remaining teeth and swallowed hard to keep the bark tea from coming up. "Caught in on the pepper coast, 'n' liked to died, though t'warn't no beautiful woman wantin' me to cross no river but the Devil himself on a lee shore, 'n' a cohort o' his demons jumpin' 'n' prancin' about to welcome me to Hades. But I boxhauled off that coast 'n' left them demons screechin' and yowlin' for want of my body." Crowninshield paused. "The Devil 'n' his demons thought they had me agin, but the laddie, he pulled me off the lee shore."

"Tain't yere body th' Devil wants," Jabez said dryly, "but yere everlastin' soul. Boxhaul off one coast, get caught in th' rip 'n' a fretted sea with a high wind directly off th' water, 'n' find yereself cross th' breakers. Just puttin' off the inevitable, Mister Mate. Most like the laddie here didn't do ye no favors by savin' yere life. We slugs o' crew had no idee how to treat ye, 'n' had Damon cupped ye with that rusty razor o' his'n, would hae poisoned yere blood, most like. But we slugs would hae given ye our cane rations, much as Beelzebub would allow us, 'til th'

Devil came out in them boats like th' Kroomen o' Cape Palmas use to bring th' slaves through th' surf. 'N' ye would hae gone to yere maker's judgment drunk as any lord ever sat in Parliament."

"I saw the Devil any number o' times whilst languishin' on Banana Island, but the lad here kept him at bay. Got to be a purpose in that, Jabez McCool," Crowninshield said, advancing and leaning anxiously over Geoffrey's hammock. "Devil didn't get me a second time. The lad's luck. This be the last good voyage we all want 'n' we can quit the trade."

"Mate's right," Amos spoke up. "I'm quittin' the trade, set myself up with a public house in Newport, 'n' I won't even get in a wherry to cross a river. Unless it be spanned by a stout bridge, I'll content myself on land. Marry myself a wealthy freed woman 'n' attend church regular. Become a right pillar o' th' gentlefolk in Newport, I expect."

"Kin't wash th' scent o' th' *Bride* 'n' her cargoes off yere hide with any amount o' soap 'n' water," Jabez said sorrowfully. "No more than Pilate could, no more than I. Stained through to our very souls with th' curses o' th' woeful cargoes shipped we be. But th' boy here, why his father ever had th' notion to send so delicate a lad to sea on a slaver be mystery complete beyond ken."

Amos laid a palm against Geoffrey's forehead, heavily beaded with perspiration, and uttered a low whistle. "Can boil an aig on th' lad's head, so hot it be."

Crowninshield crouched closer against the hammock and fished the scrap of rumbowline canvas from the kid of tepid rainwater collected from the leach of a sail. He squeezed excess water from the scrap of cloth and daubed Geoffrey's face with it. "He ain't gonna die, is he, Jabez?" Crowninshield asked fearfully. "He looked out atter me when nobody else would atter Beelzebub thumped me with th' inch o' my mortal life."

Jabez shrugged. "I've been around th' Mohammedans on these coasts enough to hae learned a few words o' their speech. Insh'allah. Means, close as I kin tell, Mister Mate, if God wills. Reckon if'en God—assumin' there actual be such—wills th' lad will live. If'en not," Jabez shrugged, causing Geoffrey's hammock to move slightly, "if'en not, well then, if'en not." But then Jabez McCool said in a low, low voice that may have carried through Geoffrey's delirium, "Insh'allah! Insh'allah!" Jabez sighed and placed one hand protectively on Geoffrey's convulsing body. "Don't want to force more o' th' bark tea on the lad just yet, Mister Mate, but belike he's forgot his manners, being so sick 'n' all, 'n' would be mortified to know he's befouled himself. So if'en ye could bear a hand, we kin get him swabbed 'n' daubed all Bristol fashion, 'n' shifted into another hammock, th' which may make him lie th' more comfortable whilst we await th' time for th' next infusion o' bark tea."

‹ XVI ›

⚜ ⚜ ⚜ ⚜ ⚜ *oseph Frost thought it a pity that Benedict Arnold,*
⚜ **J** ⚜ *preening like a peafowl in his sea blue tunic with the*
⚜ ⚜ *single gold epaulet of a Continental Army briga-*
⚜ ⚜ ⚜ ⚜ ⚜ *dier general gleaming on his shoulder, had to hold his*
bullion-trimmed tricorne in his hands and bend his head to
accommodate the low overhead of the abbreviated stern cabin
of the *Congress* row galley. Joseph had a full belly of fried trout,
bannock bread and fresh coffee, and he was quite content with
his lot in life. He had willingly accompanied Captain Seth Warner of *Trumbull* to the *Congress*, Arnold's flagship now that he
had transferred from the notoriously crank two-masted schooner *Royal Savage* to the more maneuverable *Congress*. Juby had
paddled the two of them to the flagship, anchored in the bay
south of Valcouer, or Valcour, Island, in the small birchbark
canoe just after first light. Juby handed the large bundle of
neatly folded flags to Joseph after they had transferred out of
the canoe onto the gun deck of the *Congress* by the simple expe-
dient of tying the canoe's painter onto the rough platform that
passed as the starboard channel board, then climbing into the
chains and aboard.

"You be better'n me to pass out these flags, Master Joseph,"
Juby said with great dignity. "I thinks that this gallie's stern
cabin gonna be on the small side to accommodate all the gentry." Joseph followed Warner into the closeness of the cramped
stern cabin. The only illumination came through the larded

paper that passed for stern windows and a phoebe lamp giving off more smoke than light in the fetid air.

Arnold seated himself on one of the two 18-pounder cannons set up as stern-chasers, and Joseph idly wondered how those smashers could possibly engage the British from their rearward position. The captains of Arnold's heterogeneous fleet crowded in. Joseph noted with amusement that the commanders of the heavier vessels gravitated toward the forward part of the small cabin: Hawley of *Royal Savage,* Captain Dixson of *Enterprise,* and Simons of *Revenge,* the two-masted schooner that Joseph, Juby and Samuel had helped build at Ticonderoga under the overall direction of Colonel Jeduthan Baldwin, a gifted marine architect as well as an engineer for constructing fortifications. After them came the commanders of the row galleys: Warner of the smallest galley, *Trumbull,* James Arnold of *Congress,* now the flagship, and hooded-eye Thatcher of the *Washington.* Carrot-haired Davis of the cutter *Lee* had ranged himself with the captains of the gundalos: Mansfield of the *New Haven,* Simmons of the *Providence,* Sumers of the *Boston,* the diminutive, soft-spoken Ulmore of the *Spitfire,* Joseph's friend Benjamin Rue of *Philadelphia,* who smiled and grinned at Joseph, Captain Grant of the *Connecticut,* the florid-faced, balding Grimes of the *Jersey,* a flannel rag bound round his head with a poultice to calm his abscessed tooth, and the sepulchral Reed of the *New York,* though her crew had just voted to rename her the *Success.* Somehow Brigadier General David Waterbury, second in command to Arnold, and the stout but deep-bottomed Colonel Edward Wigglesworth found themselves on a bench immediately in front of Arnold.

"All right," Arnold shouted hoarsely, eyes ablaze with an intensity that to some of the men in the cabin, which reeked of turpentine and rum, may have appeared to border on the insane, "life's hard and then you die, and that is the way it is. The British fleet has been reported off Cumberland Head. She's headed by *Inflexible,* a three-masted full square-rigged ship, the largest ever afloat on the Lake. She mounts eighteen 12-pounders and is under the command of John Schank, one of the most able officers the Royal Navy has in North America. It was he who pressed for the disassembly of vessels below the rapids on the Richelieu and their transport in sections to St. Jean." Arnold's lower lip curled defiantly. "The rapids at Chambly have been our allies as much as the approaching winter. But make no mistake about it, Schank is a formidable officer requiring our strict attention, for he brought *Inflexible* to St. Jean and got her back together in less than one month.

"The next in might might be the schooner *Lady Maria*. She is under the command of Lieutenant John Starke. *Maria* mounts fourteen 6-pounders, and she is the flagship and ships Governor Carleton and the senior Royal Navy officer on the Lake, Commodore Thomas Pringle. Next her be the *Carleton* schooner, named as you'd expect for the governor himself. *Carleton* mounts only two 6-pounders less than the *Lady Maria,* and a chap named Dacres commands her. Next her be the hoy *Loyal Convert,* which armament of seven 9-pounders could be considered puny until you realize we don't own a vessel mounting seven 9-pounders.

"But then, gentlemen, and we need not number the gunboats with 24-pounders, 18-pounders, 12-pounders, 9-pounders in their bows—they are too numerous to mention—then comes the radeau *Thunderer,* whose cannons—I wonder to speak of them—six 24-pounders, six 12-pounders and at least two howitzers of unknown calibers." Arnold smacked his fist on the mess table in the stern cabin. "Now, *Thunderer* encompasses enough of a platform to have her own furnace for heating shot to heave in our direction. She also has a detachment of Hessian artillery aboard to midwife her cannons in giving birth to death and destruction. But I shall make so bold as to say *Thunderer*'s poor sailing qualities will keep her downwind of any action—so long as we maintain the weather gauge." Joseph could not help but note that Arnold was exceedingly cheerful as he delivered his ominous tidings.

"Gentlemen commanders, I am sending around to every vessel a pipe of as wholesome a rum as ever came out of Jamaica. I wish it were a side of beef and two sides of pork, but rum is all our Congress can find to send its fleet afloat on Lake Champlain as a stopper to the might of England and her German mercenaries." Arnold made a deprecating gesture. "Ask our Congress for a three-masted frigate, ship-rigged all proper and mounting thirty-six 9-pounders, and Congress sends a rude bateaux of exceedingly green wood—which I know something about, seeing I took a slew of them up the Kennebec the year past. Ask Congress for a hundred proper seamen and you'll get a dozen cow-herds, all a-blushing like maids. Ask our Congress for honest sailcloth and cordage, and you'll get a bedsheet and a yard of ribbon . . ." Arnold stopped abruptly as joyous cries sounded from the main deck.

"Aye, that'll be the men greeting the pipe of rum brought aboard. Captain Rue, I'll trouble you to go out deck and attempt the arduous, perhaps dangerous task of salvaging for this council of war a bucket of rum and a ladle of some kind. I believe we are prodigious short of golden goblets for this mess.

"Now, gentlemen commanders," Arnold resumed, "we ain't never had no luxuries, and precious few necessities, and the few necessities that have come our way, well, we've had to scrap tooth and nail for. But, God's teeth, we've built a fleet of fifteen vessels committed to war, with two hundred and twenty cannons spread among them."

Arnold paused for effect. "That is, if we count every swivel gun capable of throwing a pound of metal in some fashion when given fire as a proper cannon. I've enumerated the size of the force ranged against us. The British can hurl at least twelve hundred pounds of iron at us, while we are hard pressed to muster a total of six hundred pounds. And be not forgetting that behind Carleton's ships will come ten thousand British regular troops, two thousand Germans, and close to five thousand Indians, half or more from the western tribes and all in a lather to garner scalps." Arnold gestured dismissively. "There are also a thousand or so Canadians compelled to the British colours, though they are seeking every opportunity to find berths away from encounters of the close and deadly kind. All toted, gentlemen commanders, there are more than eighteen thousand British soldiers and murderous auxiliaries, all well armed and fed, embarked on the Lake seeking to reduce Tyonderoga and Mount Independence to smoldering ruins. With that goal accomplished, they would press on to do the same to Albany, and then down the Hudson to join forces with Billy Howe in New York and provide fresh forces to fall upon General Washington from his extended flank."

Arnold's nostrils flared and his eyes shot sparks. "Aaah, Captain Rue, careful on the ladder! That bucket is certainly overflowing! Aaah yes, that salt-glazed tankard will serve admirably. General Waterbury, perhaps you will quaff a cup of rum to the success of our arms, then pass the bucket and cup to your right. Now, gentlemen commanders, how stand you in regards to my plan to spread our forces in an arc in this bay between the Isle of Valcouer and the western shore, let the British rush past us, then bait them into attacking our forces and fighting the wind at the same time? This is a council of war, gentlemen commanders, so all voices are welcome and much solicited. Colonel Wigglesworth, I'll value your comments exceedingly."

Wigglesworth paused, his hand outstretched for the bucket of rum and salt-glazed cup. He waited to speak until Waterbury had passed him both bucket and cup and he had taken a long draught of the rum. "Well, General Arnold, you kin trust the British to be British. They don't hold no truck with us *colonials* 'n' they're bent on harrying south up the Lake, expecting to find us in front of Crown Point or Tyonderoga. With such overwhelming force likely they don't have no proper scouts out looking for us tucked in here. This here bay ain't the optimum to meet the British, but while I certainly ain't no sailor, I kin't say I've seen much seamanship in your cow-herds, General. Rather than engage the British on the open Lake and have to work sails as well as cannons, I'd opt to make 'em come to us. And from what little I know about sailing vessels, it'll take some doing for 'em to come at us all at once."

"Well spoken, Colonel!" Arnold cried. He took the cup of rum proffered to him and pretended to drink deeply, though

Joseph saw that he actually drank little before thrusting the cup into the bucket and passing it on. "General Waterbury, as my second in command, your sage advice carries especial weight. How counsel you?"

Waterbury swallowed hard several times and coughed loudly, his prominent Adam's apple moving up and down fiercely. "Well, General Arnold, I don't much hold with bein' embayed in a hot corner when we're plainly outgunned. Your intelligence, just shared with us, reveals the British forces to be much superior to our'n. My preference is to meet the British on the open lake, and if we get the worst of it, run for Tyonderoga with our remaining ships."

An angry murmuring rose from the captains, and Mansfield of the *New Haven* gundalo fairly shouted, "Colonel Wigglesworth's right. We've a bunch of lubbers for crew, though I've come to love my men dearly, and I daren't shake out a sail unless the wind be from directly astern. If my men be able to make their mark, I'd rather it be with every man serving a cannon and letting the British come agin us."

"Or perhaps heaving on a spring cable so's to present a full broadside to the enemy, then pivot and present a smaller head-on target, eh, Captain Mansfield?" Arnold said with evident satisfaction. He continued quickly: "Gentlemen commanders, with the great respect due General Waterbury's counsel, we must take cognizance of one overwhelming fact." Arnold paused and turned to Joseph. "Perhaps Volunteer Frost, who has striven mightily to instruct us in the rudiments of serving the iron charges whose freight is our sole purpose, though he has no command of his own, may be able to offer insight into what that one overwhelming fact is." Arnold arched an eyebrow. "Comment, Mister Frost?"

Joseph tightened his grip on the bundle of flags in his lap and swallowed hard, though not as hard, he figured, as General Waterbury. "Well, General Arnold, if the British get through to Tyonderoga and reduce the fortifications there—or more likely, I'll avow, our forces withdraw in the face of overwhelming force—then they will have settled the business. The British will cordon off the northern states from the southern states. They'll strangle the northern states, then move on the southern. By year's end the British will have taken up General Washington, and the Congress, and they'll be heaped with chains, uncivilly battened in the holds of British warships, and transported to Britain. They'll be given sham trials and condemned as rebels out of hand, then given the privilege of stretching new hemp." Joseph fumbled with the ties of the bundle and plucked up one banner, which he half unfurled, though he wisely kept his seat and did not attempt to stand.

"It don't matter what happens to us, General Arnold," Joseph said with all the earnestness he could muster, "so long as we stop the British, keep them from advancing up the Lake. Keep them from reaching the Hudson. Keep them from attacking General Washington from the rear. If we can do that, though we lose every ship, every man in this fleet, well, we'll have given General Washington the time he needs to throw off the habits of that low and miserable Congress and recruit and train the men needed to turn back the next onslaught." Joseph stopped speaking, intensely aware of his own embarrassment.

"A volunteer, gentlemen commanders, a volunteer's counsel," Benedict Arnold said softly. "A volunteer who obtained bunting and sewed banners fit to be displayed on our ships."

"Oh no, General," Joseph protested quickly. "Juby obtained the bunting from Portsmouth, though I know not how, and Samuel Stonecypher did the cutting and sewing. There are sixteen banners of the Flag of Grand Union here."

"Please be good enough to pass one banner to each of the gentlemen commanders, Mister Frost. I take it the sixteenth banner is for the *Liberty* schooner that brought our fleet the barrels of rum and some flour, and I've dispatched back to Tyonderoga for additional provisions. I shall safeguard *Liberty*'s flag until it can be delivered to Captain Pumer." Arnold gravely accepted the flag Joseph passed to him. "Is this fellow Juby, who obtained the cloth embarked with us? I would fain have his be the hands that raise these colours over this vessel."

Arnold turned to the assembled captains. "Gentlemen, the

wind is now half a gale out of the northwest, the best point for the British fleet to clothe every mast with all the canvas that can be dressed. But if we disperse our forces in crescent fashion, with every ship on a spring-cable, bows facing into the wind prevailing, we can present full broadsides to the enemy. Then we can pay off the springs and let the cannons firing aft do their work." Arnold's excitement fairly illuminated the cramped cabin with the crackle of lightning.

Captain Grimes dipped the salt-glazed mug into the now sadly depleted bucket of rum and drank off half a mug in one long swallow. "Damnable tooth," he snarled to no one in particular. Benjamin Rue grasped the bucket and disappeared up the ladder to the main deck.

"I make so bold to suggest the row galleys keep their sails in reefs 'n' be smart with their sweeps," Seth Warner said laconically as he masticated a wad of tobacco. "Same for the gundalos. Sweeps can work us all in firin' position pert smart, then swivelin' stern or bow to the British whilst we reloads. Reckon we kin be the catamount in the cave fightin' off the dogs." Warner smiled a sleepy smile. "Dogs kin get almighty swatted 'n' kilt dead by a angry catamount." Warner yawned but quickly reached out to grasp the mug as Benjamin Rue came hustling down the ladder with a fresh bucket of rum.

"Don't have no idea how you intend to deploy all us, General," Seth Warner continued, "but I'd truly appreciate your seein' your way clear to let my *Trumbull* anchor the east side of your crescent, closest to Valcouer Island. I think we be of a mind that the crescent present a saber's edge to the enemy."

"The most exposed point, the most honorable!" Arnold enthused. "*Trumbull* shall certainly have it!" Arnold spied a carpenter's satchel below a stern window, pawed through it and produced with a grunt of triumph a large piece of chalk. "Here is the disposition I envision." With bold strokes of the chalk on the bare larboard side of the hull he sketched lines to represent the bay between Valcour Island and the New York mainland. "*Trumbull* shall anchor the eastern tip of our scimitar of vessels, though Captain Warner shall hold out of musket-shot of the island, for sure as bears shit in the woods the British will land soldiers and Indians on the island to pot at us. The gundalos shall be next in line, juxtaposed so: *Boston, Providence, Connecticut, New Haven, Jersey, New York, Philadelphia, Spitfire.* Behind the gundalos we shall position this *Congress, Washington,* and *Revenge. Lee* and *Enterprise* behind us, and *Royal Savage* in front! We'll send her out once the British have swept past to draw them back to our crescent!" Arnold sketched bold dashes on the raw hull to indicate the positions the fleet would take up.

"General," Waterbury said diffidently, "be there any way the British kin come through the passage a-tween Isle Valcouer 'n' the New York side and come on us from our rear?"

"They may send canoes and shallow draft gunboats down the gut on us," Arnold said soberly. "Nothing drawing more than six feet can make it over the shoals. We'll have to be looking over our shoulders, but just as they'll have to come at us piecemeal from the front, the British will have to come at us piecemeal from behind. However, gentlemen commanders," Arnold paused and looked at every captain in turn: "those of us, the *Savage, Trumbull, Washington* and this *Congress,* that have a turn of speed under sail or sweeps, we'll sortie, fire off a few cannons, then return to our positions demarcated, and the British will try to beat into our hornet's nest. Odds are more than even the British won't even think about looking for our back door." Arnold's eyes continued to strike fires that illuminated the stuffy, confining stern cabin. "Now gentlemen, you may wish to send men ashore, either island or mainland, to cut small trees to dress our vessels, the better to disguise our true natures as the British fleet sails past in all its pride and majesty. We shall also consider how we should affix spring lines for the best advantage."

⚙ ⚙ ⚙ ⚙ ⚙ E O F F R E Y F R O S T , S T I L L E X T R E M E L Y
⚙ G ⚙ U N S T E A D Y O N H I S P I N S , T H E F E W
⚙ ⚙ T E E T H L E F T I N H I S G U M S S U B J E C T
⚙ ⚙ ⚙ ⚙ ⚙ T O F R E Q U E N T A N D U N G O V E R N A B L E
chattering, stood a respectful two paces behind Wick Nichols on Nichols' quarterdeck and watched the nondescript land
draw closer. The shore appeared to be more mud than sand,
with stands of tall grasses that grew from stagnant pools of
water just above high tide waving extreme tassels at their tips.
The only human-created structures visible were a mud and wat-
tle wall perhaps ten feet high, and a half dozen huts—miserable
hovels indeed, most likely the squalid dwellings of fishermen
who plied their trade from the slovenly, twisted pirogues pulled
up on the shore. The wall ran in either direction for a good one
hundred yards. At intervals behind it low roofs thatched with
palm fonds were visible. Beside what Geoffrey perceived to be
a portcullis entrance into the wall several elaborate multi-hued
flags atop long staffs hung limp in the humid air.

Wick Nichols snapped his telescope closed with the satisfied
snick of smooth brass sliding into closely fitted tubes. "The flags
by the barracoon give credence to the fishermen at Grand Popo
who advised that King Tegbesu had enjoyed much success in
interior wars against tribes refusing to acknowledge his suzer-
ainty. Though I confess it difficult to cypher the full import o'
the flags, and it be worrisome that King Tegbesu has ventured
so far from his capital city, which lies a hundret miles well above

this coast." Nichols' eye fell on his twin brother, who was seated on the barrel of a cannon, fanning himself in the cloying heat with a large hat woven of sennet. "Brother mine, I collect we shall gather up a full cargo from this miserable port of Quidah. It behooves you to make ready your appliances for gauging the health of our purchases."

"Oh, brother, I've long been ready to test the flesh to be shipped," Damon cackled, throwing his head back, all his teeth showing. "Think you we should construct the barrier now?"

Nichols shook his head. "Do you not feel the eyes upon you? There are many, brother, though where their owners are secreted is most difficult to discern. The bushes along the fore-shore to larboard of the pirogues are capable of concealing a score of spies, and we cannot in turn spy them. Best we . . ."

"Deck there!" the lookout in the foremast starboard shrouds shouted, one arm crooked into a ratline and the other arm pointing excitedly: "Some 'uns comin' around the fort! Larboard side!"

"Let go the anchor," Nichols ordered. "Douse the fore tops'l and slack away on the fore topmasts'l. Pay out a scope o' thrice the depth 'n' snub her to."

"Eight fathom with this line," Black Amos shouted, shrewdly eying the marker just below his fist. "A right comfortable six fathom beneath the keel."

"Pay out no more than twenty-five fathom o' cable," Nichols commanded. "Get that fore topmast stays'l in, damn your eyes!" he shouted at the men gathered at the foremast sheets and hauls, and he brandished his staff. "Want to drive us onto the shore, do you? I've seen men down with the pox 'n' scurvy handle sails better."

The remaining scrap of fore top sail was being fisted up quickly, and the foredeck hands wrestled the triangular fore topmast staysail down its stay with alacrity, fearful that Nichols might stride forward and smite them with his staff. The best bower was let go, plunging into the water with scarcely a splash, while one of the foredeck hands, a wizened Dirk Covens from somewhere in the Massachusetts colony, stood by the starboard fore riding bitt. Covens bitted the cable, throwing a coil in a figure eight around the bitt. The *Bride* pivoted daintily around her anchor as a fluke took the ground and the cable came taut, smoothly checking the *Bride*'s slight headway to a complete snub, with the land starboard side-to some quarter of a mile away.

Nichols extended his telescope, brought it to eye, and focused on the party just rounding the left corner of the barracoon. He let out a low whistle. "Amazons, by God! 'N' though that pig bein' carried in that hammock be blacked by the sun, he's a Christian, sure. What mischief this?" Nichols thrust the glass toward Geoffrey. "Here, youngster, tell me what you descry. I'll hold my tongue for the nonce."

Geoffrey lay the barrel of the telescope atop a ratline in the starboard main shrouds and carefully focused on the group emerging from the lee of the barracoon. He scarce believed his eyes. Twenty women, ten on either side of a hammock-palanquin borne by four men walking briskly, two each fore and aft, followed by two boys running desperately alongside to hold aloft a canopy of light cloth to keep the occupant of the hammock in shade, were marching grimly toward the beach, where a light surf—nothing like the surf pounding on the outer bar—broke gently. The women were marching in rigid step, exact cadence, heavy muskets all slanted at the same precise angle over their right shoulders. They were identically dressed in some severe costume of heavy, dark brown cloth tied off by a wrap at their waists; heavy black belts of leather crossed their breasts; and bayonets were thrust into scabbards hung from their belts.

The troop of women marched to within a precise twenty yards of the beach, then at some unheard, unseen command stopped in precise formation and grounded their muskets in unison. A third urchin, smaller than the two spreading the sunshade, jogged over the crest of the sand dune to the left of the barracoon. In the ellipse of glass Geoffrey saw that the lad clutched a stool and a basket. The urchin slid to a stop beside the palanquin and hastily set the stool on the sand. The two sunshade bearers lay down the shafts of their canopy long enough to assist the occupant to hoist himself laboriously out of the hammock-palanquin. With a contemptuous nod the man dismissed the men who had carried his corpulent bulk to the beach. He waddled to the stool, scratched his nether parts luxuriantly before seating himself, then held out an imperious hand. Immediately an ornate goblet was held out to him by the smaller urchin, while the two boys scrambled to hoist the sunshade. Geoffrey was appalled at the man's garments, or lack of them. A few pieces of canvas comprising a twisted girdle of dirty cloth and a scrap of rumbowline canvas for a shirt were his only raiment.

"I twig him to be a white man, Captain Nichols, though fierce burned by the sun," Geoffrey said. "He seems indifferent to our appearance."

"I think he be not as indifferent as he appears," Wick Nichols said, with a grunt of satisfaction. "I surmise him to be an emissary of King Tegbesu, no doubt, Christian or not. I had dealin's with Tegbesu three years past, and he's a right bad 'un. Surprised he still lives. He has a power o' enemies. Good for us, though, as he never was one to tolerate the middleman, the factor, be it French, English or Portuguese, when he had captives to trade." Wick Nichols shouted toward the waist: "Mister Mate, hoist out my gig as fast as 'em slugabeds we've coddled this entire passage can rig the lifts. Please to hoist up a chest of gimcracks 'n' make sure a basket of cowries be included. My normal bargemen to their oars 'n' the supernumerary 'n' I be goin' ashore directly."

Wick Nichols beckoned the first mate closer. "Would not be amiss, Mister Mate, was you to load 'n' train our starboard cannons, quiet-like, you ken? Bring the cannons to bear on the parley 'n' be ready to consign 'em to hell at the first sign of treachery." Nichols leered at Geoffrey. "Most like by the time Mister Mate gets these miserable pieces to spit their wads we'll be spitted through the gizzards with the bayonets o' 'em women who live only to serve their king. Now, jump below 'n' shift into the rig you wore ashore at Bence Island; got to look the dandy for Tegbesu's emissary. "'N' jump quick," Nichols glared, "we be pricked for time if we've to get a cargo here."

Geoffrey self-consciously waited until the four bargemen had run the bow of the gig well onto the sand beach before stepping onto the shore. He was wearing his shore-going finery of velvet coat, sateen breeches and silk stockings since there was only a short distance to cover, a fact Geoffrey keenly appreciated since it took all his strength to cram his feet into those shoes. He followed a respectful two paces behind Nichols, who deliberately took no notice of the armed women drawn up in ranks on either side of the wretchedly dressed corpulent white man. The man made as if to drop the goblet, but the urchin was there instantly to catch it. The man got to his feet, though the urchin had to assist mightily to heave his bulk upright.

Nichols stopped and bowed. "I bid you a pleasant day, sir. My name be Nichols, master of the trading vessel *Bride of Derry,* three months out of the Rhode Island colony." He acknowledged Geoffrey's presence curtly. "'N' this be my vessel's supernumerary."

The white man clapped his hands and the urchin from somewhere produced two additional stools. These stools were lower than the stool upon which the white man seated himself, Geoffrey discovered as soon as he settled on his, and in a flash of insight he realized the difference in height was a negotiating ploy. "I am Lyons Bennett, first Privy Council to Tegbesu, King of the Quidah, the Oyo, the Allada, the Savi, and all the people of Danhomé." Bennett pawed aside the scrap of shirt, the better to scratch his very hairy chest, and Geoffrey saw a heavy chain of some bright yellow metal encircling the man's neck. He brought out a louse and cracked it noisily with his thumbnail. "You wouldn't happen to have a tailor aboard your vessel, Captain Nichols, what could whip up a suit of Christian clothes?" Bennett asked hopefully.

"The *Bride* be possessed of a capital sailmaker, sir, 'n' given the proper cloth 'n' time enough I'm certain he could tog you out the equal o' any Liverpool merchant. But Sails be busy sewing up a complete new main course to replace one was split in a heavy blow a week a-fore landfall, 'n' unlikely he be free to do tailorin' work until we've filled out a cargo. Then he can most likely whip up a coat of best Midlands broadcloth, not that light taffeta stuff 'em women be wearin'."

Geoffrey knew perfectly well that the *Bride of Derry* had not lost a main course during any storm and realized that Wick Nichols was playing his own game of dissembling for advantage.

"It be devoutly to be hoped, Captain Nichols, that I can treat with your sailmaker in the most expeditious manner possible for a suit of Christian clothes. I find I am unable to abide the clothes worn by the people in these parts." Lyons Bennett disdainfully flicked a rag of rumbowline canvas over his belly.

"For sure, 'em heathen got no idea a-tall about proper garments for Christians," Nichols said amiably. "I twig from 'em flags over the barracoon that King Tegbesu be in residence sommers nearby, 'n' not in Abomey."

"And have you been to Abomey, sir?" Bennett said suspiciously. "If so, when?"

"Three years past. Two other ships' masters 'n' I journeyed the hundret or so miles to Abomey to negotiate our cargoes since the local factors didn't have nothin' worth bargainin' for." Nichols peered shrewdly at Bennett. "I did not mark your presence on that trip, Mister Bennett, o' that I be sure."

"I entered the King's service as Privy Council but two years ago, Captain Nichols," Bennett said stiffly.

"Well, it was sure some sight seein' all 'em skulls set 'round the royal palaces, 'n' seein' the way 'em skulls was collected."

Geoffrey noticed that Wick Nichols was rubbing his palms surreptitiously on his breeches, leaving slightly damp stains of perspiration on the cloth, and thought that passing strange.

"You are correct, Captain Nichols, that King Tegbesu is nearby. He was forced to chastise the Yoruba people, whose former king insulted him grossly. King Tegbesu took the field personally to lead his armies. There was a great battle some forty miles north of where we are now taking our ease so comfortably. King Tegbesu pursued the remnants of the fleeing Yoruba villains so vigorously that, finding himself so near this coast that he had never seen, His Majesty decided to select himself the captives for sale to the English, French and Portuguese factors. The king was greatly pleased to receive intelligence from Popo that your vessel, disappointed at having found no goods for trade in the Popo barracoons, was destined for Quidah. The king will allot you the choicest of the captives—assuming you are able to meet his prices, of course. After which he will trade next with the Portuguese, then the French, and lastly the English."

"Your countrymen," Nichols said incisively, "for your tone be that of someone born within sound o' the chimes o' Westminster."

"Winchester, Captain Nichols. Unless you are fortunate enough to be born on our noble isle the accents of Westminster and Winchester be indistinguishable. Quite distinguishable of course for those honored with pure British birth."

Nichols ignored the rebuff. "What goods of trade would most interest your king, Mister Privy Council?"

"King Tegbesu is interested in many goods, Captain Nichols," Lyons Bennett said slowly. "Silks and velvets among cloths; beads of coral; of course, cowry shells from the Maldives not far from India. Strong drink of various persuasions—no beer or wine, of course, the peoples of these parts manufacture their own from the palms and various fruits. Brandy from France is always appreciated. But of late King Tegbesu especially longs for more gunpowder for his muskets. And he longs for small cannons that can be easily transported by horse or camel, then set up quickly on the battleground to bring consternation all the more readily to his enemies."

"Aye," Nichols said reflectively, "your king was all-fired set when last I set eyes on him at Abomey to fashion an army after the European model, 'n' he was receivin' a right smart number o' muskets o' Dutch 'n' Swede origin."

Bennett swept his arm vaguely to include the formidable-looking women soldiers. "In the main King Tegbesu has succeeded in fashioning an army after the European model. The King's Guard, some of whom he commanded to accompany me as I was dispatched to greet you, are armed with Dutch muskets acquired two years ago, at the time when I came to my appointment. Clumsy but sturdy." Bennett snapped his fingers and the urchin immediately placed the goblet in his hand. "They were defective in their locks, a matter the merchant-captain who drayed them all the way to Abomey failed to communicate to King Tegbesu. Happily, King Tegbesu has in his employ a blacksmith who was able to cypher the defects in the locks and alleviate them."

Bennett paused: "The captain who deceived King Tegbesu so hideously, having heard, erroneously, that King Tegbesu had been deposed, called last year to trade." Bennett took a long quaff from the goblet. "The captain and all his crew were taken off to Abomey, and their skulls now grace the courtyard in one of King Tegbesu's palaces." Bennett gestured vaguely toward the west. "I believe the charred timbers of their vessel, such as may be yet undisturbed by wind or water, may be found just at the surf line half a mile in that direction."

Bennett snapped his fingers again, and one of the urchins brought a clay pipe, with the shaved tobacco in its bowl already smoldering. "Would you care for a pipe, Captain Nichols?"

"Thankin' you allus the same," Nichols said, "but in the ways o' takin' baccy I've learned to content myself with a good chaw o' plug or twist. Safest way aboard a ship." Nichols made as if to search his pockets for a twist of tobacco. "I have gunpowder, cowries, cloth from the Midland looms, iron bars, much cane of the highest quality distilled in Boston and Providence—'n' I may be persuaded to part with some o' the cannons that be my armament. But was I to be so persuaded, the cannons would command a great price."

Lyons Bennett sighed: "Were you but able to communicate to King Tegbesu the formulary for gunpowder you would have your own palace and a thousand slaves to attend you."

"Eh?" Wick Nichols cocked his head quizzically. "If'en I was to set up a powder works Tegbesu would set me up with my own household 'n' slaves? How much powder would your king expect, say, per year?"

"You must present any such proposal directly into the king's ear, Captain Nichols, though naturally I shall be your translator. I cannot say what your reward might be. And if you were to offer the services of an armory, capable of casting cannon balls, assembling muskets, casting cannons . . ."

"I might possibly set up a powder works, Mister Privy Council," Nichol said, though not testily. "A proper arsenal would over-reach me, I fear. But the millin' o' gunpowder be somethin' possible, yes, it be somethin' that be quite possible. If you tell the truth, I could set up on this coast 'n' leave the sea for good. Though I would have no need for one thousand slaves, a dozen at a time would suffice."

"Were you to mill powder for King Tegbesu, Captain Nichols, you would be elevated to a kingship second only to that of King Tegbesu himself."

⚜ XVIII ⚜

"**G**od's bones! Regard them, flying southward ever as fast as wind permits, with no pas op over the shoulder! Expecting to find us on the open Lake, like so many clodpates scurrying toward Tyonderoga!" Benedict Arnold, standing next to the helmsman at the tiller, exulted, using the Dutch word for lookout. Beside him on the quarterdeck of the *Congress* row galley Joseph Frost peered southward with dread into a cold, sullen, overcast sky and horizon merged together in the color of ashes from a dead cooking fire. From the New York to the Vermont shores Lake Champlain was a long curved line of sails, abrupt hideous fangs of various hues, from pristine white of virgin number two canvas to weathered dingy gray of sailcloth taken from warships left below the rapids at Chambly. Joseph gripped the fife rail to keep from being thrown forward or backward as the bows of *Congress* plowed into the iron-gray swells spinning off into whitecaps and spume that fairly smoked and stung when it lashed the faces of the crew of *Congress*. Interspersed among the warships were dozens, no, hundreds of large birchbark canoes—*canots du maître*, master canoes, the largest canoes built by the western tribes. The canoes would completely disappear in the wave troughs, then rise on the sullen crests, and Joseph could see that every canoe was filled to overflowing with heavily armed, fiercely painted Indian warriors.

Joseph heartily wished for a telescope, but no one aboard *Congress* owned a spyglass, so Joseph peered intently through wind-whipped, tearing eyes at the sails perhaps two miles in front of him. The largest was a three-masted ship, and slightly behind it were two schooners with hulls painted bright orange, sailing in line. Slightly ahead of the gaggle of canoes and a mile behind the two schooners were gunboats, at least two dozen of them, each one close to forty feet long, broad beamed, at least twelve feet, a single mast with a shoulder-of-mutton rig and one heavy cannon in the bows. Heavier and with much greater beam, the gunboats were taking the waves better than the canoes. With a desperate heart, his knees flexing to the pitch and roll of the row galley, Joseph gave up counting the bateaux loaded with infantry troops and scattered in haphazard order toward the Vermont shore after he had enumerated fifty.

Arnold strode up to Joseph, frozen to the fife rail, and clapped the youth on his shoulder in amicable fashion. "Ain't it grand, volunteer! One *pas op* over their shoulders when the notion strikes the officers aboard the ship and schooners and first they won't recognize us as ships, but islands come detached." Arnold flung out an arm to take in the short spruce trees, many still with their branches but others shorn as bare poles and bound in bundles similar to the fasces Joseph fancied the lictors of ancient Rome bore to clear a path for the magistrates. Arnold had the trees gathered and tied in place while the fleet waited in the bay formed between the New York mainland and the bulk of Valcour Island. The fasces provided a crude form of camouflage and concealment, though they were somewhat incongruous now that the row galleys were underweigh, with lateen sails billowing far above the spruce boughs. Joseph was glad that Arnold had not ordered the fasces jettisoned when the row galleys swept out of the anchorage in pursuit of the British fleet, for he took a modicum of comfort from the thought that the bundles of poles might provide some slight protection from musket shot.

"By the Almighty!" Arnold blew on his reddened, chapped hands to warm them. "When they finally put down their dainty teacups and deign to throw a glance north'ard, they'll think we're backed into a corner. God pity them!" All the same

Arnold glanced speculatively at the foremast and mainmast lateen sails, for the *Congress* was under sail for the first time in her brief life. *Congress* was running before the wind prodigiously, the sails ballooning well to starboard, though thanks to the propulsion forces at work on the lateen sails the row galley was heeled to starboard only very slightly. "Flatten the leech on both sails inboard," Arnold shouted to the hands clustered about the masts, using cupped hands as a megaphone. Then to the helmsman: "Point her directly at the three-master." He clapped Joseph on the shoulder again and pointed to the gunboats and bateaux floundering far behind the wake of the *Inflexible* and *Carleton*. "We'll shape a course as if to cut off the bateaux from their protectors. I expect someone will throw off a gun within the minute. Soon as that happens we'll run directly at the bateaux, discharge a broadside toward them, bear on for the time it takes us to reload and run out again, then run back to our anchorage, engaging the canoes on the way."

Arnold fair skipped down the ladder from the quarterdeck to *Congress'* gun deck, completely oblivious to the seasick men all around him. As Arnold had presciently observed, a moment later Joseph heard the dull report of a warning cannon. Anxiously he scanned the massive curving line of sails, searching for the source of the sound, and saw a ragged blossom of cannon smoke rapidly borne away by the raw wind. The warning shot had come from the *Maria*, slightly to larboard and astern of the *Inflexible* and *Carleton*. Arnold beckoned imperiously for Joseph to join him. Vaulting over the fife rail, Joseph kept his feet easily and joined Arnold as he strolled forward the length of the gun deck, hands clasped behind him in the identical mannerism of his brother, Geoffrey.

"Is your piece double-shotted?" Arnold inquired of the gun captain of the forward larboard cannon.

That miserable thin creature, barefoot and clad only in ragged duck trousers and a thin singlet of worn jersey, blew his nose noisily and contemptuously between thumb and forefinger. "No, Genr'l, but we kin make her so pert smart," the gun captain said.

"Do not let me hinder you unduly," Arnold said, though loud enough to be heard for all the gunners crouched around their cannons. "But please to run in your cannons, add grape, langrage, anything that falls readily to hand, and pick a target from among the gunboats now broad to larboard. Presently I shall order 'wear ship and about' but a-fore I do, I expect each of you to sink the gunboat that you fix upon. You men!" Arnold now addressed the gun crews of the starboard side. "As we come about to starboard . . ?"

"Hold on, Gener'l," the captain of the number two cannon said irritably. "You'll accept we're all lubbers 'n' ducks' feet, and while I conceit, well I believe I conceit, your meanin' of starboard is that we turns to the right, bear in mind we conceit less about naval matters 'en you 'knowledge 'bout the backside of the moon, er some such."

"Advice well taken," Arnold said cheerfully. "We shall indeed be turning to our right in a matter of moments. During the maneuver the larboard—the cannons of the left side of our vessel—shall discharge their shot as a clear target shows. Once we are through our jibe and pointing as high into the eye of the wind as ever we can as we begin our run northward, your cannons on the right side will likewise align on the gunboats between us and the Verdmont shore. You are to select a particular gunboat or bateau, whichever be believed you can strike, and train upon it most meticulously."

Arnold beckoned all the gun crews to gather round him and drew Joseph into their irregular ring. "I believe all of you know Mister Frost here. He's the only one among us who's actually smelt and been blinded by smoke from gunpowder in a free-for-all tussle at sea. While all of you are free to direct your pieces as you see fit, if you wish to consult him about the trim of your cannons, please do so." Arnold clapped Joseph familiarly on the shoulder. "Now then, here is our plan." Joseph was quick to note that whatever plan Arnold had in mind, he intended the men to think that they had a hand in its conception. "The British officers in the large vessels ahead ran right past our anchorage because they was convinced we *colonials*," Arnold fair spat the word, "ain't no idea which end of the musket to put to our shoulders. Our plan is to turn right about, first giving the gunboats and bateaux a generous bashing with the left-side cannons. Once we are through the turn right about, the star . . . the right-side cannons will seek their targets. When our stern is directly pointed toward the British we'll unleash the twin cannons in the stern cabin toward the capital vessels."

Arnold attenuated his voice, and instinctively the gun crews drew closer. "Now, our plan as we run back to our anchorage is to plow right through the master canoes laden with Indians. We'll be going upwind, and we'll have to sweep quite a bit later on, depending on how high to the wind we can come with these lateen sails. We can run brisk downwind, but close-hauled as ever we can, we can't come higher to the wind than five points.

"But as we shift sails and plow through the Indians we've got to kill as many of them as we can. Understand that! We want the cannons loaded with grape and langrage, gunner's dice— Mister Frost helped clip up a heap of dice from old nails. Swan shot, anything we've got."

Arnold faced the gun crews defiantly. "Now think on it. We'll lick the British for sure, and they'll slink back to their remote islands; but the Indians, they still going to be here. We've got to kill a bunch of them. Wish we could kill all the bad Indians. The Pequots from down my way in Connecticut be fair on their way to being white men. But every thieving, murthering Indian we leave alive as we plow through them canoes is an Indian can sink a hatchet into your granny's skull, then snatch her scalp. So we've got to employ the swivel guns to their highest use. We've got to keep them murthering pieces so hot as we pass through the canoes that somebody'll have to piss on 'em to keep the powder from going off when we shove down the charge. Understand me now? Men at the cannons and men at the murthering pieces so's we dispatch as many of them painted devils to hell as we can on our run back to our anchorage at Valcouer Harbour."

Arnold cocked his head, and his slate-gray eyes searched the face of every man in turn. "It ain't gonna be pleasant, this work we've got to settle with the Indians. But you've all got to understand that every Indian warrior of the Algonquian tribes meets his Manitou at the bottom of this Lake is one less Indian warrior to ravage our frontier towns." Arnold broke off at the concussion of another cannon and turned toward the *Maria,* whose officers had finally looked over their shoulders and sighted the American vessels. "All right, forget her for the nonce. She's got to come about before her cannons can present any threat to us, and with our lateen sails we'll be quicker by spades. To your crews, gunners!"

Joseph stepped to the bows of *Congress* and collided with Captain James Arnold, hardly older than Joseph, who was gazing fixedly at the British vessels. "Have you any idea how to put this row gallie about?" Captain Arnold asked in a low, pleading voice. "Help me if you can, for all love. I've experience with square-riggers, but devil take these buggers with these slovenly settee rigs."

Joseph glanced upward at the short foremast, with its lateen yard angled at a precise forty-five degrees to the mast. The yard in its parrels depended from the starboard side of the foremast, and the foresail and mainsail were drawing handsomely, bellies taut to starboard. "I'm nowhere near the mariner my brother is, Captain, and now ain't no time to wonder if this be a settee rig, or some fashion of a crossjack yard." Joseph was quite certain that since the sails were triangular, without even the abbreviated fourth corner of a lopsided quadrilateral, the rig was the true lateen, though his knowledge of sails and their handling was woefully inadequate. "But sure as the good Lord made green apples in May, no way can we tack. General Arnold's in the right of it that we must wear ship. The science of trigonometry tells us that as soon as the helm moves so the wind comes directly over the stern the yard will tilt to the vertical, enabling us to swivel the yard to the other side of the mast. Then as soon as ever we can, we must move the shrouds to the weather side. We won't be sailing on a bowline, but we should fetch reasonably close to the bay before Valcouer Island with the sails set a-larboard."

Captain Arnold nodded soberly. "You and I'll have to handle the yard and throw the tack at the foot to larboard, then trim the leech and move the shrouds. Ain't nobody else can handle the sails, though sweeps will be what wins us to our anchorage."

"Ware ship, soon's the larboard . . . the left cannons fire!" Benedict Arnold shouted. Immediately the number one cannon, a 12-pounder, fired. The two 6-pounders that were guns number three and five fired within the second, and the bows were pointed directly at the *Maria* half a mile away. The stern was dead before the wind, and James Arnold and Joseph tailed onto the luff tackle as the lateen yard swung to the vertical. They wrestled the luff to the other side of the foremast and let go, running back to the foremast and repeating the maneuver for the main sail. The bows swung into the wind as James Arnold and Joseph tightened the starboard shrouds and slacked the larboard shrouds.

The bows pointed up into the wind, and the helmsman was about to over-correct too far to starboard; already the foremast lateen sail was beginning to shiver. Leaving James Arnold to tend the leech points, Joseph ran up the ladder to the small quarterdeck and seized the tiller from the confused helmsman. "Not quite so much helm to starboard . . . to the right," Joseph said tightly, realizing that the helmsman was as frightened and scared as he. "Here, we'll hold on this point of sail, with the leeches standing as firm as they are now." Joseph grinned at the helmsman, who gripped the tiller tightly to control the living thing it was. "We've only two miles until we're snug in Valcouer Harbour. Then we can laugh at the Royal Navy and the entire British Army!"

The two 18-pounders in the stern cabin beneath them crashed, startling them both, and Joseph looked southward quickly, seeing the round shot cut neat holes in *Maria*'s sails, though with no other damage that Joseph could discern. Men were running to the swivel guns on the *Congress'* quarterdeck, both sides, and Joseph saw that the bows of the row galley were coming up on the loose raft of large canoes. Several Indians stood up in their canoes, aiming muskets, their top weight causing the canoes to slew and heel. The nearest canoes were less than twenty yards away on either side of the row galley when the swivels began to bark, proper murthering pieces indeed. Canoes began to spill their contents of screaming, frightened Indians into the frigid waters of Lake Champlain.

"Reload! Reload those swivels! By God, and those cannons, too! Remember you're doing God's work!" Joseph heard Benedict Arnold shout. "Mind the *Washington!* Don't put any shot into her! And the *Trumbull's* just half a length behind her!" Joseph had never guessed that swivel guns could be reloaded so quickly, and he saw all manner of projectiles, nails, small stones, buttons, beef bones, loose musket balls, poured into the squat muzzles, and then the monkey-tails swung 'round to train on a particular canoe. The firing was hot, and it was accurate, and the rough-built *Congress* left a trail of carnage of destroyed canoes and corpses in her wake as, close-hauled as possible, she bore up toward the harbor between Valcour Island and the New York shore.

The swivel guns were firing incessantly, as were the cannons to larboard and starboard as well as the 18-pounders in the stern cabin, a deafening cacophony that had the helmsman on his knees, praying. Joseph gripped the tiller of the *Congress* row galley and kept her bows dead-on toward the crescent of gundalos tensely awaiting the galleys and *Royal Savage.*

"All right, near enough!" Benedict Arnold shouted, satisfaction evident in his voice. "Brail up sails! Get the canvas off her, and run out sweeps. Gunners, keep your men feeding their charges. The British ships will be standing in close ashore before we can draw breath."

Sweeps were out, two men to each, and the lateen yards came down with crashes, the canvas fisted frantically over the yards and tied off, then tripped vertical with the luff blocks to clear the decks. Joseph threw the helm hard over as *Congress* ran past the small buoy that marked its anchor. A boat hook dipped up the cable, spliced on, and *Congress* snubbed to her anchor.

"Spring lines! Carry out the spring lines through the stern

ports! No time for star-gazing. Make ready to turn us broadside-on! By God, we've kicked over the bee-hives most proper!" Arnold shouted to the crews of *Congress, Turnbull* and *Washington*. Joseph turned anxiously southward, searching for the *Royal Savage* schooner. She was standing half a mile due south of the anchorage, close-hauled on a starboard reach. Joseph remembered that *Royal Savage* had no sweeps. *Royal Savage* turned into the wind.

"I should have remained aboard her," Joseph heard Arnold murmur. "Before God, Hawley's no idea of judging the wind! I lie! Hawley's a right mariner. Mayhap he's trying to lure one of the British vessels onto the ledges just beneath the water on the southern side of this bay." Arnold took the ladder to the quarterdeck two steps at a time and stood beside an equally anxious Joseph. "No! No! Watch your wind!" Arnold momentarily hid his face in his hands. There was a tangle of ships standing into the bay; foremost among them, Joseph saw, was the large, implacable three-masted ship *Inflexible*. "All right, let's welcome them proper!" Arnold shouted, and the entire starboard broadside of *Congress* erupted into smoke and round ball. *Royal Savage* began a tack to starboard, but chain-shot from *Inflexible* beat upon the schooner, bringing down rigging and clearing the quarterdeck. Then one 12-pound ball tore into the mainmast, and the mast began to sway uncontrollably, causing the *Royal Savage* to lose way. A strong gust of wind from the north staggered the schooner and without anyone at her helm *Royal Savage* took the ledge at the southern tip of Valcour Island. Joseph saw both her masts pitch forward as the schooner settled onto her larboard side.

A moment later a ship's boat was somehow slid down the hull and men began to crowd into it. When the boat was full, men continued to clap onto the sides, so that the boat was almost submerged or over-tipped. "By God, I hope they make it!" Benedict Arnold rasped as he stood beside Joseph. "By God, I had Hawley pegged as a better sailor than he proved to be! By God, they are my men, but by God," he confided to Joseph, "I should have brought my books of account and day books aboard with me. I've enough problems with the Congress trying to sort out when such-'n'-such was done, and why such-'n'-such wasn't done, and why don't I have the papers to show when and why such-'n'-such was done, otherwise hang me for misprision of office. Next to tits on a boar hog, the Congress is the most useless appendage ever suspended from a body."

"Oh! The British have stove in Hawley's longboat!" Joseph cried. "Perfidy, thy name is Carleton."

"We was potting Indians and redcoats fast as we could reload bare thirty minutes past," Arnold reminded Joseph tightly. "Captain Arnold, men to the sweeps! The sweeps! Buoy the anchor and spring cables. We'll sweep out and engage, then dodge back into our crescent formation." The cables were quickly buoyed and *Congress,* her crew plying their sweeps in a most businesslike fashion, left the reinforcing protection of the defensive crescent and headed into the thickest of the coven of gunboats little more than one hundred yards away, pressing vigorously toward the American line.

"Make sure all starboard cannons are loaded, and swivels too, Mister Frost," Benedict Arnold ordered. "Captain Arnold, get all hands on the starboard sweeps to head her around to larboard, then get gun crews to the starboard cannons as soon as they bear proper and each gun captain chooses a particular gunboat to engage. We'll progress to larboard for two rounds per crew, then sweep about and exercise the larboard crews." Captain James Arnold strode up and down the gun deck and repeated Brigadier General Benedict Arnold's instructions in a hoarse, high-pitched voice sharpened by battle-lust.

"Gener'l, men in the water, men's from the *Royal Savage,*" Juby shouted from a position in the bows, and it was true, men tossed from the destroyed longboat Hawley had managed to launch were directly ahead and to the left of *Congress.* They were no longer attempting to swim to Valcour Island but were swimming toward *Congress.*

"More to larboard ..." Benedict Arnold caught himself: "Captain Arnold, please be so kind as to direct the men to trend more leftward. Let's get these souls aboard ever as fast as we can." Sweeps were thrust out toward the men struggling in the frigid water, and clinging one or two to the sweep they were hauled near enough to *Congress'* larboard side to be plucked aboard by men leaning and lunging desperately across the bulwarks that stood only three feet above the confused and turbid waters swirling to the south of Valcour Island. The first man Joseph fished out of the water was the Pequot Indian, Broadhead, who was a surprisingly poor swimmer and would have perished in another minute.

Broadhead found a small piece of charred cartridge flannel beneath a gun carriage and used it to wipe his mouth. He felt about his garments and smiling happily brought out his large silver snuffbox, which he extended to Joseph. Having no breath to spare, since he was busily engaged in pulling another man aboard by the nape of the man's jacket, Joseph shook his head quickly, tumbled the man aboard and reached for another desperately floundering arm.

"All right! We've fetched 'em all!" Benedict Arnold thundered. "Get 'em on their feet and on the sweeps. Nothing like tugging on a sweep to get sluggish blood a-pulsing!" A ball smashed into the starboard bow not a yard from where Juby sat, clutching the ancient musketoon that Joseph's uncle William Pepperrell had taken on the 1745 expedition to Louisbourg. Two feet of bulwark disappeared in a dense cloud of splinters and the carriage of the number three cannon was mangled into kindling. At least an 18-pounder, Joseph allowed, in his professional judgment, and more likely a 24-pounder from one of the gunboats. In a glance he took in the fact that half the gun crew of the number two cannon had been either killed, wounded or stupefied out of their wits by the destruction of the one cannon ball. But the number two cannon was unscathed.

Joseph pulled broken bodies and wounded, dazed and screaming men out of the recoil track of the cannon and sighted down the tube. The schooner *Maria* loomed up a quarter of a mile away. A grim-faced Benedict Arnold was beside him. "Help me with this quoin, Matross, and find some match," Arnold grunted as he wrestled with the elevating quoin. "Captain Arnold! One stroke more! Move us forward no more than one foot!" Joseph scavenged in the destruction wrought by the one opportune cannon ball and found a smoldering linstock. He blew the slow match into a white-hot ember, then extended the linstock to Arnold.

Arnold crouched to the left of the cannon, his tricorne twisted, his right cheek all a-sweat and streaked with a heavy smudge of burnt gunpowder grime, a wild predatory gleam in his eye. Arnold braced his back against the bulwark and pushed with his feet against the left side of the carriage to skew it with great labor one inch further to the right. Then he triumphantly stabbed the glowing slow match onto the touchhole and rolled out of the way of the cannon's recoil. Joseph followed the ball's arc with hungry, predatory anticipation, expecting the ball to strike *Maria* on her quarterdeck, or slightly below. To his dismay the ball passed over the quarterdeck. There was no time to dwell on the miss.

"Reload, let's reload! God's eyes, help me reload this cannon!" Arnold cursed. Juby scurried over with a flannel bag of powder, but first Joseph seized a sponge, thrust it overside to ensure it was properly wetted, then vigorously swabbed the cannon's tube. At Joseph's nod Juby thrust the bag into the muzzle and Joseph seated it home with a rammer, plucking a ball from the rack nearby and letting it roll down the tube, following the ball with a wad of tow tamped down fiercely.

"Tail on," Arnold grunted, and painfully aware there was no one to help them, Joseph and Juby pulled desperately on the tackle and blocks to run the cannon, ever so slowly and ever so grudgingly, up to its port. Joseph found the vent prick and the gun captain's powder horn. He pricked the cartridge bag and trickled a thimbleful of priming powder into the vent. "That three-master's our target," Arnold said grimly, pointing with his chin at a vessel slowly moving toward the *Congress* under topsails braced around as far as they would go. "She'll be the *Inflexible*. You're the matross! If it would not unduly discomfit you, move down the starboard side and keep the crews firing. If you find any spare men send them to me. Otherwise your man and I'll work this cannon!" Arnold pulled the quoin rearward beneath the cannon's breech, struck the cascabel with his fist to elevate the muzzle, twitched the starboard tackle to traverse the cannon slightly, then brought the smoldering linstock down on the touchhole. The priming powder hissed for half a second before the flame communicated to the main charge and the cannon bellowed most satisfyingly.

"Hit her right at the waterline, by God!" Arnold pumped his fist in satisfaction. Leaving Arnold and Juby to work the number two cannon, Joseph moved down the starboard side of the *Congress* to assist the frightened, numbed men of the gun crews to come to scratch and serve their charges. And serve their charges they did, with an increasing zeal and determination that went far in substituting for dexterity and long acquaintance with the iron beasts they husbanded. Joseph found himself shoulder-to-shoulder with the second captain of the number four cannon, a 12-pounder, moving up to the gun captain's position because his predecessor's decapitated body was being heaved overside. Two days earlier Joseph had devoted a morning to drilling the *Congress'* gun crews *en masse* and this particular fellow, a loose-limbed farmer at least twice Joseph's age, had impressed Joseph with his ineptitude. He had not been able to distinguish between a sponge and a rammer and had stood calmly by as a loader thrust the ball and its wad into the muzzle, then followed it with the flannel bag of powder as if that was the one true way God intended cannons to be loaded.

But though the man worked slowly in the din and smoke and confusion that was the confined gun deck of *Congress,* he worked with precision, shouting orders to the loader, the sponger, the assistant loader, orders they obeyed without question. Joseph helped the new gun captain run up the tail-rope through its blocks while the other men of the gun crew heaved on the side tackles. Without wasted motion the man pricked the powder bag and dribbled just enough priming powder from the gun captain's horn into the touchhole. He pulled Joseph out of the cannon's recoil path, made one final adjustment and fired the cannon.

Joseph had been too occupied assisting the gun crew of the number four cannon to think about the gun captain's target but saw now a British gunboat one hundred yards away attempting to work around the *Trumbull* galley. The 12-pounder ball struck the forty-foot-long gunboat's starboard bow, and a second later the gunboat was enveloped in a scud of sullen dirty-orange flame, shot through with the most garish streaks of red. The ball must have knocked some source of open fire into a barrel of gunpowder, igniting it. The gunboat disintegrated into individual, shattered planks that heaved upward from the lake's surface, and Joseph watched in horror as he recognized bodies and parts of bodies rising among the splintered planks. One tangled body that rose higher than the others was that of a slip of a boy still clutching a drum.

The crew of number four cannon raised a shrill, raucous cheer, but the gun captain, hollow eyes rimmed with powder residue, thin lips crumpled around the toothless cellar-hole of his mouth, swiftly recalled them to their duty. Joseph winced involuntarily as the next cannon sternward fired, but even over the ear-splitting snarl of sound he heard Arnold's triumphant cry: "She's turning! *Maria's* falling off! She's hauling her wind!"

"That was some prodigious shot, sir, a most propitious shot," Joseph Frost said with all sincerity, laying his hand with some hesitation upon the acting gun captain's perspiration- and gunpowder-grimed forearm. His mind's eye still retained the frightful image of the youth's body, like that of a doll thrown up in play, rising in the explosion above the shattered gunboat.

"Name's Drinkwine," the farmer said, smiling uneasily around his ruined mouth. "Ain't never had no drink o' wine, though. All we'uns in the Berwicks ever knew wus cyder 'n' rum from Jamaica." Drinkwine peered at Joseph through rheumy eyes washed pale by a dozen malignant diseases. "Would treat it uncommon kind could ye scare up a jug o' somethin' sharp to cut the taste o' this powder. Balls up in a man's mouth somethin' fearful."

"Devote yourself to the service of your piece," Joseph said.

"I'll return presently." He scuttled toward the one hatchway and its abbreviated three-step ladder that led to the lower deck, reflecting as he did so that the material distinctions between the row galley and the gundalo were the extra length of the main deck that afforded additional cannons; the stern cabin, no matter how cramped, against the restricted aft cuddy of the gundalo; and the enviable fact that the row galley's covered lower deck afforded the powder magazine the luxury of some modicum of greater protection than an open deck.

In the gloom, thankfully without artificial illumination of any sort that the farmers or fishers largely comprising Arnold's forces might improvidently have improvised, though the pounding of the cannons' firing overhead echoed shockingly, Joseph quickly located the puncheon of rum earlier hoisted aboard *Congress* through Arnold's largess. He started the bung with a horse knacker's maul and spilled the contents into a bucket with inward converging sides designed to hold slow match. Joseph's questing hands fell upon a pewter bowl set through its handle with a rawhide thong, and a second later he was on the gun deck just as the number four cannon fired again.

But Joseph went first to Arnold, kneeling by the number two cannon, and Juby, dipping up the rum in the bucket as he advanced. "Ain't cut that with no water, have you?" Arnold demanded suspiciously.

"Never in this life, General," Joseph protested.

"Good. Then first sip to your man. He's fair dropping, him and me running up this 12-pounder all ourselves. Thirsty work, as you doubtless ken." Arnold remarked ruefully: "You could have brought up a load of cartridge same time's you brought up the rum."

Joseph handed the pewter bowl first to Juby. "Here, Baba . . ."

Juby, the bowl almost to his lips, dashed the rum violently aside, the alcohol raining upon the deck. "Master Joseph! Nobody but the Tai-Pan permitted to call me *Baba*. Not Master Marlborough, not you! Believe on it!" Juby glared malignantly at Joseph.

"Your pardon I beg, Juby," Joseph said miserably. "I intended the name only as a measure of my deepest respect."

"Well, okay, then," Juby said grudgingly. "But give the bucket first to General Arnold; he's a mite peaked."

Arnold held up the pewter bowl and rose laboriously to his feet. On the gun deck of *Congress* Joseph alone among the crew knew what that effort, a battle against the pain of wound and of gout, cost. Arnold staggered aft, holding aloft the bowl. "Men of the *Congress!* Congressmen!" Arnold snickered. "What fighters you are! Catamounts for sure! But should we living imbibe a-fore those who have died so nobly on this deck?" Arnold continued to hold aloft the bowl: "No! Though I pronounce, you must answer! The first libation for us living, or the first libation in memory of those who have within the last minutes given their lives for their new country? Speak quickly! This bowl grows heavy!"

"Tribute first the dead, Gener'l!" someone toward the stern shouted. Another man shouted the words, and then everyone on the gun deck of *Congress* was shouting the words: "Tribute first the dead, Gener'l!" A cannon ball thudded into the hull at the waterline, and Captain James Arnold darted to the hatchway and disappeared below to inspect for damage. Benedict Arnold stepped to the bulwark and amidst an eddy of powder smoke solemnly and slowly poured the bowl of rum into the lake. Then he dipped the bowl into the bucket and gave the bowl to Juby.

Juby took one swallow. "'Nuff for me, Mister Arnold. I ain't never had no head for strong drink," he said, handing back the bowl. "I'd appreciate the loan o' the bucket once it be emptied so's to dip up some water."

Arnold walked down the starboard deck, pausing at every cannon and passing around the bowl without any sense of urgency. The number two cannon was taut in its breeching tackle, so Joseph seized a sponge and set to swabbing the bore. Juby thrust in the flannel bag of powder and a wad, and Joseph fiercely rammed the charge home, withdrew the rammer to let Juby tip a ball into the muzzle, then seated the ball atop the over-powder wad. They worked inside a cocoon of the constant rattling crash and thunder of cannons around them. "Ain't a hull lot o' wrapped powder in that case, Master Joseph," Juby said, his breathing labored as they each wearily took up a side tackle. "Appears it's bein' shot off pert smart."

Joseph knew to the cartridge bag how much gunpowder Arnold had been able to scrap together for the fleet, and yes, powder was being shot off at a fearful rate. But Joseph was of the opinion that the individual vessels of the fleet would fire away their shot, ball and grape, before their powder was exhausted. He suddenly realized just how critically important iron works such as those at Saugus were to the prosecution of war. Arnold was beside them again, though he leaned far out over the bulwark and dipped up a bucket of water before hauling on the tail tackle. He made two careful adjustments to the lay of the piece before motioning Joseph out of the line of recoil. Juby was drinking noisily and gratefully from the bucket as the cannon grumbled.

"God's eyes!" Arnold bellowed. "The captain of *Carleton* got balls of brass!"

Joseph impatiently fanned at a skein of powder smoke dispersing slowly in the chill air. Now the schooner was working its way ever so slowly on a close reaching tack with the wind from starboard toward the crescent of American vessels. He realized just how clever Arnold had been to bait the British into this narrow bay, with its shallow water abounding in ledges just beneath the surface, such as the ledge that had already claimed *Royal Savage*. Only one vessel at a time could approach Arnold's vessels, arrayed in their protective half-moon line.

"He's going to maneuver himself into a hot corner," Arnold bellowed. "Once he's come to bisket-toss he's going to anchor and put out a spring to train a broadside on us." As Arnold spoke an anchor was let go from *Carleton*'s stern and the British schooner yawed to starboard as her helm was put up. "We've got her, by God!" Arnold pounded both fists on the bulwark in momentary excitement, then ran along the starboard cannons. "Aim, aim right at her forefoot and bows! Don't let her get a bow anchor overside!"

But the *Carleton* did get a bow anchor overside, arresting her slight forward motion and pivoting her around her bows so her stern came on slowly. Two dozen cannons from *Congress, Trumbull, Lee, Revenge* and *Washington* simultaneously belched their shot toward *Carleton*. Three balls blew out great gouts of wood from the larboard bow, the swaths of splintered wood showing strangely yellowish-white against the pumpkin-colored paint of the hull. A fourth ball snipped the anchor cable. The remainder of the shot thumped into the hull or smashed bulwarks into kindling. *Carleton* heeled visibly.

"Sweeps! Out sweeps!" Arnold shouted. "Men to the sweeps! We're taking the fight to the *Carleton*." To Joseph: "Take whatever men you need and get up the anchor. It's the only one those clodpates in the Continental Congress thought a ship would need, God damn their lights! We daren't buoy it, so we must take it with us!"

Joseph, Juby and a slightly wounded man from Drinkwine's gun crew won the anchor with the small capstern and fished it aboard—overpowered it, rather, raising it by their combined strength. The wounded man returned to his gun crew while Joseph and Juby ran to the swivels at Arnold's command. "Indians! Seeking to board!" A concatenation of shrieking, ululating Indians in a dozen or more large canoes suddenly appeared through rents in the bitter drifts of powder smoke. The Indians were plying their paddles on both sides of the canoes, really bending their arms and shoulders into the task. Their strokes, extraordinarily powerful, were propelling their crafts so swiftly in waters now shielded from the wind by Valcour Island that the waves thrown up by the canoes' bows were taller than the bows themselves.

An Indian in the closest *canot de maître* threw up his musket and aimed in the general direction of the *Congress*. Joseph seized Juby by the shoulders and bore him to the deck, plainly hearing the sibilant hiss of the bullet as it passed overhead. "Now that done whipped up my horse," Juby said grimly, gathering his feet beneath him to run to the nearest swivel, one mounted on the starboard bulwark of the quarterdeck. Juby caught up a linstock as he ran, seized the swivel by its monkey-tail, pivoting the swivel until it bore full on the nearest canoe, and touched the smoldering match to the touchhole. Amidst cries of great agony and the writhing of bodies the canoe overturned. Juby ran to the next swivel and trained it on the canoe now in the lead. The linstock came down, the swivel bucked and the spread of langrage and gunner's dice swept the length of the canoe, riddling its bark in half a hundred places with small, jagged holes and inflicting similar injuries to the Indians screaming toward the *Congress.*

Joseph caught up the musketoon Juby had fetched all the long way from Portsmouth to protect himself, opened the frizzen to ensure priming powder was in the pan, eared back the cock, brought the musketoon to his right shoulder, and fired at the canoe that was attempting to slide under the counter. "Marine marksmen to the quarterdeck!" Arnold shouted through the megaphone of his cupped hands.

Bare feet and boots slapped and thumped up the short ladder from the gun deck to the quarterdeck. Marksmen crowded to the taffrail, pushing aside the screens of spruce trees, and fired their muskets in a rippling fusillade. Joseph, frantically reloading the musketoon, saw the marksmen who were barefoot and was ashamed that he owned the shoes in which he stood. Juby reached out to take the musketoon from him. "Don't let this little gun take up with you, Master Joseph," Juby laughed. "I borrowed her, if you remember, 'n' gots to return it to where I borrowed it." Juby laughed again in great delight. "Throws a mean charge, don't she? Best you tend these swivels, 'n' let me feed this 'un."

Joseph found the bucket with the small sausages of powder for the swivels, all of a caliber, and the other bucket of gunner's dice—odd swan shot, discarded, rusted bolts, bent and cut up hinges, nubbings of horseshoe nails, and small stones. He reloaded one swivel, gave it over to Juby, and moved to the next swivel. The marine marksmen were keeping up a hot fire and the Indians were retreating, though Joseph counted only six canoes paddling fiercely away. Through the skeins of amorphous smoke Joseph saw a horde of canoes and bateaux, massing at the point of Valcour Island, take the shore, and Indians and infantry in red coats leap from canoes and bateaux and splash ashore through the waist-deep water.

Joseph turned his attention to *Carleton,* showing much the worst from her intense battering, listing heavily, her mainmast shot away below the gaff and larboard stays completely cut so the mast teetered unsteadily. The small flying topsail on the foremast had been knocked askew, blanketing the schooner sail. There was no human movement on the *Carleton.* "Backs into it, you men! Backs into it! We shall close and board her! We have her for sure!" Arnold calmly laid the number two cannon on a bateau rowing desperately toward the relative safety behind *Carleton*'s bulk. The ball struck the bateau amidships and the bateau sundered apart, spilling red-coated infantrymen into the water wholesale. The bare dozen men at *Congress'* sweeps were pulling for all they were worth but having a hard time of it, so few their number, and *Congress* was yet seventy-five yards from *Carleton.*

A head staysail ran up *Carleton*'s fore stay, but no sooner was it sheeted home than several balls pierced it. The wind had veered slightly and with *Carleton* now dead into the wind the sail refused to draw. A British officer in a blue tunic and white breeches jumped onto the bowsprit and inched his way with silent determination toward the fore stay. He reached the head staysail and kicked the stay and foot around to starboard, but the staysail still refused to draw. The officer stood exposed to every cannon, every swivel, every musket in the forefront of Arnold's fleet. The officer began to work his way back along the bowsprit to the relative safety of the schooner.

Arnold struck up the muskets of the marine marksmen standing on either side of him to spoil their aim. "Let him go," Arnold shouted loudly enough to be heard above the unattenuated hubbub. "He displayed uncommon courage, and if he lives long enough he'll be an admiral." Carleton's bows slowly began to turn eastward. "God's eyes!" Arnold cursed. "She's gotten a tow! Pour everything into her!" The matrosses aboard

Congress and every other ship in the forefront of the crescent of vessels that could bring their cannons to bear labored feverishly to throw as much weight of metal at *Carleton* as they could muster from pieces so hot that many of them were on the point of bursting.

Then *Carleton* was stern-on, and beyond her Joseph could see *Inflexible* slowly beating up as high as she could point in a series of close reaches. "Pity we could not sink *Carleton,*" Arnold said, tight-lipped, to Joseph and Captain James Arnold. "Her bulk settled in the channel would prevent the flagship with her fresh crew and eighteen 12-pounders from drawing close enough to cannonade us with any accuracy." Arnold gestured toward the bulk of Valcour Island, now growing dark in the late afternoon. "Indians and redcoats are ashore on the isle and potting at men in our vessels closest to that shore, but their accuracy ain't in it."

A cannon ball falling nearby threw up a tall geyser without a skip, and Arnold winced. "Seems the German artillery in their gunboats have gotten our range for plunging fire at least. It is time we quite this place. Captain Arnold, I'd be obliged if your crew could sweep us sternward toward our customary anchorage in the bay between Valcouer Island and the New York shore. I conceit the matrosses aboard *Inflexible* are anxious exceedingly to wound us between wind and water as consolation for the damages we dealt out to the *Carleton.* Would we had sunk her! But no matter how intense the fusillade from *Inflexible,* we have far more to fear from the plunging fire of the German artillery." Arnold's glance traveled soberly around the shattered gun deck of *Congress.* "Captain Arnold, quietly, quietly, mind, slip the dead overboard while the men who live are preoccupied with mending their cannon, or pulling on a sweep. It goes sad for me to treat men who died so gallantly thusly, but there is every presumption that the living, once their great exertions temporarily cease, shall find themselves unnerved upon seeing their late companions so lifelessly sprawled about."

❧ XIX ☙

❀❀❀❀❀ EOFFREY WAS AWED BY THE SUPERB
❀   ❀ PERFORMANCE WICK NICHOLS WAS
❀   G   ❀ PUTTING ON TO CONCEAL HIS UNEASE,
❀❀❀❀❀ FOR THE CAPTAIN OF THE *Bride of Derry*
did not lower his gaze from the accusatory eyes of King Tegbesu. "Mister Privy Council," Nichols said, speaking in a low
voice and out the side of his mouth, "you know it for a God-
damned truth that I never said I possessed within my barky the
wherewithal to construct a gunpowder manufactory. I opined
merely that a gunpowder manufactory could possibly, possibly,
mind, be a consideration in a future venture."

"God's oath, did you really say that?" Privy Council Lyons
Bennett said incredulously, in an equally low voice. "Strike me
down dead in the same wise Walt Ralegh had his head lopped off
by James One if I recollected inaccurately. But I was so fixated
on the thought of new trowsers, weskit, frock coat, shirt of silk
or cambric, I care not which, that your sailmaker shall rig for me
once your barky's main course has been made whole—oh! The
utter joy of contemplating the dress of a Christian once again!
If I was so overcome with the prospect of proper garments to
supplement my meager wardrobe that I heard not aright . . ."

Lyons Bennett disdainfully flicked a piece of filthy canvas
that failed by substantial measure to circumscribe his ample
girth and made a helpless moue. "Should that prove the case I
shall be most totally cast away." Bennett turned guileless eyes at
Nichols. "But in all events I did directly relate to King Tegbesu

the fact that you possessed the wherewithal to establish a man-ufactory to mill powder for His Supreme Majesty, and it would seem that it is the establishment of such he anticipates." Bennett leaned forward, his eyes hooded, to whisper into the right ear of Tegbesu, Absolute Master of all the environs of Danhomé, and as far around else as his retainers could subdue by force of their firelocks, swords, and lances.

Geoffrey stared forthrightly at Tegbesu, fascinated by the man who sat with supreme confidence on the throne of ivory on a dais in a tall alcove made from reeds cunningly woven together and thatched over—while his retinue, to include Lyons Bennett, and of course Wick Nichols and Geoffrey Frost, squat-ted on their heels in a semi-circle without, having absolutely no shade to shield them from the remorseless sun striking the vast arena of beaten ground inside the barracoon. Tegbesu was far more corpulent that Lyons Bennett, and shimmering folds of fat loped in diminishing terraces over his grotesque belly. Teg-besu had been drinking steadily, his goblet replenished when-ever it was held out to one of the urchins who stood respect-fully to one side, attending the king's slightest gesture, from a demijohn of some liquor. But he was very far from being drunk, and as he regarded Tegbesu's alert, intelligent, cunning and cruel gaze and the absolute self-satisfaction with which he looked out onto the world he dominated, Geoffrey Frost knew that he looked upon a brutal malevolency far, far greater than the evil contained within Wick Nichols.

"Then I must beg you to correct the erroneous impres-sion you have inadvertently cultivated in the royal mind, Privy Council," Nichols said, still in a low voice but with an edge of exasperation, "and then we must get to the substance of our negotiations. I must see your king's stock before I am ready to begin any bargaining other than the gifts already made."

"First the matter of your inability to establish a gunpowder manufactory as originally represented to King Tegbesu . . ."

"That misrepresentation, for such it is, and if in fact it was made, was an error on your part, dear Council, which you are obliged in all honour to correct upon the moment."

"Captain Nichols, I assure you that once King Tegbesu has an idea firmly fixed in his mind it becomes a truth that can neither be evaded nor withdrawn," Bennett said unctuously. "And as for those wretchedly poor baubles you brought ashore, King Tegbesu did not deign so much as touch a cowrie but contemptuously consigned the entire truck to his immediate Amazonian guard. And, as you doubtlessly are aware, having dealt with King Tegbesu three years prior, the king does not display his stock but names the prices you must pay for young men of stamina between the ages of fifteen and twenty-five. Then he names the prices for the young women between the ages of fifteen and twenty-five. Then he names the prices for the children between the ages of five and ten years, divided democratically and evenly between the sexes. Of course, any woman with a babe still at breast requires no further payment for the child, such is the long-standing rule on this coast."

"Mister Privy Council, please to make our good-byes to your king. The terms you banter are surely made in jest, but since I cannot countenance them—as against all customs of negotiation for a willing seller and a willing buyer to conclude a mutually agreeable transaction. No, that was not the way of business when I was at Abomey, so I must bid your king and master farewell and search out more salubrious factories." Wick Nichols made as if to rise.

Bennett laid a cautionary hand on Nichols' knee. "Sir, I solicit most sincerely: to shun the royal presence will be taken as a notion of the greatest disrespect to His Majesty, the consequences of which shall be an immediate *auto-da-fé* involving yourself and your supernumerary." Bennett smiled sympathetically. "The *autos-da-fé* for King Tegbesu's amusement are performed by his Amazon guards. Under their practiced hands death does not come until King Tegbesu becomes bored by the spectacle and signals the end of the amusement."

"By my soul," Wick Nichols said calmly, though Geoffrey could see the perspiration burst upon Nichols' forehead, which was thankfully shaded by his round Quaker hat. "You won't be in Hell one hour before you'll be teaching the Devil new tricks.

Had I the slightest clew that a suit of clothes meant so much to you, I would have had Sails tailor you directly."

"Was you as shrewd a trader as you lay claim to be, Captain Nichols, you would have twigged my distress much sooner," Bennett said bitterly. "You have no idea what a proper suit of clothes does to set a white man apart from these heathen. I am indispensable to King Tegbesu, but even though I be his slave he looks up to me when I'm got up to look like the merchant I am."

"I am right glad to hear it," Nichols fairly hissed, "but at present we are in great need of extraction from the quandary you have created by falsely . . ." Nichols drew out the word deliberately, and repeated it, "falsely and knowingly implying that I am immediately disposed to erect a gunpowder works."

"Oh, as for that," Bennett said with a shrug, "a word from me and your assurance that you'll deliver up all the gunpowder aboard your vessel"—the Privy Council quickly held up a hand to forestall any exclamation from Nichols—"Holding back only the barest amount sufficient to secure your safe passage, and a promise to return next year with all the appliances necessary to formulate gunpowder in the Dan-Home will satisfy the king."

"I can agree to that right enough," Nichols said, his yellow teeth showing in what for him passed as a smile. "I have fifteen barrels of finest French-corned gunpowder aboard the *Bride*. I can abide with but one barrel on the voyage home, enough to keep my swivel guns charged to command the deck when the cargo be allowed up for exercise and nourishment." He exposed even more yellow teeth as he leaned closer to Bennett. "I can have Sails cut out your frock coat as soon as the boy and I are returned aboard the *Bride,* and you shall wear it at our next audience with your master, at which time we shall negotiate a fair price for cargo. Not foregoing the fact, mark, that I shall pay only for that cargo as my surgeon shall select for being the fittest."

"Oh, that is a thing beyond reach, Captain Nichols. King Tegbesu is of no mind to bargain with himself. He has set his price for men, women and children. And you must take all he appoints."

"That was not the way it was in Abomey three years ago," Nichols said, his face close against that of Bennett's. From where he sat Geoffrey Frost could smell the foul breaths of both men.

"No, I don't imagine it was," Bennett replied, shaking his head slowly, "but three years ago King Tegbesu had a raconteur who entertained him much with stories. But the raconteur was taken off by a fever this year past, and the king has been fair inconsolable. Now, could you but present King Tegbesu with a person able to entertain him through the recitation of stories, you might conceivably change the tenor of the king's mind to commercial interests."

"Oh?" Wick Nichols said pleasantly enough, turning so that his eyes fell in measured speculation on Geoffrey. "Why, as for that, you can promise your master this moment entertainment from a fluent and authentic teller of stories, sure."

❧ X X ❧

he magazine of Royal Savage *went off with a resonating concussion. The sound pealed and slapped louder than the most intense thunder Joseph Frost, huddled in profound fatigue in the stern cabin of* Congress, had ever heard. Then the whoops and ululations of the Indians ashore on Valcour Island penetrated the void of shocking silence that followed the deafening explosion. His eyes darted to her erstwhile commander, David Hawley, seated on the cabin sole and slumped dejectedly against one of the stern cannon. Hawley did not glance up but sipped morosely from a canteen of rum.

"The state of your stores, if you please, Captain Simons," Benedict Arnold inquired of the schooner *Revenge's* commander.

Simons scratched thoughtfully at the heavy stubble of beard on his left cheek, then quietly ticked off numbers on his fingers. "I have solid shot enough for three broadsides from either larboard or starboard cannons, 4-pounders all. No grape shot at all, but enough powder to account three charges to the ten swivels aboard."

"Your stores, please, Captain Warner," Arnold asked of *Trumbull's* commander. Warner did not require the use of his fingers to enumerate his stores. "Reckonin' only powder, my *Trumbull* has less than one quarter of the quantity provided—though the rest was shot away to good effect."

The intense reddish-orange light thrown out by the burning

hull of *Royal Savage* flickered garishly beyond the open stern windows, their larded paper windows long ago blown out. "And you, Captain Dixson, how stands *Enterprise?*" Arnold soberly canvassed each of his surviving commanders individually and waited until Grimes of the *Jersey,* the last interrogated, had replied. "I see," Arnold said soberly. "We have fended off the British this entire day—indeed, more than keeping the British at bay, we have wiped their eyes!"

Arnold's gaze traveled clockwise around the small cabin, starting with Joseph, then staring directly at every man in turn. "We have wiped their eyes for sure, but at the cost of seventy men known dead, another ten missing, perhaps fifteen taken prisoner . . ." Hawley winced as that number fell from Arnold's lips—all the prisoners were men from *Royal Savage* taken by Indians and British infantry on Valcour Island. "And we have no more than one-fifth of the munitions so grudgingly allotted us by the Continental Congress sitting in Philadelphia." Arnold's gaze stopped with Simons and returned anti-clockwise until his gaze paused affectionately upon Captain Benjamin Rue. "Speaking of *Philadelphia,* that proud gundalo has been sunk, though she and her crew gave exceedingly good account of themselves, as Captain Rue will warrant." Arnold paused and stared at his dirty, scarred and chapped hands as if he had never seen them before. "Would that we still counted the gallant Captain Davis of the *Lee* cutter among our number.

"Gentlemen, if the British were not so arrogant in their assumptions of our fighting qualities, they would even now be at work among us, ferreting us out in the dark from silent canoes and bateaux with oars well wrapped in greased rags." Arnold raised a canteen of rum to his lips and took a long, tired pull. "Instead, they wait in their ships without the bay, enjoying full rations, while their infantry and their German auxiliaries enjoy their rations ashore, entertained, doubtlessly, by the spectacle and sound of their Indian allies' war dances." Arnold handed the canteen to Joseph, who pretended to take a sip, then quickly passed the canteen to Brigadier General Waterbury.

"Frankly, gentlemen, I had expected the Indians to find the

back door into this anchorage afore now, but happily they are celebrating what they doubtlessly conceit their victory over our forces on the morrow—when the British Navy will renew the attack up the cove." Arnold abruptly addressed Grimes of the *Jersey*. "Captain Grimes, does your tooth foretell tomorrow's weather?"

"Aye," Grimes said, clutching the canteen that Waterbury had just handed him. "A mumpin' cold day it'll be, 'n' a gumption of fog and low mist settlin' in now. Not likely to lift until an hour or so after mornin-rise." Grimes looked longingly at Grant of the *Connecticut* gundalo, who was slowly shaving slivers of dark, rum-soaked tobacco from a short twist into the bowl of a clay pipe with a broken stem. "Say, ain't got any of that 'bacca to spare, has ye, Grant? I swallowed my cud in the excitement of one of 'em German shots lobbed in from on high piercin' complete through the bottom of *Jersey*. Keepin' a cud against the rotten tooth numbs the pain wondrous, it does."

Captain Grant carefully sliced the twist of tobacco exactly in half and handed one piece to Grimes, who seized it eagerly, then asked for the borrow of Grant's knife to cut a proper cud.

Joseph glanced out the crude stern windows. Fog was indeed forming, for the light thrown off by the flames from the still angrily burning *Royal Savage* was greatly attenuated.

"I believe the same," Arnold said, slapping his knee for emphasis, the same gesture Joseph had noted when he first met Arnold at Crown Point. "And under cloak of this protecting fog we shall hie away ever so quietly to preserve our forces for the even harder fighting ahead."

"General Arnold . . . General Arnold . . ." Waterbury spoke haltingly, his voice quavering, one hand behind him to brace his back. Joseph understood that Brigadier Waterbury had been thrown down and injured by the same ball that had burst through a bulwark on *Washington* and given Captain Thatcher his grievous wound, from which he died. "General Arnold, we have fought much harder than anyone in the United Colonies has a right to expect of us. But our munitions are almost expended, our forces decimated. On the morrow honour will satisfy if we defend ourselves briskly so long as powder serves, then upon the expenditure of our munitions raise a parley flag and send a boat to Carleton to ask for terms."

Joseph looked away from General Waterbury in great embarrassment, and he saw all of the other captains except Grimes, busily packing his jaw with tobacco, do the same. Waterbury continued: "General Arnold, we have all fought courageously this day, sure. The British will honour us for that. It is exceedingly hard for me to recommend such a course, as you'll readily concede, but I cannot bear to surrender the life of yet another of our men when the cause is so hopelessly lost." Waterbury eagerly searched the faces of the captains gathered in the small, close cabin for agreement. Nothing he saw in their faces gave him the least encouragement.

"Thank you, General Waterbury," Arnold said gravely. "Your counsel is always well taken, but upon this footing I confess less than forthright belief that our enemies will acquiesce to benevolence. We have hurt their pride mightily, and indulge me, I conceit terms, though doubtlessly generous, would come only to those few spared the knives and hatchets of their Indian allies, even now demanding our blood."

By the uncomfortable stirring the captains made as they shifted in their places Joseph knew they all conceded it most unlikely that Carleton, or any Britisher for that matter, could exercise even a modicum of control over their Indian allies, thirsting to avenge the deaths heavily inflicted upon their tribes by the combined arms of Arnold's fleet. Joseph recalled vividly the destruction he and Juby had meted out through the tubes of the swivel guns. Waterbury must have realized it, too, for he sighed, "My advice was given with the good of our men who served with such fortitude today constantly in mind. Of course, if we can get clean away—*if* we can get clean away," Waterbury laid heavy emphasis on the *if*, "then our army is preserved to the rejoicing of us all."

"We are settled then!" Arnold said, leaning forward in his chair, all fatigue gone, gray eyes snapping in the light of the two poor phoebe lamps, whose feeble glow did not reach even to all of the small cabin's corners. "The British are regaling themselves, patching their ships, licking their wounds, confident we shall be gathered quickly like so much low-hanging fruit on the morrow. Not even one boat rowing guard across the bay. No attempt to come at us from the back, no attacks launched to keep us awake and in constant fatigue. Our order of departure shall be . . ." Arnold paused to turn and rummage in the carpenter's satchel that had earlier yielded a piece of chalk. He turned the satchel upside down and eagerly seized the large lumps of chalk that tumbled upon the cabin sole. "Volunteer Frost! Do you and your man still have access to that small canoe that fetched you so swiftly between our ships as you sought to train matrosses?"

Joseph had been admiring the skillful way in which Arnold brought his fleet captains around to his way of thinking. It was as masterful a display of the ability to command others as his brother, Geoffrey, had displayed during his private revolution to free American prisoners of war from the gaol at Louisbourg. Something that Geoffrey had once said came unbidden to mind: "The proper governing of a ship, if she is to be kept clear of the breakers, is never an exercise in democracy."

"I beg pardon, General Arnold," Joseph said hastily, bringing himself to the present. "I was thinking on my brother. So far as I am aware the small canoe still swims."

"Good," Arnold said, handing the lumps of chalk to Joseph, then dusting his fingers. "I charge you and your man . . ."

"Your pardon, General," Joseph interposed quietly, "but he ain't my man, he is his own man, and his name is Juby."

"I charge you and Juby," Arnold continued unperturbed, "to paddle with the utmost quietude to every vessel in this fleet. To the stern of every vessel, where you will inscribe a broad band using this chalk. You will inscribe it in a place, one foot below the taff rails for the row gallies, and to the larboard side of the rudderposts on the gundalos." Arnold turned to his commanders. "Captains, among your equipage each of you must have a horn lantern. If any vessel is deficient in this article, please acquaint me with the deficiency and I shall find some means to remedy the lack."

Arnold's full lips turned up in a beatific smile. "One hour from now, gentlemen—I regret my only timepiece is this abominable turnip that had more than one good dash upon the decks today, though fortunately no wetting . . ." and Arnold pulled a very large silver watch from his waistcoat and shook it ruefully. "One hour from now, gentlemen, we shall unmoor without sound, not even the slightest drip of water from fluke to mark our departure as the anchor be won. Captain Warner, you command the smallest gallie, but to you is given the most earnest rôle. I wish your gallie to sweep silently as possible from this anchorage, through the present cloying fog—long may it last—steering close as ever possible to the New York shore. You shall lead us through the British fleet and thence onto the broad Lake, whence we shall make all possible speed to Tyonderoga. We shall gather beneath the battlements of Mount Independence, and mauled as they have been, I misdoubt the British shall wish to contest the Lake's passage this autumn."

Arnold cocked his head and listened attentively for a moment to the ululations of the Indians on Valcour Island. "I fancy few British infantry will get much sleep tonight, given that infernal caterwauling. All the better for us." He turned his triumphant gaze upon each captain in turn. "Captain Hawley, you have through inadvertence lost our *Royal Savage,* and the row gallie *Washington* has sadly suffered the loss of Captain Thatcher. I wish you to remove to *Washington,* General Waterbury still aboard as my second-in-command should any mishap befall me."

Hawley lifted his head in disbelief, and Joseph wondered that Arnold—who had to know that Hawley's poor seamanship had hazarded *Royal Savage* to her grave—would yet entrust another vessel of his small fleet to the man. "I accept with gratitude, General Arnold, but I am reliably informed there are no matrosses remaining aboard *Washington* to point her cannons."

Arnold fixed Joseph with a stern eye. "And will you repair aboard *Washington* to point cannons for Captain Hawley?"

Joseph swallowed hard. He did not like Hawley at all, did not trust the man, in fact. But where would he and Juby be the most useful in the fighting retreat to Crown Point and Ticonderoga? "As soon as Juby and I have marked the sterns of all our vessels with signs that even the blind can discern, General, we shall go aboard *Washington* and serve Captain Hawley as we have served you this day."

"Elegant! Simply elegant!" Arnold said, smiting both thighs in delight with a sound very much like that of thunder. "Get you overside with your chalks and delineate our vision. Signal me when your messages have been writ large on the sterns of our vessels! Now captains! Order your crews that silence must rule! Keep your wounded quiet, mind. Gag them if need be. Reliable men as lookouts in your bows, and give them any sweeps you can spare if you must fend off from ledges. And if you must fend off, do so without a word, even if a rock scrapes all the way through to your guts! Your smallest, most agile men as runners, to carry word from the lookouts meriting course corrections. Attend most closely to the shielded light seen only at the stern of the vessel in line ahead! Alter course exactly where the vessel in line ahead alters course, and not a second nor a fathom before!

"Captain Grimes! Sir, a salute to you and your tooth, that regardless of its ache has foretold the state of weather that shall allow us to slip away quietly, ever so quietly from our guardians! We must all look to the simplicity of our orders, for ambiguity leads to miscalculations. And for all that, we shall foregather below Crown Point."

XXI

EOFFREY FROST SAT ON THE VERY LOW WOODEN STOOL, KNEES DRAWN UP AL- G MOST INTO HIS FACE, HIS RIGHT HAND CUPPING THE ELECTRIC HURT OF HIS left elbow where Wick Nichols had bent the young bones so unmercifully and cruelly to emphasize the prospects of obtaining a cargo in Quidah might well turn on his prowess as a story-teller. He grasped and kneaded his elbow with stiff fingers in a vain attempt to alleviate the pain. He continued to gaze directly at the broad, unblinking face of King Tegbesu, though his gaze from time to time wandered down to the king's incredibly small and delicate hands, folded primly over the man's gigantic belly.

"And *Jehanne la Pucelle,* or simply the *maid* or *Joan the maid* when translated literally from the French language, Mister King, was never taught to write or read her native language. Nor do cyphers, being that she was a woman, and women of her times were not considered the equal of men, though there's pity in it, if you but cogitate on the matter for even a moment. The maid was the youngest of five children, and she was trained in the gentle, womanly arts of spinning, weaving and sewing." Geoffrey spoke slowly but as loudly as his lisping, youthful voice would permit, so that Lyons Bennett could translate his words accurately—Geoffrey devoutly hoped that Bennett was trans-lating his words accurately. Geoffrey was acutely aware that the two dwarfs, the yellowed skulls of long-dead monkeys stuck atop their scepters, their bodies as soot-stained and squat as the three-legged kettles standing in the ashes and coals of a nearby fire, who crouched menacingly on either side of King Tegbesu were balefully willing him dead upon the moment. Tegbesu leaned forward and whispered into Bennett's private ear. "His Majesty is anxious to ascertain what is meant by the terms spinning, weaving and sewing?" Bennett said after a moment.

Geoffrey Frost elaborated sufficient for Bennett to advise the king suitably. "Amazing, His Majesty confides, young man," Bennett said, sniffing. "His Majesty is acquainted with the terms, but such procedures are performed by slaves."

"The maid had not yet attained the age of fourteen when she began to hear voices, or as I believe should be termed 'counsel' . . ."

"His Majesty wishes to know the social condition of this woman you call 'the maid,'" Bennett said imperiously. "Exactly what was her station? And if you will indulge me, elaborate upon whatever 'council' she was receiving."

"Gladly, Your Honour," Geoffrey said patiently, not daring to glance to his right, where fifty feet away in brilliant sunlight Wick Nichols, as a sign of the king's complete indifference and exclusion, sat directly in the deep dust of the arena, no stool for him and preserved from the sun only by his heavy felt Quaker's hat. "If the malevolent dwarfs were to carve me into giblets at their master's nod, would Nichols at the least intervene to lash their flesh with his cudgel before the first knife would strike my breast?" Geoffrey asked himself philosophically. He continued aloud, "*La Pucelle* was a peasant lass, unlettered, 'tis true, but selected for her piety to receive the extreme honour of communications from the saints . . . which Your Honour may ascribe as *counsel* from supernatural aspects."

There was a pause while Bennett whispered hurriedly in Tegbesu's ear and received comments from Tegbesu in turn. "King Tegbesu inquires into the character of these voices."

"Certainly, sir. Though *La Pucelle* was reluctant to identify them directly, it was evident to those with whom *La Pucelle* shared her revelations that she was in direct communication with Saints Catherine and Margaret, and Saint Michael."

Another hurried exchange of whispers. "And these voices were accompanied by *apparitions* of the angelic beings described?"

Geoffrey shook his head slowly. "Please advise His Majesty that the chronicles are silent on that aspect, Your Honour. No one then or now can attest what it was exactly *La Pucelle* saw or heard. But she doubtless received communications that informed her the country of her birth was distressed by powerful enemies, but whether it was voices or apparitions, or both, I am unprepared to say, being that I was not a presence there."

Geoffrey spared a glance at the two dwarfs attending the king, and his soul shrank. He could feel them both gnawing heartily at his liver.

Tegbesu leaned forward attentively—and smiled, a queer smile awash with malice, but an inquisitive smile nevertheless. He spoke a few words directly to Geoffrey. Bennett translated immediately. "His Majesty asks if the voices the maid heard were the utterances of a god."

"Yes, Your Honour," Geoffrey said simply. "The voices were doubtless the utterances of the one God, though this one God is known by divers names to divers people."

"Go on!" Bennett prodded. "This maid of yours went off to do battle with the occupiers of her country, is that your tale?"

"Yes, sir," Geoffrey said.

"And where was this maid's country, and who were the despoilers of the maid's country?"

"*La Pucelle*'s country was France, Your Honour, and the despoilers were the English under the command of King Henry the Sixth."

"Faith!" Bennett said explosively. "I collect now I have heard of this sorceress, this false prophetess! You are describing the infamous witch and heretic Joan of Arc!"

"I acknowledge readily that in certain ages and times honesty, simplicity and faith are judged to be heretical, Your Honour," Geoffrey said stiffly. "But King Tegbesu, your master," Geoffrey drew out the word *master*, "has requested the entertainment of a storyteller. Unlike Scheherazade with her artful tales of Sindbad, Ali Babi or Aladdin, whose exploits may be the work of fiction, I chose to relate to your master true tales that my mother solemnly related to me." Geoffrey's voice quavered for a moment, and he bit his lower lip sharply with the few teeth that remained in his head. The telling of the story of the *maid of Orléans* was simple. Maman had recited the story of deceit and the betrayal of the young woman by her ungrateful monarch often enough. He longed to be away from this violent place and comforted by his mother's arms.

"His Majesty is distressed to hear your tale, young man," Bennett said severely. "His Majesty avers that you have concocted a tale redolent with witchcraft and superstition."

"On the contrary, Your Honour!" Geoffrey remonstrated immediately. "I was brought to mind of this tale by the view of your master's guard of women, whom I take it are sworn to defend him with their lives, should such be necessary. I merely recite the honest story of a young woman who defeated men in fair battle. The men, unable to explain her having beaten them fairly in defense of her homeland, conspired to fix her death by crying her a heretic, witch, and bride of Satan."

Geoffrey saw King Tegbesu leaning forward all the more attentively. He spoke a word to Bennett, who said, "King Tegbesu desires to know the fate of the maid."

Geoffrey managed a smile. "Sure, Your Honour, this tale is not a new one to your ears. You should easily provide the fate of Saint Joan of Arc."

Bennett stirred uneasily, then spoke a few words into Tegbesu's ear. Tegbesu did not seem particularly alarmed by the revelation. "King Tegbesu wishes to acquaint you that your story is entirely believable. Indeed, compatible with the virtues he knows reside in the women who form his personal guard. Now, having heard this tale, King Tegbesu inquires if you have other tales to relate—King Tegbesu desires you to be informed he enjoyed this tale of a woman warrior, general, and soldier most heartily. But he insists that your tales not cease now, for in addition to knowing the outcome of this formidable woman warrior, he is desirous of other stories equally entertaining."

"I wish in all matters to be shown attentive to the wishes of your master," Geoffrey said, his ears buzzing with fatigue and his eyes as scratchy as if filled with sand. "I myself hear voices—though I cede them not as voices dispatched by the Deity—but echoes from a recent illness." Geoffrey inclined his small body in what he knew Bennett would interpret as an exaggerated bow bereft of honor appropriate to King Tegbesu's station, but he was past all caring and could only with the greatest difficulty rise to his feet from the damnably awkward and cramped low stool. When the King of Danhomé took his regal departure, as soon as his back was turned, the two dwarfs darted out and in a few brief seconds struck Geoffrey repeatedly, savagely, with the monkey skulls atop their scepters, until they were shattered into yellow shards, before scampering away. Geoffrey, his body insensible to the blows, sank to his knees in the dust but contained his moans and sobs.

XXII

oseph and Juby had completed marking the broad bands of chalk in some fashion upon the sterns of all the vessels of Arnold's small fleet. Joseph's heart had been pierced by the cries and moans of the wounded men huddled in their woeful sorrow and grievous pain within the wooden walls of the row galleys and gundalos. How he wished Doctor Ezrah Green, back at Ticonderoga, would have seen his way clear to have accompanied this expedition, or even better, the half-Indian shaman Hymsinger, and Ming Tsun, his brother's best friend in life. Those paragons would quickly have alleviated the sufferings of these sore, wounded men! Joseph was mystified that Juby was paddling ever so quietly toward the *Trumbull*. "Juby," Joseph leaned toward Juby in the bow and whispered ever as low as he could, "why are we returning to the *Trumbull?*"

Juby did not deign to answer until their canoe was tucked under the low bows of the *Trumbull* galley. Instead, he reached into a pocket for a lump of chalk and carefully drew an eye, a most fanciful eye it was true, but an eye nevertheless, on the larboard bow just beneath the forward bulwark. Then with a minimum of paddle strokes, Juby swung the canoe around the bows to the starboard side, where he drew another eye, exactly the same size as the one he had drawn on the larboard side. "Why, Master Joseph," Juby whispered conspiratorially with a lopsided smile that passed unnoticed in the engloomed fog, "we be but paintin' eyes on the lead gallie to see us through this fog. It is somethin' that the Tai-Pan and Ming Tsun know full well from the far-off China. We demand that Captain Warner lead us unerrin', lest we can do be provide eyes for his ship to see her way."

"Your logic is impeccable, Juby," Joseph confessed quietly. "If my brother and the wise Ming Tsun endorse the practice, then it boots much merit. Now let us locate the *Washington*." Joseph would have much preferred to continue with Arnold. He distrusted David Hawley, for the man was utterly devoid of any abilities to inspire and was even less of a mariner than Joseph. But Arnold knew that Hawley was in need of a matross who could load and lay a cannon, and Arnold had ordered him and Juby into *Washington* for the good of the fleet. The canoe drifted past the *Trumbull*'s stern just as Seth Warner silently positioned a tin lantern on its nail, driven in just below the taff rail. Colonel Wigglesworth, swaddled in a double wrap of canvas, hat jammed down over his ears, stood morose and sniffling on the other side of the tiller, saying nothing.

Warner opened the shutters, liberating the brief aroma of heated tallow and a spill of light sternward. "Advise me, Mister Frost, if the candle can be observed from beam's end," Warner said quietly.

Joseph paddled half-a-dozen strokes off *Trumbull*'s beam, then as silently ghosted up to Warner on her quarterdeck. "The candle itself cannot be observed, Captain Warner, but the light falls upon the water and would be discerned, save for the fog that surely shall be our salvation. General Arnold's last orders are to keep as close to the New York shore as ever you can. There is five fathoms of water—beyond plunge of sweep—ten yards off the shore. When you sense you are free of the ledges around Valcouer Bay, you may shape a course southeast by south, though large. And God's speed to you."

"Exactly so, Mister Frost," Seth Warner whispered, then said quietly to his crew: "Out sweeps, and for God's sake row dry."

Joseph and Juby waited in their small birchbark canoe for Arnold's fleet to move past, as slowly as time arrested. As ordered by Arnold, *Trumbull* was the first to glide away, as silently as a wraith under Warner's stern but benevolent command. *Enterprise* followed next, all the sloop's sails tightly furled and her ghostly crew working mightily to sweep without sound. Then the gundalos *Connecticut, Jersey, New York, Boston, Spitfire, Providence, New Haven* — Joseph heartily wished that *Philadelphia* was in the line, and wondered on which vessel of the fleet Benjamin Rue was now serving. Then the cutter *Lee* moved soundlessly past, and here came the schooner *Revenge,* followed closely by *Washington.* Of course, Joseph knew that Arnold in *Congress* would be the last in line to pull in the latchstring.

Juby pointed silently with his paddle, and Joseph acknowledged with a quick J-stroke that brought the stern of the canoe around to point toward *Washington.* Time to go aboard the vessel into which he and Juby were commanded. In a trice Juby had tied on the canoe to the taff rail, and the two of them were clambering over the starboard bulwark, having left Uncle Pepperrell's musketoon in Arnold's care, their only baggage a worn canvas bag that contained a few stale and moldy scraps of bannock bread.

Since they had been aboard *Congress* with Arnold the entire day, Joseph and Juby were not particularly made welcome by Captain Hawley. Brigadier General Waterbury was just wrapping himself in a thin flannel blanket and disappearing down the ladder to the stern cabin when Joseph and Juby hoisted themselves over the starboard bulwark. Captain Hawley had a more substantial boat cloak in which to wrap himself, and his self-righteous, rigid stance beside the helmsman at the tiller conveyed his disapproval of minions thought sent to carry reports back to Arnold about him. Joseph was long past caring about others' opinions of him, so he and Juby settled themselves between two 12-pounder cannons on the larboard gun deck. They shared the meager lumps of hard, stale bannock, and, amazingly refreshed though bone-weary and pierced by the bitter cold, Joseph curled himself into a fetal position and was immediately pulled into the whirlpool that was the sleep of the utterly exhausted.

At midnight he and Juby were roused to relieve the men on

one of the sweeps. Joseph did not remember anything of the monotonous racking back and forth of the sweep, for he actually labored while still asleep, as a somnambulist. At dawn—that is to say, when the darkness began to attenuate enough for nearby objects to be perceived dimly—the day was overcast and there was no real sunrise—he and Juby were relieved and they made their way back to the small space between the 12-pounders that the other crew members had, by unspoken assent, ceded to them. When he awakened fully two hours later Joseph had to clench his teeth to keep from crying out from the pain of his bleeding, blistered palms. He had thought his hands, toughened and thickly callused by three months of continuous hard work with adze, axe and hammer, were proof against further blistering. Joseph was sadly wrong, for his hands were shaped into claws splotched with dried blood that took great effort and pain to bend. It took Joseph a good five minutes to fumble the buttons to his breeches open enough to stand in the break of the gun deck and void his bladder overside. During that time he had ample opportunity to survey the Lake, and Joseph was not pleased by what he saw. He passed his observations to Juby as they once again took their places at a sweep.

"We are rowing into an infernal wind directly hard out of the south, which means we ain't able to raise a sail at all, 'cause we did we couldn't point high enough into the wind to keep in mid-lake and would find ourselves driven close ashore." Joseph grasped the sweep's handle and swung it lustily, figuring the quick immersion in swift darting pain was less overall than the gradual working into it.

"Been meanin' to ask, Master Joseph, just what that curious thumpin' I've been hearin' long-times be. Sounds like carpets on a line bein' dusted." Juby, after pulling too quickly on the sweep and catching a crab, caught the rhythm of the stroke and settled into a long, steady pull with Joseph.

Joseph listened, for a moment, puzzled, then laughed. "Why, Juby, that lugubrious sound you hear akin to a cacophony of caulkers exercising their irons and mallets is nothing more than the pumps' drawing. Think of it, Juby! Even on these row gallies so crudely thrown together, we were yet able to fit pumps to keep the bilges dry." Joseph laughed. "We may argue to change our lot at the next shift and take a turn plying the pumps. The motion is more up and down rather than the present forward and back. We may find the pumps more to our liking, though as I collect their locations, we would be hunched under the deck, unable to stand erect. We would be out of this damnable cold wind, though."

"I appreciates the wind, though it be most cold, Master Joseph," Juby said calmly. "I'd appreciate it a heap more if we had some knowledge where we be rowin' this barge."

They learned soon enough that Arnold was directing his fleet to the anchorage at the northern side of Schuyler's Island, where they were for a few blessed hours spared the hard wind from the south. But there was no surcease from labor. Arnold ordered practically every man able to lift a hammer or prick a needle to work mending hulls, masts and yards, and patching sails. Joseph, however, busied himself with an inventory of *Washington*'s munitions. Both in garlands on deck and in the cramped hold he found ten 18-pounder balls, twenty 12-pounder balls, and twenty 6-pounder balls. The bar shot and grapeshot had been fired away by Captain Thatcher, now dead. There were enough chopped-up spikes, hinges, bolts and nuts as langrage to load each of the ten swivels with one good honest charge. After Joseph filled exactly enough flannel bags to make charges for the balls he had inventoried, half a barrel of gunpowder was left. He duly reported his efforts to Arnold.

Arnold was just sealing a dispatch in a wrap of canvas. "You and your man want to take this message to General Gates at Tyonderoga?"

Joseph shook his head. "I may not be much of a matross, General, but I be even less facile with a paddle. Reckon I'd better stay and point cannons for Captain Hawley."

Arnold nodded his head in appreciation. "Then I shall give the small chaloupe tender of *Congress* to Captain Grimes and half a dozen men who ain't wounded in the arms or back and can heft an oar. They can be away on the minute." Arnold answered Joseph's question before he could ask. "*Jersey* is barely afloat. *Spitfire* ain't in no better shape, so I've ordered Grimes and Ulmer to get their cannons out of them, with whatever stores they may have, and into *Congress*. The crews will be apportioned among the fleet—please mention this to Captain Hawley, should he want more hands, when you return to *Washington* to fetch over that half-barrel of powder. *Congress* and *Washington* will be the rear guards. I have already sent the surviving gundalos southward. I had a good look at the British thirty minutes ago from *Congress'* mainmast. Wounded as the mast is, I climbed most lightly, I assure you!" Arnold permitted himself a soundless chuckle. "The British discovered our withdrawal belatedly, and the same strong wind from the south that hinders us so keeps the British embayed near Valcouer. Carleton is no doubt apoplectic that we have slipped him the goose, and berating himself for lack of proper sentries posted! But he cannot sail down upon us in this wind."

Arnold turned to Broadhead the Pequot Indian, who was standing nearby. "Mister Broadhead, please to get the chaloupe overside while I inquire of Captain Grimes. If you know a half dozen men wounded elsewhere than backs, shoulders and arms, I would be pleased if you would point them out to me."

The gundalos *Spitfire* and *Jersey* were so pierced and wounded they needed little encouragement to sink once their armaments and munitions, sails, cordage and anything else of value to the Continental Army had been transferred into *Congress* and their hulls towed a bare hundred yards off the beach of pebbles and sand. *Washington* and *Congress* won to short cables connecting them to the gundalos, the unbitted cables came aboard, and the two gundalos were riding gunwales awash and down heavily by the heads, slipping into waters that were thirty fathoms deep, as *Congress*, *Washington* and *Trumbull* began their weary sweeps southward up the Lake.

"Master Joseph," Juby said quietly, as he handed Joseph a handful of raw potatoes sliced fine, skins and all, that he had found somewhere, "seems we's been rowin' all night to reach the harbour we's just quitted. Can you estimate how far we've rowed since we left that place where all the heathen Indians was keepin' up such a din?"

Joseph hungrily crunched on the astringent slices of raw potato while he calculated the straight-line distance from Valcour Bay. "Well, Juby, you've been tugging on that sweep for some hours now. You should have a good estimate of how far we have traveled."

Juby deftly thrust a slice of raw potato into his mouth and kept the stroke without fouling the sweep. "Well, Master Joseph, Tai-Pan talked often, that is, whenever he was home from a voyage, about some island by the name o' Helena, Saint Helena. Always spoke o' it as a capital island for sure. We should have pulled somers close to Saint Helena, I apprehend."

Joseph tossed another slice of raw potato into his mouth with some difficulty, for he was unable to flex his fingers—perhaps "hooked" the slice of potato, speared on a fingernail into his mouth would have described the motion more accurately. He chewed for several seconds, letting the juice of potato and saliva run into his throat deliciously. "For sure, Juby, my brother Geoffrey has often described the beauties of Saint Helena. A place to shelter and provision after weathering the Cape of Storms. I do not know how many thousands of leagues that fair isle lies to our southward. But, Juby, in all conscience, ten hours of incessant sweeping has won us no more than eight land miles. Another forty miles lie between us and Crown Point."

So the exhausted, near-lifeless crews of the tiny fleet continued to tug pathetically, mechanically, at their long sweeps, frequently catching the crabs that fatigue and inattention always bring, pointed directly into the wind ever building from the south.

Joseph was vaguely aware that vision was limited, so he reasoned that night had fallen. When he knew he could row no more he kept Juby at the sweep while he kicked and cursed two men curled around the number four cannon into grumbling, profane wakefulness. But the two men acknowledged their duty, albeit grudgingly, and changed places with Joseph and Juby at the sweep. Joseph and Juby in turn sought the fragile shelter of the bulwark against the sleet that began to pelt. Despite the oppressive cold and lash of wet sleet, Joseph and Juby came together for mutual warmth beneath an abbreviated rectangle of rumbowline canvas upon which the sleet beat like a drum, though they slept oblivious. They were called to the sweeps again after sleep so profound their eyes were shuttered with gum—'twas as well so—while their backs, shoulders and arms strained to the lift, push, shove, dip and tug of sweep so hard that joints and sinews creaked and popped.

Again there was no proper dawn, just a first faint lessening of the dark, and then a gloomy gray broth of fog and rain mixed with sleet. Joseph was thinking of food, and the thought of food kept him tugging on the sweep, the thought of food and the fact that Juby, who was at least thrice Joseph's age, was dead asleep on his feet from exhaustion. Though Juby's hands, as stiffened and splotched with dried blood and great gaping broken blisters as Joseph's, still rested on the sweep, it was Joseph alone who pulled. And he was comforted that his reservoir of youthful strength could accommodate his companion's exhaustion.

"Aye, Juby," Joseph thought as he gazed fondly at Juby's death-mask of a face, "how many times you must have carried me when I was but a child, all without my caring or acknowledging, because you were a slave, and such was expected of you." Joseph had no idea how many men still served under Arnold's command now abroad on Lake Champlain, but he was glad to know two noble souls counted among them, Arnold and Juby.

Gradually, as the fog dispersed, Joseph saw Brigadier General Waterbury, peering northward, huddled in conversation with Captain Hawley on the quarterdeck of *Washington*. "Matross, if it would not incommode you, I would be pleased if you would see to the state of our cannons," Hawley said, just loudly enough for Joseph to hear him.

"Immediately, sir," Joseph said, springing to the work he was coming to know so well. He went round the row galley quickly, ensuring the muzzle-lashings were appropriately fixed to the eye-bolts on either side of the ports and that the mid-breeching ropes were properly seized to the cascabels, with trucks free and train-tackle coiled down properly. He scrutinized the arrangements of rammer, handspike, sponge, vent prick, powder horn, then the quoin lying upon its bed, and the nearness of shot and a linstock of slow-match. Some of the cannons showed they were better served than others, and certainly their preparations spoke volumes about the attitudes of the gun crews.

"We are set to give good account of ourselves, Captain Hawley, needing only to set matches a-light, bring up the cartridge and stand to our pieces," Joseph said, mounting the three short steps to the quarterdeck to give his report. To the northward Lake Champlain was overspread with sails from the Vermont to the New York shores. He judged the British were still five miles to the north, but their sails were filling with a strong wind from the northwest, while the *Washington* and the five other vessels of Arnold's fleet were hogging badly into a strong wind from the south.

A glance around showed the *Congress* half a mile to the southward, a stalwart collie shepherding the gundalos *Boston, Connecticut, New Haven* and *Providence. Enterprise, New York, Revenge, Lee* and *Trumbull* were nowhere in sight. "All that God-damn rowing, and we are only now abreast of Willsborough," Waterbury cursed. "An all-night run with the men standing to their sweeps so handsomely, yet we have covered only twelve miles from Schuyler's Island." Waterbury shoved his hands into his coat pockets, not crediting Joseph's presence on the quarterdeck at all. "How stands the water in our hold, Captain Hawley?"

"I have not sounded this last half-hour, General," Hawley said contritely. "I shall take the measure now."

Joseph glanced northward and saw that one British ship was already hull-up. And it was a ship of three masts, not a schooner. It could only be the *Inflexible,* mounting eighteen 12-pounder cannons.

"Well over one foot of water in the hold, General Waterbury," Hawley confessed anxiously when he reappeared on the quarterdeck.

"You should bring all the prepared cartridge to the gun deck, less it be rendered useless!" Joseph cried. Both officers turned vehemently upon him, and Joseph shrank back to the taff rail, finding there a rag of a linen shirt that he quickly tore into strips to bandage his hands, without asking anyone leave.

"Captain Hawley, be kind enough to launch the chaloupe and appoint a reliable officer into her. We must send to General Arnold for permission to put the wounded into the chaloupe and send it off to Crown Point, then run this sieve ashore and destroy it."

Joseph listened, mouth agape. Waterbury had no intention of fighting when he still had an augmented crew of one hundred and twenty-five men and powder and shot enough for ten good rounds from every cannon aboard *Washington*. Men enough to work the pumps, sweep as need be, and fight both sides of the row galley!

The chaloupe was quickly on its way to the *Congress*, which had fallen back to wait for *Washington* to sweep closer. Arnold was preparing to raise both fore and main lateen sails. Joseph signaled for Juby's assistance, and they crept into the cramped hold, sloshing almost knee-deep in water, to bring up the buckets containing the sausage-like flannel bags of gunpowder. No one was manning the pumps and the buckets of cartridge were already floating in the chill water.

A quick glance to the northward when they emerged on deck revealed the *Inflexible,* topsails, jibs and forecourse all filled to bursting, tearing down on *Washington* at a great clip. Joseph placed buckets of cartridge between every two cannons on larboard and starboard sides and saw the *Congress* hoist her lateen sails, now that the wind from the north was finally reaching the American fleet. The chaloupe, under oars alone, was coming up with a boil of water under her forefoot. The chaloupe ranged past *Washington,* then made an amateurish and very uncoordinated turn, with many crossed oars and curses, to coast parallel off *Washington's* larboard side—screened by *Washington's* bulk from the approaching British warships. A tall scarecrow of an officer wearing the tattered remnants of an ensign's uniform stood up in the stern sheets and formed a speaking trumpet with his hands.

"General Arnold commands we press on to Split Rock, where the row gallies and gundalos may form a defensive line at the narrows! General Arnold believes we shall bring the British to check for yet another day." The ensign was very earnest and willing to fight. Joseph was sorry he did not recognize the man.

Inflexible's larboard side was obscured by a ragged embroidery of sullen dirty-gray smoke, with rosettes of reddish-salmon-orange appearing randomly within it. Cannon balls skittered across the toilsome, fretted waters, most defeated by the cross-grained waves, though at least one striking *Washington*'s starboard hull somewhere between wind and water.

"Gr-gr-great G-G-God! The British have gotten our measure!" Waterbury stuttered, his face the color of the morning. "Captain Hawley, we must haul down our colours! Please make it so!"

Joseph, disbelieving, mouth agape, held up a bucket of cartridge. "General Waterbury, we still have the means to give a good account of ourselves against the British!"

The *Inflexible* was yawing, a most unseamanshiplike maneuver though it would bring her bows around and lay her on a southeasterly heading that would permit her starboard cannons to bear on *Washington*. "Quickly, Captain Hawley, I beg! The next broadside shall surely sink us!"

Hawley dashed to the pennant halyard, reeved to the mainmast top, from which the Cambridge flag, or the flag of Grand Union, was hoist and seized the halyard. "A minute, Mister Hawley," Juby said, and there was something ominous in his tone that gave Hawley pause. Juby stood with one foot on the bottom step of the ladder to the quarterdeck. "You 'bout ready to surrender your second command General Arnold done give you without firin' so much as one shot agin the British. Don't seem fittin' somehow that you pull down that flag you ain't had no hand in the makin'."

"Juby's right!" Joseph shouted. "You are ready to surrender

while you have yet to fire a shot, while you still possess the means to resist!"

"Hear him! Hear him!" half a dozen voices echoed from the gun deck. "We ain't fer surrenderin'!"

"I need not consult you," Waterbury said coldly. "And it is your own safety that concerns me, for in the next cannonade from that monstrous ship we all shall surely perish."

"General, we've got ten cartridge each cannon!" Joseph cried. "So we don't use the larboard cannons, in that case we've got twenty cartridge per cannon and can surely give good account of ourselves."

"I alone am responsible," Waterbury said in a thin, dispirited voice. "Captain Hawley, you have heard my orders. Strike our colours. I must yield in good conscience to spare the lives of those under my charge."

"Mister Waterbury," Juby spoke in the saddest of tones, and a gust of wind tore off his cap and revealed his coif of kinked hair the color of cotton, "my kind know somethin' 'bout givin' up when the means o' resistance be still at hand. We reckons you kin surrender 'em as wishes to surrender, but they be some among us ain't ready to surrender." Juby walked two paces to the pennant halyard, taking the halyard from Hawley and carefully lowering the Flag of Grand Union until he could clutch it. Juby pushed the wooden pegs of the banner through their hauls and bundled the flag into his tunic. "I bid you good day, Masters, for I be off to take up with General Arnold."

"Ye ain't off by yerself! Waterbury may be surrendered, but we ain't!" a dozen angry men from the gun deck snarled as one. One man jumped to the larboard bulwark and shouted to the men in the chaloupe: "Veer alongside 'n' take us off! We've had a bellyful o' these cowards!"

Inflexible had yawed enough for her starboard cannons to bear on *Washington,* and the broadside roared out as Joseph expected it would, despite the fact that *Washington* had struck. Grapeshot snapped along *Washington*'s starboard side like a lash. The man who had jumped to the larboard bulwark was swept away. Joseph grabbed the nape of Juby's coat and pulled him to the quarterdeck a second before he thought the cannons would fire and was on his feet as soon as the short broadside had been gotten off. "The canoe!"

Joseph jumped to the stern counter and saw with great relief that the small birchbark canoe he and Juby had husbanded all the way from Ticonderoga was unscathed. He untied the painter and ran it forward to the break between quarterdeck and gun deck on the protected larboard side. The chaloupe was already there, and men were leaping over the bulwark into the smaller boat. Joseph and Juby tumbled into the canoe, Joseph in the bow, and found their paddles.

Joseph found himself looking directly at the scarecrow of an ensign in the chaloupe's stern sheets. "We can take some men in this canoe, should they venture."

The ensign grinned, showing rotted teeth in a face that had yet to know a razor. "Got sixteen, eighteen in here already—no more ain't comin'. Reckon the rest aim to be capons. Arnold's got more men than he needs, so south we be, up the Lake ever as fast as we can fly fer Tyonderoga, but ye might wanta head fer the flag. Arnold's alus got a use fer a cannon pointer."

"Good luck to you!" Joseph shouted hurriedly, craning his neck to get a bearing on *Congress* and estimating that she was half a mile away, on a wing-and-wing run due south. She might be hard to catch. A glance over his shoulder showed him the towering masts of *Inflexible*, her hull still largely concealed beyond *Washington*, though the tip of her bowsprit was coming into view. Joseph savagely dug his paddle into the water, then faltered as excruciating pain shot up both arms. A splinter of wood blown out of *Washington* by *Inflexible*'s cannonade floated nearby; he scooped up the chip and bit down on it hard, the better to bear the pain. Joseph leaned to reach as far forward as he could with his paddle and dragged the stroke as far rearward as he could, turning the blade as the paddle reached the extent of its leverage to lift it cleanly from the water, then plunged it into the water as far forward as he could reach.

The canoe shot forward like a dog run from a back stoop by threat of scalding water. Within ten strokes Joseph's breath was coming in short, shuddering gasps; within twenty he was lightheaded, with his vision constricted as by blinders on a horse's bridle. After thirty strokes the scabs that had formed over his broken blisters had broken open and blood was seeping through the tatters of shirt Joseph had used for bandaging and padding his hands. The splinter of wood snapped in his jaws; he spit out the fragment and shifted the larger piece with lips and tongue between his teeth, then bit down again.

At one hundred strokes Joseph lifted his head long enough to see if his line toward *Congress* still held true. Yes, the line held true—but *Congress* was perceptibly further south, heartbreakingly further south. Joseph dipped his head and closed his eyes against the spinning, whirling lights of the surreal world in which he existed. And he stroked and pulled, and he stroked and pulled, feeling the canoe *live* beneath him as Juby stroked and pulled with equal fervor and quite determination.

The round shot ranging from *Inflexible* threw up a geyser of water twenty yards in front of the canoe and they ran directly into the heavy spray, taking a lot of water aboard. Joseph's head snapped up, fastening upon the *Congress,* which was much farther southward than his last observation, disconcertingly so, almost enough to cause him to relinquish paddling in hopes of overtaking the row galley. "It is strange the British are playing bowls with *Congress* at such long distance," he wondered idly, "though it would hinder *Congress* wonderfully if the British could knock over a lateen yard, or even bring down a mast." The next ranging shot threw up its geyser thirty yards to the left of the canoe, and Joseph still had not grasped its portent. Then the third ranging shot plunged into the lake ten yards behind the canoe, bringing home to Joseph the awful certainty that the cannons of *Inflexible* were ranging on the canoe.

Joseph immediately dug his paddle hard into the water on the larboard side, calling desperately for Juby to stroke the same, pulling the canoe's bows in a swirl of water to larboard until the canoe lay at a right angle to its former course and stroking feverishly until the canoe pushed into the water still disturbed by the ranging shot. Joseph shifted his paddle to the starboard side and set the canoe once again on a southward heading. The next cannon ball plunged within one yard of the place on the Lake the canoe had occupied twenty seconds earlier.

"This is wrong! This is entirely wrong!" Joseph said to himself, almost incoherently. "Waterbury struck! It is the deepest perfidy to continue firing once a vessel surrenders!" But another ball, fired at a lesser elevation, skipped and skittered like a flat stone, rather than plunged, across the Lake's surface ten yards from the canoe's starboard bow. Joseph paddled hard on the starboard side to turn toward the shot, gambling again that his maneuver would confuse and throw off the aim of the *Inflexible*'s gunners. The Lake ahead of the canoe erupted into a ragged curtain of water. Painfully, Joseph turned his head and, unbelieving, saw not only *Inflexible* but *Maria* and *Carleton* behind him by no more than half a mile, angry blossoms of dirty black smoke obscuring their gun ports.

"Back! Juby, for all we're worth!" Joseph reversed his paddle and desperately pivoted the canoe around its stern, stroking southward for fifty yards, then made another despairing turn toward the Vermont shore, feeling what little strength he still possessed waning, ebbing rapidly. He spared a look at Juby, taking enormous heart from Juby's determined efforts. But Juby, at thrice Joseph's age, was tiring also, and his timing was half a stroke off. The waters thirty yards behind the canoe were a confused, conflicted welter of spume thrown up by plunging, ricocheting cannon balls. A ball skipped across the wave tops alongside, close enough that Joseph could have reached out and touched it.

"Arnold's haulin' his wind!" Juby rasped, momentarily raising his heavily perspiring, ashen face: "'N' he's turnin'!"

Joseph risked a glance southward, and yes! The lateen sails of *Congress* were being furled even as her sweeps were running out and the clumsy row galley was crabbing in a turn to starboard. With a glance northward Joseph's eye momentarily caught the arc of a round shot's trajectory some twenty yards above the Lake. He wished he were half as good at mathematics as Geoffrey, for his brother could calculate the exact spot where the shot would impact on earth or water with just a half-second's observation. It occurred to Joseph that a matross of his standing should be able to make such calculations also, and he concluded the ball would strike the surface of the Lake at least fifteen yards behind and slightly to the right of the canoe. He would not have to worry about that particular ball, but Joseph scanned the sides of the British warships bearing down on the canoe, anxiously watching for the loft of shot. The *Maria* was almost bow-on, coming with all plain sail drawing from the wind astern, her bows shouldering aside prodigious wreaths of water. He would not have to worry about *Maria* for the moment; she could not bring a cannon to bear, though so fast was her approach that Joseph knew the canoe could not outdistance her and *Maria* bid fair to run them under within ten minutes.

"What day o' the week would it be, Master Joseph?" Juby asked thickly.

"Juby! This ain't no time to be asking about the days of the week!" Joseph glanced southward, just in time to see a larboard sweep on *Congress* snap.

"I's got a right to know what day o' the week it be, Master Joseph," Juby pursued doggedly, his voice coming from a great distance.

Joseph thought fiercely while at the same time anxiously scanning *Inflexible* and *Carleton,* both preparing to jibe and fall off the wind momentarily to present their broadsides. "It's Sunday," Joseph said shortly.

"Ah, Sunday," Juby said with lugubrious satisfaction. "The woman who bore me was regarded highly as a seer—something much as your grandmother—and she cautioned me on more than one occasion that I would die o' a Sunday." The Flag of Grand Union Juby removed from Hawley's hands aboard the *Washington* had partially spilled out of his coat; he paused a moment to throw the entire flag in a coil over his left shoulder and tie it off, bandoleer fashion.

"We'll both die if we don't ply our paddles more assiduously," Joseph shouted, a glance southward being sufficient to divine Arnold's intent. "Arnold's bringing *Congress* around so's he's got a broadside to throw. Once we're under the protection of her broadside we can fetch *Congress* easily—so long as Arnold can dissuade *Maria* from running us under!" Joseph plunged his paddle into the water on the canoe's starboard side, as far forward as he could possibly reach, and pulled with all his strength. Behind him Juby plied his paddle on the larboard side, as they stretched out for *Congress* with all they were worth.

All the sweeps on *Congress'* starboard side were pulling double-time to bring the row galley bow-on toward the Vermont shore and present her larboard broadside. There! Though she was not quite all the way around, *Congress'* cannons began to grumble, the number one cannon firing first with a stab of dense smoke that was startlingly black against the gray Lake and the gray sky. Joseph heard the shot pass overhead with a sibilant sound like that of the quick rip of cloth. Three cannons fired in sequence and *Congress* began moving forward, turning as she came. Joseph estimated that *Congress* was less that four hundred yards away, and he bent his shoulders and back to the task of pulling the canoe closer toward the row galley.

Joseph glanced up just once to keep his line toward *Congress* and observed with great gratitude that she was tugged around enough to present her starboard broadside. The distance between the canoe and the row galley was less than three hundred yards. Joseph never heard the four round shots whistle overhead plunge downward almost simultaneously, throwing up a barrier of turbulent, tempestuous water that rode beneath the canoe's bows, raising them at an incredibly steep angle and then turning the canoe violently leftward, overthrowing it and spilling Joseph and Juby into the frigid waters of Lake Champlain.

◈◈◈◈ XXIII ◈◈

◈◈◈◈◈ EOFFREY FROST TOTTERED UNSTEADILY
◈   ◈ JUST INSIDE A THICKET OF REEDS AND
◈ G ◈ COLLAPSED FULL-LENGTH ONTO THE
◈◈◈◈◈ DIRTY SAND AND LITTER OF CANE HUSKS.
His body was wracked with dry heaves that produced nothing but an intense, agonized aching in his guts and the alum
taste of bile in his mouth. He knew he was not coming down
again with fever and ague; he was in total despair at the horrors
he was seeing. Long lines of naked men and women, joined
two-by-two by their necks in the yokes of wooden coffles, each
coffle pair connected to the coffle ahead and behind by a five-
foot length of rope, had been filing out of the Quidah barracoon since before sunrise. Naked children, bawling their utter
despair and desolation, wandered aimlessly underfoot. These
people were the property of King Tegbesu—slaves—and they
shuffled in a lane between Amazon warriors of Tegbesu's personal guard down to the foreshore. Damon awaited them,
Damon and his twin brother, Wick Nichols, who had purchased
King Tegbesu's property for brightly colored cloth, cowries,
iron bars, liquor and gunpowder. On the foreshore these miserable exemplars of humanity were forced to kneel while they
were uncoffled. Then, gripped firmly on either side by two of
the strongest seamen from the crew of the *Bride of Derry*, they
were led, one by one, to Damon, who prodded each, forced
open the mouth, critically examined teeth, slid groping hands
over arms and legs, explored the most private parts.

One man defiantly locked his jaws, refusing to open his mouth for inspection. Nonchalantly, apparently acquainted with such resistance, Damon lifted an iron poker from a fire of driftwood burning merrily nearby and applied its glowing tip immediately to the man's lips. Damon scrutinized the man's mouth, now opened in a silent, agonized scream, shook his head and thrust the man aside. Muscular guards from the barracoon immediately encoffled the man again.

"Laddie, I say, laddie, ye must come out. The selection ain't gonna take much longer, 'n' the captain bids to sail on the outgoin' tide, that'll give us just enough daylight to see us safe through the bar." Jabez McCool spoke soothingly, beseechingly, from outside the fringe of reeds. After a moment with no reply Jabez thrashed into the reeds, located Geoffrey by feel, and dragged him out by an ankle. "Laddie," Jabez said urgently, once Geoffrey's frail body lay stretched on the sand, "ye must away 'n' aboard the *Bride* before this hour passes. Beelzebub has intelligence that his bloated majesty o' Dan-Home wants to keep ye as his teller-o'-tales, his slave, 'n other words, like that great barrel o' shit 'n' chittlins claims to be the Grand Vizer, er such. 'N' Beelzebub can't do nothin' fer ye if'n barrel o' shit finds ye still ashore. We's got to get ye aboard the old *Bride* afore King Tubby discovers ye on his land. Beelzebub fancies King Tubby's taken quite a shine to yere tales."

Jabez grasped Geoffrey's emaciated upper arm and hurried him toward the ship's barge that was pulled up on the shore. They skirted the party around the driftwood fire and Geoffrey's heart sank even further when he saw that a smiling Holly was cheerfully wielding a branding iron. A crewman Geoffrey recognized as Lamb Wilkes threw a slave to the sand, then placed a heavy foot in the small of the slave's back to bear him down. Another crewman rubbed a piece of tallow on the man's upper right shoulder. Lamb Wilkes placed a sheet of greased paper over the shoulder and Holly thrust the red-hot iron against the greased paper. This particular slave writhed in pain but made no sound as the logo "B/D," surmounted by a small cornet, was seared permanently and prominently into his flesh. Geoffrey gagged at the stench that was heavy in the air. Jabez pushed him into the barge, already filled with wailing slaves, then tumbled him into the bilge. Jabez picked up a woman, wailing mightily from the pain burned into her shoulder, and thrust her atop Geoffrey Frost.

"Shove off, 'n' be quick about it," Jabez hissed to the bargemen. "Capt'n sez get the laddie aboard 'n' stowed outa sight 'n his cabin." Jabez paused and looked carefully at the woman. "Put this 'un 'n with the laddie. I mark her as one of the comfort women due me. All ye! Keep yere graspin' paws 'n' slick peckers away from her, ken ye?"

When the barge reached the ship Geoffrey scrambled through the waist entry and reached for the hand of the slave who Jabez had designated as his comfort woman. He was surprised to see that a chest-high wooden barricade of heavy timbers had been erected across the deck ten feet forward of the entry. First Mate Wolcott Crowninshield, flanked by crewmen armed with muskets, roughly cuffed men into one group near the barricade and women into another group near the mainmast. Then he studiously ticked a piece of chalk against a slate divided into columns. Just in front of the barricade a heavily perspiring Black Amos stood by a small anvil turned on its side, a pile of U-shaped shackles, and a separate pile of short iron rods, their rust covered over with a slathering of greasy slush from the galley.

Two male slaves at a time were brought to Black Amos. He fitted a shackle just above the right ankle of one man, another shackle above the left ankle of the second man, and deftly thrust a rod through the four eyes in the ends of the shackles. Black Amos butted the round head of the bolt against the anvil and with a minimum of hammer blows skillfully turned the shank of the bolt into a rivet that joined the two shackles together. He grunted, and the two men now joined at their ankles were dragged away. Two more men were led up. Black Amos slipped a shackle on the first slave without pausing.

"Here, youngster," Crowninshield said gratefully, holding out the slate, "ye can now earn yere keep as supernumerary."

"Beelzebub seys stow the lad in his cab'n," one of the barge-men who was prodding male and female slaves with the point of a cutlass to mount to the deck shouted. "'N' Jabez picked out this 'un as an allowed comfort woman, so she can go along, too."

"The youngster'll be of more use on this deck keepin' the tally," Crowninshield protested.

"Beelzebub contemplates the king has taken a likin' to the lad," the bargeman shouted. "He knows a power of stories, Mate. Lord knows young Geoffrey's tales have fastened our attention by the hour during off-watch. Little wonder King Tubby, as Jabez calls him, mot want him sequestered 'mong these blackamoors."

Crowninshield shrugged. "Get ye below then, lad. Later ye can cypher out the accounts proper. I fear I have mangled them poorly."

Geoffrey reached timidly for the young woman's hand. She shrank back. Crowninshield sniggered. "McCool alus had a good eye for a woman make a prime comfort. I'm disposed to pre-empt his namin' this woman his."

"Ain't none of that, Mate," Black Amos called out sharply, paused in mid–hammer strike: "Women enough for all, be no shortage of women. Let Jabez keep what he claims." Black Amos looked the young woman up and down, then spoke a few words in a guttural tongue with a musical "clop" at the end. Startled, the young woman hesitated, then answered in the same tone. Black Amos uttered three or four words.

"She is a Ouémé, Geoffrey, from far in the interior. I have told her she may trust you as she would her eldest brother." Black Amos smiled bleakly. "My mother was a Ouémé. She never knew who my right father was." He shrugged and recocked the arm holding the hammer. "Not that it made any difference." Black Amos struck the shank of the bolt viciously, riveting it over the shackle in one blow. The young woman timidly held out her hand to Geoffrey, and with even greater timidity, he took her hand gently and led her down the companionway to Wick Nichols' cabin.

Geoffrey was acutely aware of the woman's nakedness, and twigged she was mortally embarrassed thereby. Once they were in Nichols' cabin Geoffrey rummaged around in the captain's sea chest and winkled out a fine cambric shirt he had never seen Nichols wear. He handed the shirt to the woman, his face carefully averted, then found a short length of silk that would serve admirably as a belt.

The sashes of the great stern windows were raised, and Wick Nichols' best telescope lay on the master's desk. Geoffrey took up the telescope and focused on the shore, panning slowly along the beach until he located Lyons Bennett. Bennett was splendidly dressed in the latest Liverpool fashions, at least the fashion conjured up by Leslie Curtin, the *Bride*'s sailmaker. All that Bennett lacked to make him a proper dandy was a good black neck cloth and a pair of shoes. The man had gone barefoot so long that he could not, to his great chagrin and no matter how hard he tried, force his feet into any shoes fetched ashore from the *Bride* to satisfy his vanity. At least Wick Nichols had laid hands on a proper tricorne with a broad red-velvet strip bound around it to gift Bennett. Bennett and Nichols were conversing amiably, to all appearances. A puncheon of some strong drink stood between them, but Nichols was drinking little. It was obvious to Geoffrey as the puffed, ravaged features of Lyons Bennett were brought close through the miracle of convex and concave glass lenses joined in a collapsible metal tube that Bennett was near—if not already past—stupefaction.

The lines of slaves trending out of the ominous barracoon had tailed off. The fires where Damon and Holly kept their irons hot flared high in sparks as someone threw on several billets of driftwood. The shimmer of heat rising like a curtain reminded Geoffrey of the heated iron. He threw aside the glass, then pulled open and rummaged through several drawers of the captain's desk until he located the small fragrant cup of Dutch porcelain packed with the pure spermaceti wax Wick Nichols kept to massage the backs of his hands as protection against the sun cankers. Geoffrey pantomimed gathering a dollop of the salve on his forefinger, pulled aside the tatters of his shirt to expose a shoulder, and made rubbing motions on his shoulder.

The woman understood the pantomime upon the instant, took the cup of spermaceti wax with a sob, turned her body decorously, and applied the salve to the brand mark that would remain on her flesh for the rest of her life.

Geoffrey resumed the telescope, scanning in vain for King Tegbesu, fearful that he would actually espy that cruel and absolute monarch. But the Privy Council was the ranking member of the Court of Dan-Home present on the shore in front of the Quidah barracoon.

Another barge was putting out from the strand, so heavy with human freight that its gunwales rode a precarious six inches or less above the lagoon's surface waters, fretted now with the interplay of currents, light, contrary wind and the building tide. The ellipse of the telescope suddenly carried the images of the two dwarfs who had so lately seemed King Tegbesu's favorites that they could, with impunity, flagellate Geoffrey Frost. The dwarfs, pushed close against each other on a crowded thwart, were clasping each other tightly and bawling mightily. Geoffrey felt a twinge of pity for them, then put them out of mind, for Holly, at Damon's direction, was throwing various implements into a chest, which he then hoisted easily onto his shoulder and marched down to the captain's gig, now occupied by four dejected slaves and four oarsmen. Damon clambered into the gig and Holly pushed off, holding the bows confidently in his massive hands, standing in the shallows while the waves purled and broke around him.

Then, with many a formal bow and flourish between them, Wick Nichols took his departure of Lyons Bennett, being escorted in fine fashion to the lagoon's shore by urchins who ran desperately to keep pace with Nichols' strides in order to keep the Privy Council's umbrella interposed between the sun and the stern countenance of the captain of the *négrier Bride of Derry*.

The gig was alongside the *Bride* in five minutes, possibly less. Wick Nichols boosted the four slaves cowering in the bilge onto the main deck and was on deck himself a moment later. "Where is our supernumerary?" he said sharply. There was no need for Wolcott Crowninshield to send for Geoffrey, for Geoffrey had heard the remark and quickly presented himself to his captain.

"Glance your last upon fair Quidah, young Frost, at least during King Tegbesu's reign." Nichols smirked with a wolfish grin. "King Tubby so desires your services as a raconteur that he gave up two of his jesters as evidence of his fine regard. Return ashore and you shall be taken into his retinue and honoured as the First Privy Council has been honoured, with all that he wants and nothing that he wishes. While establishing a gun-powder mill on these shores is among my contemplations, I would not establish it for the benefit of so harsh and ungrateful a potentate—for his avarice does corrupt the trade, and there are many plotting to depose him. Their quantity of merchandise for our markets will doubtless be commensurate with their gratitude, if given the wherewithal in firelocks and gunpowder to oust him."

"I trust my captain informed His Majesty with all tact and modesty that my parents are adamantly opposed to my pro-longed absence on a foreign shore," Geoffrey said defensively.

"Such arguments, if pressed ardently upon a statue, perhaps might cause stone to weep, but Tegbesu was given to under-stand that the price for your presence in his entourage would be as many slaves as we have this day shipped delivered to Quidah this day one year hence." Wick Nichols turned away to confront his first mate menacingly. "Mister Crowninshield, why was not our *Bride* brought up to short anchor for prompt weighing once you observed me putting out from the shore? Why are not hands already aloft, awaiting the commands to make sail? We are heavily laden and must pass over the channel through the bar at the height of the tide, else spend another day in this fetid lagoon—which is not beyond the reach of canoes freighted with Tegbesu's soldiers, should his mind so change. Bestir yourself, Mister Mate, we must not be slack in stays! Hands to the cap-stern this moment!"

Wick Nichols plucked the crude, smudged tally slate from

Crowninshield's hand and gave it to Geoffrey. "Here, young Frost, busy yourself translating Mate's pitiful efforts at accounting into some useful manifest—and see to getting this stock properly in irons and stowed below." Wick Nichols shoved a finger into Geoffrey's chest. "Understand, young Frost, that Tegbesu would never commit absolutely to five hundred prime slaves, the majority of them men, in his barracoon at Quidah this day one year, in exchange for a teller of tales. Would he have done so, in trade for one youngster," Nichols cupped Geoffrey's face in his palm and drew the youth closer, "your father and mother would have been disconsolate to learn that some disease, unnamed but prevalent in these parts, had borne you away." Nichols surveyed the portion of the *Bride*'s main deck abaft the barricade. "And there is no man here who would— ever—mock the tale."

oseph fought his way to the surface before the waves thrown up by the round shot subsided and looked around wildly; neither Juby nor the canoe was visible. *He kicked off his shoes, shrugged out of his coat,* and swam as rapidly as he could toward the disturbed water. Snatching a breath, he arched his body and dived. Immediately he was under the water Joseph saw the canoe, a vague whitish blur completely awash just beneath the surface a short way off. Joseph was a good swimmer—Marlborough Frost had insisted upon it—but he knew with a terrible certainty that Juby had never swam a stroke in his life. He forced himself to keep his eyes open and scanned in every direction, pulling himself deeper with frantic thrusts of his arms, twisting every second thrust to a new direction, then just as his ears popped with the pressure of his depth Joseph thought he saw a dull flash of white. Juby's white poll!

Joseph pulled himself deeper, chest creaking, lungs consumed by fire, twisting phantasmagoric shapes and swirling bursts of color filling his vision. Whatever he might have glimpsed had slipped deeper into the Lake. And Joseph was seriously disoriented. He had dived so deep that he could not tell up from down, nor side from side. His vision was completely clouded, his eyes throbbing hideously with a pain that reverberated in his skull, and his heart pounded so strenuously that it threatened to burst from his chest. Joseph willed himself to be calm. He could claw his way in any direction, but that direction could be downward, or sideward, as well as upward. He acknowledged that Juby was beyond his reach, already an initiate into the great mysteries of death, and there was nothing else he could do—except survive, if he could, as Juby would want him to. He spread his arms and legs and stretched his lower jaw. The pain in his inner ears lessened and his vision cleared partially—enough so that Joseph could vaguely distinguish shades of gray in the murk.

Joseph had no way of knowing how long he had been under water, but he knew his remaining life was counted in seconds. He relaxed his arms utterly, his eyes following them intently. Yes! There was some slight shudder of buoyancy! Or was his body sinking deeper into the Lake and his arms, unrestrained, were trailing above him? Well, either way, his arms pointed the direction he must go. Joseph convulsed his body and thrashed his legs like scissors, at the same time beginning to claw with his arms in the direction he believed the surface lay—the direction the surface had to be!

The desire to breathe, to open his nostrils and draw in air, was overwhelming. Surely his lungs could filter sufficient oxygen out of the choking water to lessen the great weight pressing his chest. Joseph had reason enough left to resist that impulse and grimly clawed his way toward a gray that was lighter than anything surrounding.

He broke the surface of the Lake so forcefully that his body came half out of the water, inhaled one explosive breath, and slipped beneath the waves again. Joseph struggled up, paddling and gasping like a dog, utterly spent. "Matross! Ware the shaft!" Joseph's head spun around at the shout, and he saw the *Congress* fifty yards away, bow-on, sweeping for all she was worth. The butt of a sweep was launched toward him, though it fell woefully short. Joseph wearily turned on his back and moved his arms languidly, just enough to keep himself on the surface for a moment's rest, wondering that he was somehow still alive and at the same time aching with sorrow and bitterly blaming himself for Juby's loss. Had he not run away from Portsmouth in such despicable fashion Juby would not have had occasion to follow him to this Lake, in whose depths his body, shrouded with the Flag of Grand Union, lay.

A cannon ball skipping across the wavelets a yard from Joseph recalled him to his duty, regardless of how spent and grief-stricken he was. He rolled over and struck out hard for the *Congress,* seeing immediately that she was readying to fire the few cannons that comprised her starboard battery and then slipping beneath the surface like a seal to shelter his ears from the assault of the thunderous, concussive peals. Then his out-stretched, flailing hand struck the blade of a sweep, gripping it with a fierce tenacity that only death could have overcome, and he was drawn swiftly toward the *Congress.* In a moment Joseph was heaved aboard with as much ceremony as a speared trout being landed.

Arnold knelt on the deck, pillowed Joseph's shoulders against his knee, and held a battered copper ladle to Joseph's lips. "Dare not spill a drop," Arnold commanded. "It's the absolute last of the rum aboard, but all the men agreed you should have it." Joseph almost choked, then gratefully drained the fiery contents of the ladle. "We ain't seen your man, and if he didn't come up when you come up, ain't likely he will," Arnold said grimly. "All the men begrudge his loss exceedingly; color of skin ain't got nothing on it when it comes to dying for what you believe in." Arnold pulled Joseph to his feet roughly and in the general direction of a starboard-side 12-pounder. "Help me point this cannon. These men on the tackle got all the will and zeal in the world, but they lack experience, seeing's the matrosses you trained all be dead."

Joseph glanced to the north and was shocked to see the *Maria,* water parting briskly beneath her forefoot, bearing down on the *Congress.* The British schooner was less than two hundred yards away. Joseph threw himself on a sponge-ram, painfully tearing away from his hands the strips of shirt that had served their purpose as crude padding, in order to grip the sponge-ram with greater finesse. He swabbed the bore of any lingering incandescent fragments of charred cloth or unburned powder that might ignite the cartridge soon to be thrust into the tube. Joseph almost overturned the bucket containing the heavy flannel sausages of powder in his haste to seize a charge with his unpliant claw of a hand. But he fumbled the charge into the muzzle and grimly thrust it home with the rammer, pounded down a wad, seized the nearest ball that looked like it weighed twelve pounds, tipped it in the muzzle and sent it home.

"Double shot!" Arnold said through clenched lips that hardly moved. Joseph found another shot and tamped it down, then joined Arnold in running the cannon to its bowse. Arnold fiddled with the quoin on its bed while Joseph eased off or snugged up a carriage tackle, recognizing this particular carriage as one he and Stonecypher had built and aided by an enthusiastic coterie of sailors who had absolutely no idea of what they were doing. "Stand clear!" Arnold rasped, finally satisfied, and he pricked the vent as Joseph shooed the inept gun crew out of the path of recoil. The *Maria* was pressing for all she was worth and was just shy of one hundred yards away. Arnold, standing well to the right, stabbed the linstock down and the double-shotted cannon bucked in protest.

Joseph watched the brief blur of one ball as both shot smashed into the figure of the head immediately beneath the bowsprit, sheering the bowsprit and tearing away the fore stay and preventer stay hearts. *Maria*'s foremast, the full press of course, top sail and topgallant no longer kept in proper balance, toppled forward in a confusion of roiling sailcloth, flying blocks and dropping yards. "That fair wrapped their britches around their legs!" Arnold shouted as *Maria*'s way fell off. "Sweeps out! Run us south again. Marksmen to the quarterdeck. Pepper the men going forward for damage repair for all you're worth. Matross, catch up that bucket of cartridge and get down to the cabin to work the two 18-pounder sternchasers."

Arnold laid a hand on Joseph's arm as Joseph snatched up the bucket of flannel-encased cartridges, and spoke in a low voice no one could overhear. "Joseph, husband that powder carefully, for we have scant aboard, and we are a long, long twelve miles north of Crown Point."

The men at the sweeps got *Congress'* bows around and under Arnold's insistent urging hauled up the fore lateen sail—the main lateen yard had been shot through near the slings and jettisoned overside. Joseph settled himself in the cramped main cabin and began sorting out the various sizes of round and bar shot that had been dumped, dropped or thrown into the cabin when the matrosses serving the twin 18-pounder cannons had called for more shot. Both cannons had been fired and were at the extent of their breeching tackles, so Joseph set about loading the cannon to larboard first. The cartridges in the bucket he had brought down had been cut for the 6-pounders, in two-pound flannel bags, so he would need three bags for each of the 18-pounders. Joseph frowned. *Congress* was prodigiously short of powder; he would load only four pounds of powder and double-shot the cannons.

Somewhat queasily Joseph found himself looking at a tangle of corpses pitched into a corner, and he tried his best to ignore them. He had just rammed home a charge of powder when a sepulchral voice asked plaintively: "Shall eternally beseech Almighty God to succor ye in direst extremity was ye to fetch me a Christian drop o' water."

Frightened, Joseph dropped the flexible rammer and sponge just as he brought it clear of the muzzle and stared at the tangle of bodies. "Name's Goldsmith, Thomas Goldsmith," the sepulchral voice continued. "Took a ball in the groin first day of the fightin'. Been in this corner ever since, leg broke and all, more dead 'uns throwed on top all the time so's I've scarce drawn breath."

Joseph frantically pulled corpses aside until he glimpsed a body with eyes still open and jaw line firm. With horror Joseph recognized the next to last body he pulled off the pile, despite a growth of beard and a horrific disfiguring wound. One of his older second cousins, whom he saw but occasionally: hard-working John Frost from the Berwicks, who constructed the unique Piscataqua gundalo at a small yard on the Salmon Falls River he and his widowed mother, Joanna, owned. It was John who had convinced Arnold on the rightness of the lateen rig for the row galleys when he pitched up at Skenesboro with his three best shipwrights and his customary passion for building ships. Well-built ships. Joseph had seen John a few times, but afraid of what John might know about his affair with Hannah Devon he had kept aloof. And now his distant cousin was dead; as lost to him as Juby was lost.

Biting back his tears, Joseph rolled John Frost over like a side of salt-dried cod and grasped Thomas Goldsmith under the armpits, pulling him to the carriage of the starboard cannon. Peering into the man's face Joseph knew Goldsmith was already an initiate into the mysteries of death. He could smell death on the man's breath and in the putrescence of his gangrenous leg. "Thank ye most kindly," Thomas Goldsmith said in a croak of a voice through swollen, split lips caked with gum and set in a bloodless face. "Not a body never took no notice o' me 'til ye heard me."

Joseph frantically cast about for a container of water, any container, and seeing none he overturned the bucket of flannel cartridges, spilling them dangerously but uncaring on the rough sole of the cabin. He darted to the blown-out stern windows, leaned far out over the stern and let down the bucket. As he was hauling up the bucket, heavy with water, a musket ball plowed a bloody furrow across his right forearm and clanged against the muzzle of the larboard cannon with a musical chime. The spent, brightly misshapen, irregular star of lead plopped into the bucket of water.

Irritably, Joseph fished the flattened bullet out of the bucket and tossed it astern. There was no cup, tankard or dipper in the cabin, so Joseph tore a long rag from what remained of his shirt, dipped it in the water and squeezed the water into Goldsmith's mouth. He did so half a dozen times, then said: "Arnold's depending on these cannons to let the British know we've still got teeth. I'm going to pull you against the forward bulkhead with this bucket aside you and this piece of cloth. Can you move an arm? If so, you can have all the water you want." A round shot smashing into the stern just beneath the waterline recalled Joseph to his duty. He finished loading the larboard cannon, then fished up a flannel sausage of powder, scanning it anxiously to see if it had been wetted. Thankful that it had not, Joseph stuffed the few remaining charges into a locker athwart the rudderpost and loaded the starboard 18-pounder as fast as ever a cannon had been loaded in any navy.

Working the pieces up to their bowses without assistance would be another matter. Joseph stared in dismay at his bloody hands, no skin at all on the pads of his palms, no sensation of pain in his hands, or anywhere in his body, for that matter, but no strength either. He was utterly spent. Regardless, Joseph sat down on the cabin sole, wrapped the tail of the larboard cannon's traversing rope around his forearms, braced a foot against the ringbolt set in the sole, and began to pull the near three tons of metal and carriage that by all rights required the services of ten men. Grimly, inch by inch, his shoulders threatening to pull completely out of their sockets, Joseph Frost hauled on the traversing tackle and was still doing so when Benedict Arnold and a dozen men clopped into the cabin, filling it.

"God's eyes, as if the Devil ain't black enough," Arnold swore at the scene confronting him. "Get them dead men out the stern windows. Quick now! We need room to fight them cannons."

"Oh, General, don't mistook me for a dead man," Goldsmith quavered, though he was too weak to move from the cannon carriage against which he lay.

"Not in this life, Thomas!" Arnold said heartily, evidently surprised but pleased that Goldsmith still lived. "We'll get you ashore and down to the medical men at Tyonderoga. They may have to unship that bum leg of yours, but then you'll be pert as a freshet."

"Have a care with the way you hand those dead," Joseph said sharply to the men who had seized the corpses roughly. Without recalling them, he spoke almost the same words he had spoken three months earlier: "Don't tumble them overside like they're rocks without feeling." Shamefaced, the men took far greater pains, now handling the dead bodies gently, almost reverently. Arnold himself took John Frost's legs and helped ease that particular body out the stern.

Arnold clapped Joseph awkwardly on a shoulder and held out the shoes he had removed from John's corpse. "You'll be needing shoes soon, and I'll conceit your relative rejoices in his last gift to you. I have no hope that Gates will send bateaux in time enough to take us in tow and up the Lake to the protection of the Tyonderoga and Mount Independence. And aside what's already in bags, we are devoid of powder." Arnold glanced about the ruined cabin: "Where's that bucket of powder you fetched?"

"Both cannons loaded, double-shot, and the powder—enough for three charges—be in that stern locker."

"I see, you needed the bucket for another purpose," Arnold said with understanding. "All right, you are the senior matross present. These men are under your orders, which are to keep up as incessant a fire to keep the British armada at bay as you are able to maintain. I shall send down all the powder from the gun deck since we are standing in to Ferris Bay on the Verdmont side ever as fast as the men can sweep. It would mean unconscionable delay to turn for a broadside. Ferris Bay is shallow and their draughts will keep the British capital ships from following directly. We shall run the gundalos and row gallies onto the shore, burn them, and march south to Mount Independence." Arnold knelt and placed a palm on Goldsmith's forehead. "Why, Tom, no fever a'tall! And Volunteer Frost here, he's as handy with an adze as he is with a cannon. Likely he can whittle you out a leg of wood will serve as good as your wounded one."

Arnold stood to take his leave. "You and your men will be free to come on deck when you've fired away every kernel of powder, and . . ."

"And we'll bring Tom Goldsmith with us, General Arnold," Joseph said, finishing the sentence for Arnold, who had one foot already mounted on the ladder, his face screwed up in thoughtful worry. "He won't be left behind." Joseph would have said more but a bar shot fired from the nearest British warship scythed away a three-foot section of the starboard counter timber without throwing a single splinter inward. No one in the cabin was injured, and the upper counter planking, with its eyebolts for the cannon tackle, was thankfully spared.

"All clamp on the starboard cannon running tackles," Joseph barked, the words of command coming easy. "I'll dog the traversing tackle." He gathered the tail rope around his stiff fingers and strained with his utterly bottomed but still enthusiastic scratch crew to bowse the 18-pounder to its stop. "Slack all," he rasped, then "Stand clear" as he seized the quoin and searched for a target, though having the foresight to prick the vent first. A three-masted ship swam across his vision. *Inflexible!* And she was broadside-to, scarce four hundred yards away—readying her own broadside. Joseph jammed the quoin forward to depress the barrel, seized the linstock and set its smoldering glower to sizzle on the granules of priming powder, then threw himself out of the path of recoil.

Joseph did not mark the fall of shot but busied himself with the larboard cannon, adjusted its quoin to his satisfaction and touched the glowing coal of slow match to the priming powder. Joseph was free from all worry, because he had fully accepted the fact that having miraculously lived thus far and escaped drowning by no more than a second, he would likely be killed by the next broadside fired by a British warship. And knowing that he had come so close to death many times before and could well die in the next broadside freed him from worrying about death. Rather, the knowledge added an eloquent grandeur and joyous intensity to life while yet he stood upright and fought the 18-pounders with fierce delight and cruel, deadly efficiency.

◆ XXV ◆

⊛ ⊛ ⊛ ⊛ ⊛ HE PORTUGUESE ISLAND OF PRÍNCIPE,
⊛   ⊛ THE FIRST DESTINATION OF THE *Bride of*
⊛   T   ⊛ *Derry* AFTER IT CLEARED THE BAR THAT
⊛ ⊛ ⊛ ⊛ ⊛ PROTECTED THE LAGOON IN FRONT OF
Quidah, was three weeks in the *négrier's* wake when the eye-
disease appeared in the slave hold. Wick Nichols had shaped
a course to Príncipe to take on firewood, goats, chickens,
bananas, and coconuts for the crew's diet, and one hundred
bushels of manioc flour, yams, fava beans, millet, maize, pease,
and rice, seasoning salt and peppers for the diet of the cargo.
The cargo had been discharged into walled and roofed barracoons, the women and children below the presumptive age of
ten unfettered into one barracoon, and the men and male children above the age of ten, still shackled two-by-two—the men
of the *Bride of Derry* referred to them as *deuces*—into another
barracoon, with guards around.

Every day the cargo had been led, women and children in the
morning, the men in the afternoon, to a small river half a mile
from the barracoons where they were permitted to bathe. The
crew of the *Bride of Derry,* those not required to stand guard
over the cargo, freighted every water barrel the *Bride* possessed
to another small stream running into the calm waters of the
Gulf of Guinea above the town of Santo António. The barrels
were emptied, scoured thoroughly with sand, rinsed carefully,
and equally carefully filled with fresh water. The water barrels and fresh stores were then stowed and chocked to prevent

shifting in a seaway, and then the vigilant, carefully supervised reloading of the cargo commenced.

Geoffrey had taken several hours with Wick Nichols' quadrant and basic navigational instruments to calculate the exact latitude of Santo António's harbor: one degree, thirty-seven minutes north of the equator. A chart in the port captain's possession gave the longitude as exactly zero degrees, but Geoffrey's computations showed the harbor one degree east of the master line of longitude. Wick Nichols dismissed Geoffrey's astronomical studies contemptuously and set him to scribing a proper inventory of the cargo. In some wise the *Bride of Derry* had three hundred and nineteen souls crammed and packed below decks: one hundred and fifty-eight men; one hundred and twenty-one women; and forty children below the age of ten, fifteen girls and twenty-five boys.

And it was a cargo of despair and misery, particularly so for the men in the forward hold beyond the barricade, who were packed like herrings in a barrel, though methodically spoonways. Two men shackled together lay on their right sides—less stress on their hearts, it was thought—belly-to-back, heads to larboard and facing aft. Two other shackled men lay on their right sides belly-to-back, heads to starboard and facing forward, so that the drawn-up knees of the two men laying head-to-foot were thrust into the groin of the man opposite him. Two feet above the densely packed bodies a wooden platform had been hastily built as berths to accommodate more captives. As close as Geoffrey could calculate when he went into the forward holds to give the captives water, each man occupied a maximum space that was five feet long by slightly more than two feet wide, with a height of a few inches less than two feet.

Geoffrey descended into the forward hold twice a day, just after dawn and in the early afternoon, to take the male slaves water. He tied a kerchief soaked in vinegar around his nose and lower face in a vain attempt to block out the stench of feces, urine, and perspiring bodies laid out in the dim, fetid, exceedingly hot and airless hold. Geoffrey had taken a lantern into the hold the first day he brought water to the slaves, but the candle wick would not stay lit, so poor was the air. Geoffrey had computed the amount of fresh water fetched aboard at Príncipe to the gill. Now that the *Bride* had her fragile, perishable cargo and was westward bound, speed was everything. If Nichols' estimate that the *Bride* would reach the Carolina coast in sixty days, or if held back by contrary winds, unlikely this time of year, would touch at an island in the Caribbean, then each slave aboard was due a total of four quarts of water a day. There would be no washing in fresh water, of course, and of that allowance at least half would go into the gruel that fed the slaves. Of course, the women and children, who were not shackled and were on deck most of the day, did not require the same allowance, so what they did not require could be served out to the slaves in the forward hold.

"Goes you in there by yourself the first nigger thinks he can get his hands on your gullet will kill you in an instant," Wick Nichols had said, in an effort to dissuade Geoffrey from entering the hold unless accompanied by two men armed with pistols and whips. But Geoffrey persisted, and while Jabez McCool, or anyone else among the crew, refused to go into the hold with him, at least Jabez and the two comfort women he had claimed as his own would fill the pannikins from the water butts brought on deck and bring them to the opening in the barricade. It took Geoffrey the better part of one hour to haul the pannikins the length of the hold—placing his feet carefully to avoid stepping on anyone in the dense swelter of humanity—and gave each man a drink from a calabash holding exactly four gills. The slaves had retreated inside themselves and regarded him through sad, dull, resigned eyes that neither thanked nor mocked his efforts. That watched him as if he did not exist, or as if he existed but they did not.

In the late afternoon the male slaves were brought on deck, carefully, under the watchful eyes of men armed with muskets and whips. They were made to leap and move about for exercise, so much as their shackles, the confined area of the deck on the forward side of the barricade, the sheer press of numbers, and the roll and pitch of the ship as it plowed through the seaway allowed. Then food, a thick soup of millet, pease, beans and mashed yams, seasoned with peppers and larded with slush, was brought up from the galley in pannikins, one pannikin and wooden spoons enough for ten men. After the male slaves had eaten they were given another four gills of water. Then the slaves were taken in groups of two deuces to a small cleared section of deck near the fore topsail sheet bitts in front of the foremast, where a hose had been rigged. The pumps were worked and each deuce got a jet of sea water sprayed upon the two men for all of thirty seconds before being moved along in a methodical line to the forward hold, where they were secured for the night.

The evening before the eye disease appeared Geoffrey Frost had gotten excellent altitudes of Venus and the moon with the captain's quadrant and confirmed the *Bride*'s position as eight degrees west of the master line of longitude and some fifty leagues south of Cape Palmas. Cape Palmas marked the point where the strong Guinea Current melded into the true Atlantic Ocean, and the *Bride* could alter course from a westerly heading to northwest by west after another day's run.

Mightily satisfied with himself and his calculations, Geoffrey had thrown down his skimpy pallet outside the door to Wick Nichols' cabin, curled up upon it, and fell immediately asleep, oblivious to the hoarse, guttural rutting sounds emanating from the captain's cabin. Wick Nichols had appropriated for his own use at least three comfort women. Geoffrey was awakened by the confused shouts of alarm, the clamor coming from forward, but before he could collect his wits from the deep, dreamless sleep he had enjoyed, Wick Nichols, bursting from his cabin, had stepped over him and flashed up the companionway, taking the steps three at a time.

Geoffrey followed at a more leisurely pace, detouring by the galley where he helped himself to a slush cake keeping warm atop the brick hearth. He gained the deck by the scuttle immediately in front of the mainmast. The heavy door piercing the barricade—normally securely barred—was standing open. Geoffrey Frost stepped through the portal into bedlam. Three members of the *Bride*'s crew were hopping about the deck as if possessed by demons. A deuce of slaves was sprawled on the fore deck. Wick Nichols thrust his staff under one moaning body, levered it over, and shrank back.

"It be the ophthalmia for sure," Nichols said tightly. He looked around at the crew. "Who brought these men up from the hold?" he demanded. "Tell me now."

"I did, Capt'n," a crewman Geoffrey knew as Crowell Roddenbury said hesitantly. "T'was me 'n' Creen Bullock. We heard them moanin' 'n' carryin' on frightful all during the midwatch but just left 'em be until it was light enough to sort out what was actual from the skimble-skamble stuff. We fetched up this deuce so's to have a proper look in the light."

"Did you touch your eyes?" Nichols demanded, glaring at the men.

The men shuffled their bare feet on the deck and did not meet Nichols' glare. "Don't know if we did or not, Capt'n," Creen Bullock confessed.

"Damon, where is Damon, where is our ship's surgeon?" Wick Nichols looked hurriedly around the crewmen gathered in loose skeins on the foredeck, but his twin brother was nowhere in sight.

"Most like he be layin' with his comfort woman," an ashenfaced Holly volunteered, "in his cuddy just off the galley."

"Roust him hither," Nichols commanded grimly, "and fetch along two barrels of vinegar. We'll need more vinegar later, much more." Nichols kicked one of the moaning figures in the deuce savagely. "Stop your gob," he shouted: "You likely be the one who brought the ophthalmia aboard." Nichols kicked the slave again. Geoffrey shrank back against the barricade as he got his first good look at the slave's eyelids, which were scaled over with large, bleeding scabs.

"Where's that vinegar?" Nichols demanded. "We've got the eye-disease among the men and we're likely to lose every one 'less they get treated quick like."

Damon scuttled up, crab-like, naked except for a cotton shirt he was buttoning hurriedly. Geoffrey could see that he was very frightened. "We ain't never had the eye-disease 'mongst our cargoes in the past," Damon said, his voice trembling.

"Well, we sure got it now," Nichols snapped, "'n' every black bastard we have to throw overside is a plain loss of fifty pounds. What's the treatment?"

"You've sent for vinegar, I hear," Damon said tremulously.

"I did, but you're the surgeon. What's the treatment?"

"Sponge their eyes with vinegar, bind their hands so's they can't rub their eyes. Get every man out of the hold, clean the hold with vinegar and burn sulfur to draw the humours. That's the classic treatment vouched for by the learned French surgeon Surcouf, of wide experience in these matters." Geoffrey could see that Damon was exuding fear from every pore.

Holly and his mate trundled up a pipe of vinegar and half a dozen pannikins. "You, Roddenbury and Bullock, anyone else may have touched a slave, bathe your faces, particular attention to your eyes, in this vinegar, then get below and bring up the men slaves. Stretch them out along the bulwarks. The rest of you," Wick Nichols glared around at the crewmen of the *Bride of Derry*, "wet sponges in the vinegar 'n' wash out the eyes of the slaves as they come up. You, Holly, fetch along some small ropes to bind the slaves' hands so's they can't rub their eyes 'n' spread the disease."

"I ain't signed on to get the eye-disease," a crewman named Loam Beech said fearfully, shrinking back against the barricade. In an instant Wick Nichols struck the man to the deck with the terrible knob of his staff. Nichols prodded the man's ribs unmercifully with the tip of the staff until the man writhed like a snake.

"You signed on for a share in the profit attendant to landin' prime slaves in the Carolinas, 'n' that encompasses what's got to be done gets done," Nichols said savagely. Nichols dipped a calabash in a pannikin of vinegar that Holly was filling, balancing one pipe of vinegar atop another so the opened bung could gush into the pannikin. He dashed the calabash into Loam Beech's eyes and kicked the man to his feet. "You're proof against the ophthalmia! Now get below and roust up the cargo. Remember! The eye-disease be ephemeral if treated soon enough!"

Geoffrey Frost seized a pannikin of vinegar and a sponge and went to the aid of the first deuce to be brought up from the hold. He guided the sightless men to a space against the starboard bulwark, got them seated as best he could, and bathed their faces liberally with vinegar. "No, no," he told them repeatedly, as soothingly as possible, as the slaves rubbed their eyelids vigorously. "You must not do that, you will only spread the infection." Geoffrey knew the men could not understand what he was saying, but he kept his voice calm and moved to the next deuce. A fearful Holly moved in behind Geoffrey with lengths of small ropes that he used to bind the hands of the slaves to the shackles encircling their ankles so they could not possibly scratch despairingly at their eyes.

The foredeck was becoming increasingly thronged with deuces of slaves, and watching the slaves carefully, Wick Nichols permitted the deuces to be moved through the barricade once their eyes had been doused with vinegar and their hands bound. Geoffrey had labored unceasingly for he knew not how many hours, tending the men, whether they yet had the eye-disease or not, sponging their foreheads and eyes copiously with vinegar.

"Capt'n Wick, I figures we ain't got much vinegar left," Holly said, trundling up another pipe.

"Well, piss in their eyes, it's the same astringent," Nichols snapped. "What is this?"

"The last deuce found in the hold, Capt'n," Roddenbury said. "Ain't no soul below. This be the last." Roddenbury added as an afterthought: "Be 'em two dwarfs. None o' the others like 'em. Took a lot o' liberties with their fellows when they wus the king's favorites."

Nichols poked both slaves coupled together. "This bastard done scratched out his eyes," he said in frustration. He bent at the waist and peered intently at the face of the other slave shackled in the deuce. "This bastard most likely will keep. Get the irons off. Amos! Where the hell are you? Damn your black hide! I need you to remove this iron off this bastard!"

Black Amos plowed his way through the close-packed humanity, all too despairing to utter a word, only a collective low moaning like the rumble of far off thunder. He carried a hammer and a blunt cold chisel. Immediately he was beside the deuce of slaves he put the edge of the cold chisel atop the shank end of the bolt and struck the chisel with the hammer. The chisel snapped. "I'll fetch another chisel, Capt'n Nichols," Black Amos said.

"Ain't time," Wick Nichols said. "Fetch me an axe."

Loam Beech was at Nichols' side in a trice, holding out a rusty-bladed broadaxe. "Had it handy, Capt'n, agin your need," Beech said darkly.

"Holly, roll that empty pipe over here—be quick!" Nichols breathed heavily.

Holly shuddered but did as he was bid. Nichols rolled the empty pipe beneath the right leg, the shackled leg, of the dwarf who had gouged out his eyes from the pain of the eye-disease and raised the axe.

"No! No!" Geoffrey Frost screamed, a low, dull, despairing scream, and launched his frail weight against the upraised arm and its poised blunt instrument. He grasped his captain's arm, throwing off the man's aim so the axe blade thudded into the deck planking at an extreme angle and skittered out of Wick Nichols' hand. "They can both live, Captain, I'll tend them!"

Nichols snarled and batted Geoffrey away with the flat of his hand. Thrown a good four feet by the force of the blow, Geoffrey found himself atop the axe. He scrambled to his feet, gathered the axe and threw it desperately over the starboard bulwark. He was dimly aware of Wick Nichols' bulk advancing menacingly toward him. "Captain Ni . . ." he began, but his breath was driven explosively from him as Nichols' boot took him in the groin, lifted him, and threw him in an arc—the most acute nausea flooded through him, and then mercifully Geoffrey Frost knew nothing.

↩ XXVI ↪

@ @ @ @ @ rnold sent Broadhead to Congress' stern cabin to warn
@   **A** @ that the first gundalo had already run up on shore. "All
@   @ right," Joseph said, speaking with the natural authority
@ @ @ @ @ that came from one who knew his job and did it well.
He pointed to four men: "You take Tom Goldsmith on deck—
hand him gently, mind, as gently as you wish yourself handed
in like circumstance. You," Joseph pointed to two men, "collect broadaxes, hatchets, mauls and bring them hither. We
shall push these cannons into the deep so the British can never
recover them. Then we'll serve the cannons on the gun deck in
like fashion."

And push the 18-pounders overside they did, axing and
knocking out half a dozen planks of the starboard counter timber, hacking free the tackles and then launching first the starboard and then the larboard cannon across the sole and into the
void chopped in the counter. Joseph felt a deep pang of regret
as he ran the carriages Stonecypher and he had so laboriously
built across the cabin sole. He had invested many a blister and
sore muscle in their construction, but it could not be helped.
Relieved of over six tons of weight, *Congress* rode noticeably
higher in the water.

Then Joseph and his crew descended upon the gun deck and
in a riotous fever of destruction cut away and ran overside the
6 and 12-pounder cannons. "I rejoice the British shall not have
them," Arnold said, as he and Broadhead came unnoticed to
Joseph's side on the quarterdeck. A round shot fired from the

Carleton arched over *Congress* and threw up a great spout of water a dozen yards from the *Connecticut* gundalo run up on the shore. "Though it is hard to see ordnance that has served us so well away forever in the blink of an eye." Arnold sighed: "I hope Warner got away to Tyonderoga, and perhaps it is asking too much that Major General Gates"—Arnold disdainfully stressed the words "Major General"—"would have dispatched bateaux to tow our depleted fleet to Crown Point. As it is we must run *Congress* ashore to join *New Haven, Boston, Providence* and *Connecticut* in pyres funereal."

Arnold turned away. "I preserved one cartridge of powder destined for a 12-pounder and served it out to our marine force. Sufficient for three rounds per man. Our marines shall take positions ashore and dissuade any British from drawing too close. I shall thank you, Volunteer Frost, to collect some canvas for subsequent fashioning into hammocks to bear away our wounded." Arnold seized a half-pounder swivel gun on the larboard waist rail by its yoke, pulled it out of its socket and cast it as far as he could hurl it.

Joseph felt *Congress* shudder and slow as her keel took the ground. Then from the corner of his eye Joseph saw two British longboats rowing fiercely toward Ferris Bay from the northward, perilously close. *Congress* tilted slightly to larboard as she ran higher onto the ground and a fusillade of musket balls crackled from the longboats. Broadhead clutched his chest, slumped backward and tumbled overboard.

"Mister Broadhead!" Joseph shouted and followed the man overside. *Congress'* stern was only in six feet of water, and Joseph caught up Broadhead readily by the collar of his coat, swam a few strokes until the water was shallow enough to stand up, and began wading. Behind him Broadhead stumbled to his feet, pulled away from Joseph's grasp and stood up. Broadhead shook himself like a dog, water flying off him—not at all the reaction Joseph expected of a man who had just taken a musket ball in his chest. Broadhead reached into his coat and brought out the large silver snuffbox, a look of infinite pain flitting across his face. A thin brown mush of water and snuff drained from a shockingly large hole in the lid. Broadhead shook the snuffbox and Joseph heard the rattle of something heavy inside.

"This maddens me exceedingly," Broadhead growled as he turned and shook his fist at the British warships lying-to as far into Ferris Bay as their draughts permitted. "'Twas all the snuff I possessed in this world." His mouth now twisted in disgust, Broadhead cocked his arm to throw the snuffbox at the British longboats swarming across the bay like so many huge, grotesque water-walkers.

Joseph caught the Indian's arm. "Mister Broadhead, ponder upon it. Heaving the snuffbox at the enemy is small recompense for the service it has done you. Rather, preserve it as a manifestation of the Deity's sheltering hand."

Broadhead brought the snuffbox under his gaze and stared intently at the hole in its lid. His face broke into a smile and Broadhead reached out to pinch Joseph fondly on the earlobe. "I honor your wisdom, Volunteer Frost." He thrust the snuffbox into his coat. "A comforting totem to keep about me." He winced. "My breast is sore exceedingly."

Arnold appeared at the waist rail above them and threw Joseph a heaping armful of canvas. "Get the wounded sorted out," he shouted urgently. "Make hammocks with this canvas and suspend them from sweeps. Get the wounded away ever as quickly as you can. The British have their blood up, believing they can come ashore with impunity, but seeing how well our marines have behaved these last days, I doubt not their fire will dissuade any landing until we are ready to withdraw."

Arnold vaulted over the waist rail onto the shore, landed as lightly on his feet as a cat, and ran toward the half-circle of trees some two hundred yards from the bay's shore. The sunlight filtering through the bare branches of hardwood trees and boughs of pine and spruce gave no warmth. Joseph sloshed to the beach, thoroughly chilled by the wind that cut through his sodden clothing but grateful for his cousin John's shoes, which fitted him not at all well, but they were shoes. He saw a small dirk, blade snapped off a third of the way back from the tip, cast away contemptuously on the shore by someone who thought it no longer useful. Joseph could not comprehend his great fortune, but he took up the tool eagerly. He had no idea how hammocks could be fashioned from the billow of canvas, but he had an idea for fashioning carry-litters.

Joseph attacked the canvas, carving out great rectangular swatches. He stopped a man running by and demanded that he be brought a broadaxe, which miraculously the man did. Joseph detained two other men and demanded sweeps, and without quarrel they brought several of those long, heavy oars to him. Joseph smiled. If only his brother, Geoffrey, could see him now, giving orders and being obeyed because he expected to be obeyed in the natural order of things, because command and leadership were gifts, though they needed much nurturing, and those gifts must never be abused.

Joseph grasped the broadaxe, heedless of the pain inflicted on his hands, and hacked at the sweeps, cutting them in lengths of roughly nine feet. He rolled the short sides of a rectangle of canvas around the sweep lengths, pierced the lengths of canvas in three places close to the sweep and threaded strips of canvas through the punctures, tying them off hurriedly, fashioning one carry-litter in five minutes. It was far too much time. Joseph detained two men without wounds or firearms and set them to work making carry-litters.

Arnold pelted down the slope toward the *Connecticut* gundalo, shouting for Grant to get her alight. Then he darted into the *Providence*, rousted two men and sent them scuttling toward the *Congress*, awkwardly carrying a half-barrel of powder between them. Arnold met them at the *Congress*, swinging himself up onto the gun deck like the gymnast some people said he was. He took the half-barrel of powder the two men hoisted up to him and sent it on a wobbly roll across the littered deck toward the break of the waist with a quick kick. Arnold clapped a hand around the neck of matross Drinkwine, who was wandering around aimlessly with a slack-jawed, dazed look on his bowed head. "Get back aboard the *Congress* and kindle a fire; the foremast rigging's got a lot of tar in it. We've got to withdraw from this beach in the next five minutes—the British are pressing us sorely, and all our vessels built with such copious expenditure of sweat and aching muscle must be afire afore we withdraw."

Drinkwine nodded doltishly, and Arnold boosted him aboard the *Congress*. "Have you flint, man?" Arnold demanded, and when Drinkwine shook his head in the negative, Arnold pressed his tinderbox into Drinkwine's hands. "Bestir yourself, man! We've little time!"

Arnold trotted over to where Joseph and Broadhead were lowering a boy with a badly shattered arm onto a carry-litter made within the minute. "Better than the hammock I thought on," Arnold said with satisfaction. "Capital! Capital!" He turned at the sound of a loud *whoosh* as a bright jet of flame shot up the foremast of the *Congress*. The foremast tottered briefly and fell backward in a shower of sparks. Cordage and ruined spars on the fore gun deck burned brightly, and Drinkwine dropped off the larboard bow and staggered up the beach.

Joseph had been looking around anxiously. "General Arnold! I have not accounted for Lieutenant Goldsmith! He is not among the wounded we have claimed thus far!"

Arnold tripped Drinkwine with his sword as he shambled past. "Matross! Did you see Lieutenant Goldsmith aboard the *Congress*?"

Drinkwine stared at Arnold vacuously, working his ruined mouth for several seconds before he uttered a word. "Well, there was a body just where the gun deck met the quarterdeck, and the body spoke to me though I knew it was but a spirit, asking if I would take him off, or at the least throw him overside. But I, knowing that he was already dead and was speaking only as a spirit, answered that if he was not dead already he would be when the flames reached that barrel of powder . . ."

"Back! For God's sake, back all!" Arnold shouted, catching up one end of the carry-litter, Joseph the other, and they ran up slope toward the fringe of trees where the American musketeers who passed themselves off as marines were kneeling to aim at the British longboats converging on the beached remnants of the tiny American fleet. They were two hundred feet away from

Congress, panting, stumbling for all they were worth, when the flames reached the half-barrel of powder. *Congress* exploded, shattered timbers blowing outward on every side; the bows, blown off, were hurled fifty feet up on the shore. Dense sheets of flame raced the entire length of the *Congress,* drenching her in lurid colors, and propelled upward in a brief parabola was the body of Tom Goldsmith.

"Oh God, no!" Arnold sobbed. He drew his sword and looked around for Drinkwine, but the man, though shambling drunkenly some ten feet ahead of them, was carrying the forward half of a litter that bore a twitching, bloody body. "So be it," he said grimly. "Those who die outright are one thing, but those who are wounded must be recovered as best we can." He gestured toward Drinkwine. "I grieve for Tom Goldsmith, but I cannot find the heart to condemn yonder matross." Arnold sheathed his sword and ran forward eagerly. "Peter! Is that you, lad?"

"Yes, it's Peter Ferris," a thin, heavily freckled lad of no more than fourteen, dressed in butternut-colored homespun breeches and a coat to match, a shapeless wool cap pulled down over his ears, said. He got no further due to the interruption of a prolonged cannonade fired from the British capital ships. "Oh! Them varmints be firin' on the homestead! What woe!" The boy ducked involuntarily at the thunderclap of a cannon ball striking a rock outcropping nearby—a 12-pounder from the *Inflexible,* Joseph opined professionally. The ball sprayed huge shards of rock concentrically outward for a good dozen yards. Two men carrying a litter were thrown to the ground by the sting of rock, but fortunately they were well out of the killing zone of the rock shrapnel and, though mightily frightened, got to their feet uninjured.

"I'm afeared the British will extinguish the house your parents laboured so mightily to build," Arnold said, not unkindly, "and I shall much regret its loss, for 'tis a noble house in these parts. Nevertheless, I have close to one hundred and seventy men I must move off this shore and down to Tyonderoga, Peter, and I'm much afeared the British are even now ordering their Indian cohorts ashore to thwart our design. We must be away on the instant, not even paused to give our dead Christians burial."

"There are trails the red demons from Canada for sure lack knowledge, Gener'l Arnold, though I beg the loan of a firelock," Peter Ferris said, his voice quavering.

"Let me see what may be found," Arnold said shortly, turning and stumping down to a shattered barge washed up on the shore. Arnold rummaged around in the odds and ends of sail cloth and rigging cluttering the hulk and fished out—Uncle Pepperrell's musketoon! He came up the slight slope of the shore as fast as he could on his game leg, just as another cannonade screamed and slammed ashore. A concussion threw Arnold down, but he was on his feet as quick as a cat and held out the musketoon with trepidation. "It not be mine to gift, Peter . . ."

"That's fine, General," Joseph said quickly. "I had thought it left aboard the *Congress*. Juby and Uncle Pepperrell would want it employed to good effect. They both gift it willingly to kindred hands. I doubt, however, if the piece will give fire . . ."

"I know its employ," Peter Ferris said firmly, "I can tend it as we run, for run we must, not walk."

Joseph cast a glance despairingly over the desolate scene of fiercely burning gundalos and the row-galley *Congress*, thick, turgid smoke streaming ashore with great showers of angry red embers amidst the sullen billows. Bodies of men he knew and had fought alongside moved sluggishly and obscenely in the swell from the west. Joseph wanted desperately to delay long enough to bury them, honor them, but he could do no more for them than he had been able to do for Juby. He wanted to honor these men even in the horrific defeat of Arnold's small, so small, fleet, which had dared contest the Royal Navy head on.

Benedict Arnold saw Joseph's anguished gaze and paused a moment. "I do hope it may comfort you, young Frost, if we recite the service for the burial of the dead at sea, as taken from the Book of Common Prayer. I've had recourse to the verse far too often in my time as a ship's captain, though I confess memory is a curse, given the demands of the time."

"We have time, General," Joseph said, reaching for Arnold's hand, and together they knelt.

"We therefore commit their bodies to the deep, looking for the General Resurrection in the Last Day, and the life of the World to Come, through our Lord Jesus Christ; at whose second coming in glorious majesty to judge the world, the sea shall give up her dead; and the corruptible bodies of those who sleep in Him shall be changed, and made like unto His Glorious Body; according to the mighty working where by He is able to subdue all things unto Himself."

"Amen!" Joseph declared hurriedly. "As fine a memorial as we can leave those . . ." Joseph groped for the phrase. He had heard Geoffrey use it more than once. "As fine as we can leave those who have walked through the wall between life and death for our sake." He got to his feet, reeling with fatigue. But he reached for the handles of a litter and seized them eagerly. "General Arnold, send forward young Mister Ferris as our pathfinder, and willingly we follow!"

Afterwards Joseph had no memory of the journey to Tyonderoga. And that was a blessing. At some point the man carrying the front part of the litter collapsed. Joseph paused only long enough to throw the man onto the litter and then seize the forward handles and lunged forward, tugging both men in the litter, until his sight went all red and black and there came a merciful void. He fell forward, coughing and choking and spitting up bile, to his knees, and then got obstinately, obdurately to his feet and lunged forward, staggered forward. And then the litter overturned, and somehow Joseph got the two men, their limp bodies, onto his shoulders, both shoulders, and managed to stagger forward again.

Joseph made all of one hundred yards before he met the stone wall of fatigue, and he lay down for several moments, breath rasping between his teeth, courage and strength failing, then arose with a fierce roar, grasped each man by his collar, and staggered forward once again, dragging the men, screaming as loud as he could, "Juby, Juby, heed my prayer and assist me!" And then there was no sensation of pain or fatigue, and he dragged the men as easily as if they were rag dolls. And he slept. Joseph slept and yet he walked, and his feet unerringly kept the path that young Peter Ferris measured out for the exhausted, utterly spent remnants of men who had so bitterly contested the British passage up Lake Champlain, and whose vessels were now charred hulks on a bitter shore behind them. The British fleet now had unfettered range of the Lake regardless, and all their labors and sacrifices had gone for naught. "Juby, Juby, heed my prayer," Joseph whispered mechanically, and marched on, marched on, and on, and on.

"Pull up there, hoss," a voice said, a hand restraining him. "You look plumb tuckered."

Joseph Frost opened one eye with great difficulty. He was quite happy in the world where he lived. He was warm; he was comfortable. He felt very much alive. But he begrudged the thought of having to open an eye. For he knew that opening even one eye would cause the immediate loss of every sense of well-being, comfort and warmth. Joseph reluctantly forced open one eye and focused blearily and uncertainly on a short, stocky man, dressed in deerskins much like Caleb Mansfield wore. The man's black beard was shot through with a dense white streak that was remarkably replicated in the skunk pelt he wore as a cap.

Abruptly Joseph's bones dissolved and he pitched forward, saved from a hard fall only by the strong arms of skunk pelt. "Waal, hoss, you done walked a spell, that's fer sure. Your shoes done be run out of soles, 'n' the men you've been draggin', waal, one o' 'em's been dead a while, and looks like the other ain't got no hide left on his arse." But Joseph heard nothing else, for sleep, true sleep, overcame him, and he never knew that skunk pelt let him down gently onto a litter improvised from a door, or that two men bore him away.

Joseph awoke to a familiar voice. "Well, Joseph Frost, I've bound your feet in a poultice of fennel and ox lard, and that crease of a bullet on your forearm don't warrant a bandage. Suffice the self-same ox lard will heal it handsomely."

Joseph looked up dreamily into the face of Samuel Stonecypher. "Why, Samuel! I am verily surprised to find myself alive. I have never felt so close to death since I had myself smuggled aboard my brother's privateer vessel in a coffin—wherein I lay for three days beneath coils of cable that weighed down the lid and limited strictly the passage of air." Joseph stretched his limbs, his arms, his legs, hesitantly. Lo! Though his feet ached abominably, he was complete! Joseph turned his head to one side and saw that he was ensconced once again in the tent he and Samuel and Juby had shared, and he nestled on a bed of clean straw with a whole, complete blanket that Stonecypher had somehow gotten. Juby! He was alive and Juby, who had followed him to the Lake, now lay forever in it. It should have been the other way around.

The canvas flap that served as the tent's entrance was thrust aside and Benedict Arnold, his face a-bristle with beard yet untended by a razor, stumped in. Arnold maneuvered a small stool near Joseph's pile of straw and sat down heavily, precariously balanced. Without preamble Arnold said: "We gave the British one hell of a fight. Carleton looked in at the fortifications of Tyonderoga this morning. Spent an hour or more studying the cannons and men through his spy glass, and decided the season was too far advanced. Tyonderoga, with its nine thousand men, properly supported, proves too tough a nut to crack with snow already on the ground. So he is on the wing, a fair wind from the south assisting greatly, down the Lake to disperse his forces to await next spring's campaign." Arnold clenched his jaw in satisfaction. "No British ain't going overland to the Mohawk River, or Hudson's River, for that matter, this season."

Joseph digested the information soberly. "Nine thousand men, you say, General, here at Tyonderoga? What we could have done with half a thousand men more the morning the British came against us at Valcour!"

Arnold sighed heavily. "Aye, another five hundred men and more ammunition, and another three row gallies, and one or two vessel commanders less than what we had, and . . ." Arnold stopped, probably aware he had said too much. "As it is, I count eighty-two men who took their last breath in our company. The British took twice that many as prisoner, but I expect Carleton will give us back Waterbury and Hawley, not so much to appear the soul of accommodation and conciliation to us rebels, but to saddle us, to saddle us . . ."

With a discreet cough Samuel Stonecypher stepped outside the tent, to afford Arnold and Joseph a greater degree of privacy. Arnold paused again and shot out his heavy underlip petulantly. "You've done more than a volunteer should be asked to do, young Frost. Time you was on your way back to Portsmouth so's your mother can pack some meat on them bones of yours. Our affairs will abide."

"My mother lives mostly in another world, General, and I owe Juby a service I can never repay for his sacrifice, so I think to soldier on with you a while longer."

"Well, that musketoon your man fetched along has seen good service. Young Peter Ferris potted two red heathen with it defending our retreat from Ferris Bay. And surely the fact your man fetched along our fleet's battle flags will always be remembered." Arnold shrugged and fidgeted. "As for me, I've got to see to my family in Connecticut, and figure out how to square my accounts before I can think of another campaign. All my papers were aboard the *Royal Savage* when she burned, and it will try the patience of all the saints in heaven above to piece together what monies were received and what monies went where." Arnold reached out to pat Joseph's arm. "I'm going to be in the environs of Fort Tyonderoga for quite a spell, young Frost."

"I can't go back to Portsmouth just yet," Joseph said urgently, anxious that his urgency would betray his fear of facing his family, his friends; his guilt for having run in the first place; and the greater guilt of Juby's death. "This Continental Army has got to need men who know how to point a cannon."

Arnold sucked a tooth reflectively. "Aye, that Boston bookseller who learned the art of the matross from a military treatise, and who serves as His Excellency General Washington's matross-in-chief, would be God-almighty pleased to have you pointing cannons for him, young Frost. There are some major tests a-coming, and General Gates is confident enough that Carleton ain't going to sail back and lay siege to Tyonderoga this season that he's sending reinforcements to General Washington, who needs them sorely . . . though I think it would be a special kindness for your parents was you to return to Portsmouth soon as you can get about on your feet."

"I can get about good enough on my feet, if called to, right now, General," Joseph said eagerly. "Colonel Knox surely knows I can dray cannons, and under your tutelage I've learned to employ them well enough."

"Your family," Arnold began. Then he stopped. "All right, I'll ask General Gates to find a place for you in the next draft of men going south. Get you into a wagon so's you won't have to walk so much. And I'll send a letter ahead to Henry Knox telling him you're coming. But tell me, Volunteer Frost, what do you think now about this business of fighting a war?"

"It's gross injustice, fear, hate, lust, sickness, stupidity, dishonesty, avarice, and stupidity doubled, all lumped in with futility and despair and death, and I don't like it at all," Joseph Frost said forcefully, meaning every word he uttered.

"Yes, war is all that, and more, and maybe we ain't never going to see the end of it," Arnold said, getting wearily to his feet. "Least that's what the Scriptures say, though I've always hoped the Scriptures was wrong in that regard. But wars only get won when we send our best men to do the fighting. Hell of a thing to have to say, but I'll tell you one thing, your man, Juby, understood that, and he was the best there was." Arnold rested a hand lightly on Joseph's shoulder for a brief moment. "Luck to you, volunteer, 'cause the British done chewed up a hull lot of our best men, and we're in mortal danger of running out." Then Stonecypher held aside the tent flap and Benedict Arnold was gone.

"Kin't rightly tolerate the thought of goin' back to my wife and daughters this moment," Samuel Stonecypher said. "I might as well carry on with you to see if this Knox fella you've praised to the skies actually knows which end o' the cannon to pint at the British regulars."

EOFFREY WAS BROUGHT TO HIS SENSES
G ONLY AFTER THREE COPIOUS PANNI-
KINS OF SEAWATER HAD BEEN DOUSED
ON HIM. HE HAD NEVER FELT SO ILL
in his brief life; he was far more nauseated than the seasickness
that had engulfed him at the beginning of the voyage, far more
wretched than the bout with malaria. His groin was afire with
pain, and he had no feeling in his legs. A heavy hand slapped his
cheeks, and Geoffrey started up—and vomited.

"Not on my deck, you don't!" Geoffrey recognized the
voice of Wick Nichols. He attempted to focus his eyes, but
only vague shadows swam in the lurid pain of his miasma. He
slipped back into unconsciousness. Another pannikin of seawater sluiced over him. Someone grasped him from behind
and hoisted him to his feet. The pain in his groin overwhelmed
him, and Geoffrey retched, though nothing came up. Slowly
his eyes focused, and in the confusion of sight returning he did
not at first comprehend the spectacle of Jabez McCool's body
sprawled like a broken doll in a small space on the foredeck
cleared of shackled deuces of slaves. Geoffrey gasped painfully,
unwilling to keep his horrified gaze off the corpse lying face up,
a thin tendril of blood oozing from a great purple bruise on
Jabez' forehead.

Another slap and Geoffrey focused, with the greatest difficulty, on Wick Nichols, the right side of his face awash with blood
and his nose bent askew and bleeding profusely still. Nichols

was tossing his cudgel from hand to hand, and Geoffrey knew that Nichols intended to club out his brains.

"Don't hurt the boy, Capt'n," the voice of the person holding him upright implored. "He didn't mean nothin' by it." Mate Crowninshield!

"This boy mutinied against his lawful captain," Wick Nichols spat in great agitation, his eyes bulging, staring, and spittle flecking his lips. "He encouraged a mutiny, signaled that lump of offal, McCool, to attack me unawares, struck off my ear with the chisel he snatched up, intending to smite my head crown to chin, he did. Knocked out my teeth, he did! Clung to me like a cat on a mouse, he did! 'Til I gained my staff and brained him with the knob, I did! Cub raised his fist against his captain!"

Geoffrey only vaguely collected the densely packed deuces of moaning slaves. He did not see the two dwarfs. He finally broke his glance away from the grotesquely skewed body of dear, dear Jabez McCool, from Poole, the gentle voice who had befriended him when he was sick unto death in the manger at the beginning of this voyage from horror to horror.

"Get that gurry overside, and then we'll deal with this'n as the laws against mutiny demand." Wick Nichols glared at Geoffrey. And Geoffrey Frost knew that he looked at madness. He knew that he would shortly be dead, and that knowledge did not bother him in the least.

"Capt'n, McCool's a Christian, baptized so. We've got to give him a Christian burial 'n' all the rights of the service there belongin'. We can't just heave him overside like we do the heathen."

"Christian be damned, Mate Crowninshield! He struck his captain from behind with the base intention o' murderin' his captain, immediately after this cub raised his hand in mutiny. McCool be only a sack o' shit 'n' warrants no words out of the Book. Overside with McCool . . . now!" Nichols' face reddened like the coals of a forge swept with a blast of air from a bellows. "Then we'll deal with this'n as must meet all 'em's mutiny!"

"Capt'n, he's been navigatin' us . . ." Crowninshield began haltingly.

"Two of us can navigate, Mister Mate. We've done so on many a passage. He has set his course straight to hell, 'n' the devil'll take him."

"He's got important family . . ."

"Log book entry will show he died of the eye-disease, got while carin' so kind like for the niggers came down with the ophthalmia, as this old *Bride* began to make its northing fifty leagues below Cape Palmas. Family can't argue with facts writ down plain in the log book, with your signature alongside mine, that's right, ain't it, Mister Mate. Or perhaps you may wish to find yourself on the bowsprit with the boy." Geoffrey sensed the shudder race through Crowninshield's body, but he had no idea what Nichols meant.

Geoffrey Frost forgot his own pain and wept as he witnessed the body of his great and true friend Jabez McCool heaved overside like a sack of meal. He knew the men who trundled Jabez overside were not bad men. He knew those men were, like him, Jabez' friends. He knew that Mate Crowninshield was his friend, that Holly was his friend, but their fear was unable to stand up to the unalloyed cruelty and wickedness embodied in Pythias Nichols. Holly and Crowninshield led Geoffrey reluctantly to the bowsprit, clambering over the bodies of the slaves, whose moanings had abruptly stilled.

"Ye ever hear-tell about the punishment o' bowspritin', youngster?" Mate Crowninshield asked tremulously, once they had passed over the mass of bodies and stood at the knighthead.

"No, Mate," Geoffrey said listlessly, barely able to maintain consciousness.

"The capt'n has condemned ye for mutiny, and ye are to be tied to the bowsprit, that is, yere feet be tied 'neath the bowsprit, yere hands free. Holly's goin' to bring ye a halter o' rope directly. On that will be tied a pottle of water, a bag o' bread, 'n' a knife. Once ye are on the bowsprit ye can call out all ye want to yere former mates, but they're obliged not to answer ye. Not say a word to ye . . ." Crowninshield paused and swallowed hard. "No one can speak a word to ye, nor extend a hand to ye. Anyone does so, 'n' the capt'n hears o' it, he joins ye on the bowsprit."

Despite the pain that wrapped Geoffrey in its cocoon, he shivered at the barbarity of the punishment. "My hands will be free; they won't be tied?" He tried but failed to keep his voice from quavering, the fear from showing.

"Aye, yere hands not be tied, so's ye can grip the bowsprit. But once on the bowsprit, ain't no way ye can ever come back to the ship. Ye are out there . . . until . . ."

Holly, a most sorrowful Holly, came up slowly. He held two pieces of rope, one a short loop with a corked calabash lashed through its coach-whipping cover, a bag of hessian tied off, and a short clasp knife with the rope run through its grommet. Holly stepped on the thick coils of gammoning rope and eased his bulk onto the bowsprit, hitching his way gingerly along as far as the saddle for the running rigging before tentatively extending a foot to the bowsprit horses. It was abundantly clear to Geoffrey that Holly and Crowninshield were far out of their element.

"Follow me out, Geef-roy," Holly pleaded despairingly. "Beelzebub sends somebody else, likely tie you far out as the cap. But you kin back up to the riggin' 'n' keep hold o' the butt o' the jib-boom." Holly began to cry. "It ain't much, Geef-roy. Lordie, boy, it ain't nothin' except perhaps hangin' on to the bowsprit a little longer . . ."

"Yes, I understand, Holly," Geoffrey said. He turned and extended his hand to Mate Crowninshield. "Good-bye, Mister Mate. I anticipate we shall be shipmates again, and I thank you for your many kindnesses throughout this voyage." Geoffrey stiffly shook hands with Mate Crowninshield, then faced the bowsprit. The pain from the vicious kick to his groin still seared his body, but his sense of balance had returned. Geoffrey Frost walked deliberately out onto the rolling, pitching bowsprit, eased around the fore topmast stay, then gently lowered himself astride the bowsprit. His groin shrank from contact with the spar, but he knew that Wick Nichols was observing closely the movements of his executioners, and Geoffrey was determined to give Nichols no cause to condemn Holly or Mate Crownin-shield. He repressed the cry that rose to his lips and extended his legs beneath the spar.

"Geef-roy," cried Holly, balanced precariously on the jib-boom guy, taut beneath the bowsprit, his face ashen with fear at being so far from his accustomed galley, and at abetting a crime, "Geef-roy."

"It's okay, Holly. Do your duty as you must. Captain Nichols is watching you closely. You must give him no cause to punish you for disobedience as well." The fire in his groin was overwhelming, and Geoffrey lifted his torso slightly on the round spar. He felt Holly pass the length of rope several times around his ankles, then tie off the ends.

"Geef-roy," Holly said plaintively, "I tied the knot loose, but you know how rope swells up when it gets wet."

"That's okay, Holly, I have a knife."

"Soon's I give it to you," Holly said. He flipped the loop of rope with knife, bread bag and calabash over Geoffrey's shoulder and did not let go of the calabash until he was sure the loop was settled securely. Holly looked up at Geoffrey, his soul reflected in his round, no longer jovial face, one hand resting lightly on Geoffrey's leg. "Gar, Geef-roy, you ain't got no flesh a-tall on your bones." Then, peering up even more anxiously, he said: "You had words for the mate, Geef-roy. Have you any words for me?"

"Of course, Holly," Geoffrey said, leaning down to plant an affectionate kiss atop Holly's forehead. "The same words for you, also. I expect we shall be shipmates again, in another, a better, place."

Holly's eyes screwed up and he began to cry. Geoffrey kicked the man in the chest with his trussed feet. "Holly," he hissed, "Beelzebub is watching. Never let Beelzebub see you cry. He'll be on you like a chicken on a grasshopper, for then he'll know he's stronger than you, and he'll use that knowledge to advantage." Geoffrey drew himself erect. "Good-bye, Holly, you've done your duty."

And then Holly was gone, inching his bulk along the jib-boom guy until he achieved the relative stability of the foredeck of the *Bride of Derry*. Geoffrey Frost shifted his position tentatively on the bowsprit, felt that his perch was secure enough to lean forward and grasp the butt of the jib-boom with both hands. He willed the pain away, and the pain abated. Geoffrey ignored the cries of the hands working the ship behind him. He was divorced entirely from them, already inhabiting a new world entirely his own, a world bounded on the nearest side by the sibilant hiss of the *Bride*'s forefoot as it neatly and precisely shouldered the water aside and rose and descended on the wave crests, skimble-skamble. A world bounded on the furthest sides by the reach of eye to the horizon.

A dark squall was building to the northeast, toward the great, long-suffering continent of Africa, fifty leagues over the horizon, a continent that had known and would continue to know so much violence, turmoil and bloodshed. But the wind was coming from almost directly astern, and Geoffrey laid his head on his arms, fingers gripping tightly the butt of the jib-boom. Behind him he heard the *Bride*'s crew loose and sheet home the fore topgallant and fore topsail. Geoffrey felt the *Bride* increase her pace measurably as the sails billowed taut and pressed down the forefoot. The motion of the bowsprit was hypnotic: rise, roll, thrust, wallow, dip, all in a repetitive rhythm to which a body could adjust. For a few moments Geoffrey Frost watched a bull dolphin exult in the *Bride*'s bow wave, tail stroke lagging just enough to permit the forefoot to brush the dolphin's flukes. Then the dolphin powered ahead in a burst of speed wondrous to behold, leaping in exuberance—jumping clear out of the water twenty feet, then thirty feet, in front of the *Bride*. Geoffrey wished he could be one with the dolphin. But then, unexpectedly—he slept.

Geoffrey awoke quickly as his body started to rotate around the bowsprit. He was under no illusion about the utter impossibility of his being able to claw his way back to his perch atop the bowsprit should he slip and find himself suspended upside down, his weight causing the rope to cut into his bound ankles. The stiff wind from astern brought with it the indescribable smells of food. Geoffrey did not turn his head but knew the male slaves were being brought on deck for their evening gruel. Geoffrey willed himself not to think of the food but focus instead on hopes the eye-disease was waning. All the same, he was ravenous.

Very carefully, he untied the neck of the bread bag and exposed the side of a flat loaf of unleavened bread. He measured out half a mouthful, bit it off and began to chew the rough, partially milled grain. The bread bulked up in his mouth, and Geoffrey carefully uncorked the calabash and allowed a minute trickle of water to cross his lips. He masticated the moistened bread slowly. The taste was exquisite. The male slaves had finished their feeding and had been secured in the hold for the night before the last half mouthful of the bread dribbled down Geoffrey's throat.

He rigged a crude bridle, with the loop of rope holding the water, bread and knife around the butt of the jib-boom, then interwove his fingers into the bridle and again permitted himself the luxury of sleep. Geoffrey was awakened by the arrival, then quick passing, of a vicious line squall. The bowsprit's heel, roll and toss was far more pronounced than the movement around the *Bride*'s center of gravity. Geoffrey clung to the improvised bridle for all he was worth, and when the rain swept out of the squall in curtains, he held his gaping mouth aloft, filling his mouth repeatedly, gulping down the water, chilled with the hint of electricity, until his stomach could hold no more. He slept again, and in the morning the bull dolphin was again in place, this time with an even dozen of his fellows.

Geoffrey Frost slept as much as he could, seeking to conserve energy, but in most of his waking hours he was acutely conscious of the ship's exaggerated motion on his solitary position on the bowsprit. He had not been seasick since awakening in the manger at the beginning of the voyage, but he was not proof against the wildly pitching toss, thrust, and stomach-lurching roll and screw of the bowsprit. Geoffrey vomited wretchedly, though there was very little that could come up, since nothing but water filled his stomach. He turned as best he could and regarded the *Bride of Derry*. Her black, rust-streaked hull appeared infinitely small compared to the towering press of sail she carried as she ran before the wind steady out of the southeast. Her figurehead was nondescript, much pummeled and weathered by water and wind, and the wood most likely had not known a touch of paint since her launching. Geoffrey had often gazed at the figurehead, at least from the rear and above, when his bowels had compelled him to the heads, but he was seeing the figurehead in a fresh perspective. A wistful woman. A sad young woman. Sad and wistful because she had been a new bride wedded to a seaman and she yearned ever seaward, hoping to spy the ship bringing her beloved up Lough Foyle to Londonderry on the northeast coast of Ireland? Or sad and wistful from the contemplation of the cargoes of misery that had followed her so unwillingly from Africa to the Caribbean and the coast of North America? Despite the dinginess of her canvas, with all her plain sail taut to capture the wind, briefly the old *Bride* was a thing of beauty.

Geoffrey considered the ingenuity of the punishment of bowspriting. He had only limited water and bread, and on pain of their own deaths the crew of the *Bride of Derry* could offer no encouragement to him, much less provide succor. No, they were forbidden even to acknowledge him. Geoffrey had a knife and thus exercised control over his own life. With one smooth stroke of the blade across his wrist, Geoffrey could drain away his life in a few listless minutes. Or he could use the blade to sever the rope binding his ankles, drop into the relaxing water beneath him, not stirring a limb, and sink down into blessed oblivion. But Geoffrey Frost knew there was no despair vast enough to justify or induce the taking of his own life. He might starve to death, or die of thirst, or perhaps go mad from hunger, thirst, the sun, and the relentless motion of the bowsprit. But he would not take his own life. Wick Nichols would not have that pleasure.

Geoffrey bleakly took stock of his situation. He had three small loaves of unleavened bread in the hessian bag, a calabash that held perhaps ten gills of insipid water, and a clasp knife.

He was not overly concerned about the water. He reckoned another squall bringing fresh water in the form of rain would materialize in the next day or two. What a thumb in Nichols' eye it would be were Geoffrey to survive on the bowsprit until a Caribbean port was fetched! Highly unlikely, though. The Caribbean was weeks away, and Geoffrey's gaunt body would not last another five days on the meager ration of bread.

Geoffrey forced his breathing to slow and reached behind him to grasp the forestay just above the forestay heart. He resolutely forced himself not to dwell upon his consuming hunger. He glanced down and his sun-cracked lips smiled at the antics of the dolphins gamboling in front of the *Bride*'s crisp bow wave. Very, very slowly Geoffrey opened the bread bag and tore off a piece of bread he calculated would be half a mouthful. As he carefully folded the piece of flat bread before placing it in his mouth, Geoffrey thought of the navigation charts in Nichols' cabin. The eye-disease had manifested itself among the male slaves as the *Bride* came up on a course trending northwest, turning northwest on the same longitude, eight degrees west of the prime meridian, as the unseen Cape Palmas many leagues to the north. The *Bride* was running up the coast of Africa, and somewhere around fifteen degrees of northerly latitude Geoffrey knew that Wick Nichols would take up a westerly course toward the Caribbean.

There were islands there, Portuguese owned, as were the islands in the Gulf of Guinea. The Green Islands! Geoffrey forced his heart to maintain its normal beat as he thought through the navigation involved. He knew from his discussions with Nichols and the pricks the captain had made in the charts that the *Bride* would bring the wind directly behind her somewhere in the latitudes of the Cape Verde Islands and head directly west. But how far away were the Cape Verde Islands? As his tired, greatly undernourished brain wrestled slowly with the navigational problems, Geoffrey Frost realized the *Bride of Derry* would traverse most of the bulge of Africa before arriving in the general latitude of the Cape Verde Islands.

Geoffrey set about deducing the *Bride*'s latitude, and his

breathing faltered as he realized the *Bride* could be no further north than five degrees above the Equator. Ten degrees of latitude, each degree with sixty minutes of distance equal to one nautical mile traversed—six hundred minutes or six hundred nautical miles, that was how far to the north the general latitude of the Cape Verde Islands lay. Geoffrey struggled with an approximation of the speed the *Bride* was making over the bottom. Perhaps one hundred nautical miles in a day's run. The Cape Verde Islands lay an impossible six days north and west. With a trembling hand Geoffrey Frost fumbled the cork from the neck of the calabash and slowly, timing the movement to the whipping motion of the bowsprit, trickled a thin stream of insipid water into his mouth.

The hallucinations came with the morning of the second day Geoffrey Frost had been on the bowsprit. Behind him the life of the ship went on, his presence on the bowsprit unacknowledged. Though several times in the days that followed, when the slaves were brought up and fed on the fore deck, Geoffrey sensed that Wick Nichols stood somewhere behind him, regarding him malevolently. But Geoffrey did not turn or in any way acknowledge Nichols' presence. He was divorced from the life of the ship, and the ship was divorced from him.

Geoffrey gathered from the fragments of conversation that penetrated through the hallucinations that the eye-disease was running its course. A few still living, shrieking bodies were thrown overside without ceremony on the third day, but after that the eye-disease vanished. Geoffrey paid no attention to the routine of the ship; he was bound up in the prophetic voices. Just what the voices foretold he was unable to say. He had expected to see the woman again, the woman with flaxen hair beckoning to him from the other side of a brook, but he did not. Then, in a moment of lucidity, he thought that perhaps the voices were his own. He had presence of mind enough to wrestle off his stupor for a few moments in the early morning, and an equal gauge of time just before the sun disappeared, to reach into the bread bag and break off and masticate a small piece of bread.

And then one morning when Geoffrey wrestled away the demons and the prophetic voices long enough to reach into the bread bag, there was no more bread. He spend the better part of a span of time—he had no idea how long that span of time was, nor did he care—delicately turning the bread bag inseams out and with his tongue carefully licking the jute for any crumb that may have been left. He hardly had the strength to lift the calabash, but it did not matter, for sometime during that day the *Bride of Derry* ran through a squall. Geoffrey was greatly refreshed, for his body was one livid sunburn. But the sunburn's torture resumed when the *Bride* ran out of the squall, and the relentless sun smote him mercilessly. By the time the blessed night fell, Geoffrey realized that the voices were those of the dolphins, and with a start he realized that he had been talking to the dolphins for days and days.

There they were, playing a mere four feet beneath him, the same dozen dolphins, plus the one great bull, indelibly marked with a crescent-shaped scar on the top of his head, immediately in front of his blow-hole. Geoffrey attempted to talk to the dolphins, but his tongue had swollen to fill his entire mouth. But the dolphins continued to talk to him. He tightened his fingers around the butt of the jib-boom spar and slept without dreaming or hallucinating the remainder of the night and the entire next day. Then he awoke just after the sun set on what he guessed was the last day of his life. Geoffrey reckoned the time was passing seven of the P.M. He raised his head to scan the evening sky. A crescent moon, with an orange-colored Mars— brighter than any star and not very far from the moon—greeted him. He noted that Mars was in the constellation Virgo, and in the cloudless night sky he dwelled for several pleasurable minutes upon the presence of Spica, the brightest star in Virgo.

High in the eastern sky the Milky Way was a glittering, elongated oasis; and in the northeastern sky Geoffrey recognized the bright stars Altair, Vega, and Deneb as they made up the summer triangle. Geoffrey smiled, and something small, something infinitesimally small and light, brushed against his right cheek. He felt carefully with his fingers until he encountered the animal. It climbed obligingly upon Geoffrey's forefinger, and he regarded it for long, uncomprehending moments in the pale light of the crescent moon, until he recognized it as a ladybug. The dolphins frolicking in the waves beneath him were talking to him again, and he clearly understood everything they were saying. Geoffrey Frost sought along the rope halter until he found the clasp knife and struggled to draw it open. The hinge was greatly rusted and his efforts were puny. But at last the blade laboriously opened, and with studied care and patience Geoffrey Frost reached below him to saw at the coils of rope encircling his ankles. At last, after infinite labor, one coil parted under the dull blade, and the rope fell away. An exultant Geoffrey Frost relaxed his grip and dropped into the warm, dark waters hissing beneath the bowsprit.

HISTORICAL NOTE FOR BOOK 4

The wooden vessels from the age of classic sail would not be permitted to enter any modern harbor. Maritime protection agencies would proclaim any vessel propelled solely by wind an unacceptable hazard to navigation, and no maritime agency would license such vessels for the routine transportation of passengers and cargoes between ports, domestic or international. The vessels themselves would be condemned as unfit, intolerably crowded, immensely uncomfortable, filthy and unsanitary beyond belief or description. The skipper of a moderately equipped sport fisher or cruising vessel, rarely venturing out of sight of land, with navigational aids such as Global Positioning Satellite receivers, radar, digital fathometers and weather chart facsimile receivers would blanch at the thought of remaining at sea overnight if forced to use only the quadrants and sextants, hourglasses and chip logs that were the ordinary navigational instruments of the period.

Parents of students enrolled in American primary schools may be pardoned their skepticism that Geoffrey Frost, not yet ten years of age, could have been exposed to mathematics through geometry, Latin and conversational French, and be able to hold his own in discourse with elders. Unfortunately, our contemporary society has deliberately designed its formal educational systems to make learning as difficult as possible. But children are capable of learning at a much higher level, and the children of Marlborough and Thérèse Frost received all the educational benefits available to prosperous merchant families of the era. Dame schools and private tutoring began at ages well below those at which today's children begin school, and much longer hours were spent in study, and without leisurely summer or holiday breaks. The children of the privileged were not consulted about the contents of their curricula, much less given a voice in its selection. Children were empty vessels waiting to be filled with knowledge and expected to become productive members of society at a much earlier age than is the norm today. When he was entered on the muster list of the *Bride of Derry* Geoffrey Frost possessed the education expected of any youth of his age and circumstances.

Exposure to the monstrous horrors of slavery awakened in the young Geoffrey moral outrage that any human would consider his station so superior as to deign to hold another as an absolute chattel. The soulless institution and its abhorrent trade was something he would crusade against his entire life, for Geoffrey knew with the clear insight of a child that such barbaric practice, accepted, abetted and fostered by white and black alike, was the antithesis of humanity.

Joseph Frost did not lack for courage; his service with Knox and his stowing away in a coffin aboard his brother's privateer proved that. But his courage temporarily deserted the impressionable young man when he thought he had brought the most appalling shame upon two families. Joseph, prepared to die—hopefully in some glorious cause—to atone in some small measure for his guilt, threw himself into an obscure military campaign devised and prosecuted solely by the tireless efforts of the iconoclastic and charismatic Benedict Arnold.

Accuracy in accounting for the signal events that shaped our Revolution requires that the importance of the naval battle waged on Lake Champlain be celebrated and remembered. Though well and courageously fought, the small, ill-supplied fleet Arnold had collected was overwhelmed by vastly superior British forces. While Arnold initially derided the qualities of the crews who manned the fleet he single-handedly created, their conduct could not have been more exemplary. The defeat of the small naval force raised by a Continental Army Brigadier General delayed the British efforts to divide the revolutionist States for one extremely critical year. While ironic in the contemplation, it is nevertheless true that our infant country's preservation was assured by the incalculable services of one whose subsequent unpardonable treason irrevocably made his name synonymous with conduct of the most traitorous hue.